Also by Sam Barone

The Eskkar Saga:

Science Fiction:

Please feel free to contact the
author with suggestions and comments

www.sambarone.com

Earth Besieged - Formatted for CS - Ver 12 – 10-21-2020

Earth Besieged

by

SAM BARONE

Planetary Defense Force

Earth Besieged

Part 1 - Initiation

Chapter 1

On September 17, 2052, scientists detected and monitored what they believed to be the first extraterrestrial event in the solar system. A fleet of five alien spacecraft – think destroyer size – emerged from a previously unknown and unsuspected opening in the space-time close to the planet Jupiter. Less than a minute later, a much larger alien spaceship – think battleship size – also exited from the wormhole.

A space battle erupted between what turned out to be two separate alien species. Three of the first five alien ships were destroyed before the larger ship took a hit and exploded. The two survivors, their intentions unknown, headed toward the inner planets. Earth was clearly their destination.

Suddenly Earth was not alone in a potentially unfriendly universe.

Nine days later, on September 26, Earth fought its first space battle against invading aliens. Two alien species, the Halkins and the Tarlons, lent their assistance to Earth against the warlike Ktarrans. The conflict lasted little more than forty minutes, but in that brief span the west coast of North America suffered almost twenty-five million casualties. Farther west, Japan, Korea, and China endured an even higher level of devastation, with thirty-plus million dead or wounded. Entire cities burned to the ground, their inhabitants trapped by the flames. Many more on both sides of the Pacific Ocean would die in the subsequent days from injuries, starvation, or the outbreak of disease.

On the plus side, three enemy alien (Ktarran) spaceships were destroyed. A fourth Ktarran, uninvolved in the attack on Earth, departed the solar system via the wormhole in space near Jupiter.

Without the assistance of the Halkins and Tarlons, Earth would have been devastated and conquered by the Ktarran Empire. That help resulted from the work of two linguists who established communications with the Halkins and Tarlons at the New International Space Station. Major Joseph Delano, USMC, and Dr. Duan Lian of China created a rapport with the aliens. Together they led a team of specialists who, working with the Halkins and Tarlons, devised a plan to defeat and destroy the three Ktarran warships.

The Alliance – China, United States, and Russia – fought the desperate battle. Despite years of conflict and friction, the three great powers had formed a loose union twenty years earlier in 2033. The rise of international terrorism, which reached its peak in 2031, gave the three major powers the impetus to form the Alliance and bring enforced peace and security back to the world.

Since far too many rogue nations had gained possession of nuclear, chemical, or biological weapons, the three nations decided to take direct action. By 2033, each Alliance member had suffered at least one major event from a WMD. Working together, they initiated a two-year program designed to destabilize those nations supporting or threatening international terror.

To that end, the Alliance overthrew governments, destroyed military facilities and arms production centers, and established firm borders. Weapons, including nuclear ones, were used ruthlessly to stamp out the terror states. Nearly two million people died before rogue nations got the message – the Alliance would destroy any government or group that threatened global peace and security.

Each Alliance member established its own sphere of influence. China became supreme in Asia, Russia extended its reach to Turkey, Kazakhstan, and the Ukraine, finally achieving its long-sought goal of a Mediterranean port. The United States allied itself politically with Canada, Iceland, and the United Kingdom. The rest of already-fragmented Europe and the Middle East were ignored. South America and Africa became resource suppliers for China, Russia, and the United States.

After formation of the Alliance, political ideology meant little, economic growth and stability everything. Any persons or nations that opposed the Alliance soon learned to keep their dogmas to themselves. After 2033, an uneasy peace settled over the world. The Alliance remained determined to avoid threats to its sovereignty at any cost. With the exception of small nuclear programs in Israel and France, the rest of the world surrendered or destroyed their weapons of mass destruction.

At first most of the nations of Earth denounced the new coalition, as it enforced world order from the barrel of a gun. But despite the imperfect solution, somehow peace took hold. With the threats of war and terrorism held at bay by the Alliance, countries found it easier and cheaper to grow their economies and help their citizens. For almost twenty years, no major outbreaks of war or terrorism occurred.

Despite their common goals, occasional frictions arose among the three members, but these were usually worked out. No single country, not even China with its vast military, could dominate the other two. But by 2052, the political leaders who had founded the Alliance were gone. A new generation took their place, and different sources of friction developed between China, the United States, and Russia.

One stabilizing development helped keep the peace. Permanent sites for science and mining were constructed on the Moon. From that vantage point, inter-system space travel also opened up the vast resources of Jupiter's moon, Io, to planet Earth. Prosperity increased across the globe. The world remained secure until the aliens arrived.

After the alien battle of September 26, 2052, a new challenge faced the Alliance – the barbaric and warlike Ktarrans would return, this time in force, and Earth would be overwhelmed. Thanks to the instability of the Jupiter wormhole, the Alliance had seventeen months to prepare for the Ktarrans' return. But once again, Earth would need not only the superior technology of the Halkins and Tarlons but their military assistance as well.

Adding to the urgency of the request, genetic analysis of the Halkins and Tarlons revealed that humans had a close kinship to both alien species. Mankind had evolved from the same genetic stock as their visitors. Embarrassed humans discovered they were merely offshoots of the same ancestral genera.

The Halkins and Tarlons naively assumed that Earth would speak with one voice for its defense. But within days of the victory, conflicts within the Alliance frustrated the aliens. Finally the Tarlons demanded that Major Delano and Dr. Duan, the linguists who had coordinated the destruction of three Ktarran battleships, be placed in charge of the planet's defense. If not, the

Halkins and Tarlons would abandon Earth to its fate. A deadline for their departure was set for seven days.

China and the United States refused to accept the ultimatum, unwilling to cede any of their authority. Three days passed with no progress. Delano and Dr. Duan Lian remained confined in their respective countries, unable to communicate. Their individual governments suspected the aliens had influenced their minds, possibly even taken control. It fell to the Russians to break the impasse.

Chapter 2

The Kremlin – Sunday, October 20, 2052, 9:05 p.m. MSK

Newly-elected president of the Russian Federation, Air Force General Anatoly Arseny Demidov took his seat at the head of the black walnut conference table with more than a little reluctance. Or perhaps distaste better described his feelings. He recalled an old story, told many times, about how Joseph Stalin consumed several glasses of vodka before every meeting. The strong drink made it easier to forget about yesterday's gathering and the people he'd condemned to death. And easier to not give a damn about those he would sentence to death today.

Demidov, however, remained cold sober. If and when he started needing a drink before a meeting, he would just shoot himself in the head and get it over with. Better that than waiting for someone to kill him.

Today's political session would determine his fate. Less than three weeks ago, at the height of the battle to defend Earth, General Demidov had assassinated the president of Russia, shooting the fat fool in the back of the head. That well-placed bullet saved the planet from catastrophe, but of course no good deed goes unpunished. Demidov had expected to die for his desperate act. Instead he'd become a hero to the Russian people, the man who defended the Motherland from an alien assault.

In the last three weeks, Russia had survived the assassination of its last president, an attack by aliens on the planet, and the chaos of its frightened citizens. Faced with such a crisis, Demidov, former Commander of Russia's Air and Space Forces, had been unanimously selected by the Council of Ministers to take over the Presidential Office. Temporarily, with the unspoken understanding that if he screwed up, he'd be gone.

But even with former President Garanin dead and buried, the Council of Ministers didn't possess the real power in Russia. President Demidov did have the support from several ministries, enough to make him a serious, but not all-powerful, political player. His grip on the reins of power remained tenuous and could slip at any time.

The Ministers' decision didn't constitute a hand-off of power or even a real election. That show process would take place at some later, indefinite date. Demidov recalled one of Stalin's sayings. "The people who cast the votes decide nothing. The people who count the votes decide everything."

The majority of grateful Ministers had chosen Demidov because he was the hero of the hour, the General who had saved Russia from the alien attacks that devastated China and the United States. His close association with the other Alliance partners, China and the United States also influenced his selection. Demidov had negotiated directly with the Halkin and Tarlon species, the so-called "good aliens," and his rapport with Colonel Delano, the American who helped save Earth, remained very strong.

How much weight those pluses still carried remained to be seen.

Demidov carried his sixty-six years well. His grizzled hair and Stalin-styled mustache looked good on his tall frame. Despite his present popularity with the people, Demidov knew his leadership of Russia could vanish at any time. With the alien attack repulsed and the danger in abeyance, he remained little more than a figurehead. That situation needed to change.

The three men facing him at the same table held the real power. In effect, these were the ones who counted the votes. This inner circle would make the ultimate decisions. If Demidov wished to survive, he would need to bend them to his way of thinking, obtain their support, and enlist their collaboration. The three power brokers must become four, with Demidov as their head. A daunting prospect, to say the least.

If he could manage that major miracle, Demidov just might survive long enough to save Russia a second time from the gloomy future that it now faced. Either that, or someone would be putting a pistol to the back of *his* head.

He smiled at the thought. The almost forty-year-old P-96S automatic pistol he'd used to kill the previous President now rested in his desk drawer. Refurbished and cleaned, the familiar weapon slipped into his jacket pocket whenever he left the office. It might not be much of an insurance policy, but he felt more secure carrying it.

"Good evening, gentlemen, and sorry for the lateness of the hour," Demidov began. "I have been looking forward to this meeting ever since the defeat of the Ktarran invasion."

Field Marshal Shuvalov grunted at the polite lie. "As have we. The stakes are high, and we need to plot the right course for Russia."

Shuvalov, short and stout, commanded all the ground forces in the Russian Federation. A little more than seventy years old, he'd been consolidating military units for years. His staff and senior officers remained intensely loyal, probably the only reason recently deceased President Garanin hadn't removed him. The field marshal believed in the old ways, and he remained as dangerous as a wounded bear. His mind stayed sharp, and his enemies frequently disappeared without a trace.

"The power structure within Russia needs to be united," said Minister of Defense Anton Oreshkin. His thin face and jet black mustache looked out of place with his bald head. Behind his back, many called him the Undertaker. Appointed to his post three years ago, Oreshkin had been marked for removal by former President Garanin and saved only by the arrival of the alien crisis.

Oreshkin controlled all of Russia's nuclear missiles, as well as chemical and biological weapons. He had the launch codes. Even now, two aides waited outside the conference room, each with a portable terminal connected to every missile silo and pad. One aide worked for Demidov while the other reported to Oreshkin.

"Yes, it does," Demidov said. "As I said before, I am willing to step aside, if the three of you are united. In any case, I will step down if the Alliance is not supported in its defense against the alien threat."

"Step aside? Unthinkable," Minister of Internal Affairs Sergey Borodin said. His wavy brown hair attracted attention. His face portrayed a cheerful countenance with a broad smile that revealed gleaming white teeth. A glance at the man's penetrating brown eyes painted a different picture. Years ago a mid-level political officer joked that Borodin's eyes resembled those of a shark, and the nickname stuck. The officer had died not long afterward from an unexpected heart attack. A great pity for one so young and with such good prospects. After that, no one uttered the word in Borodin's presence.

"If I may speak freely," Borodin continued, "even if you were not the people's current hero, you are irreplaceable. The Chinese won't trust any of us, and the American General Klegg has already voiced his support. He's running the American military now, he and that woman Spencer."

Demidov nodded. Borodin spoke the truth. But the situation remained fluid and could change at any time. Demidov knew Borodin was the real power in the room, despite the innocuous title. The secret police and the spy services, internal and external, remained a powerful force inside any country. The man had friends and connections everywhere.

Politically savvy, highly educated, and a brilliant strategist, Borodin would soon have risen to the top with Garanin gone. No doubt Borodin considered Demidov's sudden ascension an unfortunate accident, a transitory impediment to Borodin's ultimate political rise.

For a moment their eyes met, and Demidov glimpsed his future. One mistake and Borodin would be the one in charge. But not today, Demidov thought. Today Borodin needed to choose wisely.

"You saved us the trouble of getting rid of Garanin," Oreshkin said. "The imbecile was out of control . . . wanted to leave the Alliance. The Chinese would have been leaning on the Siberian border within a year."

"My men could have held them at the border," Shuvalov said.

"Yes, they could," Borodin said. "For a time. But I do not think we can dare fight a conventional war with China. Unless we wish to incinerate each other."

That, of course, remained the problem, Demidov knew. The vast population and massive armies of China could only be defeated with nuclear or other weapons of mass destruction, which China now possessed in plenty along with multiple means to deliver them. To attack China, the planet's major superpower, was to commit suicide.

The two countries were natural enemies, and in the past had fought several small wars and countless border skirmishes and incidents. Too bad Russia had wasted so many years worried about the West and the Americans, who were no threat to invade Europe and march on the Motherland or attempt to seize Siberia's vast resources.

Demidov knew that the conflict of ideas between Russia and the United States had driven the Russians' military paranoia. China, of course, had similar ideas to those of Russia on how to rule its people. That made it seem like a lesser threat, but the opposite proved true. China always had one eye on Siberia. So much time wasted, so many opportunities lost, Demidov thought, because Russia kept looking for enemies in the wrong places.

"What about these aliens?" Oreshkin had no interest in discussing war scenarios involving China. "Are they a real threat to us?"

All eyes went to Demidov. "Yes, they are. In seventeen months the Jupiter wormhole will reopen. The Ktarrans will return the moment that happens. They will come in force, fully prepared, and they won't be caught by surprise a second time."

"Can we defend ourselves from these creatures?" Shuvalov shook his head. "I still find it hard to believe that they wish to feed on us, like cattle."

"You saw the pictures?" Borodin made it a question.

The two dead Ktarrans recovered from the Space Station spoke for themselves. Analysis had confirmed that the Ktarran diet was exclusively meat. A seven-foot-tall velociraptor come to life, highly intelligent, and with an appetite for living flesh.

"According to Colonel Delano and Dr. Duan Lian, and backed up by our own Colonel Kosloff and Dr. Maksim Mironov, the physicist," Demidov said, "that is exactly what we can expect. The Tarlons estimate that the Ktarrans have, spread over their empire, two hundred ships such as those three that came here. Perhaps the number is even larger. By the way, both men spoke highly of Colonel Delano, and said that he frequently sought their input and advice. Kosloff and Mironov are in the building, should any of you wish to speak with them.

"Later perhaps," Borodin said. "Right now we have to find a way to stop these aliens."

No one spoke. The thought of even twenty such ships attacking Earth was too much to deal with. Five or six ships might be more than enough to destroy ninety percent of the planet's population while leveling every major city. Human extinction loomed, either that or abject slavery of the few survivors.

Demidov broke the silence. "As I see the situation, we have two problems. First, we must work with the Alliance to defeat the next alien attack. We cannot negotiate with the Ktarrans, nor can we surrender to an expansionist species that looks upon us primarily as a food source or potential slaves. We have angered them greatly. They will want to make an example of Earth, to keep the rest of their empire under control." He took a breath.

"Assuming that it is possible to defend the planet, that the Alliance is successful, we will still face the second problem – Russia's survival."

"You think the Alliance," Oreshkin asked, "would let the aliens destroy Russia?"

Demidov looked at each face. Oreshkin and Shuvalov didn't fully grasp the situation. But Demidov saw that Borodin did. "No, that is not likely," Demidov said. "But to defeat these aliens, China and the Americans will have to place their entire economies on a war footing. They will build spaceships and weapons. If the Ktarrans are driven off, America and China will have hundreds of these ships and thousands of new weapons. They will rule the planet from space, and Russia will be left behind."

"We can build ships as well," Oreshkin said. "We can mobilize . . ."

"It won't be enough," Borodin said, glancing at Demidov. "Both China and the United States have stronger economies. They also have much larger populations to support a war mobilization. If the Americans and Chinese utilize every part of their industrial output, Russia simply cannot keep up with such an effort. We lack both the people and the resources.

"So what are you saying?" Shuvalov's eyes went to Demidov, then to Borodin and back again.

"To survive and retain our equal position within the Alliance, Russia must build a vast fleet of these new spaceships," Demidov said. "That means we must mobilize all our people and industrial resources to produce nothing but ships and weapons. Think about it! Ships that can reach Jupiter in days, not months. Enough power to transport huge cargoes, even entire asteroids. That is what the future holds for us if we can take advantage of it. It might be the rebirth of Mother Russia."

"But you say that Russian production cannot keep pace with China and the United States?"

Oreshkin's question drew all eyes back to Demidov. "I believe I have a solution to that problem, but we will speak of that later. First we must commit to complete mobilization of our own resources."

Borodin nodded approval. "I agree. We must start at once, and we must equal the Americans and Chinese production with regard to ships and weapons. Nothing must be held back. If we can establish a powerful fleet of our own and maintain parity within the Alliance, we will be able to take advantage of the resources and prospects offered by the asteroid belt and the moons of Jupiter. Not to mention any new opportunities offered by the wormholes. More important, we will retain equality within the Alliance."

The alien species had reached the solar system through a wormhole, a distortion in space that allowed near instantaneous travel from other star systems. However the wormhole located near Jupiter was unstable. It appeared and disappeared at what seemed to be semi-random intervals. As of now it had closed and would not re-open for another seventeen months. Or so the Tarlons and Halkins claimed.

"You know what you are asking for?" Oreshkin looked dubious. "Total mobilization of our entire population. What if the people refuse?"

"They will not," Demidov said. "If the choice is temporary hardship versus certain death, they will accept the sacrifice."

"Some will resist," Oreshkin argued. "Others will shirk their duties."

"Stalin knew how to win the people's support in times of crisis," Shuvalov said. "The moment anyone questioned or opposed him, he stood them up against a wall and had them shot. If some fools protested, he had them shot, too. That included those who failed to do their utmost, and any who sought to take advantage of the situation. What was done once can be done again. I do not want my grandchildren eaten by aliens."

Borodin nodded in approval. "If we are to survive, as a planet and as a country, we must be even stronger and more ruthless than Stalin. Without ending up as he did."

Demidov knew all too well how Stalin met his end. Wine poisoned with warfarin, a blood thinner that also served as rat poison. It took him four days of agony to die.

Oreshkin glanced around the table. The others nodded in agreement. "Very well. What should we do?"

"First, we have to stop the Americans and Chinese from getting us all killed," Demidov said. "Their stupidity has made the Tarlons and Halkins ready to abandon us. We cannot win this war without alien technology and help. We need to do whatever is necessary to keep them cooperating."

"The Chinese are still in disarray from the attack," Borodin said. "My sources say that many don't trust Secretary Liu's niece. They claim she is under the influence of Colonel Delano and the Americans."

Demidov laughed. "I believe that's exactly what General Klegg thinks, that Delano is under alien control or the influence of Lian and China. Neither country wants to yield any authority to our newest Romeo and Juliet. If this foolish impasse continues, the Tarlons will leave and we will all be destroyed. So it falls to us to change Alliance thinking."

"And how will we accomplish that?" Oreshkin asked.

"By doing the unexpected," Demidov said. He removed a notebook from his briefcase, flipped it open, then leaned closer. "I did not want these notes entered into any computer, at least not yet. Here is what I think we must do."

Demidov had spent most of the last twenty-four hours preparing his material. Now the new Russian President spoke for nearly forty minutes. His talking points generated plenty of comments and criticisms. That lasted another three hours and required the use of two whiteboards. When the four men finalized the plan, each of Demidov's listeners had a smile on his face.

"It is a good start, President Demidov." Borodin used Demidov's title for the first time, a subtle hint that the new President would remain in control. "The full support of the Internal Affairs Division is at your disposal."

"I agree," Shuvalov said. "The armed forces of Russia will support whatever course of action you require."

"As will the Ministry of Defense," Oreshkin added. "It will at least add some humor to the situation."

Everyone laughed. "Only a Russian could enjoy this," Demidov said, returning his notes to the briefcase. "Now we must prepare for our meeting tomorrow with General Klegg. In less than three days, at midnight, Washington time, the aliens intend to depart. We all have much to do, and little time to waste."

Chapter 3

Washington, D.C. – Sunday, October 20, 2052 – 7:15 p.m. EST

Lieutenant Colonel Joseph (Joe) Delano, United States Marine Corps, stared at the unadorned off-white walls of the VIP guest quarters in the Pentagon basement, only about a hundred yards from General Klegg's teleconference room. Even in jest, no representative of the hotel industry would ever use the term VIP in connection with this dump. The local Ramada Inn rented rooms by the hour that boasted larger and more luxurious accoutrements. But for the military brass and their senior staff in need of temporary digs, these single-room accommodations proved more than adequate.

As he lay on the bed wearing only a T-shirt and underwear, Delano wondered how many sweaty generals, after a quick call to the wife explaining that duty kept them at the office, had pounded their female aides into the overly-soft mattress. He imagined he could feel the indentations. All in all, a foolproof flop system. Even if a suspicious spouse or significant other phoned the Pentagon switchboard, the audio-only call would simply be routed to the cheating husband's room. As long as no one giggled, the caller would never be the wiser.

Thanks to the Pentagon's tight military security, there would be no snooping detectives, unfriendly cameras, video chats, text messages, or suspicious partners. And no worry about accidentally bumping into someone you knew at the Hilton, or a cop shining a flashlight into the back seat of your government SUV.

Unfortunately, Delano shared his dreary room and its well-used mattress with no one. Nor had he requested the lodgings. He did, however, have two armed MPs standing watch outside the door. Security staff had disconnected the room's communication links, taken away his private phone and tablet, and installed two cameras to "monitor his health." He could understand that logic. Anyone suspected of alien control merited being held incommunicado and kept under close surveillance.

For his first twenty-four hours after arriving back on Earth,

NASA and the military doctors subjected him to every conceivable examination – X-ray, MRI, sonograms, brain scans, etc. They'd even pumped his stomach, hoping to find extra-terrestrial bacteria. The fact that the docs found nothing wrong didn't really seem to convince them. They just believed the alien influence was well hidden. No doubt they wanted to look even more closely, though Delano doubted their probes could extend much farther.

Aliens, of course, couldn't be trusted. Large swaths of the western United States, as well as China and Japan, had recently been devastated by the Ktarrans, aggressive creatures who had entered the solar system with the goal of taking over the entire planet. The fact that Delano and his team, with the help of the two friendly alien species, the Tarlons and Halkins, had saved Earth from total destruction meant nothing.

Earth's governments, represented by the Alliance of China, Russia, and the United States, had no experience dealing with intelligent sentients from outer space. Unfortunately their first and only contact had dragged them into an ongoing interstellar war, one that likely meant the end of human civilization. Delano sometimes wondered if the Alliance thought that option a better outcome, rather than cooperating with friendly aliens to save the planet. Maybe the Alliance had prepared a planetary suicide option.

With nothing to do but stare at the walls for the last two days, Delano considered his future, or lack of one. He'd gone from being the hero who saved the world to political enemy number one in the Alliance and its various dependent entities. Instead of enjoying a pleasant vacation in the south of France with his amour, Lian, he remained half a world away, locked in this room, under observation, and cut off from all communications. If General Klegg hadn't wanted to keep Delano available at the Pentagon, he'd probably be staring at the ceiling in some maximum security mental hospital under an assumed name.

Lian probably endured much the same situation. She, too, remained under tight wraps because of possible alien mind control. At least her uncle, the premier of China and general secretary of the ruling Party, had taken charge of her care, keeping her at his home for security concerns, i.e., house arrest. So she likely had better quarters, food, and entertainment selections available, possibly even a view of her uncle's gardens.

Even if she had access to a phone or computer station, Delano had nothing on his end to complete a link. He kept reaching for his non-existent phone.

Being under alien mind control might be bad, but a worst situation was possible. Delano could be under the influence of the Chinese ruling party, represented by Lian. No matter how he tried to spin it, he couldn't find an upside. *I'm doomed.* He hated having no control of his fate.

Someone knocked on the door.

"Go away!" Delano had no interest in company. In the last ten hours, he had refused to speak with a major, a colonel, and a brigadier general. The first two had been merely annoying, but when the overweight Army general barged in and demanded cooperation, with the threat of incarcerating Delano, he lost his cool.

Issuing a few threats of his own, Delano grabbed the puffed-up fool by the collar and ejected the fat bastard without actually employing his fists. Still, for using his hands on a superior officer, Delano could face an Article 90 charge under the Uniformed Code of Military Justice. When he thought about a court-martial, Delano decided he should have punched the man in his prominent nose. *Yeah, real smart, that idea.*

"Colonel, it's me, Gunny Stecker. Steve's with me. Let us in."

Delano jumped off the bed and opened the door. "Hey, good to see you guys!" He felt himself smile for the first time in days. The stoic guards remained in place, but said nothing. Apparently some worthy soul had authorized Delano's two visitors. *Hallelujah*!

Once his former team members stepped inside, Delano frowned at the guards. "*Kreténi!*" They would not understand the word, but would no doubt catch his drift. Delano slammed the door shut. Somehow the word "assholes" sounded better in Czech.

As one of the top linguists in the world, Delano had done plenty of multi-lingual swearing in the last few days. With too much time on his hands, he'd analyzed the world's profanity situation and concluded that the energetic and upbeat people of the Czech Republic had made significant linguistic contributions in that area.

"So they let you out?" Delano knew Gunny and Steve had

been quartered in the two remaining "suites" down the hall. *Just as a precaution,* he'd been assured.

"Yeah, about an hour ago we had our final debrief," Stecker said. "Some lieutenant said you were still on lockdown but that we could visit you. Practically insisted. Didn't expect to catch you with your pants down."

"Wasn't expecting visitors," Delano chuckled, pulling on his trousers.

"We'd been here sooner, but we decided to stop at the PX first," Steve said, grinning as he held up a bulky nylon carry bag.

"No!" Delano's eyes widened. "You've got booze?" He hadn't had a drink in almost four days.

"Good stuff, and all the fixings." Stecker's familiar West Virginia drawl sounded comforting. "Didn't want to drop in on you empty-handed."

The room didn't have a kitchenette, so Steve Macey, Army Sergeant First Class, Electronics Command, dropped the bag on the coffee table and began emptying its contents. The first item turned out to be a large bottle of Bushmills Black Bush Irish Whiskey, quickly followed by a liter of spring water, a plastic platter of beef jerky, two large bags of potato chips, and one each of pretzels, nachos, and cheese puffs.

"I think we've got all the major food groups," Steve said, tearing open a bag of potato chips. Tall, thin, and without any trace of a beard, he always looked ready to fall asleep. He'd been everyone's choice for a data expert to help Delano establish communications with both aliens and Earth. "Gunny insisted on the water and the plastic glasses. I was for just passing around the bottle." He laughed, practically a giggle, and joined Stecker on the room's only sofa.

Delano dragged up a chair and faced the two men across the flimsy coffee table. "They let you bring this stuff? I've been living cold turkey for more than three days. Not even a decent cup of coffee. One level up from bread and water."

"The bastards!" Steve ripped open a bag of chips. "Cruel and unusual punishment, if you ask me." He stuffed a handful of chips into his mouth. "Have some jerky. It's my favorite."

Delano had to grin. Steve Macey had been instrumental in establishing communications with Earth's first visitors from another world. Only twenty-four years old, Steve technically out-ranked the Gunny, nearly five years older.

"Have you two heard anything more about the Halkins?"

"Zip. Nada." Steve passed around the chip bag.

Nearly three days had elapsed since the Halkins issued their ultimatum to the Alliance. After a month of non-action, the Halkins insisted that they would deal only with Delano and Lian. If that did not happen, the Halkins threatened to depart and leave Earth's billions to their own fortune.

That announcement had rattled the Alliance, but not enough for its leaders to devise a solution. In less than four days, the Halkin ship would depart the solar system. That would leave Earth helpless against the Ktarrans.

"We only got our clearances back today." USMC Gunnery Sergeant Stecker was a member of Marine Recon Force. He stood well over six feet tall, with powerful arms and shoulders and close-trimmed sandy blond hair in the regulation Marine buzz cut. Everyone called him Gunny. A small arms and explosive specialist, he'd accompanied Delano to the Space Station, tasked by General Klegg with blowing it up if necessary and making sure no one fell into alien hands. At least not alive.

"Major Mitchell, Klegg's aide, wanted us to loosen you up. So we said we'd be glad to chat with you," Gunny said, "but we wanted a drink first, and nobody objected too much. In fact, I think we're supposed to get you oiled so you'll talk to General Klegg."

"Not going to happen, and nothing to say anyway" Delano said. "I told them I wanted my job back in Paris, or they could discharge me. But either way I'm done with talking. By the way, they're probably listening to every word we say."

"Don't care. Worst they can do to me is send me back to Recon." Stecker had filled three glasses with whiskey, and now he added a splash of water in each. "Only way to drink good whiskey is with a little water."

"Thanks. Never really been a whiskey drinker." Delano took a cautious taste. "A little rough."

"No, this is very expensive Irish whiskey," Stecker insisted. "Surprised the PX carries it. Take only small sips until you get used to it. Five minutes from now, you're going to love every drop."

Delano took a second and much smaller sip. "It may grow on me. Now, tell me what's going on out there."

"Not much." Steve's high-pitched voice made him sound like

the ultimate nerd. Thin and gangly, his army greens looked baggy, and he probably didn't have a real muscle anywhere on his body. "The president is still flying all over what's left of the West Coast, making stupid promises of relief to the victims and blaming the Alliance and our military for the disaster. The fool can't even bury the dead, let alone help the living. Food and supplies are barely trickling in. People are still dying out there, especially the old and anyone needing medications."

The Ktarrans had bombarded the West Coast of North American from San Jose in Costa Rica to Mexico City to Oakland. Thirty million Americans had died, and millions more in Mexico.

"Yeah, it's real bad," Gunny agreed. "California got fucked big time."

"Half the country thinks they got what they deserve," Steve said. "Smug bastards."

Delano understood the feeling, but they were Americans and needed help. California had dominated the United States politically for many years. Now it wanted the rest of the country to bail them out, right now, and no matter what it cost. Steve, coming from New Jersey, had little sympathy for the Golden State and its tony inhabitants.

No matter what his individual feelings, Delano recognized the fact that California, with its thirty-three military bases and dozens of high-tech industries, remained vital to the defense of the country. Not to mention the naval base in San Diego or the critical harbor in Los Angeles. Both had sustained heavy damage, and both needed to be operational as soon as possible. Their resources were necessary for the coming war with the Ktarrans.

"So, Colonel, what are you planning to do?" Gunny Stecker paused to take a healthy swallow. When he lowered the glass, his eyes fixed on Delano.

"Not up to me," Delano said. "I'm just a linguist who got lucky. And I've tried my best to reason with the Halkins, told them I couldn't do what they wanted. Lian tried, too, but her uncle cut her off." Delano shrugged. "Now it's up to Klegg and his boys to figure out how to deal with our new Tarlon and Halkin friends."

General Langdon Klegg, the Air Force Joint Chief, had led the fight against the enemy alien spaceships. Even before the advent of the Ktarrans, after the initial contact, the president had given Klegg full martial authority over national security. That had expanded to include not only the military, but all state and local security services.

Thirty days ago, Klegg had plucked Delano from his soft gig in Paris. He'd been stationed there little more than a month, acting as chief translator for the American Embassy. Klegg, desperate for a physically fit, military linguistic expert, promoted Delano to Major and shipped him up to the International Space Station. Klegg told Delano he had full authority from the Alliance to establish communications with the approaching aliens. Fortunately for Earth and Delano's team, the arriving aliens, known as the Halkins, proved moderately friendly. He and Dr. Duan Lian, the chief linguist from China, established a basis for communications and initiated a dialog in less than two days.

That's when Delano and Earth first learned that an attack fleet of Ktarrans was on its way, and that Earth was doomed, certain to be enslaved or destroyed. Somehow he and Lian managed to persuade the Halkins, now joined by a second species known as the Tarlons, to risk their own lives and ships to help defend Earth.

The breakthrough in communications with the Tarlons and Halkins made it all possible. Delano and Dr. Duan Lian had indeed accomplished an extraordinary feat that won the trust of both species.

Meanwhile General Klegg had achieved miracles by getting Russia and China to work with the United States. Delano's team, still on the Space Station, had come up with a rough plan, and Klegg had hammered it home. But defeating the three Ktarran warships required a heavy cost in human lives and population centers. Even worse was the knowledge that the Ktarrans would almost certainly be back in seventeen months when the wormhole reopened, and that they possessed hundreds of powerful ships.

So Earth needed to mobilize the entire planet's resources and work with the friendly Tarlons and Halkins. But after days of fruitless talks, the Halkins decided that Earth's rulers were hopeless, and demanded that Delano and Lian take charge of the planet and lead its defenses. The Halkins reasoned that Delano and Lian had led Earth's military response before, and saw no reason why they should not do so again. The Alliance received seven days to agree to these terms. Otherwise the remaining Halkin ship intended to depart Earth and abandon it to the

Ktarrans.

That simplistic demand sent the Alliance leaders into a rage. Suddenly Delano and Lian had morphed into alien-lovers or even worse, alien supporters. General Klegg and Delano, standing toe-to-toe, exchanged more than a few angry words. Delano ended up being escorted to the VIP quarters under guard, charged with multiple violations of Article 89 of the Uniform Code of Military Justice. Nothing much had changed since then, while the clock kept ticking.

"Well, Colonel, you should start thinking about how to get Earth out of this mess," Stecker said. "You did it on the Station. I'm sure you can come up with another good idea or two."

"Gunny's right, Colonel," Steve said. "The Alliance is going to figure out sooner or later that without the Halkins and Tarlons, their precious Alliance ass is grass. That means they need you."

"Doesn't much look like they want me around," Delano said. "Besides, what do I know about defending the planet? I'm just a Marine linguist. It's more likely that Klegg will toss me in the brig than put me in charge of planet Earth."

"The Alliance is running out of time," Stecker said. "If they don't include you in the negotiations, Earth is looking at a big time FUBAR." The Gunny refilled Delano's glass. "Just start thinking about it. I'm sure Lian is already doing that. When the pot boils over, you don't want to be standing around with your thumb up your butt and nothing to say."

"Just remember us when you need help," Steve said, splashing water into Delano's whiskey. "No matter what, you're going to need a comms guy and a bodyguard or two."

"Nobody I'd rather have than you two," Delano said, returning the compliment. Then for the first time in days the wheels started turning. What the hell was Lian doing? She had to be putting pressure on her uncle. Maybe she could figure out how to make the most of the mess the Alliance had created.

The rest of the evening's gab session passed with more talk about the alien crisis. Aside from the food riots on the West Coast, crowds of alien haters and religious fanatics filled the streets throughout the country. New political organizations formed overnight, each one different but all demanding something from the government. Everyone protested the continuation of martial law, and the National Guard was regularly called out to support the local police. The situation, as Delano's drill sergeant often said, remained in a state of flux.

Around ten o'clock his two visitors stumbled out the door. Delano, head buzzing from the unfamiliar whiskey, glared at the guards. "*Mange merde*," he shouted, before slamming the door shut and slumping down in his chair, a half-full glass of booze in his hand.

The Gunny and Steve were right. Like it or not, the Alliance might have to cave to the Halkins' demands. So maybe Delano should start thinking about the problem. He'd done nothing but feel sorry for himself and ignore politics for the last three days. The crisis might be coming right back in his lap at any moment.

At first he didn't think there was anything that he, a jumped-up Lt. Colonel with good language skills and a near-eidetic memory for sounds and words, could do. Less than a month ago he'd been a captain. Klegg promoted him to major just to give him some rank on the Space Station. After the battle, Congress voted him another grade, a promotion they now probably regretted. Not a thing in his background qualified him to make planetary-wide economic, industrial and military decisions. Even so, was anyone else better qualified? What would you do, if you had the power? *What would you do if you were Dictator of the world?*

No, better not use that word. Too much negativity, though to the ancient Romans who coined the word it merely meant a temporary military leader. Maybe something like War Planner, or Invasion Coordinator, perhaps even Supreme Arbiter? After all, that person would have the entire resources of the planet at his disposal. That included experts in every field of science, industrial production, computer intelligence, and military capability.

So this *El Supremo* might not need to know that much. With the planetary knowledge base available, all you might really need to do is select the right experts, tell them what you needed, listen to their advice, and then monitor their performance. Delano frowned at the thought. If these people screwed up, started cheating and bribing, or couldn't get the job done, you couldn't merely fire them or put them on trial. That wouldn't send the right message, nor would there be enough time for that.

Thinking of messages, Delano knew he had one powerful weapon. As a planetary hero, he could speak to the world using any of a dozen methods, from TV to radio to the Internet. No matter what Klegg threatened, people would at least listen to

Delano's words. Sooner or later he'd demand access to a communications network.

He must think like a battlefield commander. Develop the overall strategy, work out the tactical plans, identify the proper teams, ready the correct weapons, manage the logistics and turn the subcommanders loose. Then monitor closely for results. At the first sign of possible failure or non-performance, replace the weak links in the human chain. The penalties would have to be harsh to keep everyone focused on the ultimate goal – saving the planet's population from destruction. On the battlefield, deserters and other trouble-makers could be executed on the spot. Earth's armies had done just that for thousands of years.

Suppose you had all that power? What would you do first? Ideas began to bubble up through the alcoholic haze. Each thought led to another, which linked to the next. Two hours later, he'd filled half-a-dozen sheets of paper with possible scenarios and many questions.

Just after midnight, Delano glanced at his barely legible notes, surprised at what he'd managed to jot down. The task, of course, was impossible. But after you accepted that fact, decisions actually got easier. Tired, he considered the big question. *If I were running the defense of Earth right now, what my first step?* Well, that choice was easy enough – get some sleep.

He weaved his way into the tiny bathroom and washed up. The haggard face in the mirror caught his eye, and Delano stared at himself. Few women called him handsome. The charitable ones used words like "rugged" or "strong." Tonight, needing a shave and bleary eyed, his face insisted that someone else had helped save the planet. His dark brown eyes appeared inadequate for the task at hand. Did the guy in the mirror really stop an alien invasion? Could he do it again? Or was he just a quitter, looking for the easy way out?

Suck it up, Marine. "OK," he answered himself. "I'll give it a try."

Bone-weary now, he gulped a glass of water and staggered into bed, almost too tired to remove his trousers.

No matter what General Klegg felt or demanded, Delano knew he could play a pivotal role in Earth's survival. His relations with the Tarlons and Halkins guaranteed that. Those species wanted someone they could trust, and he and Lian had proven themselves. Without that trust, the friendly aliens weren't going to commit precious resources and time to save a disorganized and ungrateful Earth from destruction. That, too, needed some thought. Right now it was time to get some shut-eye.

But before he fell asleep, or passed out, he wasn't sure which, Delano ordered his sub-conscious mind to think about what he could do. Tomorrow might bring a whole new set of problems, and he still considered himself good at resolving issues. Saving the Earth from destruction might be problematical, but he would let his liquored-up brain work it out while he slept. It might even come up with a good idea or two.

Chapter 4

Beijing – October 21, 2052 10:00 AM CST

In her suite at her uncle's house in Beijing, Dr. Duan Lian paced the thick Baotou-Suiyuan rug that partially covered the flooring of delicate teak planks. The antique rug dated from the 1920s, but she gave it no thought. There were many such luxuries in the private residence of the leader of China.

In the last six days, Lian had worn a rut in the expensive carpet, and it would probably need restorative services to return it to its former pristine state. Whenever she grew tired of walking back and forth, she would stand in front of the walnut framed mirror over her dresser and frown at her image.

Tall and slender, Lian had beautiful and expressive brown eyes. Her mother had told her young daughter they were her best feature. The rest of her face showed sharp lines that gave her an athletic, almost fierce look. She could move with grace, thanks to two years of ballet training in high school, abandoned when she grew too tall. Lian preferred her black hair in a pony tail, and habitually wore nothing more formal than shorts and T-shirts. Many considered her features plain, but a flashing smile made her quite attractive. And she dressed up well. Lian never had any trouble catching a man's eye, when she made the effort.

Now the mirror showed nothing of her softer side. Only anger and frustration stared back at her. After helping to save China from complete destruction – helping save the rest of the planet as well – Lian now found herself a prisoner in her own home. While not strictly confined to her rooms, guards accompanied her every departure, and she could not leave the grounds.

Enough was enough, she decided. The face in the mirror nodded agreement. She picked up her phone and called her uncle. At this time in the afternoon, he would be in his office, working. Usually he answered within three or four rings, but this time twelve passed before he answered. "Yes, Lian? I'm quite busy at the moment."

"Uncle, I want to see Sergeant Shen. Please have him sent to my rooms."

"Lian, now is not the time for such things. Until certain issues have been resolved, you must have patience."

Lian had wasted more than enough days patiently waiting. "If Shen is not here at once, I promise that I will escape. I will find a way, and I will get on the internet and tell everyone what is going on here."

Before he could reply, Lian broke the connection. She took a deep breath, and walked out to the small balcony. Her suite was on the second floor, and as a child she had occasionally climbed down the decorative railing to reach the ground. But when she leaned out, she saw two soldiers in impeccable uniforms standing almost immediately below. Polished black leather belts held their holstered sidearms. Both looked up and smiled.

"Damn!" Since her schooling in Los Angeles, Lian had learned to swear in English, and now preferred it. Being one of the top linguists on Earth had its advantages. The guards below might not understand, but they would get the message. She went inside and resumed her pacing. Escaping would not be easy.

Twenty minutes later, a knock sounded on the door. Grateful for the interruption, she crossed the room in three strides and flung open the door.

"Dr. Duan," Sergeant Shen said, bowing. "You wish to see me?"

Three guards stood behind Shen, and they looked alert and capable. They had to be. Shen was an Eagle soldier, one of the toughest fighters in China's army. Chosen as her bodyguard, he had accompanied her on the First Contact mission aboard the Space Station.

Without hesitation, Lian reached out, grabbed Shen by the shirt, and jerked him into the room. With her other hand, she slammed the door shut behind him. Before the guards could react, she turned the bolt. They would have to break down the door to get in, and they wouldn't do that without her uncle's approval.

"Shen, I'm so glad to see you. I knew you were somewhere in the house, but they wouldn't let me visit you."

"I was confined to quarters," Shen said. "Only my wife was allowed to visit. They thought I might be under alien influence."

"Idiots!" Her hair swirled around her face. "A bunch of frightened old women!"

Shen had killed four Ktarran fighters in less than two

seconds, right in front of Lian's eyes. So of course they suspected him of . . . whatever?

Thinking about that moment crystallized her thoughts. Suddenly she knew exactly what she wanted to do.

"Shen, I want you to teach me how to use a firearm," Lian said. "During the battle, I did less than nothing. You gave me a gun, but I saw that you and Delano didn't want me to use it. You were both afraid I might shoot myself. Even the American Med-Tech fired hers during the battle with the Ktarrans."

"Not very effectively, I heard," Shen smiled. "But I would be glad to teach you, Dr. Duan, if they hadn't confiscated my pistol. In fact, they took all my weapons."

"First, from now on please call me Lian. Second, I will get us a pistol and you will show me how to use it. The situation on the Space Station was intolerable. Both you and Delano were ready to kill me at the first sign of trouble. I felt helpless and useless, unable to protect myself. So I will learn to shoot, and you will teach me."

"Do you think they will let us have a gun?"

"One way or another, they will," Lian said. "And if they don't, you will teach me how to fight using a knife or just my hands. I never want to feel such helplessness again."

Shen glanced around the room. No one was banging on the door, or threatening to break in. With alien paranoia everywhere, they had certainly bugged her room. So they overheard Lian's comments. She doubted they would give Shen a gun, certainly not one with bullets, but Lian could be very forceful when she wanted something.

Shen took only a moment to decide. "Working out with you will be far better than staring at the bare walls of my own room. You are athletic and strong. You should make a good pupil."

"Good. When can we start?"

He shrugged. "We can start now. The bed comforter should make a good mat, and we can start with some basic movements. You understand that proficiency under pressure takes time, often years of practice, to master?"

Lian nodded. "We have time. Almost seventeen months before the Ktarrans can return. That takes us to March of 2054. By then I want to be well-trained in both firearms and unarmed fighting."

"But will you not be busy dealing with the aliens? Aren't you and Col. Delano going to take charge of the planet's defense?"

She laughed. "I doubt that will ever happen. I'm a prisoner in my own house. But sooner or later they will get tired of keeping me locked up."

"You understand that unarmed fighting will not be effective against the Ktarrans? I do not think I could kill one with my hands. But in that much time, there is much we could do. It's unfortunate that we did not recover any of their bodies. It might have given us a way to fight them."

Big and ugly brutes, the Ktarrans resembled oversized velociraptors more than anything else, with leather-like skin and claws to match. Unlike the Tarlons and Halkins, the predatory Ktarrans were a distinctly different species. Thinking about them made her shiver.

"I think we will find there are plenty of humans who might want to harm me," Lian said.

"Do you intend to return to Col. Delano?"

She met Shen's eyes. It was a bold question, but she didn't hesitate. "Yes, if he will have me. Then we can face the aliens together. And when that day comes, I hope you are by my side."

Shen smiled. "I would be honored. Now, let us begin."

They worked together for nearly three hours. By then Lian could barely stand. The days spent in space and the week of idleness at home had softened her once-firm muscles, and she struggled to overcome her weakened body.

No one had bothered to answer her demand for a pistol, even an empty one. So Shen instructed her in hand-to-hand combat, simple moves he'd learned as a boy. When that grew boring, Shen used her comb to simulate a knife, taking her once again through many of the same moves.

"Remember, a knife fight is often deadly to both fighters," Shen explained. "So you must always be prepared to defend yourself as well as attack."

Finally she decided to rest. After escorting Shen out the door, Lian went to the bathroom to wash the sweat from her face. She frowned at the face in the mirror. It would take time, but she would harden herself into someone strong and capable. Lian returned to the bedroom, a towel in her hands which she used to dry her face. Shen, of course, had not even raised a sweat.

Lian vowed that someday Shen would sweat as much as she did. Her days of being a helpless person were over.

Chapter 5

Washington – Monday October 21, 2052 7:00 a.m. EST

General Langdon Klegg sat in the Pentagon's communication center, a room he'd come to know all too well. The fact that the basement facility possessed comfortable, state of the art teleconferencing equipment no longer meant anything. Everything in the underground chamber annoyed him. The lighting, the cameras, the blinking lights, the monitors, the technicians, even the air conditioning. Though he knew filters kept the air clean, he still thought he detected the smell of fear that had hung in the room for the past month.

Shortly after receiving his third star, Klegg had joined the Joint Chiefs as Commander of the Air Force. On his way up the Washington ladder, he'd worked closely with NASA and the private space industry. Klegg had received the initial information on the alien ships that had fought a battle in our solar system, and his effective response resulted in the head of the NSA recommending Klegg take command of the alien situation under full martial law.

He initiated the alien first contact protocol, assigning responsibility for that to then Captain Joseph Delano, USMC. Working with the Alliance, Klegg and Delano had ended up fighting a Ktarran invasion force. Despite winning a victory in that conflict, Earth suffered devasting losses in Mexico, the American West Coast, and throughout Japan, China, and Korea.

Shocked by the heavy loss of life, the president of the United States, Mathew M. Clark, blamed Klegg for the disaster. But the Chinese and Russians, representing two-thirds of the Alliance, had voiced their support for General Klegg, as had Dr. Vivian Spencer, head of the NSA. She threatened to resign if Klegg were removed.

Klegg didn't worry about removal. He did worry about President Clark, making wild claims in California about the relief effort and threatening to pull the United States out of the Alliance.

In his middle fifties, Klegg had started his career as a fighter pilot, and flown until his vision had weakened. Tall and physically fit, he boxed for exercise. White hair gave him the distinguished appearance of a natural leader. He'd moved rapidly up the Air Force chain of command, earning his first star before age forty. In due time two more stars followed. The appointment to the Joint Chiefs two years ago completed his personal career goals. He had looked forward to retirement in another few years. The alien arrival had changed all that.

Now he sipped his third cup of coffee while he waited for the next conference call to begin, this one requested by Russia. Seven in the morning, Washington, D.C., equaled 3:00 PM in Russia and 6:00 PM in Beijing. During the alien crisis the time differential hadn't mattered much, as everyone in the Alliance leadership pretty much ate and slept in their respective teleconference rooms.

"Comm link is going active, General," his aide announced.

Klegg glanced at one of the large digital clocks mounted high on the wall, behind the bank of teleconference cameras aimed at him. Right on schedule, seven o'clock.

The door opened and NSA Director Vivian Spencer slipped in, carrying her own coffee in one hand and a large brown briefcase in the other. "Morning, Lang. Sorry to be late." She took the seat beside him. Other than Klegg's aide, Major Mitchell, no one else attended.

An attractive woman in her mid-forties, she could display an eye-catching smile that complimented her short brown hair. Spencer had been appointed as head of the NSA only a few months ago by President Clark. Rumor claimed she was one of his mistresses, but even if true, she'd stood firm with General Klegg against him. After that, Spencer and Klegg developed a relationship during the crisis, and they'd grown close.

"Just starting." He gestured toward the monitor, now displaying the familiar images of China's General Secretary Liu along with his senior military advisor, Air Force General Zeng.

Before Klegg could mutter more than "hello," the Russian monitor went active. To his surprise, this one displayed four men seated side by side, all facing the same camera. Something must be up. Klegg recognized only two of them, newly-appointed President Demidov and Army Field Marshal Shuvalov. The CIA had nicknamed Marshal Shuvalov the 'Iron Bear.'

"Good morning, General Klegg, Dr. Spencer." Demidov spoke English, the usual language for such calls. "And good evening to you, General Secretary Liu and General Zeng." Everyone exchanged the usual hellos as Demidov continued. "Joining me today is Russia's new advisory council. You all know Marshal Shuvalov. You may not have met Minister of Defense Anton Oreshkin or Minister of Internal Affairs Sergei Borodin."

Klegg had read their dossiers, but had not expected any of them to rise to the top of the latest Russian regime. Clearly a new power structure had formed around Demidov, and the foreign affairs experts at the State Department would have to redo their research and attempt to decipher the new political order. Nobody at State expected Demidov to survive, not after assassinating his former president. More polite greetings were exchanged. Klegg glanced down at the table. Dr. Spencer had scribbled two words on her legal pad – "Watch Borodin!"

"I would like to speak to the most urgent situation," Demidov said. "The Halkin ship will be departing in a few more days. We, and I include the Russian people, want to know when the Alliance will be accepting the Halkins' suggestion. A position of a unified planetary leader must be declared at once. Only then can construction of ships and weapons begin on a planetary scale. Russia is ready to do her part. Colonel Delano is obviously as qualified for the role as anyone, and he enjoys the support of the Halkins and Tarlons. So, when are you going to name him to the position?"

A grenade tossed into the room couldn't have shocked Klegg as much. Beneath the table, his hand turned into a fist. The Chinese seemed just as surprised. What the hell was going on in Russia? Was Demidov still running things, or had this so-called advisory council taken over?

"You know that situation is not workable," Spencer said. At the same time, she placed her hand over Klegg's fist, hoping to calm him. "We are still working to resolve that issue so that the Alliance can assemble a unified committee to deal with the Halkins."

Demidov smiled. "Of course. I quite understand. But meanwhile time passes and we get no closer to a solution. Nor will the Halkins cooperate with a committee. Colonel Delano should be attending these meetings." He shifted his gaze to Secretary Liu. "Of course, your niece should also be present, but I understand your reluctance to keep her involved."

The Russian's eyes returned to General Klegg. "So, I would like Colonel Delano to speak to the Halkins and explain that Russia is willing to accept his authority over our military forces, scientific development, and industrial production. We are confident that the Halkins will accept Delano alone, if he is nominated by the Alliance."

"President Demidov," Klegg began, "this is premature. We still have time to negotiate with the Halkins."

Demidov brushed that aside with a shake of his head. "We do not wish to continue negotiations without Colonel Delano. The Halkins trust him, and by extension, they will trust us when they know we have agreed to their terms. Meanwhile, we need Colonel Delano's help translating the technical plans for the new ships and beam weapons. We have already initiated the first steps for that process. So we want you to produce the Colonel, right now. He is, I suppose, somewhere close at hand, perhaps even in the Pentagon?"

Klegg started to reply, but Dr. Spencer cut him off. "Just what steps have you initiated, President Demidov?"

"Ah, of course," Demidov said. "Perhaps Minister Oreshkin can explain our preliminary measures."

Oreshkin leaned toward the camera, the slight adjustment increasing the size of his face on the monitor. "We have assigned a team of engineers and production specialists to study the Halkin and Tarlon ship designs, as well as the data from Jiuquan."

Prior to the arrival of the aliens, miners on Jupiter's moon, Io, had discovered an ancient space craft. Transported to China's primary testing facility at Jiuquan, engineers from all three Alliance members had already probed deep into its design secrets, desperate to learn the technology of its fusion power drive. After the Ktarran defeat, the Halkins also gave Delano's team design specifications for building beam weapons and power generators.

"When this meeting ends," Oreshkin continued, "President Demidov will begin daily press and national broadcast speeches so that the Russian people understand what is required of them. Many sacrifices must be made. Our first step will consist of ceasing all non-military production. Every factory in the Russian Federation will be ordered to retool and prepare for new manufacturing. That means no civilian vehicles, appliances, or other consumer goods will be produced. No military tanks or aircraft. Only space ships, weapons, and systems required to operate both."

Oreshkin paused to consult his notes, and Klegg jumped in. "Minister Oreshkin, if I may say, Russia does not have the facilities to construct ships and weapons systems on the scale required without help from the Alliance."

"Yes, that is true," Oreshkin said. "Which is why, just before this meeting, Marshal Shuvalov initiated a general mobilization order for the military. Reserve units will be reactivated and moved to the western front. In a day or so we will be contacting the governments of Switzerland, Poland, the Czech Republic, Germany, and Finland. Those countries will be asked to join the Russian Federation, but only for the duration of the alien crisis. With the full support of their industries and scientific skills, Russia will be able to construct the ships, systems, and weapons it requires."

The western front? Shuvalov was calling it that? "The Europeans will never agree to such a demand," Spencer said. "It is . . . unthinkable."

"An invasion of aliens was unthinkable," Demidov said. "If you think the people of Russia are going to sacrifice everything while European nations sit idle or continue profiting, you are very much mistaken. Russians will not work around the clock while the Swiss build cuckoo clocks and the Germans manufacture luxury cars." He turned to Marshal Shuvalov. "Perhaps you can explain this better than I."

Shuvalov leaned back, not forward. His gruff voice sounded harsh. "Russian troops will cross the border of any country – make that every country – that does not agree to support us. Strike forces and mobile air units are being readied. If resistance is encountered, tank divisions will enter that country, then seize and occupy any critical factories or research facilities. While our ground forces should be sufficient, if necessary air and naval units will be called in. If resistance continues, tactical nuclear weapons will be employed. After the first few examples, I expect there will be little opposition."

"You are using the alien threat as an excuse to invade Europe," Dr. Spencer said. "The Alliance, the nations of Europe will never permit it." That had remained a main plank of the Alliance since its creation. No member could expand beyond its current borders.

"Really?" Demidov's voice sounded as hard as Shuvalov's.

"The Alliance will resist Russian efforts to prepare for the alien invasion? Your so-called free press, Dr. Spencer, will be delighted to hear that. Perhaps you should consider the alternatives. Without the help of our Russian fighters, the Ktarran ship would still be destroying your country. Without Russian help, the aliens cannot be defeated. If the European countries accept our solution, there will be no need for a single Russian soldier to set foot outside of the Motherland. So I would be careful with your words, Dr. Spencer. You may find yourself on the wrong side of the argument."

"Threatening to use nuclear weapons on European cities is not reassuring the Alliance," Dr. Spencer said.

"If the Europeans are not willing to help the war effort, then they and their factories will be of no use to anyone," Demidov said. "The survival of the Alliance nations is at stake. Remember, the threat will grow with each day. Do you think the people in China and your United States will care what happens to Europe? Already in Russia there are riots and demands for action."

Spencer started to reply, but this time Klegg halted her. "I think we should ask General Secretary Liu what he thinks about all this."

Throughout the conversation, the Chinese had said nothing. Now all eyes went to Secretary Liu. "China will not permit any troop buildup along our frontier," he said.

"I thought Minister Oreshkin made himself clear," Demidov said. "The mobilization and troop movements will be only on Russia's European borders. There will be no change to the Sino-Russian region. No increase in troops, no buildup of equipment. In fact, military units may be withdrawn from that area, to serve in the western region."

Secretary Liu stared at Demidov for a moment, then turned to Klegg's camera. "President Demidov has made at least one good point. We need Colonel Delano in this meeting. I suggest you send for him, General Klegg. If Delano speaks to the Halkins on behalf of the Alliance, it might buy us some time."

Klegg opened his mouth, then shut it. If he didn't produce Delano, the Russians would simply contact the Halkins themselves. They had the translation software and the comm frequencies. Not to mention that their astrophysicist Dr. Maks Mironov had already participated in several technical discussions with Halkin and Tarlon scientists. Having Delano in the loop could actually help to slow down the Russians before they did something rash.

"I suggest we take a sixty-minute break," Klegg said. "I need to brief Colonel Delano and bring him up to speed."

"An excellent suggestion," Demidov agreed. "If he is not present when we reconvene, I will contact the Halkins and inform them that I suspect Colonel Delano is dead and request them to deal with us directly."

Before anyone could protest, Demidov gestured to someone off-camera and the Russian link went dead.

Klegg gritted his teeth at the threat. Damn Delano. Somehow the obdurate bastard seemed at the center of every crisis. "Secretary Liu, I suggest that you bring Dr. Duan into the conference as well. Colonel Delano has been, let me say, somewhat uncooperative since he's been unable to communicate with her."

"I will consider that," Secretary Liu said. "Do you believe that Demidov means what he said? He will march into Europe to seize their factories?"

That was the big question. "Yes, Secretary Liu, I think the power structure in Russia has just changed. Demidov seems more confident and in control. He obviously has the support of the key ministers. Those four are the Russian government for now."

"I agree. But we did not expect him to solidify his position so rapidly," Liu said, "or even to survive as President." He frowned. "The Alliance cannot let Russia negotiate directly with the aliens. We would lose all leverage."

"Let's hope we can solve that problem as well," Klegg said. "Now if you will excuse me, I have to eat some crow and speak with Colonel Delano."

Chapter 6

October 21, 2052, Beijing

The moment the technician severed the connection, General Secretary Liu Quisan slammed his fist on the table. "Damn the Russians! How dare they threaten to ignore us! They will work with the Americans?" With a snarl, he ordered the room cleared, leaving him alone with General Zeng.

Liu took some deep breaths. He had to restrain his temper. "Have we detected any movements on the border?"

Zeng shook his head. "No, nothing. We'll check again. But even if General Shuvalov gave the order a few hours ago, not much would be visible from our satellites so soon."

The weight of China's woes, the fractured Alliance, possibly even the entire planet, rested on Liu's shoulders. A quarter of his country lay in ruins, including the capital. Soon-to-be-arriving aliens threatened to destroy the planet. Now the Russians, unaffected by the recent conflict, seemed poised to initiate hostile actions on their European border.

Meanwhile, the Chinese Army, ordered to support the nation's emergency relief effort, threatened to revolt against Liu's decrees. Across the country protestors and mobs of angry and frightened citizens demanded guarantees of safety from further alien attacks. In fact, the situation had grown so tense that he had turned to General Zeng for military forces to guard the temporary government headquarters. And Zeng was not a particularly strong supporter of Liu's policies.

To make matters personal, President Demidov had practically brushed Liu's niece, Dr. Duan Lian, aside, deeming her unimportant to the new planetary structure. Many of China's citizens considered her a traitor to her country, an agent of the United States, as personified in Colonel Delano.

"The aliens trust Lian," Zeng kept his voice calm, "as much as they trust Delano. You have to bring her into the negotiations. If you do not, then the calls for her head from within China will only increase. Meanwhile the aliens will demand to know why she has been removed, especially since they specifically requested her."

"If she is involved," Liu said, "she will support whatever Delano proposes. She is clearly under his influence."

"It may be so. But that sword can cut two ways," Zeng argued. "Delano may be as much under her spell. I do not believe that she will fail to support both her country and the head of her family." He waved his hand, brushing aside the matter of the star-crossed lovers. "Our real problem is the Russians."

Russia had always been the weakest link in the Alliance, a geographically vast nation with a small population and limited production capacity. Its strength lay in its weapons and the will to use them. Both men knew that if the Russians seized eastern Europe with its modern fabrication facilities and skilled labor force, in time the Russian Bear would be as strong as China and the United States.

"I smell Borodin's hand in all this," Liu said. "He will work through Demidov until he has what he needs, then seize power himself."

"Yes, most likely," Zeng agreed. "But that is in the future, after the aliens are dealt with. Remember, Demidov is no fool. He will not leave himself vulnerable to such an obvious trap."

"You're correct, but that problem is for another day." Liu shook his head in disgust. "Nevertheless, place our military forces along the Russian border on alert. If one Russian soldier takes a single step in our direction, I want to be ready to respond."

"The last thing we need now is a border incident," Zeng said. "Hopefully the Russians understand what our reaction will be. I will make certain they do."

"Now I must speak with Lian," Liu said, "and make sure she appreciates what is at stake."

*   *   *

In her quarters, Dr. Duan Lian paced back and forth, trying to find an outlet for the anger and frustration that threatened to overwhelm her. Lian hated anyone or anything impinging on her privacy or freedom of movement, yet here she was, a prisoner in her own house and watched constantly.

Comfortable as the accommodations were, she hated not being able to walk outside or stroll alone through the ornamental gardens. Nothing prevented her from leaving her rooms, but whenever she stepped outside, two or more armed security guards trailed behind her. They watched her every move and stayed within two meters at all times. Uncle Quisan, the General Secretary of China, had ordered – well, strongly suggested – that she remain within the complex. She'd protested, but to no avail. He'd urged patience, the one course of action guaranteed to further enrage her.

Her uncle should have known better. A few weeks after her seventh birthday, Lian and her mother had moved into her uncle's residence. Recently appointed to the position of General Secretary of the Chinese Party, he wanted his sister to manage his household. Even as a child, Lian wanted to help her uncle. She had already mastered several Chinese dialects, and her teachers recognized their precocious pupil's linguistic ability. Since she belonged to an elite political family, Lian received the best possible education, one that included the latest international techniques.

By the time she entered university, Lian had attained recognition as one of China's top linguists, fluent in the ten major dialects, old and modern, and had mastered Korean, Japanese, Hindi, and another dozen lesser known vernaculars. She studied in Paris at the Sorbonne, and in the United States at UCLA. Her European travels added many more languages to her repertoire. Unlike Colonel Delano, who she considered more of a dilettante in his approach to learning new languages, Lian studied the history and culture of entire geographical regions and eras.

That training helped her master the languages of the alien Tarlons and Halkins, and she delved into the subtleties of nuance and accent. With Delano's help, they established a working knowledge of the aliens' language. They worked side-by-side unlocking the strange tongues in a remarkably short time. The shared danger and stress of Earth's First Contact situation had thrown them together. Before she knew what had happened, they had fallen in love, for the first time in her twenty-six years of life.

When the aliens arrived in the solar system, she'd been furious to discover she'd been excluded from those being considered for First Contact assignment. There might be a few others in China with more experience, but all were too old or infirm to withstand space travel. Only a shouting match with her uncle reluctantly persuaded him to let her join the program. In the end, the fact that he could rely on her judgment changed his mind.

And now he didn't – couldn't – trust her. For nearly twenty years, she'd thought of his dwelling as her home. Her uncle – for all practical purposes he was her father – believed she might be under alien or American influence.

Almost four days had passed, and she hadn't participated in any of the Alliance conference calls. Security had even reprogrammed her phone and tablet. She could call her uncle or her mother, but no one else. Blinking security cameras monitored her bedroom and the sitting room she used as an office.

She didn't find any cameras or microphones in the bathroom. But spy cameras had gotten so tiny that they were almost impossible to detect. Perhaps her uncle had drawn the line at that. The pressure on him had come from the Politburo Standing Committee. Currently at eleven members, every five years they selected the General Secretary of the Party, the ultimate ruler of China. Her uncle had led the country for almost fifteen years, and until the alien attack he'd enjoyed wide support from the ruling committee and the people.

The Ktarrans had changed everything with their devastating attack on Beijing. The common people wanted someone to blame, and her uncle's political support rapidly deteriorated. He now had to tread lightly with his supporters, while his critics became more outspoken. As long as there remained a chance, no matter how remote, that Lian could be under alien influence, he agreed to keep her under observation.

During her isolation, Lian wanted most of all to talk to Delano. Her feelings for him hadn't lessened. Instead her attraction had grown stronger. But he above all remained off limits. Everyone in China remained leery of his influence, some going as far as calling him the American devil.

On board the Space Station, already reconciled to their likely deaths, Lian and Delano had become intimate. When the Halkin ship rescued them from the wrecked Station, they continued the relationship. However, her country, ravaged by aliens, had no tolerance for anyone friendly to aliens. Or a woman who might be under the influence of an American lover.

Someone knocked on the door, and Lian took her time opening it. To her surprise, her uncle stood there.

"Lian, in thirty minutes there will be another conference call. The Russians have demanded that Colonel Delano attend, and I want you there as well."

He might appear impassive to others, but Lian could see the worry in his face. "What's happening, Uncle?"

"I am not certain, but prepare yourself," he said. "Russia is making demands. We may need your presence. Come to my office. We'll talk there."

One look at his face told Lian a new problem had arisen. "I will be ready." More than ready, she thought. Once in the meeting, she would insist on speaking with Delano. If they said no, she would refuse to deal with the aliens. That threat, she decided, would be all the support she needed.

Five minutes later, Lian sat across the wide teak desk in her uncle's office. The antique writing table, hand-carved for the royal court several hundred years ago by one of China's most skilled craftsman, was priceless. For all she knew, other rulers in China's past had sat there for the same purpose – making critical decisions about the country's future.

Despite the comfortable chair, she remained perched on the very edge, upright and barely restraining her impatience. Being confined to her quarters for the last four days had increased an already stressful situation.

For nearly twenty years, Lian had watched her Uncle, General Secretary Liu Quisan, direct China's affairs, internal and external, from this very room and using the same historical desk. In her childhood she often sat on his knee while he read papers and reports, until the inactivity turned her into a mischievous and squirming young girl. Lian knew he appreciated the tradition and history the polished wooden surface represented, almost as much as he enjoyed her childish demands to help her Uncle "work" at his job. She loved and respected him all the more for it.

But today the situation had reversed. Now she represented part of a problem Uncle Quisan had to resolve. The stakes were high, nothing less than the survival of her country. To advise him, General Zeng remained his constant companion, though he sat beside Lian. Zeng's face held no familial love or trace of affection. Behind Lian, discreetly inconspicuous, were two of Zeng's guards. They had only one reason for being present in the room – herself. As long as Lian lingered under the suspicion of alien mind control, she would be watched, her words and actions studied.

After days of examinations and medical tests, her uncle Quisan no longer suspected his niece of any such influence. Even

General Zeng had come to terms with her status, but many in China's Council of Ministers still had misgivings. The ministers had insisted she be monitored at all times. Zeng had agreed to be their eyes and ears, until all such doubts resolved themselves.

"Uncle, you must allow me to communicate with . . . Colonel Delano," Lian began. "The Tarlons and Halkins will soon depart from our solar system. They must be persuaded to remain and assist in Earth's defense. Otherwise our fate is sealed."

"Lian, we cannot permit this yet." She recognized the tone, the reassuring voice that had guided his people through many crises, and far longer than the sixteen years he'd been General Secretary. His appearance reinforced his image as a strong mentor, literally the most powerful man in the world. Liu Quisan spoke with the authority of his office. He'd ruled China for many years. Liu looked like a leader, with his rimless glasses and straight brushed-back, black hair.

"Uncle, you must let me work with the aliens," Lian urged. "They want to help, are willing to help, but you must give them someone to work with."

"And that would be you and Col. Delano," General Zeng said, speaking for the first time. "You want our people, our government to yield so much authority?"

Where her Uncle stood tall and imposing, General Zeng Weimin was thin, with an almost emaciated appearance. With his wispy gray mustache he looked more like a starving Buddhist priest than a powerful military leader. In fact, scholarly study of English history and its language was more than a mere hobby. It helped him understand both his allies and potential foes.

"No! We did not ask for this!" Lian struggled to keep her voice under control. They would not listen to her if she became emotional. "Find someone, anyone who can speak for the Alliance. It may not be too late to convince the Tarlons to accept a single voice. Colonel Delano and I will support your choice. But you must do something!"

Her uncle shook his head. "We will discuss that later. In twenty minutes, there will be another conference call with the Alliance, and you must be present. The situation remains uncertain, and we are still considering many options."

Speaking rapidly, he explained the crisis. For once, Lian had no words, as the import of the political emergency, precipitated by the Russians, washed over her.

"For the first time since the alien demands," Liu continued, "Colonel Delano will be in attendance, and you must take your place as well. So you must let us guide you in this, Lian. If the ministers feel that you are under alien or American influence, they will demand you be removed. My support among the Council has weakened. The people are angry and afraid. Many blame me for this disaster. If it were not for General Zeng . . ."

"Then name General Zeng to lead the Alliance," she said.

"I have already offered the Council General Zeng's name, as well as two others that might be acceptable to the Alliance," her uncle said. "I argued that he has been involved since the very beginning of the aliens' arrival, and that he worked cooperatively with the Americans and Russians. But the ministers were adamant against giving anyone from the military such power."

"Nor would the Americans, let alone the Russians, accept me in such a role," Zeng added. "I am not a diplomat or someone who can deal with political matters. I suggested your uncle, but the ministers are uncertain, not to mention that the Americans and Russians would never accept his authority."

"Then give Delano the authority," Lian pleaded. "At least until you choose someone more acceptable. Then we can begin our preparations. Once the world unites against the Ktarrans, you and the Alliance should be able to find someone to replace him."

"That may be possible. The full Council is still discussing the matter," her uncle said. "But it may not matter. The Americans are doing nothing. In fact we have received reports that they will withdraw from the Alliance. Many in America have been told we did not do enough to stop the Ktarran attack."

"And they are even more angry at Russia," Zeng added, "for not being attacked at all. The Americans are fools."

"And no one supports this man . . . Delano," her uncle said. "Not even his own countrymen. General Klegg has him under guard at the Pentagon."

Lian stared at her Uncle. "Is that why he has not contacted me?"

Quisan sighed. "Yes, I suppose. It would not have been permitted. General Klegg did not want him talking to you, or to anyone for that matter."

The knowledge that Delano was not free lifted a weight from Lian's heart. She had not believed he had forgotten her so quickly, but doubts had troubled her. Her first intelligence briefing had described him as a rugged Marine, tall and athletic, who sought the company of women. His picture, in his Marine captain's uniform, gave the impression of strength rather than someone attractive to the opposite sex.

"I want to speak with him," she said.

"Unfortunately, I must ask the Council of Ministers for permission," Quisan said. "They were most firm about that. Perhaps it can be arranged after today's meeting with General Klegg and President Demidov."

Reading her uncle's face, Lian knew there was no point in arguing. His position as General Secretary of the Party might already be in jeopardy.

"Very well," she said. "I will wait until then." Lian rose. "General Zeng, please help my uncle. He has the best interests of China at heart."

Without waiting for an answer, she left the office, leaving the two men alone.

"Your niece believes in you." Zeng shook his head in frustration. "She knows I have not always supported your policies. Yet she would turn this power over to me. I find it hard to understand."

"Each man must make his own way in life," Quisan said. "Without your leadership in the crisis, China would have fared much worse. You have done more for China in the last few weeks than anyone knows."

"As has Lian, it seems," Zeng said. "Perhaps it is time for us to trust her judgment. It may be Colonel Delano is not as foolish as his leaders. If the American President and General Klegg are against him, it may prove helpful for us to support the Russian position regarding Delano and Lian."

"Such ideas may not win you more friends in the Council," Liu said. "But I for one will respect your opinion."

"I do not believe your niece seeks power, or will abuse her authority simply because of an American lover."

"In that we agree," Quisan said. "Yet I wish that Colonel Delano were old and fat and not a handsome Marine." He, too, shook his head. "After the next meeting with Klegg, it may be time to take a new stance."

"Yes, it will be interesting to hear what Demidov thinks," Zeng agreed. "Assuming he remains in power. There is a good chance that he, too, will not survive."

Zeng shrugged. "This meeting should answer many questions."

"Beware the old saying," Quisan said. "May you live in interesting times."

Chapter 7

October 21, 2052, 7:35 a.m. EST, Washington, D.C.

The steady pounding on the door woke Delano, but before he could drag himself out of bed to find out who it was, the lock clicked and General Klegg strode into the room. Delano, still in his skivvies, sat on the edge of the bed and stared at his early morning visitor. Delano's head ached from too much whiskey the night before, his throat felt dry, and he really wanted to sleep a few more hours.

"Hope you don't mind me waking you up," Klegg said, his words only a little less than a snarl. "Get dressed. You look like hell. General . . . I mean President Demidov wants you to join the daily conference call."

Klegg's surly words provoked Delano even more than the abrupt entry into his room. "Not interested. Close the door on the way out."

"You're still begging for a court-martial, aren't you? Now either you get dressed, or I'll have those two guards come in, put you in cuffs, and drag your sorry ass to the conference room. You can talk just as well in your underwear."

"You do what you have to do, General," Delano said. "Like I told you before, you either send me back to Paris or put me in the brig. But I'm done talking to you."

Klegg took a half-step forward, then stopped, his hands balled into fists.

Well, this should get me a ticket to the brig or the hospital. But Delano no longer cared. The urge to rearrange the man's face proved too strong to resist. He stood and faced his superior. Klegg might be more than twenty years older, but the man boxed for exercise and looked in shape. The outcome, as Delano's drill instructor used to say, remained in doubt.

The two men glared at each other. Then Klegg relaxed. When he spoke, he had his voice under control. "I'll make some allowance for your hangover, but I thought you wanted to talk to Lian. She's included in the conference. I'll tell her you're too busy packing for your trip to the San Diego brig, if it's still standing. Maybe she'll visit you there for the next twenty years."

Lian! That changed everything. For the chance to speak with her he'd gladly endure another useless conference, even one with Klegg calling the shots. "OK, give me ten minutes to shower and shave."

Klegg snorted. "Hurry up. Things are happening, and Demidov doesn't seem in the mood to wait." He turned to the two guards watching the proceedings with interest from the doorway. Both faces showed disappointment. Watching a fistfight between a four-star General and a Lt. Col. would have made their day. "Get him to the conference room as fast as possible." Klegg stalked out, muttering under his breath.

But Delano scarcely heard the words, already heading for the bathroom and a wake-up shower.

He needed almost twenty minutes before he actually took a seat in front of the cameras, a coffee cup in his hand. The wall clock said 8:21 a.m. He found himself sitting beside NSA Director Vivian Spencer. Delano nodded a polite hello, which she ignored. *Well, fuck you, too.*

"What's on the agenda this morning?" Delano took a cautious sip from the cup.

Her head snapped around. "Didn't Klegg brief you? What the hell have you been doing?"

"No, Klegg didn't . . ."

"Fuck . . . never mind. Listen, Delano," she said, "Demidov has asked for you. He wants you to come to Russia and take over the mobilization of the entire country and initiate contact with the Halkins. And by the way, Russia is planning to move into eastern Europe and seize critical industries there. Demidov wants you to talk to the Halkins and agree to their terms. I can't believe it, but apparently he's willing to place the Russian military and economy under your, and the Halkins, control. And if you don't cooperate, or aren't available, Demidov intends to deal with the Halkins himself."

Delano's first reaction was to ask if she were serious, but the look on her face told him not to bother. "What about Lian? The Halkins wanted her, too."

"I think Demidov is being cagey," Spencer said. "He asked for her as well, but in a lukewarm way. To all appearances he doesn't care if she works with you or not." She shook her head. "Brilliant! I can't think of a better way to convince Secretary Liu to include her."

Jeez! Delano had been out of the loop for less than seventy-two hours, and the Alliance, already bickering among themselves, appeared ready to fall apart.

The comm link went active early. Delano glanced up to see General Secretary Liu, General Zeng, and Lian on the monitor.

General Klegg, across the room and discussing something with his aide, Major Mitchell, joined Spencer and Delano facing the cameras. Klegg didn't waste any words. "Welcome back, Secretary Liu, General Zeng."

This time General Zeng took the lead. He didn't even wait for Klegg to take his seat. "General Klegg, are you considering letting Colonel Delano deal with the Russians?" Zeng's faultless English, acquired during his studies at Harvard, always sounded out of place coming from his Chinese peasant features.

"Yes, I am," Klegg said. "I don't like it, don't like any part of it, but it's either that or Demidov starts talking directly to the Halkins. He's got the software and the frequencies. We'd have no way to stop him, or even know what was going on."

"I just updated the President," Dr. Spencer said. "He's fully involved with the situation in California, and frankly he doesn't give a damn about friendly aliens right now. He's not happy with the Alliance, and not at all pleased with the idea of Colonel Delano running anything. Regardless, General Klegg and I discussed it, and we think it's best to agree, at least temporarily. We can always pull Delano out of the loop if things get out of hand."

Zeng shook his head. "Your President's actions are unfortunate." He whispered something to Secretary Liu that the microphone didn't catch.

Liu spoke up. "It's almost time. If Delano is involved, then Lian must be as well. She will join the discussion."

Neither of the Chinese leaders bothered to notice Delano, let alone say anything to him. They probably thought he'd contaminated Lian somehow, after defiling her body. He couldn't wait to hear how the Russians treated him. At least he could see Lian, and he knew a big smile had spread across his face. Maybe they could speak after the session ended. *Yeah, sure, they're just going to let the two of you shoot the breeze. Asshole!*

* * *

The Russian end of the communications link went active at exactly 8:30 a.m. Obviously the Russians didn't intend to waste any time. Delano recognized Demidov, the new president of the Russian Federation, but not the three hard-case men seated beside him. The oldest, wearing the uniform of a Russian Army Field Marshal, sat smoking a cigarette, a real tobacco stick. The others wore civilian clothes that might have come from the same bad tailor – boring dark brown or dull slate gray.

Delano might joke at their clothes, but the four Russians appeared nothing to laugh about. Sharp, intelligent eyes bored into the camera. Even Demidov, who had smiled often during the crisis meetings, now seemed covered with granite. Definitely not a happy group. *Well, I should fit right in.*

Demidov took in Delano and Lian's presence, then got right to the point.

"Colonel Delano," the Russian president said, "it is good to see you again. Congratulations on your promotion. Have you been briefed on Russia's position regarding the aliens' demand?"

"Not really," Delano answered, "just that you wished me to speak to the Halkins and Tarlons on your behalf."

"That is partially correct, Colonel," Demidov said. "But what we really want is to place the military and industrial resources of Russia under your control, so that you and the Halkins can start preparing us for the next Ktarran assault. I am now formally requesting that you come to Moscow at once, to meet with our leaders and civilian advisors, speak to our countrymen, and begin the mobilization effort."

Stunned, Delano hesitated, and before he could speak, Minister Oreshkin spoke.

"The situation is unique, Colonel Delano," Oreshkin said. "The Russian people need to hear from you, directly and immediately. There is much confusion. Soon unrest will begin to grow. Our countrymen must see and listen to you. Otherwise the full deployment of our resources will not be accepted. Coming from you, with the support of the Halkins, the message to the citizens of Russia will be better received. The state of affairs here is . . . fluid, to say the least. If we, the Russian government, attempt to do this without your support, there will be endless and needless resistance. It is unfortunate, but in this matter our people will trust you more than they do us. Meanwhile, we want the construction of these new spaceships to begin as soon as possible."

Demidov took over. "We must convince the Halkins that we are doing our utmost to prepare for the next Ktarran arrival."

"I don't know what you expect from me, General . . . I mean President Demidov." Delano glanced at General Klegg, but saw no help there. What the hell was he supposed to say? He had no intention of going to Moscow to be some figurehead. "I will be glad to work with you, help you talk with the Halkins, but I can do that from here just as well."

"No, that will not be satisfactory, Colonel," Demidov said. "You must understand, if you do not come here and accept the role that the Halkins demand, thousands, maybe millions of people are going to die. There will be major opposition both inside Russia and in Europe. We want those ships to be built and those weapons readied, and we can only do that with Halkin support. Which means you must take charge, without any conditions or reservations. At once."

Delano glanced at the Chinese monitor. Secretary Liu and General Zeng's faces revealed nothing, but Lian's hands told a different story. During the tense days of negotiations aboard the Space Station with the aliens, Delano and Lian had established many ways of signaling to each other, both on and off camera. Now her right forefinger lifted slightly, the signal for assent. If it had been tucked in, the meaning would be the opposite.

She wanted him to accept the Russian proposal. Delano looked toward Klegg and Spencer. Both stared stonily at the cameras, refusing to look at him. Still no assistance there. Delano felt his jaw tighten. *Here we go again. I am so screwed.* "President Demidov, if it is approved by General Klegg, I will be glad to come to Moscow and assist you in any way that I can."

"Excellent," Demidov beamed. "General Klegg, how soon can Colonel Delano be ready to leave?"

Klegg forced a smile to his face. "Assuming I can find transport, I can have Colonel Delano aboard a jet in a few hours. Is that quick enough, President Demidov?"

"Yes, of course," Demidov said. "But if you can't find a plane, we will send an Antonov An-168 for him."

Demidov had been a general in the Russian Air Force, so of course he knew his planes and their availability.

Delano looked at Klegg for the third time. Still nothing. *Well, then, fuck it all.* "General Klegg, I'd like Sergeants Stecker and Macy to accompany me. They can help me set up communication links. And President Demidov, I'd like to consult with those Russians who were aboard the Space Station. They have a unique viewpoint and I trust their judgment."

Klegg hesitated, then nodded. "A good suggestion. My aide, Major Mitchell will also accompany you. He can act as liaison with the Pentagon."

Naturally they weren't going to let him go off on his own, with just his own people.

Klegg wasn't finished. "I would remind you, President Demidov, that Colonel Delano has a tendency to do things on his own. You may be asking for more than you anticipate."

"Yes, I suppose you're right, General Klegg." Demidov smiled. "Colonel Delano has, how do you say it, the defects of his qualities."

"If I may suggest," Secretary Liu broke in, "I think my niece Lian should also be present. She will be most helpful in any alien talks."

"That would be even better," Demidov agreed, with just the slightest trace of reluctance. "With both working with the Halkins, we should make rapid progress."

"You will be responsible for her safety," Liu said. "I would not want anything to happen to her while in Moscow."

Demidov glanced at Minister Borodin, who nodded approval. "She will be quite safe, General Secretary."

"Since Russia has already decided on its course of action," Liu said, "China and the United States must now decide on our policies toward the Halkins. General Klegg, I will call back within the hour. And now I believe that Lian wishes to speak privately with Colonel Delano."

Everyone forced a smile. Demidov muttered his goodbyes, and the Russian link went dark.

*   *   *

The private talk with Lian didn't amount to much. They knew that their conversation was being monitored at both ends. Without the luxury of privacy, the discourse remained strictly platonic. He wanted to say more, but the awkward situation put him at a loss for words. Fortunately, he sensed the bond between them remained, and few words were required. They chatted politely for a few minutes, before Lian summed up the session.

"I will see you in Moscow," Lian said. "We will have much to talk about." *In private.*

Her smile warmed the words. Delano nodded. "Yes. In Moscow, then."

She broke the connection. For a moment Delano just sat there, trying to sort everything out. Soon he'd be on his way to Russia as a . . . what the hell was his status? For all he knew, the Russians might toss him in jail or keep him and Lian under lock and key, using them for some unfathomable purpose or political propaganda.

Before his thoughts became too gloomy, the door opened and Klegg and Dr. Spencer returned. Delano frowned. *Now I'll get my marching orders.*

Klegg pulled his chair back, while Spencer sat next to Delano. "Do you understand what's happening, Colonel?" Klegg's voice no longer sounded truculent.

"Not really," Delano said. "Sounds like I'm going to Moscow to give some speeches and contact the Halkins."

"We think it's a lot more than that," Dr. Spencer said. "It's likely that the Russians will give you full authority to deal with the Halkins and to direct the Russian economy. They want to mobilize the country, put it on a total war footing, just as Stalin did when he fought the Nazis. This way, if anything goes wrong, you and Lian will be the ones taking the blame. The Halkins and Tarlons will like that arrangement, however. So they will do everything they can to assist both you and Russia."

"That part doesn't sound too bad to me," Delano offered. "We do need to prepare for the Ktarrans."

"Yes, we know," Spencer said, resignation in her voice. "Demidov has forced our hand. In the next seventy-two hours, we need to convince the United States and China to accept you and Lian as the final authority on planetary defense. Global mobilization is coming, which means you'll be making serious and strategic decisions, life and death decisions. You and the Halkins and the Tarlons. And don't fool yourself, people are going to die. Hundreds, perhaps even thousands. No matter what choices you make, things will get ugly across the globe."

The thought sobered Delano. But something had to be done, or the Ktarrans would insure that everyone died. With the human species facing extinction, the good of the many had to outweigh the good of the few. That mistake could not be corrected. "Dr. Spencer, General Klegg, whatever I do, I'll try to save as many as I can."

"I believe you will, Colonel," Klegg said. "And I think the only way that this arrangement is going to work is if you treat everyone as fairly as possible." He took a deep breath. "Dr. Spencer and I will speak to the president. Hopefully he'll accept the recommendation that the United States remains under full martial law, with you as the military and industrial leader of the nation, at least for the duration. But I want to warn you, President Clark is not happy with any of us right now. We may all be out of a job by tomorrow."

Delano knew that Clark was an asshole. "And the Chinese? Will they go along?"

"If we do, they'll have to," Spencer said. "Dr. Duan Lian's acceptance by the Halkins means they have a seat at the big table. They won't like giving up any authority, but they'll realize what they need to do. It's either that, or the aliens work with us and the Russians, and leave China out of the loop. Assuming, of course, that Klegg and I can convince the president. He's been, uh, less than pleasant lately regarding anything to do with aliens."

That's a job Delano wouldn't want. He actually felt sorry for Klegg. *Well, almost.* "I'll do my best," he said, then added "Sir."

Chapter 8

October 22, 2052, 00:15 MSK, Star City, Russia

Fourteen hours after the conference call ended, the US Air Force C-20M landed at Chkalovsky military airport, located near Shchyolkovo, thirty-one kilometers northeast of Moscow. Local time was a little after midnight. General Klegg diverted the aircraft from flying medical supplies to California, and ordered it to Andrews AFB. There it refueled and picked up Delano and his three traveling companions.

No matter how great the crisis or urgent the need, the American military would not embarrass itself into using a Russian plane.

As before, Gunny Stecker was ordered to provide security for Delano, with Sergeant Macey to establish communications. Major Mitchell, meanwhile, would spy on Delano and report everything back to General Klegg. Or so Delano believed, though maybe not in those words. He thought Mitchell a little pompous, but Klegg obviously liked and trusted him, so maybe he wasn't all bad.

A month ago Delano had been the junior officer to Mitchell, but now that role had changed, with Mitchell being the junior. As always in the military, Delano knew things could get worse. With his usual bad luck and poor timing, they probably would.

The flight from Andrews to Shchyolkovo lasted only nine hours. It turned into a non-stop planning session, with the four passengers exchanging ideas, suggestions, and research. Mitchell turned into a valuable asset, using the internet and the military databases to check on facts and figures. Everyone slept for the last two hours, waking up when the big plane bumped down onto the runway. The weary but somewhat refreshed travelers deplaned as ready as they could be, given the jet lag factor.

A Russian helicopter, rotors turning idly, waited to lift them to the Star City complex. The chopper generated far too much noise for any real conversation, and the provided hearing protection didn't seem to do much. The ten minute flight ended soon enough. A Russian Air Force colonel, his great coat belted around him, waited to receive them. But the first surprise of the trip occurred when Delano climbed out of the chopper and found Lian and Sergeant Shen standing a few steps away.

Before Delano could recover, Lian was in his arms, holding him close, as close as they had held each other on the Station, awaiting death to overtake them. For a moment, he felt awkward. "Lian, it's good to see you . . ."

She stood on her toes and kissed him. Delano dropped his bag, wrapped both arms around her, and returned the kiss. *The hell with everybody. It wasn't much of a secret, anyway.* None of the bystanders said anything, though most had smiles on their faces.

Lian broke the embrace, and Delano shook hands with Sergeant Shen before they all crowded into a minivan. A five minute drive took them into the Star City complex, to the facility where then-General Demidov had directed the Russian efforts against the Ktarrans. And rumored to be the place where, according to Mitchell, Demidov had put a bullet in the back of President Garanin's head. Delano didn't care about that – old and unimportant news by now. The cold night air had them all moving quickly inside, where Delano and Lian found another of President Demidov's aides waiting for them.

"Welcome to Star City, Colonel Delano, Dr. Duan. I am Major Pushkin," he said, extending his hand to each of them. "It is a pleasure to meet you both. You've had long trips and must be tired, so I will take you to your quarters and let you get some sleep. We will meet tomorrow morning at ten o'clock. Of course, if you need anything, please let me know. Guards will be posted at either end of the corridor, to make sure you are not disturbed."

Entering his room, Delano had a moment of déjà vu. The cheap furnishings reminded him of his VIP quarters beneath the Pentagon. He wasted no time. After dumping his bag on the bed, he left his room. Ignoring the guards, he entered Lian's room, conveniently located next to his, and locked the door behind him. A connecting door would have been better, but after what they had endured, neither one worried about convenience or propriety. They'd become lovers on the Station where there was little privacy and later on the Halkin rescue ship, with aliens who didn't know the meaning of the word.

What they did worry about were the listening devices almost certainly installed in the chamber. Lian punched up some music on her tablet, making it loud enough to be distracting, before they crawled naked under the covers. Pulling the thick comforter over their heads, they held each other close. The room held a chill, and Lian shivered in his arms.

When Delano whispered in her ear, the language he chose was the same one they had used on the Station, the Yue dialect of the Cantonese region. Not that either of them had much to say. As the bed warmed up, Lian stopped trembling. They made love, frantically at first, then more slowly and tenderly the second time.

Afterward, satisfied for the moment, they lay in each other's arms.

"Joe, do you know what to say tomorrow?"

"Not really. But at least I have some talking points. We did a lot of thinking during the flight in, and the Gunny and Steve had some interesting ideas. But I'll need your help. This is all so . . . terrifying."

"Whatever you need," Lian said. "But my uncle insists that I be at your side. He expects me to be your equal in the decisions and negotiations. My country must not be slighted."

"Well, your uncle is going to be disappointed," Delano laughed. "You are going to be a lot more than just equal. At least a dozen times on the plane, someone said 'Lian can handle that.'"

He kissed her again. "I don't know how this is all going to end, but we will do this together – every assessment, every decision – we'll resolve them all together. I'm already convinced that this is the only way this whole planetary defense thing can work."

"Good." She returned his kiss. "Then we can forget about tomorrow. For now," she moved her hand down his chest, "we need to make up for lost time."

*   *   *

At ten o'clock in the morning, Delano and his team settled into chairs around Demidov's long conference table. Along with the Russian President, his three top ministers were there, each accompanied by an aide of his own. Demidov sat at one end of the table, facing Delano and Lian at the other. The three aides, all with somber faces, took their places just behind their respective ministers, ready to take notes or answer questions as needed.

Everyone exchanged polite greetings. The ministers appeared wary of Sergeants Shen, Stecker, Macey, and Major Mitchell being present, though none of the four spoke much Russian. Stecker and Shen carried their sidearms, and the security people hadn't liked that idea. Before it became an issue, President Demidov had overruled his personal guards. After that, aside from some uneasy glances, no one said anything further about the men or their weapons.

Delano started right in, glancing down at his notes. "President Demidov, first, let me say that I'm aware of the significance of your request for Dr. Duan and me to meet with all of you. The world political and military situation is unique, and I hope that whatever difficulties arise, we can work together to deal with them. Russia has been the first to grasp the magnitude of the danger that faces Earth. Lian and I are grateful for your support."

"We appreciate your words," Demidov said. "We have prepared a list of specific items Russia requires from the Halkins. The designs for the Halkin ship and power source are our first priority. And their weapons, of course."

"A good starting point," Delano cut in before the President could continue. "But even at this preliminary stage, I think we should anticipate the planet's full requirements. May we give you some of our first ideas?"

Demidov's face seemed to harden, but he restrained himself. "Yes, of course."

Here we go. "Starting with space craft, I believe we will require six types of ships to meet the Ktarran invasion. First, we need some type of 'lift to orbit' vehicle, a space jeep or cargo truck so to speak. That will be used to deliver cargoes and people into low-earth orbit. Second, we will need a freighter to transport the materials to the Moon, where more jeeps can unload the vessels. Third . . ."

"Why the Moon, Colonel Delano?" Minister Borodin asked. "We intend to build our ships here on Earth, in Russia."

"Unfortunately, that is not practical." Delano took care with his words, not wanting to offend the first one to question his ideas. He'd been well-briefed about Borodin on the flight. "The fighting ships, if they are to be powered by the anti-matter engines, cannot operate inside a planet's atmosphere. Nor can they really be tested on Earth. And it seems wasteful to add a second set of engines merely to lift the vessel into orbit. The Halkins and the Tarlons build their fighting ships in space or on a low-gravity moon."

"You are certain of this?" Demidov sounded doubtful.

"Yes. During our flight to Moscow, I communicated with the Halkin ship. I spoke with the Tarlons chief technical officer, Jarendo, for some time and he confirmed this."

The notion that Delano had communicated with one of the three senior Tarlon members aboard the Halkin vessel jolted the Russians. Since the ultimatum, only Ahvin, the lower-level Halkin female, had spoken to any humans. She had refused all requests to pass on questions or plans to either the Halkin Captain Horath, or Talmak, the Tarlon leader, without the approval of Delano and Lian.

"If I may suggest, President Demidov," Delano went on, "you might prefer to let me finish my opening remarks. It may save time and answer many questions."

"Continue, Colonel Delano." Demidov was frowning now.

"The third type of ship we will need is a small, two-seat attack craft. It will be able to launch missiles and carry a single beam weapon. I think of this craft as an equivalent to a torpedo or patrol missile boat. It will be both fast and agile. A highly maneuverable ship that is sufficiently hardened should be able to dodge beam weapons or even survive a brief contact.

"Fourth, we will want a larger attack craft. I expect this would be similar in size and armament to the Tarlon ship, with at least three beam weapons. It must also be capable of carrying missiles."

Delano paused, but no one said anything. *Don't lose them now.* "With these two types of combat ships operating within the solar system, we believe we can best defend the planet. Since none of these vessels will be sent on long voyages or through the wormhole, they won't need to carry large supplies of food, water, and fuel. That means we should be able to pack more weapons and bigger engines to provide higher maneuverability and utilize stronger plasma screens. And build them quicker."

"So you do not envision building larger ships?" Demidov asked. "May I ask why?"

Don't step on his ego. "For us, larger means slower," Delano said. "The Ktarrans are very experienced building oversized ships, and their vessels will exceed anything we can construct and test in the time available. If we follow the basic blueprint of the Tarlon ship, our testing needs will be greatly simplified. Therefore we should be able to construct more vessels."

Delano looked around. No one challenged him. "Our battle theory is that we will need to be smaller and faster. Think about the Japanese Naval Forces in World War II. They had the largest battleships afloat, but they proved largely ineffective. If we are to defeat the Ktarrans, we must present them with tactics and equipment that are unfamiliar to them."

No one said anything. *Damn, did I hit a nerve?* If he couldn't get past his first session with these men, all hope was lost. The silence dragged on until Field Marshal Shuvalov cleared his throat.

"The colonel's ideas seem correct to me," Shuvalov said. "If we try to match them ship for ship, we will invariably lose. We should not attempt to fight them using tactics or weapons they are familiar with. Even tactics that the Tarlons might recommend. They have, after all, failed to stop the Ktarrans."

Like the voice of God, from heaven above. "Thank you, Field Marshal," Delano said. "We hadn't talked about actual fighting yet."

"And smaller ships with smaller crews can be constructed and repaired faster, similar to our T-34 Tank." Shuvalov paused to let that sink in. Everyone at the table knew all about the famous World War II battle tank that turned back the German invasion. "I expect these ships will take heavy losses, you understand that?"

"Yes, I suppose they will," Delano said. *People will die, just like Klegg said.*

"How many of these combat ships do you foresee?" Minister Oreshkin asked.

"As many as we can build," Delano said, "at least one hundred of each type. We have to assume that the Ktarrans will send a strong force. They won't want to risk another failure. The Halkins estimate that at least one hundred enemy ships will form the invasion fleet. They have plenty of time to gather and prepare sufficient forces. Since they don't expect the war to be a long one, they will have no problem temporarily diverting ships from other locations within the stellar quadrant."

"All this construction will need to be carefully coordinated with China and the United States." Delano took a breath. "Everyone knows Russia builds rugged aircraft and ships. Pound for pound, we want our ships to be tougher and faster. They will need to resist high acceleration, possible nuclear blasts, EMP radiation, and particle beam weapons. One of our goals is to produce an equal number of ships for each member of the Alliance. That will allow our fleets to work together efficiently and fairly."

"I do not believe we can construct so many ships of unknown design," Minister Oreshkin said. "We would need the plans and construction crews in place. Even the small ships you describe are far larger than a battle tank, and we do not have the capacity for so many."

"I understand, Minister," Delano said. "That's why we are hopeful that the United States and the European nations will join with you. We must have their expertise in metallurgy, production, testing, and system design and integration."

"And if your Americans do not join with us, what then?" Demidov's voice sounded harsh.

"Earth will not survive the next alien encounter," Delano said. He motioned to Lian.

"I spoke with my uncle shortly before we landed," Lian said. "He hopes China's Ruling Committee will accept the Halkin suggestion of appointing Colonel Delano and myself co-leaders of the planet's defenses until the invasion is resolved. If my government joins with you, the Americans will have no choice but to follow."

"China has the most capacity for building nuclear missiles," Delano said. "With engineering help from the Tarlons and Halkins, we'll improve both the design and durability of such weapons. Nuclear weapons expertise is one of the two specializations where Earth probably exceeds or equals alien technology."

"What is the other?" Oreshkin asked.

"Computers and software," Delano said. "Other alien species have never developed such advanced computer hardware and software. We believe," he waved his hand to include his companions, "that is a tremendous advantage. It gives us an edge that the Ktarrans won't expect. And of course we'll need powerful computers for the drones and rail gun platforms. That is a field in which my country still leads the way."

"You expect to use drones in a space battle?" Demidov said.

"Possibly, if it's feasible. Small craft with hardened surfaces that can accelerate rapidly and change direction. Not even the Ktarrans have unmanned fighting ships, since they never developed the required computer technology. Without anyone aboard, the drones will be able to perform maneuvers impossible for a human crew. I expect they will carry various types of weapons, including rail guns. At close range, say a hundred kilometers, a rail gun under computer control could be devastating. In the vacuum of space, projectile speeds could be significantly faster than what we have available today."

"Rail guns are still problematical," Shuvalov commented. "Will they operate in space?"

The rail gun as a weapon had encountered almost as many problems as the fusion engine. Their primary usage remained aboard naval vessels. They functioned – China had made advances proving that – but even after forty years of development, issues remained.

"I showed the Tarlon technical expert, Jarendo, a typical rail gun design," Delano said. "He was quite curious. He believes the design would work better in space than on land, if we can manage the recoil. With the coldness of space to cool the rails and DC power obtained from the anti-matter scoops, Jarendo believed an effective weapon could be developed. One strong enough to penetrate Ktarran shields."

Delano watched the Russians glance at each other. No one said anything, but he guessed they had not expected Delano and Lian to be so well prepared. The Russian agenda, whatever it might have been, was off the table, for now at least.

"You mentioned six types of space craft," Borodin said. "I count only five, including the drones. Did I miss one?"

"No, Minister, you did not," Delano said. "The sixth type of space craft is the most important. Lian and I believe that there remains a strong possibility that Earth will not survive the Ktarrans. For example, they might reach Earth and seed the atmosphere with nerve agents or biological weapons. So we believe the Alliance should also construct large interstellar transports, each capable of carrying a thousand or so humans to another star system. These people will be the salvation of the human race if the Ktarrans overrun the planet."

"How many of these . . . transports do you envision?" Borodin asked.

"I don't know, Minister." Delano sighed. "As many as we can possibly build. At least five, if we want to give the human race a decent chance to continue its existence. That way some of your families, some of your children, may yet survive. The ships would need to be self-sufficient for at least five years. That much time, Jarendo believes, could carry them to another star system, where they might access another wormhole. That would put them out of reach of Ktarran pursuit, at least for a generation or two. Of course if we drive off the Ktarrans, they could return to Earth."

"Why can't we use the wormhole off Jupiter?" Minister Oreshkin wanted to know.

"By our bad luck, or perhaps good, this solar system is like a dead-end street. The wormhole ends here, and we can only use it to go back toward Ktarran controlled space. That's how Jarendo described it, Minister. So we will need to travel through uncharted space and hope to encounter undiscovered wormholes. Jarendo said that most such openings are near planetary giants, but there are many in interstellar space as well."

"The interstellar transports will do more than provide a method of escaping the planet," Delano said. "Aside from offering hope for the future, they can be a motivator for our best and brightest to work on our defense. We must initiate and win a campaign for the support of the people. This opportunity to leave Earth should help. The fact that we are building escape ships will deliver the proper message to our people – the Ktarran threat is both real and immediate."

The first of the best and brightest would undoubtedly be members of the ruling governments, Delano knew, but that couldn't be helped. *Some things never change.*

Demidov pushed back his chair. "We need to discuss this in private. We are not prepared to agree . . ."

"If I may speak," General Shuvalov said. "I am a soldier. I understand the ways of war, perhaps better than President Demidov and Ministers Borodin and Oreshkin. To win battles, one sometimes must make deals with the devil. Short cuts must often be taken and risks ignored. If lives are lost, so be it. I believe Colonel Delano and Dr. Duan are suggesting total war.

"Naturally there are things that we will not like, tactics that we might not choose ourselves. Remember, the Chinese and Americans will come up with their own plans to wage war. In this case a particular solution, perfect or not, may be better than any attempts to develop an optimum solution. If we are not ready to accept that, then we are already doomed. Following Colonel Delano and Dr. Duan's plan may actually give us a head start. Of course Russia must work with the Alliance and others as equals if we are to achieve our goals. As your General Patton said, a good plan violently executed today is better than a perfect plan next week."

"Excuse me," Steve said. "There's a call from Beijing coming in for Dr. Duan. Should I put it through?"

Demidov appeared surprised, and Borodin frowned. Delano knew the bunker complex was considered a secure site, with no unofficial communications in or out except through the main communications center.

"Steve is, as you know, our communications expert. He has some . . . special equipment." Delano paused. "I suggest that Dr. Duan take the call here. It may be important."

"Of course," Demidov said, reverting to his usual good nature. "Let us hope it brings good news."

Steve rose and moved to Lian's side. She plugged her phone into the connector cable he offered, and the phone immediately rang.

"Dr. Duan, here." She held the phone to her ear for a moment. "Let me put you on the speaker, Uncle." She set the phone down on the table. "We are meeting with President Demidov and his ministers. Do you have any news?"

"Yes, Lian." General Secretary Liu's voice sounded grave and formal, even coming from the tiny speaker. "General Zeng is with me. We have just come from a meeting of the Central Military Commission. A vote was taken, and the Commission has agreed to meet the Halkin demands. You and Colonel Delano will lead the defense effort, at least for the immediate future."

"That is good news, Uncle," Lian said, relief apparent in her voice.

"The Council insisted on two requirements, however," Liu went on. "First you must fully share command with Colonel Delano. That means complete participation in all meetings and decisions, especially those that involve China's interests."

"Of course, Uncle. Colonel Delano has already informed me and the Russian government that we will share our authority equally."

"Good. The second requirement is that all communications from you or Colonel Delano must be presented to General Zeng, or someone he may designate, as well as myself. Neither you nor Colonel Delano may speak with me without General Zeng's presence. We must avoid any possible doubts regarding family influence."

Lian looked at Delano, who nodded. "That is acceptable," Lian said.

"Then you and President Demidov may consider that China will accept Dr. Duan Lian and Colonel Delano as the military leaders of Earth's planetary defenses until the threat is removed. Of course China retains its authority over local matters."

"Thank you, Uncle," Lian said. "Colonel Delano and I will not let you down. Is there anything else we should know?"

"Nothing. Right now the damage to Beijing and our seacoast cities and towns is our primary concern. People are still dying in the ruins of the capital. Until the city can recover, we must do all that we can to alleviate the situation."

Delano leaned closer to the phone. "Secretary Liu, have you heard anything from General Klegg?"

"Yes, but it is not . . . helpful. Apparently there is a serious problem within your government. President Clark refuses to consider the Halkin request for a unified command. He will soon be consulting with General Klegg, who we expect to be replaced. It is also rumored that President Clark wishes to declare an end to martial law, now that the aliens have been defeated. And he has notified me that he intends to withdraw from the Alliance."

Yeah, sure, the crisis is over. Delano grimaced. He might not get along with the hard-ass Klegg, but the man *had* saved the planet. So of course the idiot Clark wanted to get rid of him. *No good deed goes unpunished*. "Secretary Liu, Lian and I ask that you please contact President Clark, along with President Demidov, to persuade him to change his mind. There isn't much time before the Halkins depart. We spoke with them from the plane yesterday. They're somewhat helpful, but they remain committed to leaving in less than three days. Without their help, we cannot survive."

"Understood. We will do what we can," Liu said. "Lian, China is in your hands."

"I understand the responsibility," she said, her voice firm. "We will not let our nation down."

"Secretary Liu, we will contact you regarding resources later today or tomorrow," Delano said. "But I suggest you begin selecting your best engineers and industrial designers. We want to start building ships as soon as possible, and you need to hear all about that."

"Do not bother," Liu said. "Give the information to General Zeng. He will arrive in Moscow tonight, with a small team of experts. He wishes to meet with you and Lian. Assuming you approve, President Demidov?"

"We will be glad to have him," Demidov said.

Delano leaned back. Russia and China were coming around. Now only the US was holding up the party.

Chapter 9

October 22, 2052 08:15 a.m. EST

In Washington, General Langdon Klegg strode down the White House corridor that led to the Oval Office. Alabaster statues and gold-framed portraits adorned the beige walls, while the thick red and blue carpet completed the well-decorated waiting area. The furniture provided a last moment of comfort and eye relief for those nervously awaiting an audience with the President of the United States. At the end of the passageway Klegg saw Dr. Vivian Spencer sitting on a plush burgundy sofa. Both were early for the eleven o'clock meeting. Klegg started to take a gilded armchair across from Vivian, but she beckoned him to join her.

Sitting beside her probably wasn't a good idea, but Vivian had made up her mind. Like it or not, she and Klegg had developed a relationship, and she didn't intend to try and keep it secret. Not that a thing like that could be kept private for very long, not in this town, where everyone knew everything about everybody.

Klegg didn't really care either, as he sat beside her. What people thought or said about them no longer mattered. If their meeting with President Clark didn't change his mind, the entire planet would be in trouble, in which case Klegg's personal problems meant little. The country, under President Clark, had taken a disastrous tack, and Klegg wondered if anything could right the Ship of State.

Last night Klegg and Vivian spent their first night together, in the same bedroom recently vacated by Delano. Klegg hadn't made love to a woman since his wife died five years earlier. But he and Vivian had worked together, side by side, since the first word reached Earth of the alien incursion into the solar system. Like Delano and Lian, two people thrust into a life and death situation ended up either as lovers or haters. Their lovemaking proved satisfying and comforting to them both.

President Clark's latest actions had pushed Klegg and Vivian even closer together. They had already wasted an entire day trying to get Clark to see the light. But numerous video calls accomplished nothing. The man refused to listen to their arguments. Tempers had frayed, and finally an angry Clark shouted that he was flying back to Washington and would see them at the Oval Office at 11 a.m.

A Secret Service agent stood guard at the Oval Office door. His cold eyes stared at the two visitors. The agent didn't say a word. Normally the agents on duty pretended not to notice the President's visitors, but this one kept his gaze on Klegg and Spencer. Klegg decided to ignore the hostile scrutiny. "I don't think we're going to have much luck with Clark."

"He'd damn well better listen to us," Vivian said. "We're the only ones trying to keep him alive."

Heavy footsteps in the corridor made Klegg lift his eyes. "Oh, hell." He squeezed Vivian's hand, and they watched the newcomers arrive.

Four star General Joseph Stimpson, the Chairman of the Joint Chiefs, marched down the hallway as if on a parade ground, trailed by a pair of Army MPs, both sergeants. Stimpson strode past Klegg and Spencer as if they weren't there. Stimpson halted when he reached the Secret Service Agent. "Tell the President that I'm here," he ordered. "He's expecting me."

"Yes, General." He mumbled something into a microphone attached to his jacket. A moment later the door clicked open. "Please go in, General. The President is ready to see you." The agent's eyes moved to Klegg. "You, too, General, Dr. Spencer."

So that's how it is, Klegg decided. We're out and Stimpson is in. Klegg followed Vivian into the Oval Office, feeling like Daniel entering the angry lion's den.

Inside, Klegg saw that the President wasn't seated behind the massive Resolute desk. Instead he occupied the center position of one of the two facing sofas. Seated beside him was the Secretary of State, Kevin Wilson III. Short, stocky, and balding, he and the President went back a long way. Both had attended college at Yale, where they partied together for four years. Neither had bothered to do much studying, their grades assured by generous contributions to the University from their parents. Or so those in the know claimed.

Secret Service agents stood on either side of the big desk, professional frowns on their faces. And ready to handle any trouble.

"Good morning, General Stimpson," President Clark said.

Stimpson took the last seat on the sofa, to the left of the President.

"Good morning, Mr. President, Mr. Secretary," Klegg said. "Thank you for agreeing to meet with Director Spencer and me at this early hour." He knew better than to take a seat until asked.

But apparently Clark didn't like Klegg towering over him. "Sit down, Klegg. You, too, Vivian."

They sat, facing the trio across the red teak coffee table. Neither relaxed. Klegg resisted a sudden urge to hold Vivian's hand, just to see what kind of reaction Clark might have.

Vivian forced a smile. "Mr. President, we'd like to . . ."

"Skip it, Vivian," Clark said. "I'm not interested in anything you two have to say. It's because of you that California is a disaster, millions dead, cities destroyed. But don't think you're going to get away with it, oh, no, not this time. I'm not taking the fall."

Clark, of necessity, had approved the declaration of martial law and the final plan for the planet's defense, but Klegg knew that didn't count when the time came to assign blame. "Mr. President, right now it's more important to discuss the Alliance and . . ."

"Fuck you and fuck the Alliance," Wilson snarled, jumping into the conversation. "We're done with the Alliance once and for all. Your so-called defense plan has crippled this country. Our military has been severely weakened. Russia got off without a scratch. China took some hits, but nothing like what happened to us."

Klegg's fist tightened at the lie. More than anyone in the room, he knew the full extent of the world-wide death toll. He'd held back the Alliance forces until the counterstrike had a chance of success. He glanced at the President, but Clark just sat there, glaring. The destruction and death in China and the Far East far exceeded the United States losses. Clearly Secretary of State Wilson had taken on the role of attack dog.

"What matters now is dealing with the coming alien invasion," Klegg said patiently. "We need to work with the Alliance . . . "

"You won't be working with anyone," Wilson said. "As of now, you're under military arrest. The President is rescinding your appointment to lead the nation's military under martial law."

He turned to Vivian. "You'll face a civilian court, Spencer, but I'm sure you'll both end up with the same sentence. If you're lucky, maybe you can share a cell."

"President Clark," Vivian began, "you can't abandon the Alliance now. If we don't work with China and Russia, the Halkin ship will depart our solar system in less than three days. That means Earth will be destroyed when the Ktarrans return."

"Don't give me that bullshit," Wilson snapped, still taking the lead. "The Ktarrans got their asses kicked. They'll probably never come back, and if they do, we'll nuke 'em again. And if China or Russia don't like what we're doing, that's tough. We've still got enough nukes to send them back to the stone age."

Reason wasn't going to work, Klegg realized. "Did you talk to Secretary Liu? Or President Demidov? They know what will happen if . . . "

"That Chinese bastard!" President Clark's flushed face twisted in hatred. "He wants me to put your fucking Major Delano in charge of the United States, so that Liu and his niece can run the country through him! Well, that's not going to happen. That asshole Delano is the one who should be swinging from a rope, and he will as soon as we get our hands on him."

Clark paused to take a breath, and Wilson took over. "We planned to arrest him, too, but when we got back, you'd sent him on his way to Russia. Stimpson has already issued orders to recall him to Washington. As soon as he's here, he goes on trial, so the American people can see what we do to traitors."

"Why bother with a trial?" Klegg didn't intend to put up with any more crap. "Just hang him. Don't let the fact that he probably saved the planet from destruction slow you down."

Clark's face turned red. "I think we're done talking. Secretary Wilson has prepared a press release that will reveal the truth about your so-called hero and . . ."

One of the two Secret Service agents in the room moved toward the sofas, touching the microphone in his ear. "Mr. President, there's a call from General Secretary Liu. He insists on speaking with you."

"Fuck him, too," Wilson said. "We've already wasted enough time on his bullshit this morning."

Clark nodded his agreement to the agent, who whispered into his comm unit.

So China had already contacted Clark. Klegg wondered what

exactly had been said. "Then I guess we're done here, Mr. President. If you won't listen to us or the Chinese . . ."

"You're not finished yet," Wilson's voice rose higher. "You both are going to give one final press briefing. You'll explain to the American people what you've done, why you sacrificed so many lives, and how sorry you are."

"I don't think so," Klegg said. "You can spin your story any way you like, but don't expect me to lie for you."

"You'll do what you're told, or I'll make sure your family, your friends, are destroyed." Wilson's face had turned red with rage. "I'll use the IRS and Justice and FBI to tear their lives apart. They'll never work again. I'll show those people in California that at least we can give them justice."

Klegg started to speak, but Wilson held up his hand. "Don't think we won't," he added. "You've got a family, too, Vivian. Wonder how they'll like living in poverty for the rest of their lives?"

Clark and Wilson were out of control, Klegg realized. He and Vivian were probably only the first of their political enemies they intended to destroy. The President wanted to blame everyone but himself for what happened in California. With Stimpson's help, the military ranks would be purged, too. Anyone who had ever worked or served with Klegg would suffer. Martial law would be retained indefinitely, but under Clark's control. And with Wilson behind him, there would be no more elections.

None of that mattered. Klegg had never given in to a bully in his life, and he didn't intend to start now. Taking his time, he got to his feet. Vivian stood as well, and linked her arm to Klegg's.

"Clark, you're a bigger asshole than I thought," Klegg said. "You're going to kill everyone in this country before you're done."

"How dare you speak to me like that!" Clark rose, spittle flying from his mouth. "Don't you ever . . ."

"Mr. President." The Secret Service agent had stepped forward again. "I've just received a text message from General Secretary Liu. It's been released to the press. He's insisting that you read it at once. Perhaps you should look at it, Sir. It's only a few sentences."

"Tell that Chinese bastard to fuck off," Wilson shouted.

Clark looked shocked at the temerity of the Secret Serviceman. But the agent, Elliot Kyle from his badge, didn't yield his ground and ignored Wilson's outburst.

"Oh, for god's sake, what is it? Read it." Clark wiped his mouth with the back of his hand.

"Yes, sir," Kyle said. His gold badge crossed by a thin blue ribbon identified him as the AIC, the Agent In Charge of White House security. "To the President of the United States: Effective immediately, all American facilities on the Moon are being placed under Chinese control. American personnel and their allies living on the Moon have thirty-six hours to depart. Also, all American scientists and technical advisors working in China, including those at the Jiuquan facility, are ordered to depart China immediately. After twenty-four hours, any that remain will be arrested. In addition, all trade between the United States and China is halted. Chinese cargo ships at sea are ordered to return to their homeports. Finally, the Ministry of Finance is directed to promptly collect, in yuan, all monies owed by the United States to the Chinese government. If the financial instruments are not promptly redeemed, China will begin confiscating all US property and factories in our country. This official government bulletin is being transmitted to the leader of every country in the world and all major international news services. End of text."

Klegg watched the faces of Clark and Wilson. Both looked shocked. Anger almost immediately replaced that emotion.

"By God, they can't do that," Clark said. "How dare they?" He strode to his desk and touched the intercom. "Put me through to the Chinese General Secretary. At once."

Klegg glanced at Vivian, then smiled. He turned to Wilson, since he seemed to be running things. "You two just don't get it, do you? The leader of the most powerful country on the planet wants to talk to you, and you're too busy engineering the end of mankind to take his call."

"You close your fucking mouth," Wilson snarled. "You're the cause of all this."

"Shut up!" Clark roared at them from behind his desk. He grabbed his private phone. "Rose, are you through to China yet? What? No, put him on the line." He covered the mouthpiece. "It's Demidov." Clark didn't bother to put it on the speaker, but the call lasted less than a minute. Suddenly Clark slammed the phone down hard enough to shatter internal components.

"Demidov says Delano and that bitch Lian are holding a press conference in thirty minutes. The Russian Council of

Ministers is attending, and the speech will be broadcast worldwide, as well as beamed to the Halkin ship. Demidov says we should watch." Clark shook his head.

"That's all? What else did he say?" Wilson was at the President's side, standing behind the desk.

"Nothing!" Clark shouted. "Fucking nothing. He hung up on me!"

Klegg laughed, a good hearty chuckle. "You thought you could just quit the Alliance with an alien invasion coming? The Chinese are throwing us off the Moon. Know what that means? No more helium-3, which means no fuel for spaceships or beam weapons. China and Russia will get all the fuel. And without our engineers and scientists working at Jiuquan, we won't get the latest alien technology."

The Jiuquan site held the nearly intact space vessel found buried under the rocky surface of Jupiter's moon, Io. During the crisis, China had agreed to let Alliance engineers and scientists study the alien craft.

"They wouldn't dare, goddammit," Wilson shouted. "We'll blow the hell out of them."

"President Clark," Vivian said, "who is running the country? You or Secretary Wilson? Maybe you should let China and Russia know who's really in charge here. Assuming you find out."

Klegg laughed again. Vivian had a big smile on her face.

"Let's get out of here, Lang," she said. "I want to see Delano's press conference. It'll be very interesting."

Wilson, his eyes bulging in his now-crimson face, moved around the desk and in front of Vivian. His arm reached out and shoved her back so hard she nearly went down. "You're not going anywhere except to a jail cell, you bitch."

Klegg caught Vivian with his right hand and held her upright until she regained her balance. Then he took a step forward and shot out his left arm, a straight jab that landed square on Wilson's thick nose. The Secretary of State staggered two steps backward. Only the President's desk kept him from going down.

By then the two secret service agents had intervened, moving between the two men. "General Klegg, Dr. Spencer," Agent Kyle said, "I think you'd better wait outside."

Vivian, hanging on to Klegg's right arm, agreed. "Yes, Agent Kyle, we should. The smell in here is getting bad."

Elliot opened the door. The two MPs outside moved, ready to take them into custody and march them off to God knew where. But General Stimpson leaned out the door. "Hold them here for now," Stimpson ordered. "Don't let them consult with anyone. I need to talk to the President."

Klegg shrugged. "Didn't know the asshole could talk." Klegg took his former seat on the sofa and Vivian joined him. The two MPs stood on either side of the sofa, hands on their holstered weapons.

Vivian addressed the Secret Service agent still guarding the door. "Since we can't call anyone, how about turning the TV on?"

"You're not supposed to talk to anyone," the agent said.

"We just want to see the Russian news conference," Spencer said. "You should, too, since you and your family's lives are involved. You might want to know what your President has gotten our country into."

The agent's face revealed nothing. But he picked up a remote control and activated the wall-mounted TV, already tuned to a local TV news station.

"General Stimpson said they weren't to communicate with anyone," the younger MP said, his voice hard and threatening.

"They're just watching TV," the agent said, but apparently he didn't like the MP's tone. He activated his microphone. "Bill, this is Mike outside the Oval Office. Why don't you and a couple of the boys join me."

So much for the MPs, Klegg decided. In less than twenty seconds two more agents arrived, moving into positions facing the sofa and the MPs. A third agent halted in the hallway, about twenty feet away. A second field of fire, Klegg noted, in case anyone started something. Close enough for accurate shooting, but far enough away in case of trouble.

Klegg glanced at the TV, where the DC newscaster's blank face showed he'd just received the text message from the Chinese government. He looked as stunned as the President had a few moment ago.

"Viewers, I was about to lead off with a major story about the United States withdrawing from the Alliance. But that news is now eclipsed by a chilling announcement from the Chinese government. Their military forces on the Moon are moving to occupy all US and European research and mining bases. They intend to hold all personnel until they can be returned to Earth.

These actions are being taken as a result of President's Clark's decision to leave the Alliance. An unofficial source in Beijing has confirmed this decision, and stated that the United States' refusal to join with the Alliance in defense of the planet is the cause. Further information is arriving and will be passed on as soon as it can be verified. Now we are switching to our news reporter in Moscow, where Marine Colonel Delano and Dr. Duan Lian are preparing to address President Demidov and the people of Russia. Colonel Delano and Dr. Duan's speech is also being streamed worldwide."

Klegg leaned back and crossed his legs. "This should be good, Vivian. I can't wait to hear Delano."

"Wonder what he'll say?" Vivian asked.

"Not a clue," Klegg said. "But I'm sure he'll manage to piss off Clark."

She laughed, and snuggled up against his shoulder. "Good for Delano."

On the TV, the picture changed into a feed from the Kremlin, informing the audience about the upcoming speech by the new leader of Earth's Planetary Defense.

"Knowing Delano," Klegg said, "I'm sure it will be interesting. And now he'll have the chance to piss off half the planet."

Chapter 10

Moscow, October 22, 6:00 p.m. MSK

Delano adjusted his tie, using the mirror in what television people in the US called the green room. His Marine green uniform looked drab, but the still-new silver oak leaves shone on his shoulders. How much longer he'd be allowed to wear them remained to be seen. A few hours earlier one of President Demidov's aides informed Delano that the US Military Police worldwide had received orders to place him under arrest and return him at once to US territory.

Fortunately for Delano, the American military didn't have any troops or MPs in Moscow, except for a few Marines at the Embassy. He doubted they would attempt anything so foolish. Even if they did, Gunny Stecker would stop any arrest attempts. Nor would Minister Borodin's secret police let anyone interfere with a person summoned by the President of Russia. Not to mention the unknown number of Russian troops surrounding the TV facility. Delano decided he felt quite safe in Moscow.

Lian stood next to him, adjusting her hair. Her high heels raised her up almost to Delano's eyes. She wore a basic red and gold dress, the colors of her country, setting off her trim figure. Around her waist she had on a white, blue, and red sash, the colors of the Russian flag. The sash had come from Minister Borodin, a suggestion "to add a Russian flavor to her presence." She hadn't brought anything formal with her, just the one garment in case she and Joe found time to go to dinner somewhere.

Delano took a deep breath and looked at her reflection in the mirror. "I think you can stop fussing with your hair." He'd spoken nothing but Russian all day, in preparation for tonight's speech. "You look stunning."

And she did. Delano remember his first sight of her, jet-lagged, wearing her baggy travel shorts and a rumpled T-shirt, with her hair in a ponytail. He remembered thinking some makeup and a designer outfit might improve her image. Well, that turned out to be a good guess.

A Russian lieutenant, his green army uniform spotless,

entered the room. "They are ready for you, Colonel Delano, Dr. Duan."

Show time.

Lian faced Delano. "I'm scared to death."

"Me, too," Delano agreed. "Remember the worst they can do is laugh us off the stage. Or maybe shoot us." *Not funny.* He offered her his arm. "May I escort you to the podium, Dr. Duan?"

She took his arm. "Don't let go of me. I'm afraid I'll trip in these heels."

He leaned over and kissed her ear. "*Bonne chance.*" The French phrase seemed most appropriate. Delano nodded to the smiling lieutenant. "We're ready."

Delano felt prepared. Together with two of Borodin's best writers, Lian and Delano had worked almost seven hours on the speech. Now they just had to deliver it and hope for the best.

They left the room and walked with care down a well-scuffed linoleum floor. At its end two smartly-dressed Russian army sergeants opened the double-doors and held them wide.

They stepped through the opening into a blaze of white lights. Crowd noise from the two hundred VIP guests, seated in the studio, greeted them. On the floor in front of the stage, eighty or so reporters and TV crews, most of them Russian or European, focused their cameras. Delano had to concentrate to avoid squinting. Lian's hand tightened on his arm. *At least everyone will be looking at Lian, not me.*

President Demidov, dressed in a dark brown suit and wearing the same sash as Lian, waited for them in the center of the stage. He shook Delano's hand vigorously, then greeted Dr. Duan with a courtly bow, followed by the customary European triple kiss. With a shock, Delano realized the noise washing over him had turned to applause and cheers. No doubt the Russians had packed the audience with government supporters.

Demidov guided them up the four steps to the brown wooden podium displaying the gold double-headed eagle on a red background, the emblem of Russia. The wide lectern had enough space for two to stand side by side, a single microphone centered between them.

Demidov remained below the podium. He faced the audience and held up his hands. The crowd quieted. "Members of the Russian Ministry, heroes of the world's fight against the Ktarrans, distinguished guests, and of course representatives of the media. It is my great pleasure to introduce Lt. Colonel Joseph Delano of the United States Marines, and Dr. Duan Lian of the People's Republic of China. Dr. Duan was recently awarded the Meritorious Service Medal by her government, as was Colonel Delano, for their actions aboard the International Space Station that helped save the planet from destruction. I may add that today our Council of Ministers unanimously voted to honor them both with the Hero of the Russian Federal Republic medals."

The audience, composed almost entirely of members of the Russian Federation and the news corps, applauded even louder at that news. The medals, the highest the government could bestow, meant that the Russian government officially approved of Delano and Lian's actions on the Space Station.

Delano glanced to his left, where only six seats were positioned, the row at a slight angle so those seated could see the podium without strain. These held the remaining "Heroes of the Space Station," their freshly-earned medals hanging from their necks. Closest to the podium sat Professor Petrov, along with Colonels Kosloff and Mironov. The next three seats held Sergeant Shen, Gunny Stecker, and Sergeant Steve Macy.

To the right of the podium were sixteen seats, separated into two rows for the members of the Russian Council of Ministers. Two seats held General Zeng and Senior Colonel Jang, representing the government of China. They appeared somewhat uncomfortable with the raucous audience. Their blue uniforms caught the eye, standing out alongside the Ministers' business suits. Both had copies of the speech, since neither man spoke Russian fluently.

Next to Zeng and closest to the podium, an empty seat waited for President Demidov. The symbolism of the President's chair, and his refusal to ascend the podium, announced visually to everyone watching the honor he awarded Delano and Dr. Duan.

Demidov waited for the noise to cease. "But this is not the time to talk of medals and honors. China and Russia, in fact our entire world, face a grave and deadly danger. To say that the planet itself faces destruction is not an overstatement. To address this mortal threat, China and Russia are temporarily uniting our two great countries under the joint leadership of Colonel Delano and Dr. Duan, as suggested by our alien allies. Together they will lead Earth's efforts to defend herself from the coming Ktarran invasion, expected within the next 18 months."

Another round of applause broke out, and Delano licked his dry lips. He'd never experienced anything like this, with the probing eyes of eighty cameras and even more microphones aimed at him. Every word he uttered would roll out over the airwaves and across the fiber optic cables that made up the Internet, to be distributed to the world.

President Demidov took his seat, and Delano realized he was on. *Don't screw this up, you idiot.* He took a deep breath, stared briefly into the bright lights, then glanced down at his notes.

"Ladies and gentlemen, Dr. Duan Lian and I thank you for this opportunity to speak to the people of Russia and the world. Dr. Duan and I have prepared a statement, which we will now read to you. As many of you are probably aware, neither of us has any experience in dealing with the news media or even public speaking. So please bear with us, and at the end we will take a few questions."

Delano shifted his notes on the podium, centering them beneath the single microphone. "First, I would like to say that not long ago I lived in Moscow for two months, and in that time I learned one lesson very well, the same lesson that history has taught us. The people of Russia are as brave as anyone in the world. They never back down, they never give up."

Cheers and applause erupted at those words. Delano saw the pride in the faces of the Russian reporters and cameramen. "Second, I would like to explain how Dr. Duan and I were chosen to speak for Earth. The aliens, that is the Tarlons and the Halkins, risked their ships and their lives to help save our planet. Without their assistance, our world would even now be ground to dust under the three Ktarran ships. After our joint success, they offered to unite with us in our struggle against the Ktarrans. This is a war that they have been fighting for more than two hundred years, a conflict that has forced them again and again to retreat against the ever-growing and powerful Ktarran Empire. The Tarlons and Halkins, along with several other alien species, now look to us to help stop the menace that threatens Earth and their worlds. In a way, they may consider our planet to be another Stalingrad, the final line that the Ktarrans must not pass."

Delano's flawless Russian impressed the audience. He might have been born and raised inside the Kremlin. Borodin's speech writers made certain his words utilized only the most current and literate Russian. His linguistic ability would help sway those listening to the grave warning he and Dr. Duan were delivering.

He shifted aside and Lian took his place, steadying herself with a hand on the lectern. Her voice sounded as serious as Delano's. "The aliens' offer to fight at our side is not made out of any altruistic sentiment. As much as we seek their help, they recognize in Earth our ability to wage war against aggressors. They believe that we can help them win a victory and halt the Ktarrans' steady expansion. But the Tarlons and Halkins quickly grew confused with our planet's multiple governments. They consider it a critical defect that Earth is the only large-population world that does not possess a single, unified leadership to speak for the planet in times of danger.

"After three weeks of fruitless negotiations," Dr. Duan went on, "the Halkin leader decided that our multiple nations structure would not prove successful in a global war. Since Col. Delano and I were instrumental in negotiating and developing the battle plan with the Tarlons and Halkins, and because of our success against the Ktarran mothership, they determined that we should speak for Earth in the coming war."

She turned to Delano, and he picked up where Lian left off. "Russia defeated the overpowering might of Napoleon, and destroyed Hitler's vaunted German Wehrmacht in the Second World War. Now the people of this great land face another grave threat from hostile aliens, and once again they have accepted the challenge that faces our planet. As with Napoleon and Hitler, the adversary's strength appears overwhelming. And so China and Russia must show the world their strength and courage to face the common enemy."

Delano turned to Lian, and she took up their presentation. "Unlike Col. Delano, I have no military skill, and so I cannot talk of armies and battles, bravery and deeds of valor. But I can speak to the coming conflict, a frightful event that now confronts every person on Earth. I saw with my own eyes the viciousness of the Ktarrans, felt the paralyzing pain wash over me from their neural weapons. I watched as Sergeant Shen and Col. Delano fought through their pain to save the Space Station. Together they shot and killed five aliens who had come aboard to take us prisoner."

Her somber words quieted the audience. Everyone in the room and across the globe would have witnessed the Ktarrans' brutality. In every country, crowds of fearful people cried out for their governments to make them safe. Warfare on a global scale, affecting every man, woman and child, presented a new conundrum.

Delano knew Lian's Russian was as good as his, and would be just as appreciated. He recognized from experience that foreigners were always suspect, unless they could speak the local language, or at least make a reasonable effort to do so. The crowd's attention remained as fixed on her as it had on him.

She went on. "One of the contributions I can make to this approaching conflict is my ability to deal with both the Tarlons and the Halkins. On the Space Station, Delano and I earned their trust, and they committed their ships to the battle to save Earth. No matter what you might hear, our planet could not have survived without their assistance. They risked their own intergalactic ships and lives against overwhelming might to help the people of Earth. To save ourselves, we must work closely with the Tarlons and Halkins in the future, while addressing our common needs in the face of the coming invasion."

"Our alien friends, of course, have their own interests," Delano took over. "They help Earth to help themselves. But as Dr. Duan and I have discovered, the Tarlons and Halkins are both basically peaceful species, and not suited for warfare. They have been forced to learn to fight, but have been driven back again and again by the aggressive Ktarrans. The Tarlons had colonized six planets, the Halkins four in our stellar quadrant. Five of those planets have already fallen to the Ktarrans. On each captured planet, ninety percent of the population was exterminated, while the remaining survivors are kept for breeding so that they can provide a living food source for their captors. And yes, it is true that they are carnivores who prefer to eat the living flesh of their conquered species."

"This is the future that faces Earth," Lian said. "The Tarlons and Halkins hope for a Ktarran defeat, one convincing enough to stop or at least slow their advances throughout the galaxy. But they understand that a divided world cannot resist the Ktarrans. Again, I repeat we are the first planet that either species has encountered without a single leadership body. All the other worlds, by the time they achieve space travel, speak and act as a single unit. The concept that Earth, under the threat of such an existential danger, would not unite under a planetary command is incomprehensible to them."

"When we first achieved effective communication," Delano

said, "they thought the Alliance spoke for all of Earth. At that time, we did not try to explain our political structures to them. After the battle, when they learned how much of Earth is not part of the Alliance, they began to doubt our resolve. They watched as days passed without any progress. After weeks of nothing concrete, they informed us of their decision. If Earth could not unite on its own, they would depart our solar system. They would remain only if Dr. Duan and I represented Earth's defense. In other words, if Earth could not choose a single leader, they would do it for us."

"No one was more shocked at hearing their decision than Col. Delano and I were," Lian said, "when we heard their request. The Alliance governments, as well as those not members, were naturally unwilling to cede their authority to anyone, let alone two linguists. Attempts were made to get the Tarlons and Halkins to change their position. Meanwhile the days rushed by. At last, less than forty-eight hours ago, the Russian government took the lead to break the impasse that threatened, that still threatens, Earth's safety. As President Demidov explained, in matters of planetary defense, Col. Delano and I are as qualified as anyone in Earth's military. Russia then advanced our names, and the Chinese government has now accepted us as well. We are humbled by this new role. We believe that love for our planet and its people will guide and direct our decisions and actions."

"To that end," Delano continued, "in the last few hours we have initiated meetings with Russian and Chinese military and industrial production leaders. We have developed an initial plan to produce fighting and support ships to defend the planet. These new ships will be powered by engines based on alien designs, but improved with our world's computer resources. With these vessels, we intend to fight the Ktarran invasion and provide planetary security. Industries across the globe will be mobilized to produce the ships and equipment needed to fight. New programs will be developed to train the men and women who will fly and fight them. Nothing will be held back."

"However, even with the full support of the governments of Earth," Lian said, "we cannot be certain of victory. The Ktarrans possess a vast fleet of enormous fighting ships, any one of which is capable of destroying three or four Tarlon vessels." She paused, glanced at the cameras, and took a breath. "To prepare for the possibility that Earth's defenders will be unable to resist the

Ktarrans, Russia and China intend to build another type of space ship, an interstellar transport. This vessel will be capable of carrying approximately one thousand people on a voyage possibly lasting as long as five years. We will build as many of these colonizer ships as possible, so that in the event of Earth's defeat, we may be able to save enough of humanity to restart our civilization on another planet."

"These transport ships," Delano said, "powered by the alien space drives, will travel to parts of our galaxy's quadrant, that's the Orion Arm, where wormholes may be located. If new wormholes are discovered along the way, then the ships will be able to travel even further, perhaps over distances that will allow these new colonists to find and develop a habitable planet, along with the means to resist future Ktarran advances."

The crowd had quieted, not even a trace of murmuring. Delano saw that some had started checking their tablets, to learn where the Orion Arm was located and what a stellar quadrant was. "Colonizer ships will ensure that humanity survives even if Earth is overrun or destroyed," Delano added. "If our planet is saved by our defenses, the colonists can return home or continue on their voyages of exploration."

A palpable silence fell over the audience. No one builds massive escape vehicles unless you expect to use them. Cameras stopped clicking and reporters ceased whispering into their recorders.

"Yes, the situation is that grave," Lian said. "No matter how many fighting ships we manage to build, the enemy may still overpower us. Abandoning our planet may be the only way to ensure the survival of the human race."

"So, now everyone understands the severity of the threat that faces us," Delano continued. "Difficult decisions must be made, arduous actions will be undertaken. We, and I mean all of us here and in service of their governments, will be guided by the principle of the greatest good for the greatest number. We will work night and day to protect and defend the people of Earth."

"Colonel Delano mentioned the brave people of Russia," Lian said, "who resisted the Nazis at Stalingrad. I would add the heroic Chinese who battled against the invading Empire of Japan. As they suffered and strove against their enemy, so must we. But I believe the words of Winston Churchill are most appropriate for Earth at this time – in the face of this threat, we have nothing to offer but blood, toil, tears, and sweat."

"Tomorrow we will speak with the heads of state from Poland, the Czech Republic, Switzerland, Finland, and Germany," Delano said. "We will ask them to join our defense efforts. We will have much more to say to you, the people of Earth, but we also have much work to do. Over the course of the next few weeks, there will be more time to answer the many questions that will arise. But we will take a few now."

Delano knew enough to pick a Muscovite first. Fortunately, a reporter from the Russian news agency, TASS, leapt to his feet. Delano gestured to him.

"These colonizer ships . . . how will the colonists be chosen? And how many ships will be built?"

"We have not yet decided on a selection process," Lian said. "Colonists will need to possess specific skills useful to settling and developing a new planet. Our goal is to find a fair method of choosing colonists. As for the number of ships to be built, we will manufacture as many as we can, provided we can do so without impacting our construction of fighting ships."

A reporter wearing the badge of the Chinese News Service shouted out his question. "China possesses many more people than Russia. How will that affect the issue of colonizer ships?"

Delano shrugged. "I don't know. That is just one of the hundreds of details that must be worked out and agreed to by the Chinese and Russian governments." He spotted an American reporter, from the Dow Jones News Corp, a man Delano actually recognized. "Yes, Bill, you get the next question."

"Colonel Delano, you've spoken quite a bit about Russia and China. What about the United States? Since they are members of the Alliance, won't you be working with the US military?"

Delano frowned, though he been expecting the question. "I'm sorry to say that the United States has decided to withdraw from the Alliance. President Clark does not believe the Ktarrans are a continuing threat, and he is unwilling to cede any authority to anyone, including myself, Dr. Duan, or the Tarlons. That means that the United States will not be able to build advanced ships of any kind, since the critical helium-3 needed for fuel is not available in sufficient quantities on Earth. Chinese resources on the Moon are already moving to take control of all lunar mining operations. US access to the lunar bases has been rescinded, and China and Russia will take over those sites. So no colonizer ships will be built by or made available to the United States."

The response seemed to fluster the Dow Jones reporter. "I'm not sure . . . what does that mean?"

Lian leaned forward. "It means that if we, Russia and China, cannot convince the Tarlons and Halkins to stay and help with Earth's defense, our alien allies will depart our solar system in thirty-seven hours. It means we will have no support from other worlds, other species. We will have no allies from those also at war with the Ktarrans. The Tarlons have studied us enough to understand the resources needed to fight, and have realized that without the United States bloc fully participating in a common effort, a full defense of Earth is not possible."

A murmur rippled throughout the room. Lian glanced at Delano. "It also means that President Clark, for some unknown reason, has ordered the arrest and court-martials of Colonel Delano and General Klegg for acts of treason."

Stunned silence greeted her blunt statement, followed by gasps of disbelief. Lian held up her hand for silence. "If I may add," Lian went on, "the governments of China and Russia believe that the efforts of General Klegg were paramount in the defense of Earth. China and the United States suffered grievous losses from the Ktarran attack, but there is no doubt the destruction would have been much worse without General Klegg's leadership. He is a true planetary hero."

During Lian's words, President Demidov rose and joined them at the podium. "I know you have a thousand questions, but I must end this discussion now, as we all have much work to do. But I will offer one final statement. China and Russia are in full agreement on this issue – the defense of planet Earth will be entrusted to Colonel Delano and Dr. Duan. As of now, the United States stands alone. Thank you all for your participation."

Demidov flipped a switch and cut the microphone, ignoring the babble of questions from the correspondents. The briefing was over.

*   *   *

The speech had ended twenty minutes ago, and now a much smaller group sat around the table in Demidov's office. General Zeng and Colonel Jang sat side by side with Ministers Borodin, Shuvalov, and Oreshkin. For the first time, Delano had requested the presence of three others – Professor Petrov, Col. Kosloff, and the Russian physicist Col. Mironov. Delano had spoken with the three earlier, and asked if they wanted to play key roles in the new Planetary Defense Force. They agreed, and Delano notified President Demidov and the key ministers that he considered the three to be integral parts of their decision-making team. Demidov, Lian, and Delano completed the group.

"Congratulations. Your speech should get President Clark's attention," Demidov said.

Delano lifted his shoulders and let them drop. "I hope so. If we can't get General Klegg back in control of the United States, the Halkin ship will leave. We can ask them again, but I doubt they will change their minds. If they did, they know we would never trust them again."

"You delivered your message well, Colonel Delano, Dr. Duan," Borodin said. "Your words should already be impacting the people of your country. The pressure on Clark will be enormous."

"If the United States does nothing in the next few hours," Demidov said, "Russia and China will release another joint statement, declaring that we will focus the majority of our industry into building the colonizer ships. That will convey the message that we have given up, that the planet is doomed, and that we are only trying to save as many as we can."

"You are certain we cannot deal with Europe instead of the United States?" Oreshkin directed the question at Delano.

"Yes," Delano said, "Jarendo and the others aboard the ship have been studying all of us since the battle ended. They know Europe is fragmented, and unable to cooperate. And they comprehend the industrial and military power of my country. Nor do they believe Earth can marshal the necessary resources without the three major powers working in unison and leading the effort. As I said, they have never encountered a world with our size population that didn't have a single leader for planetary defense."

"Then we must hope that President Clark sees the light," Borodin said. "If we had more time, perhaps we could do something to . . . change his mind."

Delano knew what that meant. Put a bullet in Clark's brain, assuming the idiot still had one. "General Klegg and Dr. Vance still have supporters. Maybe they can do something before it's too late." It sounded lame, but Delano couldn't think of anything else to say. He remembered another Marine Corps saying – hope for the best, prepare for the worst. *Why is it always the worst?*

Chapter 11

Washington, DC, The White House – 12:15 p.m.

When the live feed from TASS ended, Klegg turned to Vivian. The entire broadcast had lasted just under an hour. The American translator had done an excellent job converting the speech to English on the fly. As far as Klegg could tell, the translation matched Delano and Lian's grave and deliberate statements perfectly. And their pace delivered the words at just the right speed for a simultaneous conversion to English and other languages.

During the speech, Klegg half expected someone to come along and cart them off to some dungeon. But either the President had forgotten about them or he had other things on his mind.

"They gave a good speech," Vivian said. "Someone from the Russian propaganda bureau must have written it."

"Not all of it. I recognize Delano's speech pattern. But I'll bet he and Lian did get help from Demidov's people. If Delano wanted to panic half the world, that speech was perfect. By not mentioning the US until the American reporter asked the question, Delano branded President Clark as an idiot who's going to destroy the planet. Now we'll have even more riots. I'll bet the White House staff is already overloaded with emails and tweets."

She laughed. "And imagine! We're both getting medals from the Chinese and Russian governments. That little touch was brilliant, considering Clark wants to convict us of treason." She sighed. "What happens now?"

Klegg glanced at Mike, the Secret Service Agent guarding the door to the Oval Office, who still refused to look at them directly. Usually those assigned to the White House quickly learned to mask their faces no matter what they heard or saw, but this time Klegg detected some uncertainty on the man's countenance. No one could listen to Delano's words and not be concerned about the future.

The two MPs, however, lacked that kind of control. Klegg saw doubt and worry in their uneasy glances. They might be Stimpson's people, but like everyone else, they had wives and children and loved ones to think about. And now they had to follow the orders of their leader who'd just been branded a traitor to the human race.

The reverberation of raised voices came through the door to the Oval Office, despite its supposed sound-proofing. Klegg couldn't make out the words, but somebody inside was shouting loud enough to push some noise through the thick door. President Clark must be having a fit. Of course he'd watched the speech and realized he had a problem. Before the broadcast, he might have gotten away with blaming Klegg, Spencer, and Delano, but now for that argument to hold up, Clark would also have to blame China and Russia.

Before Klegg could say anything about that, the door opened, and another secret service agent stood in the entry. "Bring them back in," he ordered. Without another word, the agent turned away.

"Back inside," Mike ordered as he moved closer.

"No, thanks," Klegg answered. "We're under arrest. The only person we want to see is our lawyer."

"The President wants to see you," Mike said, "so you're going in, if we have to carry you."

Klegg leaned back on the sofa. "Sorry, not interested. Tell President Clark . . ."

Suddenly General Stimpson appeared in the doorway. "Get them in here! Now!"

He'd snapped the orders at the two MPs, who stepped forward, menace in their attitude.

Klegg sighed. "Oh, what the hell! I suppose we can wait inside as well as out here."

"I don't like the air in there," Vivian said, but she rose at the same time as Klegg. "And I'm still not talking."

The MPs practically pushed them through the doorway, and Klegg saw the seating arrangement hadn't changed. Shrugging off the MP's arm, Klegg guided Vivian back to the sofa. Right away, he noticed that President Clark and Secretary Wilson looked ready to explode. A trace of blood lingered beneath Wilson's now-swollen nose and anger-flushed face. General Stimpson's face looked even redder. Clark and Wilson must have jumped all over Stimpson's ass for something.

"Did you watch the speech?" Wilson snarled the words at them.

Klegg wished the sofas were a bit farther apart. He could smell the man's bad breath across the coffee table. "Not really. Since it didn't concern us, we weren't paying much attention."

"Don't give me that bullshit, Klegg," President Clark snarled. "I saw you watching on the camera. You were hanging on every word."

"There were a few good moments," Klegg agreed. "I expect we'll use some of Delano's comments as evidence at our trial. The part about the medals was especially nice."

"You're not going to make it to a trial," Wilson said. "We're turning you over to Stimpson and he'll have you shot for treason. You instituted martial law, remember? You gave the orders that let all those people in California die."

Vivian had been studying her nails. Now she looked up and smiled at the Secretary of State. "You're even more pathetic than the President. But I'm glad to see you've taken charge, you and Stimpson. Are you sending Clark back out to California to drum up some more good PR?"

Clark ignored the gibe. "The Chinese are not going to push us off the Moon. I'll send the Space Force and Seals up there if I have to."

"If those bastards try anything, we'll nuke 'em," Wilson agreed. "They'll get wise fast enough."

"I'm glad to hear it," Klegg said. "Good for you!"

Clark's face twisted with rage. "I want Delano back here. You sent him to Moscow. You get him back. That's an order."

"You need some Valium, Mr. President," Vivian said. "Try and think things through." Her calm words only increased Clark's fury. "Colonel Delano is concerned about the survival of his country. He has just been placed in charge of Earth's planetary defense by Russia and China. You think he cares what you want? He now has the military forces of two superpowers under his finger. He can turn Washington into radioactive ash. How stupid are you?"

"You keep your mouth shut or I'll slap that smile off your face," Wilson said. "Klegg, call him and order him to return ASAP."

"Colonel Delano isn't very good at following orders in the best of times," Klegg said. "I'll make the call if you want, but maybe General Stimpson should do it. Who knows, Delano may jump on a plane and rush home, confess to his crimes, and beg for forgiveness."

"No, wait, he can't come home, not yet," Vivian said. "Remember he's speaking with the leaders of half of Europe in a few hours."

"Oh, forgot that," Klegg said. "Maybe after the Halkin deadline has passed, and the aliens have departed. Of course by then, Clark, you probably won't be running things anyhow."

"We'll target China and Russia with our missiles," Wilson said. "They can't bluff us."

Klegg shook his head in disgust. "By now every missile in China and Russia is aimed at the US. I'll bet they have thirty nukes targeted at Washington right now. You really don't get it. China and Russia are not bluffing. You even look like you're getting ready to launch and they'll melt our country into radioactive slag. Ask Stimpson. He should know."

General Stimpson looked up in surprise, almost as if he hadn't been following the conversation. He took a moment to clear his throat. "In these circumstances, Mr. President, I wouldn't advise doing anything to threaten them. You notified them yesterday that we're leaving the Alliance. That means they've had at least a twelve hour start at preparing their nuclear forces and locking in new targeting codes for their bombers, ships, and subs. If Russia and China are working together, it could be bad."

Since the creation of the Alliance, the three major powers had agreed to end all targeting, even for exercises, of any member. Before that agreement, China and Russia had three-quarters of their weapons pointed at each other. By tacit agreement, the United States had played the role of a neutral umpire in disputes along the Sino-Russian border.

Pulling the US out of the Alliance changed all that. Now Russia and China were allies in the war against the aliens. Obviously Clark hadn't thought anything through, or he would have recognized the importance of maintaining a neutral stance.

Klegg watched as Clark and Wilson exchanged glances. Stimpson, whatever he might have said to curry favor before today's meetings, wouldn't entertain the idea of all-out war against Russia and China. Especially not with half the West Coast in ruins and most of California's naval and air bases out of action.

"If you don't mind," Vivian said, "I have to use the restroom. Or maybe we could be taken to our prison cells."

"You're not going anywhere, God dammit!" Clark shouted.

"You'll stay where you are until I'm good and ready to get rid of you."

Klegg rose and offered his arm to Vivian. "Stimpson, you've really fucked up this time, listening to these two clowns. You should have told Clark it was a big mistake to pull out of the Alliance. At least our country had some leverage as a member."

"Thank you, Lang," Vivian said, rising from the sofa and accepting his arm. She started toward the door, but Wilson jumped up and moved in front of her.

"Stay right where you are," he ordered, pushing her back with the heel of his hand.

Klegg, half a step behind Vivian, leaned forward and let go with another left jab, his fist smashing into Wilson's already-bloody nose. The Secretary of State staggered backward, a fresh red streak already running from his nostrils. He stumbled into Agent Kyle, the Secret Service AIC. Wilson clung to the man's arm, until he managed to regain his balance.

"You're not a very fast learner, Wilson. Touch her again and I'll do more than tap your nose," Klegg warned.

"Arrest him!" Clark practically screamed the words.

The two Secret Service agents hadn't made a move toward Klegg. Their job was to protect the President. Secretary Wilson had his own security, but they weren't in the room.

"Sir, General Klegg is already under arrest," Senior Agent in Charge Kyle said. "Should I remove them from the Oval Office? Again?"

The simple question caught President Clark off balance. His mouth remained open. He stared at the agent as if he'd never seen him before.

"I still need to use the ladies' room," Vivian said. "Or so help me, I'll pee right here on your carpet."

Suddenly Clark straightened up. "Use the damned bathroom." He gestured to the Oval Office's private facility.

Vivian walked across the front of the desk, passing within inches of a still shocked Secretary Wilson and disappeared into the Presidential john.

Clark, meanwhile, turned to General Stimpson. "So what are my military options?"

Klegg, watching Stimpson's face, saw a man who looked like he'd just consumed a dozen three-day-old oysters.

"Short of nuclear war," Stimpson said, "there's not much we

can do. I can check with Klegg's people and NASA, but I think the Moon is a lost cause. If we try to launch a shuttle, China has plenty of time to prepare. The Chinese took over the JovCo facilities easy enough, so I don't think they'll have any problem with our bases." He shook his head. "After hearing Delano's speech, someone should talk to him first. General Klegg is probably the best one for that job."

The Swiss-based JovCo operated the freighters that ferried ore and supplies to the miners on Jupiter's moon, Io. JovCo had attempted to conceal an alien spaceship discovered on Io at their refinery on the Moon.

"Damn you," Clark said, "you said we should stand firm, that we should take a strong stance against these aliens."

Stimpson nodded. "That was before I heard the Delano's speech and saw Demidov and General Zeng nodding approval at every word Delano and Dr. Duan said. General Secretary Liu's niece was at the podium, for god's sake! Do you think he's not going to back what she said? Her words and Delano's have probably been heard by every single person in China and Russia by now. In a few hours, all of North America will have listened to that speech, and be asking the same questions and demanding answers from you. You'd better find a political solution, Mr. President. I'm afraid the Alliance has removed any possibility of our use of force on the Moon or here on Earth."

The bathroom door opened and Vivian reentered the Oval Office. "Did I miss anything?"

Klegg hadn't heard the toilet flush, but that might mean the soundproofing, at least on that door, was first rate. "Nothing much. President Clark is considering his reelection options."

"I'd still like to get out of here," she said, turning toward Clark. "There's no reason for us to be here under arrest." She moved toward the outer door, and Klegg started after her.

"Wait! I need to talk to you both," Clark said. He swallowed. "Please!"

"Are we still under arrest?" Klegg asked.

"No. Sit down, both of you." Clark took a breath, but he waited until they returned to the sofa. "Wilson, you'd better get that looked after. You're still bleeding."

Secretary Wilson hadn't uttered a sound since Klegg's fist made its second contact with his nose. He looked dazed. "No, I'm all right. I'll just wash up and . . ."

"I think you'd better go. Now." Clark's voice sounded hard. His instinct for political self-preservation overrode any friendship. He glanced at the two agents, still stoically standing with their backs against the wall. "Escort Secretary Wilson someplace where he can get that looked after."

Wilson protested, but Clark just nodded to Agent Kyle. In another moment, Wilson and his escort left and the outer door closed again. Only Kyle remained.

"Now, tell me what my options are," Clark demanded. "And I am not going to cede my authority to that asshole Delano."

"Then you have no options," Klegg said. "The time to bargain was before you pulled out of the Alliance. Now it's too late. The Halkin deadline is less than a day away. Once they've gone, everyone will turn against you. You'll be the one man who refused to help the planet. You'll be lucky if they don't lynch you."

"Don't be ridiculous," Clark snapped. "Nobody's going to do anything like that."

"Look at General Stimpson's face," Klegg said. "Ask him if he wouldn't like a few seats on a colonizer ship for his children and grandchildren. I know I would."

"Dammit, we'll build our own ships," Clark said. "We have the best technology and manufacturing . . ."

"But no fuel," Klegg growled. "What are you, too stupid to keep some simple facts in your head? No moon bases means no helium-3. No helium means no starships. No ships means no hope for anyone in this country to escape the Ktarrans. Do you think the Chinese are going to waste precious fuel on America when millions of their own people are clamoring to get aboard those ships?"

"Wilson said the Ktarran threat is overrated. We beat them once . . ."

"Right, great." Klegg shook his head in disbelief. "We barely managed to destroy three ships we caught by surprise, and that was with the help of the Tarlons and Halkins. The Ktarrans have at least 200 battle-ready ships in service. We have none. Suppose they send 50 or 100 against Earth. Do you like those odds, Stimpson?"

"You think the Halkins will abandon us?" Stimpson's voice had lost its bravado.

"Can we dare to take a chance they won't? Suppose Delano

tells them they are better off without us. You think they'll remain and risk their own necks to protect President Clark?"

"Watch your mouth, Klegg," Clark said. "I'm still running things, and I intend to keep on running them."

"No, you're not," Vivian said. "You just ended your presidency. China and Russia will never trust you again. Maybe you can save yourself by begging to rejoin the Alliance and giving Delano and Lian the authority they need."

"All of which needs to be done immediately," Klegg added. "You already have protests and violent crowds all over the country. If the deadline passes, the mob will tear you apart. No one will lift a finger to save your sorry ass."

"I still have the military." Clark's voice betrayed his worry.

"Ask Stimpson," Klegg suggested. "Think about those generals and admirals, the fighter and bomber pilots with families, all condemned to death by your stupidity. Maybe they won't take their anger out on you! Oh, no! I'm sure they'll let you stay in charge until the Ktarrans arrive to take you out."

Clark turned to Stimpson, but the General dropped his eyes. "I'm afraid General Klegg may be correct. Perhaps you should consider resigning immediately and let someone else deal with the Alliance and the Halkins."

"Never! I worked my ass off to become President of the United States and I intend to stay right where I am. We'll show those bastards in China and Russia where to get off. I'll find a way to deal with the Ktarrans, if they ever do return, maybe make a separate peace with them. But I'll be damned if I'm going to let assholes like Klegg and Delano run my country. So you can . . ."

The gunshot made everyone jump, the boom of the .45 caliber weapon deafening in the Oval Office. President Clark, a hole already oozing blood from the center of his forehead, slumped forward on the sofa, his head between his knees and nearly touching the coffee table.

Klegg, his heart racing, turned to see Secret Service Agent Elliot Kyle. The agent's weapon remained aimed at President Clark. But the man was dead, and after a moment, the weapon shifted to General Stimpson.

The door to the Oval Office flew open, and Mike appeared, his weapon at the ready.

"Stand down, Mike," Kyle called over his shoulder. "President Clark just committed suicide. Go back outside, close the door, and keep everyone out."

The agent appeared stunned, but he yielded to Kyle's authority.

Not surprisingly, Vivian reacted faster than Klegg or Stimpson. "That's right," she said. "Clark shot himself." She turned to Stimpson. "General, I think you should consider retirement. Right now. Otherwise . . ."

"There's a pen and paper on the desk, General Stimpson," Kyle said, holstering his weapon. "And as far as I know, Clark never officially signed anything ending General Klegg's command under martial law."

"It's a shame," Vivian said, her voice a little louder than necessary, "that President Clark decided to commit suicide. The stress of his many mistakes must have been too much for him. Isn't that right, General Stimpson?"

Stimpson swallowed, then stared at the corpse, dripping blood on the table. Nearly forty years had passed since he'd seen a man die. "Yes . . . yes, of course. Everyone knew he was not a well man, not since California."

"Good, then that's settled," Klegg said. "Vivian, you should contact the Vice President and let him know that he's in charge. But tell him that by your authority under martial law, you are authorizing the return of the United States to the Alliance, and that you are fully committed to having Col. Delano assume the role of planetary defense leader under the Alliance."

The grief-stricken VP was in California, at his wife's bedside. She'd been gravely injured in the attack on San Diego, and one of their married children had died, along with his family. "I'll explain the . . . situation to him," Vivian said. "I'm sure he'll agree."

Unlike the dead President Clark, the VP had a brain and a sense of decency, which was probably why Clark kept him out of the power loop since the election. And the VP had been friendly to General Klegg.

"Agent Kyle," Klegg said, "Welcome to the fight. I would like you to take charge of Dr. Spencer's security. I think she's going to need all the protection she can get."

"I'm surprised you want me around," Kyle said. "After this . . ."

"This nothing? By stopping Clark, you probably saved the entire planet. He was never going to listen to reason. And right now we need the help of all the good men and women we can get. Protecting Dr. Spencer should be your primary concern now."

"I'd like that, General Klegg," Kyle said. "As senior agent, I can assign some personnel to look after you as well."

Klegg nodded. "Good idea, at least until I can have some Air Force SFs take over. But Dr. Spencer is the priority." He turned to Stimpson. "General, I still think it's best if you take your retirement. Too many people know what you tried to do. Better get to that pen and paper. The faster we can wrap up all this the better. Meanwhile, I have to put in a call to Col. Delano and Dr. Duan and inform them that we are at their service." He shook his head. "He's gonna love that."

Chapter 12

October 23 - Moscow

Once again, Delano and Lian took the center seats. On Delano's right sat General Zeng of the People's Republic of China. On Lian's left was President Demidov. They faced a battery of cameras, and five separate viewing screens. On those monitors appeared the leaders of Poland, the Czech Republic, and Finland. On screens five and six were representatives of Germany and Switzerland, bureaucratic advisors to their respective leaders. Apparently the leaders of Germany and Switzerland were too busy with matters of state to waste time on unelected nobodies named Delano and Duan.

Well, that's going to change. "Good morning, everyone," Delano began, speaking in English. "I know that you have many questions. But we would appreciate it if you will please let Dr. Duan and I, as the leaders of the Planetary Defense Force, first read our prepared notes." He glanced down at the tablet in front of him, then back up at the cameras.

"I'm sorry to see that the leaders of Germany and Switzerland are too busy to take our call, and have instead sent their representatives. They will be allowed to remain, but we will take no questions from them. We'll attend to those nations later. For now, I want to speak to the leaders of the remaining nations. As you know, a global emergency has been declared by the Alliance. The fate of the planet is a stake. China and Russia are already gearing up to begin production of ships and weapons to defeat the Ktarran fleet. To that end, the factories and industrial complexes of your countries will need to be added to, and coordinated with, those of the Russian Federation and the Republic of China."

He nodded to Lian, and she continued the conversation, working from her own set of notes. "We are in the initial stages of developing the plans for these new ships and weapons. The Planetary Defense Force is asking your countries to join that effort. That will require full mobilization of every factory that can be converted to the wartime production of military goods. Giving up a sizeable portion of your factories means that your countries will face considerable hardship, as will China and Russia. If you agree to that, we are prepared to offer each of your nations two hundred berths aboard a Colonizer Transport."

Delano leaned toward the camera. "Listen and listen carefully. If your nations are not willing to join in defending the planet," he said, "then Russian and Chinese troops will move in and take over the factories. In that case the citizens of your respective countries will not have any access to the CTs. Nor will your people be given any considerations or compensations. If there is active resistance, military or otherwise, then the factories will be destroyed, using whatever force required, if necessary by nuclear devices. Since we have no desire to take anyone's life, there will be a three hour warning prior to the destruction."

The alphabet brigade had already begun its work. The Planetary Defense Force was the PDF, the Colonizer Transports the CTs, and the small Earth-to-orbit ships, what Delano had called Jeeps, were now Jumpers.

"In short," Lian said, "the PDF is proceeding on the assumption that you will want to devote your efforts to saving the lives of your families and yourselves. But let me state that the people of China and Russia are not going to sacrifice themselves so that you can benefit from their labor and military efforts. It is expected that some factories, regions, or even nations may refuse to join our efforts, and when that happens we will make examples of those who resist. In other words, we are not going to argue, plead, or appeal to your individual best interests. There is no time for that. If this seems harsh or Draconian, please review the photos from China and the Western United States after the Ktarran attack. That is the future that faces every person on this planet."

She paused, and looked at each camera in turn. "From today forward, every day is precious. The clock is ticking. The earliest Ktarran return date, as calculated by the Tarlons, is March 5, 2054. That's less than seventeen months away. The alternative to all-out mobilization is clear – look at Tokyo, Beijing, and Los Angeles. I trust we have made ourselves clear. This is not a negotiation."

Delano started up. "As for Germany and Switzerland, based on their relative sizes and ability to contribute to the war effort, we had planned to offer two hundred berths aboard a CT to

Germany, and one hundred seats to Switzerland. Since the leaders of those two countries could not find the time to attend this meeting, I am informing their representatives that those numbers will be cut in half. If the leaders of Switzerland and Germany do not contact us within two hours, the offer will be withdrawn completely, and they can explain to their citizens why none of them will have a chance to survive the coming Ktarran invasion."

"If there is no call received by the PDF at that time," Lian said, "the order will be given to General Shuvalov to begin moving his troops into Germany and Switzerland. Meanwhile we ask that Poland and the Czech Republic temporarily approve the use of their highways and railways to help transport the Russian troops and equipment. Additionally, some Chinese and Russian units may be flown directly into specific locations. Resistance will be immediately met with overwhelming force." She looked directly into the cameras. "I want to emphasize that all military forces of the Alliance are ready to do their part. Now it is time for your nations to do theirs."

"I think our statement sums up the high points," Delano said. "To the representatives of Germany and Switzerland, your leaders have two hours to contact the PDF. Will the technician please end the connection to those two countries at this time."

Lian smiled into the cameras. "Now, are there any questions?"

*   *   *

Poland, The Czech Republic, and Finland filled the next two hours with questions. That kept Delano and Lian busy responding to every concern. Even Demidov and General Zeng were called upon to speak. But they resolved a number of issues, and in the end all three nations agreed to support the planetary defense effort.

Delano had to stretch the truth only once, and that was when the leader of Finland asked whether the United States intended to rejoin the Alliance and contribute its efforts. But General Zeng and President Demidov nodded in support, while their grim faces indicated their approval and consent for Lian and Delano's declaration.

"Yes, we expect them to do so within a few hours," Delano said. *Fingers crossed.* He was aware that some high-level discussions at the White House were going on, but the outcome remained unknown.

Whether any of the three leaders believed him, he couldn't say. What did matter were the basic rules that they hammered out. These would become the basis of all future interactions with the PDF.

1.   The agreement for nations to join the Alliance was temporary, to be terminated immediately upon the removal of the Ktarran threat.

2.   All national borders were permanently frozen. The Alliance agreed to make no attempt to capitalize on the current crisis now, or after its conclusion.

3.   All local governments were frozen. No new elections will be permitted until the crisis is resolved.

4.   Russian and Chinese troops would be used only as needed. Their role would consist of protecting the factories, maintaining order, and ensuring production. Militaries from nearby countries would be utilized as much as possible. Local troops and police would provide support as required.

5.   Inspectors would be selected and allocated to each country, and to a specific group of factories. All inspectors would be selected from another country, to insure that no local favoritism took place.

6.   Any attempt at fraud, favoritism, sabotage, or profiteering, by anyone involved with the production of PDF materials, would be subject to an immediate death penalty and confiscation of all private goods and property. The military of an alternative nation would be in charge of any trials and executions. There would be no exceptions and no appeals.

That last item caused quite a stir. Lian hammered home the critical point. Time remained of the essence. For all anyone knew, the Ktarrans might have the technology to open the wormhole next week or next month. Anything that contributed to the slightest delay would be dealt with on the spot. Declaring that the urge to take personal advantage of the crisis would be too strong for some to resist, she demanded the harshest penalties. In fact, she said, the sooner some examples were provided, the better and faster the process would proceed.

Delano, a little surprised at these harsh words and grim tone, transmitted the final list to the three nations. Before they had time to electronically sign and return the documents, the moment arrived to make the call to Germany and Switzerland.

Lian activated the cameras, and once again Delano, Lian, Zeng, and Demidov stared at the monitors, as Otto Schaffner, the German Chancellor, and Joseph Waldman, President of the Swiss Confederation appeared. Both had angry scowls on their faces.

"This is an outrage," the German Chancellor began. "You have no authority . . ."

"Chancellor Schaffner, our authority is sitting beside me," Lian said. "President Demidov and General Zeng will confirm that. As I recall, you were the one who wanted special favors from the Tarlons. Faced with a planetary crisis, you tried to negotiate specific trade agreements to benefit Germany. So you are the one willing to sacrifice your country to your own greed. Such behavior will no longer be tolerated."

Lian sounded angry, and she kept speaking before Schaffner could get in a word. "The Alliance needs the automotive and industrial factories in Leipzig as soon as possible, and you are going to turn them over to us. If you do not agree to support and participate in the Planetary Defense, every facility on this list," she lifted a paper and waved it in front of the camera, "will be destroyed in three hours, using conventional weapons. You will be responsible for notifying everyone living within two miles of each factory. People living within that radius will have only that much time to evacuate to a safe distance."

Delano leaned forward. "After those factories are leveled, another complex will be selected, and the process repeated until Germany has no useful industrial facilities remaining, or decides to join wholeheartedly the Planetary Defense Force. Nuclear weapons may or may not be used against subsequent sites. They will be employed, however, if any military resistance is offered. Meanwhile, Russian and Chinese troops will soon be on their way. Poland, the Czech Republic, and Finland have agreed to join the PDF, and they've already given approval for any needed military passages and rail transport across their nations."

"You cannot do this," the Chancellor shouted. "The world will not permit such a use of force."

"The world is still in shock from the alien attack. The world will be more interested in why you are not choosing to fight against the Ktarrans," Delano shot back. "Germany has already lost half of their possible berths on a Colonizer. Tell that to your people. You have fifteen minutes to decide. After that, we will release the news, listing what you have done, and giving the time for the first factory neutralization. The PDF needs an example to demonstrate our dedication to saving the planet, and it might as well be Leipzig."

"Cut the German feed," Delano ordered. He turned to the Swiss President and smiled. "Are you going to berate us as well, Mr. President?"

"Switzerland has never been invaded," President Walman began, but his voice trailed off. He appeared shaken by what he'd just witnessed.

"Nor does it need to be," Lian said. "We want only coordination and control of key factories, and your country's total support. Two or three hundred Russian soldiers and technical experts can be in Zurich in less than ten hours. If you object to Russians, we can send in Chinese units. Think of them as security consultants for the Alliance and PDF. As long as your government cooperates with us, there should be little contact or friction. And I think we can agree to give you another fifty seats on a Colonizer. Say one hundred and fifty? Do you know any of your citizens who might wish to leave Earth to avoid the coming alien invasion?"

Delano, watching the President's face, recognized the signs. The man didn't want to resist. He'd heard the harsh language used on the German Chancellor, and by now he believed the threat was real. Politically, the menace to his personal power loomed large. Also, the chance to save all or part of his family aboard a Colonizer was a powerful temptation.

"Some members of my family might consider leaving the planet. I might even join them."

Lian shook her head. She and Delano had talked about that. "I'm sorry, but that is unlikely. We have not yet identified the needed skills sets required to join a Colonizer. Obviously only people with viable and needed skills can be selected. Your political background would be of little value aboard a starship. Besides, if national leaders are forced to remain, they will work harder to help defend the planet. Remember, President Walman, we could have said yes, and promised to give you a seat. But that is not what this Planetary Defense Force is all about. We will deal honestly with you, in return for your cooperation."

Walman considered that. "My daughter is an eye doctor, an ophthalmologist. Would that be considered a useful occupation?"

"I would assume so," Lian answered. "Doctors and medical support people of all specialties will be required on such a long flight. Is she married? Any children?"

"Yes, they have two children. Her husband is a software engineer."

"Then I believe that we can promise her four of the seats allocated to Switzerland."

As of now, the PDF had no idea of who should be selected, Delano knew, but the offer would be a huge bribe. An entire team of doctors and medical technicians would be needed for every Colonizer. No doubt the ships would have to take some dead weight, those politically or financially connected, but the captains could work out that problem during the flight. Once underway, a ship captain would have absolute authority. Troublemakers or useless mouths could always be tossed out an airlock.

The Swiss leader considered his options. "You say the other nations have already accepted?"

"Except for Germany, yes, Mr. President," Lian said. "Contact them if you wish. If Switzerland decides to join the Alliance, temporarily of course, you could make that announcement to your country yourself. It might increase your prestige and alleviate your citizens' worries."

"The threat is that grave? You sincerely believe this?"

"It is, Mr. President," Delano said. "You've seen the videos of California and Japan and Beijing. Two alien ships massacred over forty-five million people in less than fifty minutes. They destroyed entire cities in the process. What do you think will happen when fifty or a hundred of these alien battleships arrive? Your Alps will not protect you from a space-borne attack. Will Bern and Geneva will be spared? Or that you can negotiate with monsters who would initiate such attacks?"

"I need time to discuss this with my ministers," Walman said.

"You have one hour," Lian said. She glanced at her phone and noted the time. "After that . . ."

"Very well," Walman said. The connection went dark.

"He's in," Delano said. "Now we just have to see how stupid the Chancellor is."

After the link to Switzerland ended, Delano leaned back and sighed. "At least we've taken the first steps."

A knock on the door to the teleconference room drew everyone's attention. Demidov, General Zeng, and Lian all watched as a Russian aide to Minister Borodin entered, with Steve Macy at his heels.

"President Demidov," the lieutenant began, but Steve called out over his shoulder. "It's Klegg! He wants to talk to you and Lian!" He waved his phone.

Delano looked at Demidov. "OK, Steve, put him on the speaker."

Steve muttered into the phone, and Klegg's voice came through, loud and clear.

"Col. Delano, this is General Klegg. I wanted you to be the first to know. Sadly, President Clark committed suicide a few hours ago. Since he never officially rescinded the emergency powers order, I am continuing in command of the United States military, under the civilian authority of NSA Director Vivian Spencer. When the Vice President returns to Washington, he will take personal charge of the nation's rebuilding effort. So Dr. Spencer and I want to immediately cancel Clark's misguided directive withdrawing the United States from the Alliance. That was an unfortunate mistake. He was not a well man."

Delano didn't waste a heartbeat on Clark's demise. "Good to have you back in command, General. President Demidov and General Zeng are here. I'm certain they feel the same way."

"We are relieved to have you in charge," Demidov said. "I'm sure Secretary Liu will also be delighted." He glanced at General Zeng, who nodded approval.

"If we may rejoin the Alliance," Klegg said, "I want China and Russia to know that the United States will do everything that it can to support its fellow members and help defend the planet against the Ktarrans. Since you're in charge of that effort, we await your orders. Can you initiate contact with the Halkin ship? We've less than six hours before the deadline."

"Yes, Steve can connect us up from here. We spoke to Jarendo during the flight to Moscow."

"Do you think they'll listen?" Klegg sounded worried. "What will you tell them?"

"The truth, that we've learned our lesson," Delano said. "Dr. Duan can be very persuasive. We'll say that the Alliance is dedicating all its combined resources to building a fleet, and that we've already started enlisting other countries in that effort."

He told Klegg about Switzerland and the other European nations. "We'll be adding the support of more nations countries to the effort as soon as we can get our act together. Before we're finished, every country that can contribute to the war effort will be working with us."

"Are you going to remain in Moscow?"

"For now, until Europe gets aboard. Then we'll be heading to Beijing to speak with their leaders. After that it's on to the US, providing everything remains on track."

"I'll give the heads up to British and Canadian militaries," Klegg said. "You and Dr. Duan better make the call to the Tarlons and Halkins."

"Will do. Meanwhile, can you start the ball rolling back there? Assemble a high-level planning and administration team to mobilize the US industry. We'll need steel, mining, manufacturing, tech, hell, you know how to start the train moving."

"Have you put together any ideas, Colonel?"

"Yes, we have. We'll send you what we've got as soon as we get the Tarlons' commitment. We may need to patch you in on that."

"If you need me," Klegg said, "I'll be available. Otherwise Vivian . . . Dr. Spencer and I have quite a few loose ends to take care of. The nation needs some reassurance after your speech and the President's sudden death. All this coming after California . . ."

"Good luck, then, General Klegg." Delano broke the connection. He turned to Zeng and Demidov. "I take it that there is no objection to my country rejoining the Alliance?"

Demidov glanced at General Zeng, who smiled. "None at all, Colonel." Demidov couldn't keep the satisfaction out of his voice. "President Clark was an obstacle to the planet's defense. His, uh . . . suicide was most fortunate for all of us."

Someone had taken Clark out of the equation, Delano guessed, wondering who had pulled the trigger. *Klegg must have more friends in power than I thought.*

"With the United States' resources, management skills, and technical expertise," Lian said, "we can commence building the fleet. Now at least we have a chance."

"Then it's time to make the call," Delano said.

Chapter 13

Moscow

The call from Earth arrived less than four hours before the deadline expired. As usual, Ahvin – second wife to Halkin Captain Horath – opened the link and listened to what Delano and Lian had to say. Ahvin had been the first alien to establish communications with the humans, teaching them the trade language used as a common tongue by all the enemies of the Ktarrans.

"It is good to speak with you again, Delano and Lian," Ahvin said. "I will deliver your message to Captain Horath and the others." She left the small room now used as a comm center for messages to and from Earth. But the comm link remained active.

"I couldn't tell if she were happy or not," Delano said.

"Cautiously optimistic," Lian answered in Chinese. "I wonder if the Tarlons and Halkins were as concerned as we are." She sighed. "Do you think they would have really left? Without the wormhole, it would take them several years to reach one of their planets."

"The trouble with playing chicken is that you have to know when to drop the bluff." She looked at him quizzically, and he had to explain the American slang. "But I believe they would have left. They'd be unhappy, perhaps sad, but their minds are too organized, too logical to deal with a world full of crazy humans, all screaming to be in charge."

She laughed. "Now they only have to deal with two crazy humans. Us."

Before Delano could reply, Ahvin returned. Following her into the camera's view was Celeck, one of the three Tarlons aboard the Halkin vessel. Almost two weeks had passed since Delano had seen any of the aliens. The call from the airplane prior to his arrival in Moscow didn't count, since that communication used audio only.

Once again he contrasted the two different species. Ahvin was a female Halkin, and small compared to the male of her species. Her husband Horath – apparently Halkins could have several mates at the same time – resembled an upright grizzly bear, only with a fine coat of hair, like that of a horse and with the muscles to match. Celeck, a Tarlon, probably weighed thirty pounds less than Ahvin, even though he had about the same height, a little under six feet. But where a Halkin displayed physical strength, the Tarlons as a species were slender, with thin arms and legs and skin like fine leather. They appeared fragile compared to the Halkins, but nobody on Earth knew if the differences mattered.

Ahvin's duties as a translator were not needed, but she remained in the room. One of her assignments, she'd previously explained, was to learn as much about humans as possible. Celeck spoke in his own language, the one that Delano and Lian had struggled to learn in the little time they had before the Ktarrans arrived.

"Delano, it is good to see you again," Celeck said. "Do you bring good news? I was hoping to learn more of your languages."

Celeck was a professional scholar, teacher, and trainer. He taught Delano and Lian the Tarlon language, and watched over them as they communicated with Talmak, the leader of the Tarlon expedition, now a passenger aboard the Halkin ship. Delano guessed that Talmak had almost certainly devised the ultimatum, and let Horath deliver it.

"Yes, Celeck, Lian and I bring good news. The Alliance has agreed to your conditions, and many of the remaining large countries have begun accepting it as well. As of now, Lian and I are the leaders of Earth's Planetary Defense Force. We have initiated the first steps to mobilizing Earth's economies for a war footing."

"In fact," Lian continued, "that is the first thing we want to discuss. Delano has identified the critical ships that need to be built, and we want your help, that is, the help of your engineers and technicians. As you know, we have no time to waste if we are to assemble a fleet of ships to defeat the Ktarrans."

Celeck took a moment before he replied. "Are you certain that what you say is true? I have been reading many of your histories, and it seems that often deliberate lies are told, in order to achieve political solutions."

The Tarlons had access to all of Earth's major libraries, news feeds, and reporting blogs. Celeck possessed a quick and ready mind, and by now had absorbed a good deal of Earth's history as well as current events. He'd certainly learned enough to be cautious.

"Yes, Celeck, this is true," Lian answered. "My uncle, my kindred through my mother, leads the nation of China. They, as well as Russia and the United States, have made their commitment to this arrangement. Delano and I have established what we call a Planetary Defense Force, and we will lead the efforts to stop the Ktarrans."

"We are fully committed," Delano added. He'd expected Celeck to be more positive. "Russia has already begun the process of mobilization."

"Based on your Earth histories, it seems that there will be many who will oppose your authority, perhaps even with force. Are you and Lian prepared to resolve such situations?"

Delano understood the polite question. Translated, it meant "Do you have the stones to deal with those who oppose you?" General Klegg had spoken the truth. People were going to die, a lot of them, and this time it would be Delano and Lian pulling the trigger.

"Yes, we are," Lian answered. "My nation has learned how to use force to silence those who oppose us. We are ready to do what needs to be done."

"I will discuss this with Captain Horath and Talmak. Your world's decision comes very late, and that is not a good sign for the future. Our preparations for departure are already complete." Celeck seemed almost resigned to failure. "We will contact you when we have decided."

Celeck rose and disappeared from the camera's view. Ahvin leaned closer. "I wish you success," she said. The camera went dark.

Lian grasped Delano's arm. "Damn, do you think we are too late? Will they really leave us?"

"I don't know," Delano said. "I expected Ahvin and Celeck to be happy to hear the news. It's like they've already made up their minds to abandon us."

"Then we will be on our own," she said. "Earth will not survive by itself."

"Yes, all alone in the night," he answered. "A long, dark night."

*   *   *

Shortly after the call ended, Delano and Lian were joined in the conference room by President Demidov and Field Marshal Shuvalov. General Zeng arrived a few moments later. Last to arrive was Major Mitchell, who'd probably sent a text to General Klegg. All of them had monitored the call. No one had much to say, and the next hour dragged by while the uplink remained dark.

Demidov's aide took drink orders. Vodka for the President, Scotch for General Zeng, and Irish whiskey for Shuvalov. Delano wanted a whiskey, but he and Lian drank tea. They had to stay at the top of their game in the event negotiations turned dicey.

A full seventy-five minutes passed before the comm link went active. If the aliens wanted to drag out the suspense, they had succeeded. Delano had lost count of how many drinks the others consumed. He wondered if it had been such a good idea to give Celeck access to every document in the Station's computer. By now he and his companions probably possessed a good working knowledge of Earth's history and the psychology of its inhabitants.

The screen went active. Delano saw that the key players sat close enough for Ahvin to get them all on the single screen. Ahvin, of course, remained, to monitor the equipment. She sat at the end of the table, next to Celeck, who would do most of the talking. But Captain Horath sat next to Talmak, the leader of the Tarlons. Jarendo, chief technical officer for the Tarlons, completed the assembly.

"It is good to see you again, Delano and Lian," Talmak said. "We missed your counsel."

The words sounded friendly enough, but Delano and Lian picked up on his tone, which did not seem particularly cordial. The others present, relying on the translation software, would not detect the nuance. Captain Horath appeared particularly grim, again something the others might not notice.

"Yes, it is good to speak with you again," Lian answered. "We are grateful that you have remained in orbit while Earth resolved its difficulties."

"You are satisfied with your planet's resolve? You and Delano will act as leaders for its defense?"

Again, the translation software couldn't catch the subtle hint of doubt, or maybe condescension. Delano sensed the danger, and knew that Lian recognized it, too. For the others, the conversation would appear normal.

"Yes, we are," Lian said, a hint of firmness in her voice. "We are even now beginning the planetary mobilization."

Talmak glanced at Horath. The big Halkin had remained unmoving, staring at the table in front of him. Something passed between them, some kind of non-verbal signal. For the first time, Delano noticed that Jarendo and Celeck had kept their eyes lowered.

"When will the first fighting ship be ready?" Horath's eyes now bored straight into the camera.

"Not for some time," Delano said. "As I explained to Celeck when we last spoke, there is much preliminary work that needs to be done. For example, we will assemble all our fighting ships on Earth's moon. Before we can do that, we need to build transports capable of efficiently carrying supplies and parts to the Moon's surface. The sooner we begin working over those designs with Jarendo and Celeck, the better we will be able to develop a plan with dates and deliverables."

"You declared that Earth intended to build ships to carry humans away from the danger," Horath said. "But each such ship will mean many fewer fighting ships. If you wish our help, Earth must concentrate on constructing only fighting ships."

Lian's pinky moved slightly, their private signal for danger. Delano had already recognized the problem. "Earth, specifically every member of the Alliance, will undergo full mobilization in the face of the external threat. But before the remainder of our planet can commit to the same effort, there must be a way for Earth to save a portion of itself in case of failure."

"You yourself have said that we may not be able to resist the Ktarrans," Lian added. "In that case we must have a plan to save our civilization from extinction."

That word caused some confusion, and Celeck had to explain to the others what extinction meant. When he finished, Horath shook his head.

"No, you must only build fighting ships, if you wish our help." The Halkin captain sounded firm.

"We will build both," Delano said. "Earth has sufficient resources. A ship to transport people and cargo will be much simpler to build than a fighting ship."

"Then it may be that we cannot help you," Talmak said. "Before we risk our own ships, we must be certain of your total commitment."

"Then it may be that we cannot help you," Lian snapped. "We already have sufficient information to construct ships and weapons. With your assistance, we can build more of them and faster. But if you wish to fight the Ktarrans alone, as you have done in the past, that is your choice. You know what future your home worlds will face. The Tarlons and Halkins need Earth as much as we need you."

That probably wasn't quite as true as Lian declared, but Delano thought her quick response a good one. He reminded himself that while they might be on Horath's ship, Talmak was the one making the final decisions. Horath might be the public face of the aliens to the people of Earth, but Talmak and his allies represented the greater power.

Lian leaned back, crossed her arms, and stared into the camera. Talmak would recognize the gesture for what it meant. He'd seen it before.

Jarendo, seated at Talmak's right, leaned over and whispered something. Talmak nodded, and Jarendo leaned toward the camera. "Delano and Lian, what makes you think you can build enough ships in the remaining time?"

"This is how we construct everything," Delano said. "First we design, a step that often takes much time. When we know what we need to build, we develop plans that tell us when and where each part is needed. Meanwhile we determine construction sites and resources required. Mass production can then begin. Don't be concerned. Once the process is in place, we can produce many ships."

Jarendo didn't sound reassured. "And the people of your planet, they have agreed to support your efforts? All of them?"

Lian shook her head. "No, not all of them, at least not yet. But those in the Alliance have agreed, and the others will follow soon enough."

Or else they'll be dead. Delano didn't like the idea, but it was becoming more and more inevitable.

"When will we see the first ships?" Jarendo still sounded dubious.

"You know our process," Delano said. "First we need to construct the ships that can lift the material to our Moon. Then we will begin assembling the components there. Our estimate is that it will take at least three months before we begin construction of the first fighting ship. But during that interval, we will also be working on later phases of production."

"What comes next?" Jarendo had taken over the discussion. "Will you have enough time to build sufficient ships to resist the Ktarrans? There is so little time. We have many questions that need answers."

"You ask questions that we are not ready to answer yet," Lian said. "We will work as fast as we can, for as long as we can. The only question is, are you going to help or not? Your decision will affect our plans."

Jarendo hesitated, then glanced at Talmak, who turned back to Horath.

"Why are you considering building these smaller ships?" Horath sounded curious. "And these drones, or whatever you call them? You need to build powerful ships that can fight the Ktarrans."

Delano started to answer, but Shuvalov lifted his hand. "May I answer the Halkin captain, Col. Delano?"

"Of course, Marshal," Delano said. "Please speak slowly so that I can translate your words directly."

Shuvalov leaned back in his chair. "In my position, I command military resources of over four million men and women fighters. Russia, my country, has fought many wars over the last hundred and fifty years. In that time, we have learned that smaller and faster is often superior to large and powerful. China and the United States have similar armed forces. The Alliance countries have learned to control and coordinate not only such large numbers of fighters, but the vastly more complicated tasks required to arm, equip, and supply such numbers. Sufficient ships and fighters will be ready when we need them."

Delano had translated Shuvalov's words, placing the emphasis exactly where the Field Marshal intended. As Delano and Lian had already discovered, Shuvalov didn't say much, but when he spoke, everyone paid careful attention to his words. Delano saw the aliens could not conceal the impact of Shuvalov's numbers. They had a difficult time grasping the idea that four million sentients could be welded together into a single fighting force.

"Then you approve of Delano's ideas for small ships and these drones?" Horath's body language showed he still doubted.

"Colonel Delano has proposed a bold strategy for military

operations," Shuvalov said, "but one that I believe will optimize our planet's forces. Like all designs in their initial stages, changes and modifications based on learning will occur. That, too, is something we are used to dealing with."

Horath turned to Talmak. "Will you commit to this . . . plan?"

Talmak looked to Jarendo and then Celeck. Both nodded. "Yes, the Tarlons will remain, if Captain Horath also is satisfied."

Horath still seemed dissatisfied. "Then I will also agree, but we will monitor your progress with great care. Should you fail to achieve your goals, we will depart."

Not a resounding vote of confidence, Delano decided, but good enough. "Then Lian and I give you our thanks, Captain Horath. We will begin at once."

"What do you need from us?" Horath asked.

"In a few hours, Delano and I depart for China," Lian said. "There we must meet with General Secretary Liu and some of his ministers. On the way, we will stop at Jiuquan, to meet with the scientists from the Alliance working on the Star Rider's vessel.

That was the name given to the alien ship recovered under the rocky soil of Io a few months ago. Though only a small, two seat scout ship, it possessed a powerful drive that appeared to be something new, and different, from the Tarlon/Halkin/Ktarran technology.

"At Jiuquan," Delano said, "we will need help from Jarendo and Celeck. The sooner we can decipher its propulsion system, the better."

"Yes, we also would like to examine that," Jarendo said. "It may be something from the Ancients that we have not developed."

The Ancient Ones were those genetic parents of all three races – humans, Tarlon, and Halkin. They had left the stellar quadrant many cycles ago, after failing to stop the Ktarran expansion. With the discovery of the damaged scout, the Ancients might yet offer up some of their vast knowledge.

"Your assistance will be most welcome," Delano said. "We do not have much time."

The Tarlon Celeck had thoughtfully calculated the likely number of days remaining before the wormhole reopened and the Ktarrans returned. The expected date of arrival was March 5, 2054.

Delano glanced at Lian. They'd done it, taken the first critical step. The planet Earth, under the guidance of the PDF and the Alliance, had solidified its position. Or rather, the Alliance had managed to save itself despite its best efforts. Now came the real work, getting the planet mobilized. Many across the globe would resist or try to seize advantage from the coming crisis. How well Delano and Lian dealt with those issues would be the next big test. In one sense, the next 497 days would pass soon enough. *Now all we have to do is work our asses off for sixteen long months.*

Chapter 14

The Planet Ktarra, home world of the Ktarran Supremacy . . .

Sixty light years from Earth, another conference took place on the planet Ktarra. This stellar system held only three worlds orbiting the orange, K-class star. Though the Ktarran star was considerably cooler than Earth's sun, the Ktarran home world orbited somewhat closer, and so the surface temperature was significantly warmer. Ktarra possessed about one and a quarter the mass of Earth and a much stronger gravity.

The planet had once boasted a diversity of life forms, nourished by a jungle world of dark red and orange vegetation spread out over vast tracts of honey-colored grasslands. Rivers and mountains abounded, with many lakes and swamps beside them. The favorable conditions gave rise to a multitude of different life forms, but the Ktarrans, in their climb up the evolutionary ladder to preeminence on their world, had affected not only the ecology but the planet itself.

In less than a million years of development, the Ktarrans had killed off their animal competitors and risen to the top of the evolutionary scale. That accomplishment left them without a steady source of meat protein, and they began to fight and feed upon each other. After the passage of another million years, the urge to fight, conquer, and eat their enemies became an integral part of Ktarran genetic structure.

Unlike many other species in the galaxy, when the Ktarrans first became sentient, they saw no reason to change their savage instincts, instincts that had inevitably led them to fight and feed among themselves. Favored by natural selection with a high birthrate, and long without any natural enemies, there were always too many Ktarrans vying for the same food and females.

The Ancients had discovered them trapped in that cycle. Unlike other races in the quadrant, the Ktarrans had not been seeded with the DNA of the Ancients. Seeing the abundance of life strength on Ktarra, the Ancients' genetic engineers decided to modify the DNA of the planet's primary species.

To that end, the Ancients introduced segments of their own

DNA into the Ktarrans, fully expecting that, over time, the new additions would result in modified behavior. This procedure had been performed many times on other species, and the Ancients had a remarkable number of successes in initiating intelligence. This time, however, they were only partially successful.

The evolutionary change introduced into the Ktarran species did not have the desired result. Instead of pacifying the worst carnivorous instincts, it instead only sharpened Ktarran intelligence. The same situation might have occurred on Earth, if the prehistoric velociraptors had avoided the climatic disaster of the asteroid impact and continued developing ever-larger brains.

Within a few hundred generations, the Ktarrans absorbed the DNA and began their rise to civilization. When the Ancients returned several thousand cycles later, they found a powerful and clever species ruling the planet.

The intervention by the Ancients turned the Ktarrans into something unexpected – an intelligent hunter-species that lived exclusively on meat. These dominant and powerful creatures cared nothing for the pastoral existence so strongly recommended by the Ancients.

Worse than mere rejection of those ideals, the Ktarrans pretended to follow them. With the cunning of a far more advanced race, they deceived the Ancients, begging and pleading for more and more technology. Believing that they might still achieve their goals, the Ancients yielded up many of their civilization's secrets to the Ktarrans.

But within a few thousand cycles, as their wisdom and knowledge increased, Ktarrans achieved technical breakthroughs on their own. Learning of life on other planets, space travel immediately became their true goal, for only the meat animals of other planets could satisfy their concealed hungers.

Still committed to their ideal of pacifying the Ktarran planet, in time the Ancients finally surrendered their greatest and most precious secrets – the space drive and wormhole travel.

The Ktarrans needed no more. Trusting that the Ancients would never resort to violence, Ktarra turned on its benefactors. Within a single rotation, they murdered and devoured every Ancient on the planet, and began their assault on neighboring worlds. Their newly-built ships, fitted with weapons developed in secret, lifted off to begin the harvesting of alien species.

The Ancients, even with their great wisdom and enormous

technical skills, had blundered badly. A hundred worlds had welcomed their help, worked with them for peace and prosperity, and over time revered the Ancients as near-gods. In their pride, they assumed that the Ktarrans would do the same.

Aghast at their mistake, the Ancients could do nothing but leave. They tried to contain the Ktarrans, but would not use force against them. That was not their way. Instead they turned to their other children-races, and gave them the same technology that the Ktarrans possessed, hoping the other worlds could contain the terror unleashed upon them.

But like the Ancients, these other worlds hosted relatively peaceful species unaccustomed to the savagery of Ktarra. To save themselves, these worlds seeded by the Ancients learned to fight, but against a warlike species that preferred conflict to peace, they found themselves outmatched in arms, ferocity, and resolve.

Planets fell before the Ktarrans, and the local life forms became part of the Ktarran food supply. Over time, billions of sentients were killed and their bodies processed as food for Ktarra. Those not condemned to die were made slaves, laboring to build more technology that the Ktarrans used to continue their expansion.

Believing in their destiny, the Ktarrans intended to master and rule over every planet supporting life in the entire Quadrant.

Now a tiny world on the farthest fringe of Ktarran-controlled space threatened that inevitable growth. A backwater planet, without advanced development and accessible only by an unstable wormhole, had found a way to defeat Ktarran fighting ships, albeit with help from the degenerate Tarlons and Halkins. Those species, already facing the inevitable surrender to Ktarra, had helped the humans, but the fact remained that three ships of Ktarra had been destroyed, the worst defeat the Ktarrans had endured in hundreds of cycles.

The Ktarrans, of course, could not accept any setback, let alone one of this magnitude. To survive, the Empire must constantly expand. Something must be done. But by the time Ktarra's leaders learned of the disaster in Earth-space, the wormhole had closed, and would remain closed for some time.

In some ways, that was a good thing. The species on the newly-discovered planet could not go anywhere, trapped within their solar system. Nor could they trade with other worlds, or absorb the necessary technology in the brief span of time before the wormhole reopened. Even so, the Ktarran leaders made their plans with care, and prepared for the time when they would exact their revenge.

*　　*　　*

Pannoch Staleeck (the name translates as "Staleeck the Almighty") ruled the planet Ktarra and every living creature that dwelt upon it. Nor did his authority end at Ktarra's atmosphere. Forty-two other planets paid tribute to his name, and their inhabitants dropped to their knees to acknowledge his rule. Despite the number of planetary systems under Ktarran rule, only twelve different species existed on them, spread across the forty plus worlds. The others had been wiped out by military force or eaten into extinction.

Most of the conquered planets had been emptied of intelligent life, then reseeded with the slave species utilized by the Ktarrans – Peltors and Dalvaks. These two species survived by doing the bidding of their masters. Dalvaks provided technical knowledge and manufacturing skills, while the Peltors performed lower-level duties not requiring superior intelligence. Over the thousands of cycles since they became slaves, the habit of obedience to their ruthless masters had become almost ingrained.

Neither slave race was immune to Ktarran claws and teeth. The slightest infraction by any Peltor or Dalvak could result in death. The thought of being eaten alive kept the subject species in line.

But today Pannoch Staleeck had no interest in slaves. He sat on his massive throne, with six of his guards behind him, frowning at the three Ktarrans standing four steps below. He had met with them several times since the debacle in Earth-space. The loss of three capital ships in one encounter had shaken the Ktarran Empire. If the captains of those ships had survived and appeared before him, they would have been ripped to shreds and their flesh roasted over the cooking fire.

The only survivor had returned to Ktarra, after making a single stop along the way to refuel. That foolish weakness allowed the Peltor and Dalvak slave crews the opportunity to gossip about the defeat, and word had soon spread throughout the empire. For that stupidity, the captain of the vessel had been put to death, and his slave crew executed as well.

That situation would never happen again. New orders declared that if any Ktarran fleet or ship suffered a setback, the ship would return immediately to Ktarra. Once there, the Peltors and Dalvaks would be executed upon arrival, while the Ktarran crew would be quarantined to prevent the spread of any rumors of defeat. The worlds in the Ktarran empire must only hear of the Empire's inevitable conquests, never of its defeats no matter how minor or temporary.

By now Staleeck knew quite a bit about Earth. He'd studied every report from the ship that escaped destruction. The planet's name, size, composition, atmospherics, even a rough estimate of its population, had all been recorded before and during the fighting. Partial video of the destruction of Earth's cities had also been recorded. As part of standard procedure, that information had been transmitted to the ship orbiting Jupiter, near the location of the wormhole.

Staleeck had seen fuzzy videos of the tiny air vessels that launched missiles at his ships. Each time he viewed these images, he wanted to rip his incompetent captains apart for being so stupid, for letting themselves be drawn down lower into the atmosphere where they could be attacked and destroyed. Fools, all three of them.

The biggest fool of all was Turhan, one of Staleeck's pouch cousins. That incompetent had allowed a bomb to be smuggled onboard his flagship. Even now Staleeck's long claws twitched at the urge to dismember Turhan. Unfortunately, the animals of Earth, puny creatures even more helpless looking than the Tarlons, had saved him the trouble. Staleeck had seen the video log of the human leader screaming his challenge before Turhan's ship exploded.

Nevertheless, those humans had prepared an efficient attack in a very short time. Of course they'd been warned and coached by those filthy Tarlons and Halkins, who were even now being hunted down, pursued from world to world, and scrambling to escape Ktarran retribution. As soon as the animals of Earth were eliminated, the Tarlons and Halkins would be exterminated. That should silence the rumblings of the slave worlds, who whispered in secret about the fleet's destruction at a planet named Earth. No threat to the power or prestige of Ktarra could be allowed.

"The initial plans are nearly complete, Pannoch Staleeck," Grand Commander Veloreck said. "We have more than enough time to prepare. The moment the wormhole opens, we will begin our operation. We are developing six different attack plans and we will be well prepared for any contingency. Every captain and every ship will be trained on all of them."

Staleeck stared at the speaker. Veloreck stood between two other commanders, Jothe and Teeg. Originally Staleeck had selected four of his most powerful satraps to lead the invasion of Earth space. However, Commander Morak had been eaten for questioning Staleeck's directives one too many times.

"Do you have the final list of how many ships will be ready?" Staleeck already knew the answer, but wanted Grand Commander Veloreck to confirm the number.

"All seventy of our main battle cruisers will follow our lead into the Earth system. Another forty-six of the smaller cruisers will also participate. Only those with the upgraded fire control systems are included. Sixteen scout ships, plus ten supply and conquest vessels as well."

More than two-thirds of the total Ktarran military ships, not counting the food and supply freighters. Staleeck growled approvingly. With every one of his largest fighting ships committed to the fight, the full force of Ktarran might would be employed. He did not intend to be embarrassed by a second defeat.

The enhanced fire control systems Veloreck mentioned allowed for multiple beams to be interconnected and focused on the same target. Linking three weapons would allow the ships to ride in high orbit over the planet, safe from Earth's air ships, while delivering even more destruction than at lower altitude.

"You will make certain that nothing remains of these animals," Staleeck said.

"Of course, Pannoch." Grand Commander Veloreck needed no reminders of his orders. The commander who'd been eaten had suggested that only twenty ships would be necessary to conquer the planet. He'd also believed that some humans should be saved for study, and that their civilization might make useful contributions to future Ktarran plans.

Others had muttered the same thoughts, that Earth was a rich planet with useful technology. The death of Morak had ended all such talk. The Pannoch had decreed it. No greed of any commander would stand in the way of the brutal example Staleeck planned.

"You will notify your second in command of your orders," Staleeck said. "If you fail in your mission, do not bother to return."

"We will not fail, Pannoch," Veloreck said. "The planet will be blasted to rubble and nuclear weapons will ensure that no life reappears on that place."

Before the Earth encounter, the Ktarrans had stockpiled fewer than thirty nuclear weapons, all stored on Ktarra. They had never bothered to use them in any of their planetary conquests. Since the defeat of Turhan's command, that number would now be augmented by another thirty-five devices, each ten times more powerful than the ones utilized by the human animals. Every battleship would carry at least one atomic weapon.

If only fifty of these missiles reached Earth's surface, it would be enough to turn the Earth planet into radioactive ash.

"Good. Then you will assemble your fleet at the transfer point."

"We still have much time before . . ." Veloreck's voice trailed off as he saw the snarl on the Pannoch's face.

"You will gather them as soon as possible," Staleeck ordered. "Then you will train them until every ship and every crew member is ready. When you go into action, every Dalvak and Peltor must be fully prepared for any contingency. Remember, these humans will have learned from the Tarlons when the wormhole will reopen. They may be waiting for your arrival."

That possibility had already been discussed, and Veloreck had prepared plans for that as well.

"We will be well prepared," Grand Commander Veloreck said. "Nothing will be left to chance. When the wormhole opens, we will enter their system and destroy the planet."

"Then I look forward to your return from Earth after a quick and successful campaign," Staleeck said. "The slave planets will learn once again the penalty for defying their masters."

Part II: Mobilization

Chapter 15
497 days BKA (Before Ktarran Arrival)

Gobi Desert, China

Eight hours after the aliens agreed to assist Earth, Delano and Lian landed in the Gobi Desert. During World War II, the United States had established roving weather stations in the Gobi, to provide more accurate forecasts for the bombing raids against the Japanese Empire.

Today's flight had a specific destination – the Jiuquan Launch Center. The facility remained a restricted and secretive research complex from where many of China's satellites and lunar projects blasted off into space. The world's first quantum communications satellites originated here, as Lian explained to him.

Like any budding Marine Officer candidate, Delano had tried to stay awake through a few sessions where instructors "explained" the basics of quantum mechanics. *Pas de chance, quoi.* Unfortunately, his near-eidetic memory failed completely as he tried to grasp the difficult concepts. He soon realized you needed a solid background in mathematics to understand even the basics of the subject, and Delano had never had much luck with anything more complicated than Euclidian geometry.

Just prior to the Ktarran crisis, miners on Jupiter's moon Io discovered an alien space craft buried beneath the volcanic ash, a dead alien on board. This event turned out to be Earth's true First Contact with another species. Knowing that the find represented a vast fortune in new technology, the discovery was kept secret by the finders. A rogue crew of JovCo miners secretly transported the craft from Jupiter's space to the Moon. Half the crew died during the murderous journey.

But when the aliens arrived, the story leaked, and with Alliance approval, the Chinese recovered the vessel and ferried it to Jiuquan. Normally the Research Facility there remained off-limits to most foreigners. During the Ktarran crisis, however, China allowed teams of scientists and engineers from Russia and the United States access to the ship. For over three weeks those specialists had worked round the clock inspecting the small, two-person craft.

Already that work had started to pay dividends. Engineers had examined, studied, X-rayed, and disassembled the ship's power train. It seemed to be a type of ion drive, powered by a fusion engine of unusual design. Exact copies of its components were being replicated and printed. Meanwhile metallurgists analyzed the various materials, more than a few of which they did not recognize. Aircraft designers were the most puzzled, since the craft utilized controls that did not correspond to anything familiar.

When the miner on Io first discovered the buried ship, an dead alien creature sat at the command seat. But JovCo – the mining company that had hidden the craft on the Moon – had removed the pilot's body and placed it in storage. It remained there even now, as everyone had been much too busy fighting off the Ktarran attack to worry about one more alien species – the current body count for types of aliens now totaled four.

Delano had no interest in the dead alien pilot, though geneticists and biologists acted hysterical in their demands for access. He wanted to see the ship itself. His curiosity was more than idle – the writing on the ship's consoles interested him, and for now he and Lian remained the two top experts of alien scripts. So they asked the pilot flying them from Moscow to Beijing to stop at the Jiuquan Launch Center.

The aircraft's captain had initially refused, but Lian had ordered him to do so, despite his instructions to get them to Beijing. General Zeng, also aboard the flight, supported the two leaders of the new Planetary Defense Force. Apparently he, too, wanted to see the vessel, before the over-eager scientists accidentally ruined it or chopped it up into functional but unrecognizable pieces.

Delano hoped to spend at least a day inspecting the ship before moving on to the meeting in Beijing. Lian's uncle, the leader of China, and his ministers waited there to meet the PDF leaders. But instead of staring in wonder at the small but obviously powerful craft, Delano found himself in yet one more conference room, attending another damned meeting.

As it turned out, two of China's ministers, one for Science

and Technology, and the other for Industry and Information Technology, were already at Jiuquan, also studying the alien technology. Since they constituted two of the key people for the Beijing meeting, General Secretary Liu had decided to send two more ministers to the Launch Center. The Beijing meeting could then be held in Jiuquan, with teleconferencing links to Liu and the remaining Ministers.

Liu dispatched Wang Yonghao, the Minister for National Defense, and Chen Zhidong, the leader of State Security, on the five hundred mile trip. Both had arrived in Jiuquan shortly after Delano and Lian touched down.

The most prestigious conference room in the Launch Facility served as the meeting place. Delano and Lian sat at the head of an oval-shaped table that could easily have accommodated thirty.

White-jacketed staff members from the Launch Center's exclusive restaurant fussed about, making sure each person at the table had ice, coffee, tea, or their choice of several different types of bottled water. Polished silver gleamed on red cloth napkins. A large floral arrangement occupied the center space. Lian mentioned that the chamomile, roses, and lilac mix was supposed to exude a soothing essence to facilitate agreements.

Attending via satellite were General Secretary Liu, and six more of his Ministers, looking cramped as they sat shoulder-to-shoulder facing the camera. At the table, the four ministers sat on one side, while General Zeng and an aide sat opposite. Each minister, of course, had a personal aide, discreetly seated behind the appropriate official. The only others present were Sgt. Shen, Lian's bodyguard, and Gunny Stecker, filling the same role for Delano. They sat, not at the table, but behind and to either side of the PDF leaders.

Polite greetings and introductions were exchanged, and Delano forced himself to memorize everyone's name, title, and face. He didn't worry about the meeting. Lian would be in charge, and guide the discussion. Since China had already agreed to the PDF, Delano expected little in the way of obstacles.

That foolish assumption disappeared right away.

"I object to the presence of these armed soldiers," Chen Zhidong said. The Minister for State Security had a frown on his face. "My own guards wait outside, as is customary when senior officials meet."

Oh, merde! Delano shifted to full alert mode. The words,

delivered politely enough, didn't convey Chen's hostile body language.

"Sgt. Shen's orders come from my uncle," Lian said. "He has been ordered not to leave my side."

"He can join the others outside," Chen answered. "Or do you intend to treat us as potential threats?"

Lian rested both palms on the polished red oak table. "I can assure you that Sgt. Shen is very accurate with his pistol. He only hits what he is aiming at."

"And the American? Is he really needed as well?" Chen glanced at Gunny Stecker for a moment, then let his eyes shift to Delano. "Do you also feel afraid for your safety, Col. Delano?"

Delano knew Gunny Stecker had a smattering of Chinese, but not enough to keep up with Chen. However, Stecker spoke fluent Spanish. Delano turned his head a bit, to face the Gunny. *"No le gustan las armas."* He said the Spanish words softly, so that only Gunny and those sitting closest to Delano could hear. Whether they comprehended Spanish was doubtful. Gunny would understand the words – *he doesn't like the weapons* – and get the message.

In less than two minutes, the mood had turned unfriendly. *At least I didn't cause this one.*

"The guards stay," Lian said, leaning back in her chair. "Of course, Minister Chen, you are free to leave if you feel . . . uncomfortable." She glanced around the table. "Is there anyone else who would rather leave? Those who remain can continue working with the conference."

"Lian, you will apologize to Minister Chen." Her uncle's words sounded thin over the speaker. Apparently the Facility's equipment was not up to the latest government standards for high-quality conferencing. "We did not expect you to bring Sgt. Shen to the meeting. In fact, I think it would be best if both Shen and Sgt. Stecker waited outside the room."

Enough of this bullshit. "General Secretary, if I may," Delano spoke before Lian could reply to her uncle. "The guards are here at my request, and they will remain here. These are dangerous times, and until the PDF is properly staffed, the need for security should be obvious."

"Sgt. Shen is a soldier in the Chinese Liberation Army," Chen said. "He takes his orders from his superiors."

"I'm sorry," Delano said. "But for the last thirty-six hours,

Sgt. Shen and Gunny Stecker have been drafted into the PDF. They will remain solely under PDF jurisdiction until the alien crisis is resolved. They will not obey any orders from the Chinese or American governments."

"Your so-called authority," Chen said, "does not extend to the People's Army. What threat the aliens present does not affect our internal affairs."

On his mental toes, Delano watched the faces while Chen spoke. The air of hostility was real, and Delano intended to take no unnecessary risks where Lian was concerned. General Zeng had his hands in his lap and seemed to be staring at them, apparently ignoring the discussion. But not hostile. The other three ministers at the table all had serious looks on their faces. Delano checked the Beijing monitor, but only noticed one Minister echoing the gloomy faces in Jiuquan.

Just another power struggle. "Then I am doubly sorry," Delano said, rising to his feet. "I thought we were going to brief China's leaders and discuss planetary defense. But, if Minister Chen is unwilling to accept that premise, then the meeting is ended."

Delano looked up at the camera. "General Secretary Liu, we arrived here on your private plane. Our intention after briefing you was to continue on to the United States. I would greatly appreciate it you would send orders to the pilot, and direct him to fly us to Hawaii. Once there we can change to a Russian or American airliner."

Lian had already closed her notebook. "Uncle, we would first like to inspect the alien space craft. That will take a few hours, so could you please notify the pilot about the change in plans?"

"This is intolerable!" Chen banged his fist on the table. "Lian and the American must accept the guidance of the Council of Ministers."

"I'm afraid that we cannot do that, Minister Chen." Lian made no effort to soothe Chen's feelings. "Our agreement with the Russian and American governments is that the PDF is an independent authority, above any influence from *any* of the Alliance countries."

"Neither of you know anything about fighting a war," Chen snarled. "Lian is practically a child, and the American is nothing more than a translator, a common Marine soldier. And your idea of building ships to colonize other worlds at the expense of defending China is foolish and a waste of resources."

"I believe Minister Chen is partially correct," Lian said, picking her words with care. "Neither of us knows anything about fighting a war *on Earth*. And if we did, the knowledge would be of little use to either of us. But we have fought an alien ship *in space*, and destroyed it. What have you accomplished against that?"

Delano felt his jaw clench. *Now it's out in the open.* "Perhaps Minister Chen could take my place," Delano said. By now he had figured out the politics and the true reason for the choice of Jiuquan for the meeting. Secretary Liu had dispatched his most troublesome opponents to the Launch Facility. And the two fools had taken the bait, leaving Beijing and their power bases behind. Now all that remained was for Delano to deliver the fatal stroke.

"I am sure that President Demidov and General Klegg would be eager to agree to that," Lian said. "And the other nations of the world would no doubt prefer someone under the 'guidance' of Minister Chen. Of course the minister has not himself faced an armed alien, destroyed a Ktarran battleship, or negotiated with any of the primary leaders of the Tarlon species."

"Perhaps I can explain the situation to those willing to listen," Delano said. "It is simple enough. In sixteen months, 497 days, Earth will face a powerful armada arriving in our solar system with but a single intent, to destroy and conquer us all. There will be no negotiating, no bribing, no maneuvering with the Ktarrans."

Chen tried to speak, but Delano went on, leaning forward and fixing his gaze on the minister for state security. "Did you not, Minister Chen, see the video of Captain Turhan, the Ktarran who led the expedition to Earth? What happened to Beijing and Tokyo and Los Angeles was only a small taste of what is to come. Imagine every city and town and village in China leveled. That's what this world faces, and there may be no way to prevent it from happening."

Delano glanced at Lian, but she merely nodded. Chen, practically in a state of shock, just gaped at the two of them. Probably he'd never been spoken to like that in his entire life.

"Unlike you," Delano went on, "I am not certain we can achieve victory. That is why we must build ships to carry humans to safety. But if Minister Chen is completely confident of defeating the aliens, unlike President Demidov or Marshal

Shuvalov or General Klegg or the Tarlons and Halkins for that matter, then I am willing to yield to his expertise."

"So, Minister Chen, give us your plan," Lian cut in before the man could answer, her voice now harsh with contempt. "Tell us how you will win your victory." She looked at him with derision. "Neither Col. Delano nor I wanted this authority. It was forced on us by the Tarlons and Halkins. We would gladly give it up. Just tell us what you would do in our place. Tell the Alliance how to win."

By now Chen had lost all control. His face flushed, he rose to face Delano. "You will both be sorry for this insult. You will . . ."

"Enough!" General Secretary Liu's voice blasted from the speaker. "Minister Chen, you will sit down. Ministers, I call for a vote to remove Minister Chen from his position as leader of state security. It is obvious that he does not have the ability to deal with this situation, and China cannot afford to have such a man in a position of authority."

Nobody spoke, not even Chen, who still couldn't believe what was happening.

"I call on each Minister for their vote on removing Chen from our ranks and placing him under arrest for treason against the State." The steel was back in Liu's voice, and everyone recognized the danger signals. "I vote against Minister Chen." He glanced around the table. The Ministers had to choose – it was either Liu or Chen.

Liu looked at the Minster seated to his right, clearly one of the General Secretary's supporters. The man nodded agreement. "I vote against." The vote call moved swiftly in Beijing. One minister looked unhappy, but voted against, making it unanimous. Now it was Jiuquan's turn.

"I vote against," General Zeng said. "The situation is too dangerous for the old ways. Since we cannot guarantee victory, China and its civilization must survive, no matter what the outcome of the battle. The possibility of failure cannot be discounted."

Zeng's vote ended the last shred of resistance. The remaining three ministers present joined those who voted against. The undisputed final vote finished Chen's dream of replacing Liu as General Secretary.

"Then it is decided," Liu said. "Chen Zhidong is immediately removed from all decision making. General Zeng, can you please see to it that Chen is placed under arrest and returned to Beijing?"

"Yes, General Secretary." With those three words, Zeng announced that he had made his choice, and there was no turning back now, for any of them.

"Then perhaps we can resume the discussion," Lian said. "We have developed many ideas we want to share with the Council. Their thoughts and suggestions will be most helpful."

Delano returned to his seat, and let his gaze, the icy glare usually restricted to drill sergeants, meet the eyes of every minister in turn. *And none of you are going to challenge our authority ever again.*

Just another damned meeting.

Chapter 16
495 BKA

China

Midnight approached by the time Lian escorted Delano and the rest of their entourage into her family's home on the outskirts of Beijing. Her uncle's private house now functioned as the official residence of the President of China. The official government buildings no longer existed, thanks to the Ktarrans and their particle beams of destruction.

The dwelling, Lian's home for most of her life, remained an architectural delight. The poppy-red outer walls, topped with a golden pagoda design, first impressed the visitor. The rambling structure surrounded by a hand-tended lawn of lush green grass sprinkled with gutta-percha and dove trees, only increased the eye's pleasure. As a child, Lian believed she lived in an enchanted garden, full of magical delights and secrets.

Now Lian saw only the harsh lights the soldiers had installed to illuminate every square meter of the house and grounds. More than troops stood guard. Two armored vehicles protected the long driveway that led to the main entrance. Off to the side, she glimpsed three military helicopters, their long blades dangling listlessly in the reflected light. More soldiers and equipment would be positioned behind the house.

The drive from the nearby landing strip had lasted nearly an hour. Every road remained clogged, day or night, and not even the army could keep the homeless refugees under control. Thousands departed Beijing each day, while more thousands pushed their way into the capital, seeking friends or family. Lian had never seen such misery in her peoples' eyes.

Delano, her friend and lover, appeared ready to crash, eyes drooping as he struggled to stay awake. They both needed a good night's sleep. He'd traveled two-thirds of the way around the world, participated in six planning sessions, and spent every spare moment talking with people. General Klegg occupied the majority of that time, needing basic decisions before he could get the ball rolling in the US.

For Russia and China, both more autocratic nations, the citizen population proved more amenable to central authorities. US citizens were already exhibiting some recalcitrance, objecting not only to the continuation of martial law and the creation of the PDF, but also protesting the government's role in the destruction significant portions of the West Coast.

California remained a shambles, and the former President Clark had fanned the local populations' flames of anger by his critical remarks about General Klegg. Clark also made wild and grandiose guarantees about the rebuilding and recovery efforts. Now those citizens demanded that the government follow through on the President's promises.

With Clark dead, Vivian Spencer, the NSA Director, had taken on the unappealing job of lowering expectations. At the same time General Klegg needed support for the already unpopular announcements coming from the PDF. Even the armed forces, working around the clock to keep order and transport supplies, seemed on edge. Rumors of a military coup continued to surface.

Lian sighed. The world seemed filled with unsolvable problems. She felt exhausted, too, but at least she'd only flown to Moscow and back to Beijing, so the jet lag from the seven hour flights hadn't affected her as hard. Nevertheless, when they reached their destination, she ignored her uncle's aide and took Delano directly to her suite of rooms. The Gunny and Steve accompanied them, both looking as tired as Delano. For tonight, their guards could sleep on the sitting room floor, using hastily procured sleeping pads, outside her bedroom.

Delano protested, but she ordered him to get some sleep, and said she would join him as soon as she'd visited her uncle. Delano's eyes closed and he fell asleep before Lian left her bedroom.

Outside the suite, she found Sgt. Shen waiting, and he escorted her across the width of the house to her uncle's office. Lian entered without knocking, something she'd never done in her life, with Shen reluctantly trailing along. She greeted her uncle and his two visitors, General Zeng and Captain Wang Quangdong, Liu's personal aide and secretary.

Lian had never seen Captain Wang, but knew he was a replacement for the two aides who usually assisted her uncle, both killed in the Ktarran attack.

"Hello, Uncle Quisan," she said. Without asking, she sank into one of the four red leather chairs facing his desk.

If her uncle seemed surprised by her independent behavior, he didn't show it. "Lian, I am glad to see you."

But when Sgt. Shen took a position behind Lian, her uncle raised a brow. "I do not think we will need Sgt. Shen."

"I'm sorry, Uncle Quisan," she said, "but Sgt. Shen must stay. Colonel Delano has insisted that I go nowhere alone. After Jiuquan, it seems I need more protection in China than Russia."

General Zeng made a sound, something between a cough and throat clearing. "I apologize, President Liu. I should have mentioned that Colonel Delano gave strict orders that Shen must accompany Lian. He was very firm and I thought it unwise to argue with him, not when the goal is so worthy."

Liu stared for a moment. "We will be discussing affairs of state, and Sgt. Shen does not have security clearances."

Lian shook her head. "What is he going to do, tell everything to the Americans or Russians? Why would we even care if he did? If you don't think he has the proper security, promote him and give him the necessary clearances."

Zeng laughed. "I warned you that she might be difficult, President Liu. The flight from Jiuquan was most . . . interesting. Colonel Delano was quite upset that you used the conference to deal with Minister Chen. The Colonel said that he did not appreciate being put at risk like that, and especially with Lian in as much danger."

Liu had kept his eyes on Shen during General Zeng's words, but now he shifted his gaze to Lian. "That was most unfortunate," Liu said, "but necessary. Chen had begun to mobilize troops loyal to himself. In one more day, he would have had enough men in position to seize both you and Delano. Or to replace me."

"Yes, he was a problem," Zeng said. "Fortunately Chen foolishly left his power base to go to Jiuquan, thinking he would deal with you and Colonel Delano there. We needed to act on the opportunity."

Lian rubbed her eyes. "It doesn't matter now, I suppose. I just hope that no more plots come to pass until we're out of here and on our way to Hawaii."

"You should thank General Zeng for that, Lian," her uncle said. "Without his warning and support, all of us might now be dead or in prison."

"Delano spoke highly of you, General Zeng," Lian said. "He told me that General Klegg and President Demidov were really military people forced to act politically. But he said General Zeng was a politician who became a general."

Zeng nodded. "His instincts are strong. Perhaps he is right. I will ask him someday for his reasoning."

"Since you appear so tired, Lian," her uncle said, "let me say a few things before you retire. At noon tomorrow you and Colonel Delano will address the Politburo and Council of Ministers. I trust you will reassure them that China will be treated equally in this new and enlarged Alliance that seems to be forming."

"The Planetary Defense Force," Lian agreed. "If the threat of an alien invasion cannot unite us, then we are all lost." She reached into a jacket pocket. "Here is the speech we will give tomorrow to the Ministers." She placed a thumb drive on the desk. "It should reassure them. Colonel Delano is counting on your support. He says the real difficulty will be with the United States. The Planetary Defense Force is already meeting resistance there."

"Yes, we've been observing the chaos in California and Washington. But at this moment it is more important to deal with affairs here. If the two of you can calm the ministers," her uncle said, "General Zeng and I should be able to keep them under control, at least for a few months. By then I hope you and your PDF will have established and solidified your own power base."

Lian smiled. "We should. We have a plan to do just that."

Her uncle waited a moment, but when she didn't offer any details, he continued. "Can you keep yourself safe at the same time? I would not like to explain to my sister that you were killed trying to establish this new . . . defense force."

"Don't worry, Uncle," she said. "We understand quite well that we will soon have people and nations seeking to end our lives. They will blame us for every problem they encounter and every death that results from our decisions. So we have already started planning for that contingency as well."

Her uncle again looked at her, but realized she didn't intend to say anything more. "Then I say goodnight, Lian."

"Thank you, Uncle. General Zeng." She rose and left the room, the silent Sgt. Shen trailing behind.

When the door closed behind them, Liu turned his eyes to

General Zeng. "Well, what do you think? Can she and Delano make this work?"

Zeng nodded. "Yes, I believe they can. They learned much in Moscow, and even more from Minister Chen's foolish words and attempt to seize power. Both Delano and Lian reacted very quickly at the meeting. I was watching Delano as the meeting began, and I saw how fast he grasped what was happening. By the time they finish here and in Washington, they will have consolidated much of their future authority."

Liu frowned. "That is what frightens me. Power corrupts."

"And absolute power corrupts absolutely," Zeng finished. "And these two will have more power than Emperor Quianlong or Alexander the Great or Julius Caesar or Genghis Khan ever had. Let us all hope they can handle it."

Chapter 17
491 BKA

Scottsdale, Arizona

Mark Tilman watched his tee shot sail through the air. The golf ball landed about two hundred and ten yards down the third fairway at Troon North Golf Club in Scottsdale. The ball took a hard bounce on the dry grass, which added another thirty yards before it came to rest. Even with such a good drive, Tilman knew he'd be lucky to make par. This par five hole at Troon always gave him trouble, especially the last year or so.

Tilman had just turned sixty-four, and his body simply couldn't put out the power needed to reach the green in three strokes, at least not from the back tees. Soon he'd be playing from the Silver tees, which would shorten the hole by than fifty yards.

As a golfer, old age had crept up on him. At least he could still hit the ball pretty straight, he consoled himself. He had a four-stroke handicap, and usually parred this hole about half the time.

"Nice shot, Mark." Jim Bedford, his friend for more than thirty years, managed not to sound too condescending. He was the other half of the twosome on this beautiful desert morning in Arizona.

"Yeah, but you managed to outdrive me by thirty yards," Tilman grumbled. But the bastard usually did. Tall and lanky, Bedford could pound the ball over two hundred and forty yards, despite being only two years younger.

As Mark settled into the passenger side of the golf cart, his phone, mounted in a cradle on the dash, started to ring.

"I thought I turned the damn thing off!" Not that Tilman received that many calls anymore. Before he retired last year, he'd averaged over a hundred a day from his employees, financiers, stock brokers, and politicians. Not to mention those he labeled "open palms," meaning someone who wanted something, usually for nothing.

Without looking at the incoming call, he pressed the button that turned the phone off. The golf links were the one place where

Tilman demanded privacy. A phone call, no matter what the reason, affected his concentration.

The phone kept ringing.

He frowned, and stared at the phone. The damn thing had been off, and was still off. As far as Tilman knew, only certain high-level government agencies could override a phone's privacy setting. For the first time he glanced at the incoming caller-id, and saw the words "USAFJC" on the screen.

What the hell, Tilman decided. This hole was probably already ruined. He pushed the accept button. "Who is this?"

A deep voice asked, "Is this Mark Tilman?"

"Yes, who is this?"

"Let me see your face," the voice said.

Tilman's first reaction was to tell the caller to take a hike, but he held his annoyance in check. Activating the phone's view screen, he held it up to his face.

"Ah, yes. This is General Klegg, Mr. Tilman. I'd like you to come to Washington as soon as possible. The government . . . no, the Alliance has a job for you, if you're interested."

Like everyone else in America, Tilman knew all about General Klegg, the man who some claimed saved the planet. Others, however, had a decidedly different opinion, especially those in California. There people tended to spit and swear at the mention of his name.

"I've retired, Klegg," Tilman said. "In fact I'm out on the golf course right now."

Klegg chuckled. "Sorry, Tilman, not buying it. I hear you're bored to death. How much bridge and golf can you take? Besides, your country . . . your planet needs you."

"I've offered my services to some people in California," Tilman said. "They need all the help they can get."

"Yeah, and even with the crisis, they haven't gotten back to you. No one wants help from a hard-ass like you. It's been, what, ten days since you volunteered? And you're still cooling your heels on the golf course?"

Damn Klegg and his government snoops at NSA. No doubt they had monitored every one of his private phone calls.

Tilman recovered fast enough. He had years of dealing with problems and difficult people. He rarely let anyone get under his skin. "What's your point, Klegg? Hurry up, I need to hit my second shot."

"I've got a . . . no, my new boss has a job for you. But if you're too busy golfing to help save the planet, I'll tell him you're not interested and let you get back to your game."

In these days of martial law, General Klegg's boss was Dr. Vivian Spencer, the NSA Director. But Klegg had said "he" in referring to his superior. With the president dead – the suicide statement was so much tripe that no one with an IQ above room temperature believed it – who could Klegg's boss be?

"Who are you working for now, Klegg?" If it was that jerk Wilson, Tilman would tell them both to fuck off.

"Ah, my new boss, and yours, for that matter, is Lt. Col. Joseph Delano. And Dr. Duan Lian, the two co-leaders of the Planetary Defense Force. I assume you heard the speech?"

By now everyone on the planet had heard Dr. Duan and Delano's Moscow speech, most of them more than once. It hadn't been a politician's speech, but that made it all the more effective. "What's Delano want?"

"He needs someone to take charge of all, let me repeat that, all production of goods and services in the United States. It will be a full national mobilization. You know, to start building ships and weapons. Oh, and you'll have to coordinate with your counterparts in Russia and China. We're one big happy family now."

Even Tilman needed a moment to grasp that one. "When you say all, what exactly do you mean? All weapons production?"

"No, not just weapons," Klegg said. "Delano wants a single person to head up *all* production in the United States. That means nothing gets produced without supporting the war or providing basic necessities. No luxuries, no new automobiles, phones, games, toys, nothing. Remember the War Powers Act of 1941? Do I need to draw you a diagram?"

Tilman clenched his jaw at the sarcasm. OK, "all" meant everything under one person's control. It couldn't be done, never had been done, not even in 1941, though FDR's people had come pretty close. "I assume Delano has the authority to do this? The government is going along?"

Klegg's sigh could be heard over the breeze. "The government is out of the loop, Tilman. Delano, by virtue of his Alliance connections, is in charge of planetary defense. Anything and everything that can be shoved or slipped beneath that umbrella falls under his control. And Dr. Duan's. Think of it as planetary martial law for the duration of the conflict. Our military will provide any needed authority, at least until the PDF gets their own troops up to speed."

A new military force, unaccountable to anyone, with all the guns and muscle it needed, Tilman decided. No checks on its power, no oversight from self-important bureaucrats. Business was never going to be the same. "I'd have to think about it, Klegg."

Another chuckle floated from the phone. "Sure, take your time. I'll have a jet from Luke AFB at the Scottsdale Airport at 1800 tonight."

Tilman started to protest, but knew what the response would be – the aliens were coming, and they didn't care about anyone's retirement plans or timetable. "Can I bring some people with me?"

"Bring whoever you like. Hell, bring all your friends. The jet will seat eight."

"Damn you, Klegg," Tilman said. In his forty-plus years of business, he hadn't made more than a handful of real friends, and Klegg knew it. "I'll be there."

"Good. Welcome to the fight." Klegg broke the connection.

Tilman sat there and stared at the phone. His wife would be glad to get him out of the house and back to work. He'd been driving her crazy, moping around and pretending to be busy. She knew how much he hated his forced retirement.

"Do we have time to finish the round?" Bedford had heard every word.

Tilman glanced at the time. His wife could pack a bag for him, and he lived only ten minutes from the Scottsdale Airport. "I think we do, Jim. Because I don't think either of us will be playing again for quite some time."

"So I'm going with you?"

"God, I hope so," Tilman said. "Who else can I yell at?"

"OK, but then we better double the stakes. Might be awhile before we get to play again. Ten dollars a hole."

His friend knew all about Tilman's problems concentrating on golf when something big was in the wind. "You're on, Jim. But this time I'm going to beat your ass."

Two hours later, Tilman handed over sixty dollars. Bedford had beaten him by six holes. Someday, Tilman decided, he was going to wise up.

Chapter 18
490 BKA

When the Air Force jet landed in West Virginia, Delano let himself relax. At least he was back on US soil. In seven days, he'd flown completely around the world, supported Russia's incursion into Europe, inadvertently assisted a coup in China, and helped destroy an American president. In conjunction with the earlier coup by General Demidov in Russia, every Alliance power had undergone a significant change in government. And Delano had played a role in each of them.

He glanced at Lian, still asleep, in the seat next to his. A peaceful smile lingered on her lips. They had spent a little more than two full days in Beijing. First had been the official presentation to the Council of Ministers. Delano and Lian's speech, much the same one as delivered in Moscow, was received far differently. The Russians had applauded and cheered. Within hours, the people of that country had voiced overwhelming support.

The leaders of the Chinese government reacted more cautiously in their backing. Nevertheless, President Liu and General Zeng had control of the government, for now at least, but not the full sponsorship of the Chinese ministers. Of course China had absorbed the most damage from the Ktarran bombardment, and their historical opposition to foreign pressure or influence made them a tougher sell.

They remained suspicious of the United States. Former President Clark had blurted out many rash statements that bordered on blaming China for the disaster to the American West Coast. But the behind-the-scenes pressure of Liu and Zeng made the Planetary Defense Force acceptable, if only temporarily.

The next day, in the presence of the inner council, Lian worked tirelessly to assure the doubters, essentially all of them, that China had nothing to fear from the PDF, that she exercised as much control as Colonel Delano, and that China's concerns would be the same as those of the PDF.

While she was busy winning them over, Delano had taken a helicopter ride with General Zeng, to study the damage to Beijing.

Six hours later, Delano had a far greater appreciation for China's apprehensions. The near-obliteration of China's capital city appeared more severe than that in California's cities. The effective and stringent building codes on America's West Coast required strong earthquake and fire protections, making the secondary damage caused by the fire storms less severe. Nor did Los Angeles or San Francisco approach the population density of Beijing.

The following morning, he and Lian flew to Hawaii aboard a Chinese air force jet, escorted by four fighters. All five aircraft landed at Joint Base Pearl Harbor, where Delano and his little troop transferred to an Air Force Gulfstream. The Chinese planes were serviced and refueled, while their crews got to spend a day resting.

All in all, Delano spent less than two hours in Hawaii before taking off for the unscathed March Air Force Reserve base in Riverside, California. After a quick safety check and refueling that lasted less than two hours, they took off again. Four hours later, they arrived in West Virginia, landing at the Air Command Bunker less than two hundred miles from Washington. Klegg and others had directed the defense of the planet from this AF facility, hardened to withstand a nuclear attack.

General Klegg met the Gulfstream, and escorted the weary and disoriented travelers to their quarters, a quarter mile below ground. Delano wanted to talk, but Klegg said it was almost 9 p.m. and they might as well get some sleep.

*   *   *

Ten hours later, Delano awakened. At first he couldn't remember where he was, or the day of the week. Groggy and still suffering jet lag, he wanted to stay in bed, but a glance at the clock changed his mind. Lian, still asleep beside him, didn't wake as he slipped out of bed and stumbled to the unfamiliar bathroom.

Like most military facilities, the bunker didn't have much in the way of amenities, even less than the room in the Pentagon Hilton where Delano had been kept for days. After a quick piss, he stared at his unshaven reflection in the dull mirror over the washbasin. He looked like hell. Worse, he felt the same. For nearly two weeks he'd done nothing but sit on his ass, trying to pass himself off as someone who knew something about saving the world. Bullshit. Plain and simple. *Schwachsinn*. Yes, it did sound better in German.

At least he knew one reason why he felt like shit. Without a sound, he dropped to the deck and started doing pushups. On a good day in OCS, he'd done 75, but now he normally stopped at 50. Today, however, he found himself straining after 40 and had to push himself to add five more. Exhausted, he let his face rest on the worn carpet.

Damn. He really needed to get in shape. Otherwise all this talking would turn him into a candy-ass Marine or worse, a fat-assed civilian. He'd talk to the Gunny about some kind of routine. Besides, if he intended to return to space, he would need to be in as good physical shape as possible.

Pushing himself off the floor, he did stretching exercises until all his muscles felt the strain. Finally satisfied, he headed for the shower.

Two hours later, dressed in clean fatigues, Delano sat at the head of yet another conference table. Today, however, he actually felt good, glad to be back in the USA, happy not to be dog-tired, with no more trips planned for awhile. More important, he felt relaxed at the prospect of this meeting.

Attending were the usual suspects: Gunny, Steve, Shen, and Lian. General Klegg sat facing Delano, with two civilians seated on either side. Klegg's assistant had made place cards for everyone, and Delano saw what looked like a distinguished New York lawyer with slicked-back hair at Klegg's right: Mark Tilman, according to the signage. On the other side sat a tall, thin black man who could have passed for a retired NBA player – his name was Jim Bedford.

Glancing around, Delano started. "Are we all here, General Klegg? Is Major Mitchell coming?"

"No. For this morning's session, it's just us," Klegg answered. "Mitchell is setting up the afternoon conference call with the scientists in Jiuquan and Moscow. But I wanted you to meet with Mark and Jim privately. They're the ones I'm recommending to head up the mobilization effort for us."

Delano had asked Klegg to start that ball rolling several days ago. Now that he had a name to put to a face, Delano remembered Mark Tilman as a big-time CEO and part-time hedge fund manager. Until he'd retired, or been forced out, depending on the story.

"Nice to meet you, Colonel Delano," Tilman said. "General Klegg hasn't told me much, but he did suggest I read the War Powers Act of 1941, and some books on the wartime mobilization efforts. It's quite interesting."

Lian, who had been working on her tablet, now joined Delano in examining Tilman. The man returned their gaze, while Jim Bedford chuckled softly.

"Something funny, Mr. Bedford?" Delano struggled to keep the smile off his own face. Bedford appeared to be the kind of man you'd gladly have a drink with.

"No, not really. It's just been a long time since anyone sat across a table and sized up Mark Tilman for a job."

"I can send you a copy of my resume, Colonel Delano," Tilman offered.

"Not necessary." Delano already liked this man, too. "Klegg says you're the best man for the job, and if we start looking at resumes, someone might want to see mine."

Everyone laughed politely. "OK, this is the job, Tilman. I need someone to start building the ships and weapons that Lian and I outlined in the speech in Moscow, beginning with the Jumpers. We need those ships right now, to get construction materials to the Moon as quickly as possible."

"How will I know what to build?"

Lian set down her tablet. "We have already developed some ideas, Mr. Tilman. Maks – Colonel Mironov – has been working with the engineers in Jiuquan, and we have received some preliminary sketches." She slid a thumb drive across the table. "The first item we will need is cargo containers similar to those used on the Io to the Moon run. They are very similar to what is used to transport material across the ocean. In fact, we could utilize standard ISO containers, 12.43 meters in length and 2.59 meters high. Each container could carry about 45,000 pounds of cargo."

Klegg frowned, and glanced at Delano. "Are you sure about those numbers? That's more than twenty-two tons."

Before Lian could reply, Delano spoke. "Before we go any further, I want to make something clear. Lian is speaking to you with the same authority as I do. That's not only the way we prefer to work, it's part of the agreement with the Chinese government. When she and I disagree, and I'm sure we will, we'll discuss it ourselves or at meetings such as this. Officially, Lian represents

China's interest, and I, together with Colonel Mironov will represent Russia. General Klegg and Mr. Tilman will speak for the United States. Are we clear on that?"

"Yes, sir," Klegg said. "I meant no disrespect to Dr. Duan."

She smiled. "Do not worry about such things. I was about to tell you that the engineers in Jiuquan have studied the Star Traveler's ship, and are already reverse-engineering it. The ship uses an unusual combination ion and fusion engine that produces incredible power, almost as much as the Tarlon ships. And does it within a small footprint. Maks believes that such a design can easily lift at least thirty-five tons of ship and cargo. It can also operate within the Earth's atmosphere, something the Tarlon space drive cannot do. Since our Jumper will need to do little more than lift a single container to orbit, it will not need much in the way of life support or safety features."

"I'm not sure I understood all that," Tilman said.

Delano explained about the Star Traveler's ship, how it had been found buried beneath Io's surface. Its stubby wings indicated that it could operate within an atmosphere. If the ship delivered the power Maks expected, it should easily be able to lift 40,000 to 50,000 pounds into low earth orbit.

"So, Mr. Tilman, the Jumper will get the containers off the planet, out of Earth's gravity well, and park them in space. We still have three operational freighters that were built for the Moon to Io run, and we can use them to ferry the containers to lunar orbit, an easy run for those ships. From there, more Jumpers will take the cargo down to the surface."

"I need to see the plans," Tilman said. "Jim is more of an engineer than I am, and he can figure out the factories, equipment, and infrastructure needed to begin manufacturing."

"They're on the drive," Lian said.

"You said something about safety features, Dr. Duan," Jim said. "What exactly do you mean?"

"I mean that safety concerns are no longer the primary function in the design process," she said. "NASA has a long history of over-caution for its pilots, crews, and equipment. Russian and Chinese designs are more, shall we say, reliant on the pilot. We do not intend that these ships be over-engineered for safety. The priority is to get the cargos into orbit."

"NASA isn't going to like that," Jim said.

"They are not going to like a lot of things, but that will be your and Mr. Tilman's problem," Lian said. "Neither of you gentlemen have served in the military, let alone in a conflict. In wartime you cannot always seek an optimum solution, which is a polite way of saying that accidents happen and people die. The Russians and Chinese expect these kinds of start-up losses. So must the Americans, if we are to keep pace with their construction schedules."

"The bigger issue is mobilization," Delano said. "You're going to encounter a lot of resistance, from the labor force, the owners, unions, Wall Street, even the general population. You need to remind everyone that what you ask for is what you want, with no delays, no excuses, and no slow-walking."

"What if people refuse to cooperate?" Tilman glanced around the table. "I need to know how much pressure . . ."

"General Klegg and Gunny Stecker have already started soliciting volunteers for the PDF," Delano said. "In a week or two we'll have a mobile force of several hundred men and women ready to join the PDF and work toward its goals. So the minute you encounter resistance or problems, you let me know, and the PDF will take care of it for you."

"Such a force is also being established in Russia," Lian said, "and my uncle is searching for volunteers in China. Sergeant Shen is working on that as well. There are many soldiers in my country who have lost loved ones in the Ktarran bombardment and seek revenge. There will be no opposition to the PDF there. After a few salutary examples, managers and workers will do what they're told."

"There won't be many problems here," Delano said. "Not after we make a few public examples. The sooner everyone gets the message that the PDF means business, the better."

"So you plan to arrest people who don't want to cooperate?" Tilman looked askance at Delano. "Then what, show trials?"

"No, Mr. Tilman," Delano said. "I'm only going to arrest those who cause trouble. I intend to execute anyone who tries to impede the PDF agenda. As General Klegg reminded me when this whole thing started, people are going to die. If we . . . if I have to kill a few hundred or a thousand fools to save eight billion, then that's what it will take. I assume you saw the video of the Ktarran captain and his plans for our planet."

"Yes, I saw it. At the time, I didn't think it was real." Tilman looked at Klegg. "But it was, wasn't it? You both were there." He took a breath. "This is the way it's going to be?"

"Yes, Mark, that's how it will go down." Klegg's voice remained hard. "I have grandchildren to protect. I don't intend to let any idiot or greedy bastard get in the way of that responsibility. Anyone who isn't fully cooperating with the PDF and the mobilization is working against Earth's safety, and against my grandkids' future."

Lian broke the silence that followed Klegg's words. "If you have a problem with that, please say so now. Otherwise, Mr. Tilman, if anyone objects to the mobilization, just let us know."

He took less than a second to decide. "OK, I have grandchildren, too," Tilman said. "I'm in." He looked at Jim Bedford. "What about you, Jim?"

"I suppose all you people have been considering this for weeks. If you think this is the best way, then I'm fine with it. If I find out later that I can't deal with it, I'll let you know."

One more problem solved, Delano decided. "Good. Lian and I are spending the rest of this week reviewing fighter designs with NASA and the engineers at Jiuquan. As soon as we have some idea of what we want, we'll be getting back to you, Mr. Tilman."

"Call me Mark," Tilman said. "I have an idea that we'll be working closely together for the next sixteen months."

"Welcome to the team, Mark," Lian said.

Delano nodded. "Now, what's happening in New Mexico?"

"They've already broken ground on the new air strips," General Klegg said. "Workers are still sleeping in tents, but we'll soon have a labor force up there building quarters. The Air Force and the Army Corp of Engineers have about a thousand people on site and more coming. As soon as the runways are constructed, we'll have supply flights operating round the clock."

"Is this something I should know about?" Tilman asked.

"Yes, indeed," Klegg said. "As far as we're concerned, you should know about everything. We've selected Spaceport, New Mexico as the primary site for our new space fleet. We've already taken over most of the civilian facilities there, and the place is pretty much in the middle of nowhere. The White Sands missile testing area is next door, which will prove useful and provide plenty of elbow room," Klegg said. "Colonel Delano wanted a new site for the main PDF headquarters and launch pad." He glanced at Tilman. "Its elevation is about forty-five hundred feet, an advantage when we start lifting cargoes."

"You're planning to lift-off from Spaceport? Why not Cape Kennedy or California?" Jim Bedford's voice revealed his disbelief. "There's no support infrastructure near Spaceport, no easy connect to the sea, not even good rail service."

"Right, Mr. Bedford," Delano said. "But we've already contacted the railways and they're ready to begin laying track. But we'd prefer to move as much cargo as possible by air. In fact, our new space Jumpers can probably do double duty as cargo transports within the atmosphere. Spaceport will soon be the world's largest airport, and heavy cargo aircraft from Russia and China will be flying in and out. We didn't want anything near a metropolis, and we don't want our people being distracted."

"So you propose to develop a whole new infrastructure?" Bedford sounded dubious.

"Yes, that's right," Delano said. "I think you'll be surprised at how much you can get done with people working twenty-four hours a day. Sounds like a perfect job for you, Jim."

Lian looked at her watch, and everybody got the message. "We have to get to another meeting, gentlemen."

Delano stood. "Right. Welcome aboard, Mark, Jim. General Klegg will get you started and plugged into the new networks. Good luck."

Chapter 19
484 BKA

Six days later . . .

Colonel William Manning of the Planetary Defense Force rested his elbows on the roof of the silver minivan. Fortunately he was tall enough, six foot three inches, so that he could look comfortably through the binoculars. A tall, powerfully built black man, everyone assumed he could play basketball.

Truthfully, Manning hated the game, even more than he disliked football or baseball. Even as a kid he'd never taken to any organized sports. In high school he joined the track team and selected cross-country running. That solitary activity stayed with him. He then wasted six months in college before, bored out of his mind with the tripe that passed for education, he joined the Army. In Ranger school, he could pretty much out-run everybody in his class. He discovered a love for the military and he made captain before his twenty-sixth birthday.

He'd been out jogging in the hills behind Spring Valley when the Ktarrans attacked San Diego. After he fought his way through mobs of panicked civilians back to the base, he found his house burned to the ground. Nothing was left, not even a trace of his wife and twin daughters. The Ktarran beam weapon must have passed directly over his home. He remembered kneeling in the swirling gray ashes, still warm, and choking on the smells of fire and death. Sobbing uncontrollably, the medics had to drag him away from the site.

Hatred for the Ktarrans had nearly driven him to suicide. Then thoughts of revenge dominated his mind. But now he was a newly-promoted colonel in the PDF, one of the very first, and tasked with the PDF's and his first assignment. He'd been recruited by Gunny Sergeant Stecker, who worked directly for Lt. Col. Delano. Less than fifteen days ago, Delano had been named Planetary Defense Leader by the Alliance.

"It's an ugly job," Stecker warned him on the video call. "But it needs to be done. You said you wanted a shot at these Ktarrans. I'll give you more than a shot, if you've got the stones for it.

You'll have to recruit more people like yourself, ones who suffered losses from the Ktarrans. That should give them plenty of motivation."

Manning hadn't hesitated. The next day, he spoke personally with Col. Delano, who endorsed the preliminary assignment and the orders Gunny Stecker had delivered. And confirmed Manning's promotion to full colonel in the PDF, the second to achieve that rank. Some Air Force fighter jock named Welsh had gotten his commission a few hours earlier.

Now Manning's first mission had arrived. He carefully swept the binoculars over the office building, less than a mile away, that housed the leadership of the ITWU, the Industrial Technical Workers Union. Manning's scrutiny revealed no unusual activity around the front of the building, which seemed normal for a Saturday morning in Renton, a wealthy and idyllic suburb of Seattle.

Satisfied, he snapped the binoculars closed as he climbed back into the minivan. "OK, let's roll."

The minivan, followed by three additional and nearly identical vehicles, cruised the streets until they reached Houser Way, which they followed for less than a quarter mile. The ITWU three-story building – they were the sole tenants – had plenty of Italian marble and veined granite showing on its facade. Two massive teak doors styled like the entrance to a medieval Florentine palace provided access to the building. Union dues paid for the excessive display, nothing but the best for the union bosses.

Stopping directly in front of the main entrance, Manning exited the van and strolled inside, followed by three of his team. All four wore fatigues and light body armor, and everyone except Manning carried a rifle.

The union guard at the desk looked up in surprise at their sudden entrance. He started to reach for the phone, but stopped when he saw two of the rifles aimed at his chest.

Manning reached the counter and leaned casually against it. "Where's the meeting?"

"Meeting? There's no meeting today. It's Saturday . . ."

"I'll ask you again, and if I don't hear the truth, you're going to die right there in that chair."

The third soldier had not been idle. Once inside the lobby, she threaded a suppressor to the rifle's barrel. The guard understood exactly what that meant. With a final grunt, she tightened the suppressor, then moved behind the counter and shoved the blunt end into the guard's stomach. "Answer the colonel."

The guard was no coward, but he was no hero either. His union paycheck might be fat, but not enough to argue with a gun barrel pressing painfully in his belly. "Third floor, room 301."

"Where is that?"

The guard licked his lips. "Take the elevator up. It's just off the lobby, to the left of the elevator."

"If you behave, you may survive." Manning turned to the soldier holding the rifle in the man's stomach. "If he so much as twitches or makes a sound, shoot him." Manning pushed the transmit button on his radio. "Lobby secured. Cover the rear and any other exits. Squad one, get in here."

Manning turned back to the guard. "How many men up there? How many guns? Do I have to explain what happens if you lie?"

The words came out in a rush. "Six, maybe seven. I didn't count. Three armed guards."

Not too many to take by surprise, Manning thought. "Good. Tie him up and keep him out of sight, in case anyone walks in."

The rest of Squad One entered the lobby. Manning ordered two of the new arrivals to stay in the lobby, in case anyone else showed up. Then he and seven of his team crowded into a waiting elevator. Manning squeezed in last and pushed the button for the third floor.

A single guard was on duty at the third floor reception area, but he had no chance to make a move as the elevator disgorged eight heavily armed and armored soldiers, all carrying short-barrel automatic weapons. In moments he was down on the floor, his hands bound behind his back with plastic ties. Black duct tape over his mouth made sure there would be no outcry. Manning turned left and strolled down the hall. The first doorway on his left was marked 301 in elegant gold script. "Two of you stay in the hall. Check for another exit. The rest, come with me."

He pushed the door open and stepped inside a small anteroom, filled with four comfortable black leather armchairs and a matching sofa. Two more union goons were there, one reading a magazine, the other playing a game on his phone. Manning didn't even have to say anything. The rifles said everything. Nobody made a sound, nobody made any rash moves. He waited until the two men were disarmed and lying face-down on the floor, bound and gagged. "Ready?"

His team nodded. Manning opened the inner door and stepped into a good-sized conference room. A wall of solid glass looked out toward the green hills practically surrounding the city. Expensive artwork covered the three remaining walnut-paneled walls. Seven men looked up in surprise and disbelief that turned to shock as five more soldiers entered, their rifles covering those seated at the table.

"Everyone stay right where you are," Manning said. "Anyone who reaches for a phone or a weapon will not survive the attempt."

"Who the fuck are you?" Jake Guardino, the president of the ITWU demanded. Short and overweight, the words boomed from a deep chest. Small dark eyes dominated a jowly face as he glared at the soldiers.

The mission brief had noted that Guardino was considered a tough guy. He'd worked his way up through the union ranks leaving behind a lot of broken bones, along with reports of missing people. "I'm Colonel Manning of the PDF. I understand you're refusing to cooperate with Mr. Tilman's deputy. I'm here to change your mind."

The man seated to Guardino's left started laughing. "The government sent you here to scare us? Nuthin' and nobody scares us."

Manning glanced at him. "You must be Mr. Palmiterri. I'd advise you to keep quiet."

Palmiterri shrugged and leaned back in his chair. "Say your piece and get out of our building. We know where you live, you understand?"

"Pali, let the man talk," Guardino said. "But you soldier boys can save your breath. Go tell Tilman and his suits that if he wants production from Seattle, then he'll route all the jobs through us. Depending on how much money he's willing to donate to the union's fund, we'll decide just how many hours our members are willing to work."

"Glad to hear that," Manning said with a smile. He lifted his .45 caliber pistol from the holster on his belt. "Colonel Delano – he's the head of the PDF, in case you haven't heard – wants to send a message to people like you." The pistol rose and leveled itself at Guardino's forehead.

The gunshot boomed inside the conference room, and Manning realized he'd forgotten to put in his ear plugs. Damn. The pistol swung over to Palmiterri's head. "You said something about knowing where we live?"

Palmiterri, his mouth hanging open in shock, had to swallow before he could speak. "No, no, I didn't mean nuthin' like that. Just talk, you understand."

"Sure. I understand." Manning fired again, putting a nice round hole in the middle of the man's head. Palmiterri's head must have been softer than Guardino's, since the bullet exited the back of the skull and punched a hole in a very nice landscape, now splattered with blood, on the wall behind.

"OK, now that the message has been delivered, maybe we can talk about work rules and production schedules." Manning faced the man seated at Guardino's right. "You're Aaron Gorenstein, correct?"

"Please god, don't shoot," Gorenstein pleaded. "I'm just the union lawyer, their legal advisor. I told them not to . . ."

"Shut up," Manning said conversationally. "As of now, you are in charge of the ITWU, and you'll stay that way until we decide to make a change." He waved the pistol around the table. Anybody else think they should be head of the Union?"

The rest of the Union leadership, beads of sweat already glistening on their foreheads, shook their heads.

"Good. Then each and every one of you gentlemen will give your full and total support to Mr. Gorenstein. If any of you think you might not want to do that, you can say so now. Otherwise, like Mr. Palmiterri said, we know exactly where each and every one of you lives, including your family, your relatives, and your friends. Got that?"

Manning went back to Gorenstein. "OK, here's the drill. You've all become good planetary patriots. The ITWU will cooperate fully with all, repeat, all of Mr. Tilman's requests. That includes overtime with no extra pay if required, and as many hours a week as Tilman's people want. And make sure you tell your members about how important it is that they maintain the quality of their work and every schedule. Any attempt to cut corners, substitute materials, work a slow-down, or god-forbid a little sabotage, and every single one of you in this room will be getting a visit from me or my men. Understand me. We will kill you and confiscate every single asset you or your family has ever owned."

He glanced around the table, meeting every man's eye in turn. "Got all that? You'll be dead, and your family will be out in the streets with just the clothes on their backs, branded as traitors to the planet. Make sure you tell your wives about that. If they don't want to end up in the streets like Mrs. Palmiterri and Mrs. Guardino, they'd better keep an eye on you."

The smell of urine wafted from under the table. Manning knew someone, or maybe more than one, had pissed themselves.

"Being branded a traitor to the planet might not mean much now," Manning said, "but in a few months, those words will become a special kind of death sentence." He glanced at his watch. "I see we've finished up just in time. In thirty minutes I believe you have a conference call with Mr. Bedford, special assistant to Mr. Tilman. You will, of course, cooperate fully. A few of my men will stay behind, in case you get the very stupid idea of changing your mind. Anyone considering that? Anyone want to say anything?"

No one did.

Manning holstered his pistol. "I'll give you one more piece of advice. Don't make me come back to Seattle. I hate the rain." He turned and strode out of the conference room.

He rode the elevator down in silence. The PDF's first message had been delivered. Manning had another appointment scheduled for this evening – a banker in Oakland who was refusing to provide credit to three new companies already gearing up for the war production. The man had brazenly demanded a fat government kickback. That meeting should go much faster, and this time he'd probably only need one bullet.

Manning thought about the two men he'd just killed. Once his conscience might have bothered him, but not after San Diego. The two dead upstairs were simple thugs, who would put their own greed over the needs of the planet. He wouldn't waste a tear on them. More men like these were going to die, but better a few useless and uncooperative ones be killed in order to defend millions.

Another shock would come when the PDF bean counters confiscated all of Guardino and Palmitierri's financial assets. Any such cash windfalls would go directly into the PDF Emergency Fund. A few videos of formerly affluent women clutching a bag containing all their worldly belongings would make certain that every wife or partner in the country would keep a close eye on her significant other.

Saving the planet meant that many people needed to change their way of thinking. Gunny Stecker and Delano were right about that. The sooner everyone got the message, the less force would be needed. Earth held over eight billion humans, and if a few thousand had to die to induce the others to do the right thing, so be it.

The idea wasn't new, Manning knew. Niccolo Machiavelli had worked out the rules for leaders hundreds of years ago. Better a killing here and there, to save the majority from unrest or war. Not much had really changed since the wily Florentine councilor first whispered advice in the ear of his prince.

Word of what happened to the ITWU would soon spread, and powerful people would stop and think. The news people would be screaming the headlines within hours, but the PDF wouldn't even bother to deny it. "No comment" would be the official reply. The quicker word got out, the better. More examples would be needed, but soon enough Earth's business leaders would fall in line.

After that happened, the cheaters and profiteers would have to learn the same lesson, but that would require more time. Already plans were being developed to take care of the Mexican cartels and organized gangs in the United States. Full military force would be used to encourage them to leave the PDF alone, or face annihilation.

Manning didn't care. In the end, he would get what he wanted – a chance to go into space and kill Ktarrans. If he had to dispatch some self-serving individuals along the way, he'd shed no tears. His wife and children had been slaughtered, burned into unrecognizable ashes, for no reason at all. He hoped to kill a lot of Ktarrans.

Chapter 20
483 BKA

Colonel Matthew Ogden glanced in the mirror one last time, making sure his Army combat uniform looked crisp. He would have preferred wearing his Army dress greens, but the PDF hadn't gotten around to designing anything so formal. So the people in the new service wore standard ACUs, with different insignia.

The new patch on his sleeve seemed out of place, but it marked the only change to his regular uniform. The gold initials "PDF" hovered above the flowing streamers of red, blue, and green. The colors represented the three Alliance members. The stylized image of a fighting ship lent no doubt to the purpose of the organization.

The new emblem, which had arrived this morning, proclaimed his position as an officer in Earth's new Planetary Defense Force. He'd served in the military since joining the Army at age eighteen, more than twenty-five years ago.

In that time, he'd married and raised two sons, and four grandchildren. Only one son and one granddaughter remained alive, the rest having died in the Ktarran attack. Ironically, Ogden had been stationed in Fort Bliss, Texas, at the time of the attack. But his wife and son had taken the three grandkids to Los Angeles to visit Disneyland and Hollywood. Instead of a vacation, they found death. He hoped they hadn't suffered much. Just bad luck on their part, but that didn't matter.

He didn't like the face he saw in the mirror, but that no longer mattered either. Only the Ktarrans meant anything now.

"You're ready, Colonel." Lieutenant Pileggi had already inspected his commander's uniform.

"OK, Lieutenant, let's get this thing over with as soon as possible." The first trial held by the Planetary Defense Force was about to begin, and he wanted to send Delano's message to the rest of the country – justice from the PDF would be swift.

Pileggi opened the door of what had previously been the coach's office. He then stood aside as his commander strode past and up onto the stage of the converted high school auditorium. Ogden stepped toward the table set aside for his use.

The recording corporal snapped to attention and called out. "All rise. Planetary Defense Court is now in session, Colonel Matthew Ogden presiding."

The introduction concluded as Ogden reached the table, took his chair, and set his portfolio and tablet on the surface in front of him. Two Marines in battle dress took up positions on either side, each carrying automatic weapons. The Marines and their weapons made the appropriate statement without saying a word. This was a military trial, and neither interruptions nor violence would be tolerated.

"Be seated." Ogden let his eyes scan what had once been the local high school's home court for basketball games. The poorly performing school had closed seven years ago, and the property sat unused since then, thanks to the usual bureaucratic red tape. Now the appropriated complex would assume at least a temporary rebirth as a PDF facility, with a different and serious role to play in the coming struggle against the Ktarrans.

Ogden eyed the crowd six feet below him. About two hundred people faced him, half of them seated on folding chairs, the remainder, a mix of spectators and twenty reporters and TV crews, stood behind the seats. Upon entry to the building, everyone had received a printed card with warnings about appropriate behavior. Of course some people never learned how to read, and Pileggi had already informed his commander that three people had already been ejected.

The faces he saw appeared subdued, almost unsure. The grim, heavily armed soldiers and Marines would have frightened trained professionals, exactly the effect Ogden intended. This time there would be no security from being part of a crowd, no protection in numbers, and no safety in authority's hesitation to use force.

The auditorium could have held several hundred more people, but Ogden didn't want his troops facing a possible mob. Better to have just a large enough crowd to provide witnesses.

"This military court has been convened to try the sixteen defendants presently in custody," Ogden began. "The primary charges are for interfering with duly designated members of the PDF in the performance of their duties. Additional charges are for murder and destruction of PDF records. We will begin with the murder charges." He turned to his aide. "Bring in the prisoners."

"Yes, sir." Pileggi spoke into his intercom and within

moments a six-man squad of Marines escorted the sixteen prisoners into the courtroom. All the defendants wore orange jumpsuits and had their hands secured behind their backs, white plastic ties sticking up at odd angles and plainly visible. Nearly all were under thirty years of age, and their appearance showed that they had received few amenities in the three days of their confinement. Two Marines physically arranged the sullen prisoners until they formed a rough line, facing the stage.

Ogden glanced down at his notes. "Michael Murdock, Alesia Torres, and Ahmed Beyed. Step forward. You three are charged with interference with PDF personnel, destruction of records, and murder in the first degree. How do you plead?"

A man sitting in the first row of chairs stood and moved to the front of the prisoners. "My clients plead not guilty, Colonel. Furthermore, I challenge the legality of this entire proceeding. The Planetary Defense Force is not a duly constituted judicial entity and has no basis in United States law. It certainly has no authority to impose a death sentence, let alone . . ."

The man would have continued, but Ogden held up his hand. "Since this is the first such trial by the PDF in the United States, I will read you my credentials and my orders. Please listen carefully."

Some in the crowd murmured, and voices began to rise. "Sergeant, please remove anyone who creates a disturbance or speaks without being recognized." Ogden kept his voice firm. "If any resist, use your tasers. Don't bother to wait for my order."

That shocked the spectators and quieted them down. The meter long wand resembled a cattle prod, and a single touch would incapacitate. Multiple touches could stop a person's heart.

Ogden tapped a file on his tablet, and read aloud. "Orders to Colonel Mathew Ogden, from Colonel Joseph Delano, Commander of the PDF. The United States of America is under martial law, as proclaimed by President Simmons. Lieutenant General Langdon Klegg, United States Air Force and Chairman of the Joint Chiefs, has been given the authority to administer such martial law until the emergency is declared to have ended. In turn, for *all* matters relating to planetary security, General Klegg has ceded his authority to the Planetary Defense Force, under the command of Colonel Delano and Dr. Duan Lian."

Ogden paused and faced the courtroom. "They are, as I'm sure everyone knows by now, the Alliance-approved leaders of the Planetary Defense Force. Their directive from the Alliance is to defend the people of this planet from an alien invasion by whatever means necessary."

He waited, but no one said anything. Martial law itself required an adjustment period, and so far it hadn't quite sunk into people's consciousness. The concept that there might be a more stringent authority was even more difficult to comprehend. Ogden returned his gaze to his tablet and continued reading.

"By order of the Planetary Defense Force, as specified in writing by Colonel Delano, military courts are established to insure that the PDF's efforts and personnel receive the highest priority and support in their mission, which is the defense of the entire planet and every living person on Earth. Therefore any attempts to hinder, obstruct, or impede PDF personnel in their assigned duties or personal activities is to be considered Planetary Treason and punished as such."

Ogden glanced up from his notes. "Therefore, under direct orders from Colonel Delano, I have the authority to arrest, try, and punish anyone who hinders the PDF. These orders supersede current martial or civil laws. All federal, state, and local police and government agencies have been ordered to cooperate fully with the PDF. Exceptions, delays, or requests for clarifications will not be permitted."

"The PDF orders," Colonel Ogden continued, "have been published and in effect for seven days. Therefore the prisoners," Ogden indicated the sixteen sullen young people standing in front of him, "have committed offenses against the PDF, and will be punished accordingly."

He stared at the open-mouthed lawyer, probably at a loss for words for the first time in his legal career. "However, if you are defending these people, you should see and hear the evidence against them. Lieutenant Pileggi . . ."

Ogden's aide stepped forward, lifted his tablet, and began reading. "On Tuesday the 24th of December, the Maryland PDF was in the process of recruiting civilian volunteers for service, and at the same time disseminating PDF literature and application forms in front of Baltimore City Hall. Suddenly a crowd appeared and assaulted the three PDF staff members. They were Mrs. Sharon Daffner, Mr. Leon Mayberry, and Ms. Leslie Holman. Sharon Daffner died from injuries received, while Mayberry and Holman required hospitalization and are still recovering. The attack was both unprovoked and especially vicious."

Pileggi glanced around, but no one bothered to dispute those facts. "By the time the local police and PDF military staff arrived, the crowd had dispersed. But the attack had been recorded by two separate cameras, and several members of the crowd were quickly identified, including two by confirmed retinal scans. With the assistance of local police, the PDF forces arrested those two within hours of the attack, and used their phones to locate other members of the crowd. With electronic records available, the leaders and organizers of the attack were identified. Three of those leaders are the defendants standing before this court – Michael Murdock, Alesia Torres, and Ahmed Beyed. The video record, which I will now play, confirms that these three initiated the assault and carried out the physical violence that led to Sharon Daffner's death, and injuries to Mayberry and Holman."

An Army technician seated below the stage punched some keys on his tablet, and the video began to stream, displaying on two large monitors sitting on a second table on the stage. The defendants and spectators watched in silence. The video showed a brutal assault on the three PDF members that lasted over three minutes. Two of the accused were clearly identifiable. Several of the attackers continued to kick and punch the three victims, bleeding and incapacitated, for forty seconds after they were down.

A second video, from a different angle, confirmed the first and showed even more clearly the faces of Murdock and Torres.

Ogden ordered the tech to stop. "As prosecuting officer, are you satisfied of their guilt, Lieutenant? I don't want to waste time going over the evidence."

"Yes, sir. We have the video evidence, the phone records, and in the case of Alesia Torres and Ahmed Beyed we have their DNA evidence on the victims as well. Also six of the defendants have confessed to being paid to take part in the attack, and under oath they named and identified the ring leaders and those who perpetrated the actual assault."

"Very well," Ogden said. "With this evidence, the Court is satisfied of their guilt, and sentences Torres, Beyed, and Murdock to death for crimes against the PDF and the murder of Sharon Daffner. Sentence is to be carried out immediately."

The auditorium erupted in an uproar. Gasps of dismay from supporters and relatives of the defendants, joined by shouts protesting the sentence, overwhelmed the lawyer's protests. Everyone in attendance started talking and shouting at once. The families of the defendants and the lawyers raised their voices in remonstration. The defendant Torres sobbed, while the others pleaded for mercy. Ogden let the tumult continue for about 15 seconds.

"Outbursts are not tolerated in PDF trials," he announced. "Sergeant, restore order."

That didn't take long. Six Marines wielding wands strode into the crowd. In seconds a dozen people were paralyzed, silenced and writhing on the floor. The rest, shocked at the violent and immediate response, ceased talking.

"For your information," Ogden said, "the wands are set to maximum power, to reduce any chance of injury to my men. From this point on, anyone tased will be arrested and sentenced to a work detail at Camp Stillman. Be aware that if anyone is tased and is not in perfect health, there is a good chance of permanent injury or death."

Shocked stares greeted those words. Watching the Marines use the wands, the spectators realized that the safety of a crowd or mob no longer offered any protection.

Lieutenant Pileggi ignored the chaos. Another squad of six Marines took charge of the three convicted murderers, now trembling uncontrollably, and guided them over to the side of the auditorium. A ladder rose up, and a Marine scrambled to the top. He tossed three ropes over one of the roof support beams. Meanwhile another Marine spread out a large plastic drop cloth beneath the beam.

Prisoner Torres continued struggling, and one of the Marines tased her. The two men had already been tased, and offered no resistance. Ropes went around their necks, and were snugged tight. A trio of Marines took the other end of each rope, and simply hauled the convicted up in the air. They didn't bother to lift them high, getting their feet about two feet above the ground before securing the ropes to wall stanchions installed yesterday.

The entire process hadn't taken two minutes. Now gasps from the stunned spectators filled the auditorium. Within thirty seconds, all three bodies hung limp. Urine leaked through the jumpsuits and pooled on the drop cloth.

Pileggi had one more task. He ordered the ropes lowered, until the feet touched the ground. Approaching the deceased, he drew his pistol and fired a round directly into the forehead of each. Then he turned, faced Ogden, and saluted.

"The orders of the PDF Court have been carried out, Colonel."

"Satisfactory," Ogden said, and meant it. The Marines had time for only one walk-thru of the new procedure. He turned to the spectators. "This sentence will not restore life to Sharon Daffner, a mother of two young children and a good woman trying to serve her country and her planet. But her death is not wasted. This is an example of what will happen to anyone who interferes with or causes damage to the PDF or its staff. If there are those among you who wish to protest, do so peacefully and legally, at legitimate sites. But violence of *any* kind against the PDF or its personnel will not be tolerated."

"Now the other prisoners will be sentenced." Ogden faced the thirteen remaining. "For participating in the assault, each of you is hereby sentenced to six months of hard labor at Camp Sillman. You will be required to work up to twelve hours each day, seven days a week. Your labor will help free up those volunteers and paid laborers working to accelerate the construction of the base. In the event of *any* – I repeat, *any* – resistance or attempts to escape, disobedience, protests, even complaints – an additional six months will be added to your sentence. So understand, each and every deviation from your sentence will increase the time you have to serve."

Camp Sillman, in the wilds of New Mexico adjacent to Spaceport, had just been designated by the PDF as a training and testing facility. At present it was little more than empty desert. Now it would also assume a role as a military labor camp.

"Fit them with the restraint collars, Lieutenant."

"Yes, sir." An Army sergeant stepped forward, carrying a box with the collars. Five minutes later every prisoner had a two-inch wide band of high-tensile steel around his or her throat. Each collar contained a GPS locator as well as a remote-activated miniature taser. So far, the collars had proved nearly invulnerable to tampering or removal.

"Get them out of my sight." Ogden stood. "One last comment for those in attendance. This is not a secret court. Reporters and TV crews have been permitted to film these proceedings, so that there will be no doubt about the PDF's resolve. However, any attempt to tamper with, distort, or edit these videos or my words will be considered a crime by the PDF. If you show any part of these proceedings, you are to show the entire session. If any of my words are omitted or taken out of context, that will also be deemed an attempt to subvert the PDF. Punishment in either case will be immediate and severe."

Shocked silence answered him. Most eyes were still drawn to the three dead prisoners, already being shoved inside body bags. A few stared at him, mouths open in surprise. Well, there was a new sheriff in town, and as far as the PDF was concerned, justice would be both swift and permanent.

Colonel Ogden nodded in satisfaction. "Good work, Lieutenant Pileggi, everyone. This Court is adjourned."

A vehicle waited for him. He intended to visit Sharon Daffner's family, to offer what sympathy he could. Hopefully, he would never need to do something like this again. That was futile, Ogden knew. In the next sixteen months, he'd be sentencing thousands to hard labor and hundreds to their deaths.

Unfortunate, but necessary, he told himself. But nothing would be permitted to stand in the way of the PDF's efforts. When the Ktarrans returned, Ogden's family would be boarding a Colonizer transport. He would either join them, or take a berth on one of the fighting ships. He had plenty of time to make up his mind.

Chapter 21
414 BKA

Lian stared through the one-way mirror into the interrogation room at Chaobai Prison, the primary facility on Beijing's outskirts for female criminals or political offenders. This prisoner sat shackled to a steel chair, facing the glass, but unable to see those watching her. Her head had been shaved to a black stubble, and her feet were bare. A large bruise decorated her left cheek. Her dark brown eyes were dull and her mouth slack. She looked much older than her thirty-five years.

Unlike the other women within the facility, this prisoner wore the faded blue jacket and pants, both decorated with white vertical stripes, normally seen on male inmates. Female inmates wore darker blue jackets and trousers. Those deemed reliable or performing duties for the prison's guards and staff wore white shirts with black trousers.

"She doesn't appear dangerous," Lian said.

"Don't be deceived, Doctor Duan," the warden said. "She's a ruthless murderer. The police and security forces spent three years trying to catch her. Even so, they needed help from Interpol to track her down."

Lian had read the complete file. The three year hunt the warden referred to didn't include the eight years trying to learn the identity of the mastermind operating one of the largest international criminal networks. The document claimed that she'd killed, with her own hand, at least three police officers who'd gotten too close to catching her. Arms dealing, drug smuggling, and human trafficking across the globe had brought her both immense power and wealth.

At her secret trial, Daiyu Shan had claimed to be thirty-five years old, but no one really knew her age or where she came from. Records of her birth, if any existed, had disappeared, including the required computer data. A genetic test revealed that she had some Japanese blood, and so might have been born in Japan, where the record keeping authorities were less efficient. The trace of Japanese ancestry alone would have condemned her for any crime in China.

"Why is she barefoot?" Lian hadn't seen any other prisoners without shoes.

"Since she arrived here already sentenced to death," the warden explained, "no one wanted to waste clothes or sandals. Besides, caged prisoners always have their shoes removed, so they can't hurt themselves."

Only used for the most serious criminals, prison cages were 1.5 meters square and 1 meter high. A two meter chain was fastened to the prisoner's neck and bolted to the floor. The cage contained a small stainless steel bowl and nothing else.

Daiyu Shan had been one of the most wanted criminals on the planet, and even an attack two months ago by Ktarran aliens hadn't stopped her pursuers from maintaining the chase. Nevertheless, Lian had traveled to this prison to seek her out. Earth and the PDF forces she and Colonel Delano had established needed help in many areas. Daiyu Shan – the name could be translated as "Mountain of Black Jade" – had many valuable skills, skills that Lian wanted to use.

She turned to Lieutenant Shen, always within reach of her person. Two other PDF officers, both Russians, stood behind Shen. Two more PDF sergeants waited in the hall. "Remain here while I speak to Daiyu. Make sure there are no recordings or videos." She glanced at the warden.

"I will stop the devices," he said. "And I will make certain your are undisturbed."

"Thank you, warden. You've been most helpful."

"I lost my brother in the Ktarran attack," the warden said. "If there is anything I can do to help the PDF destroy those creatures, let me know."

Lian thanked him, then left the observation room and entered the interrogation chamber. Here the smell that she first noticed on entering the prison seemed stronger, a mix of body odor from too many people crowded together in too small a place, combined with the harsh chemicals of disinfectants. There was another scent in the room, but she couldn't place it. Perhaps the aroma of despair. She closed the door behind her and turned to the prisoner.

Daiyu's eyes had flashed at Lian's entrance, but she said nothing. Her gaze, however, fixed on Lian's uniform, with its loose-fitting jacket.

Lian settled on a straight-backed chair facing the caged woman. "Yes, it's a gun." She lifted the right side of her jacket and let it fall back. An in-waist-band holster held the small Glock. "And I know how to use it."

In the last three months, Lian had become quite proficient with the 9mm weapon. Lieutenant Shen had proved a most-capable instructor.

"Are you my executioner?" Daiyu didn't seem concerned. "I'm surprised they chose a woman. Unless you enjoy inflicting pain."

Condemned criminals were often brutally beaten, sometimes for days. When they could no longer feel any pain or provide some amusement for their jailers, a bullet to the back of the head followed. In cases where the executed had a family, they received a bill for the cost of the bullet. It served as both a reminder and warning against further transgressions.

"No, there are many others eager for that task, friends and family of those you have murdered over the years," Lian said. "Do you know who I am?"

Daiyu lifted her eyes for a moment. "Your voice . . . are you Duan Lian, the niece of our most gracious and glorious leader?"

Lian smiled. "Yes, but now I am also one of the commanders of the PDF. You've heard of that, I suppose?"

"The American and Russian conspiracy to rule China," Daiyu said. "I am surprised to see you without your American master at your side."

The harsh words didn't bother Lian. She'd heard them all, even from those in China and the government who should know better.

"We are apart far too often," Lian agreed. "But we do what we must to save the planet from destruction."

"I'm afraid I cannot help you with that. Nor are you likely to succeed. Too many in China wish you dead. Already there has been an attempt on your life."

"There have been three," Lian said. "And two on Colonel Delano. Which is why I have come to Chaobai."

"Don't expect anything from me," Daiyu said. "Even if I could, I would do nothing to assist the Chinese government."

"Perhaps you might," Lian said. "Unless you prefer not to save your daughter's life."

Daiyu straightened up, her lips tightening with anger, the first show of emotion. Then she lowered her head. "I have no daughter."

"Huiling is already in Beijing," Lian said. "Would you like to see her? Would you want her to visit you, here in your cage? I can have her brought in."

"I have no daughter."

"Huiling is twelve years old. A beautiful child, and very intelligent. Highest grades at the Swiss Academy for Humanities and Social Sciences. Yesterday she received a DNA test. Once we saw the results, she was taken from Switzerland. Even now she sleeps at my Uncle's palace. Her DNA matched yours perfectly."

Daiyu knew when to give up. Records could be forged, but DNA couldn't be disguised or disputed. "What do you want from me? I have given your police everything I know, every name, every account number. There is nothing left."

"I'm sure there are many secrets you can still reveal, but that is not what interests me. How would you like to be free, to resume your life. Within limits, of course."

"I will never be free. I cannot aid you."

"Then your daughter will be given to the Four Seas gang in Taiwan," Lian said. "You offended them when you killed their leader. I'm sure they will be grateful to have her. But perhaps the Ktarrans will end her misery."

The Triads and other Chinese gangs had inflicted horrors on the women and daughters of their enemies. Huiling would first be addicted to heroin, then used to pleasure the gang's leader and his friends. When they grew bored, she would be given to a madam in a house of prostitution. After a few years, when she grew numb with pain and drugs, she would be returned to the gang's leader and tortured to death.

"You would do that? You who claim to be saving the planet?"

"To defend Earth, there is nothing I would not do." Lian's voice now sounded cold. "If you want your daughter to live, you will have to help me in that effort."

"You want my help . . . even you cannot protect my daughter. If my enemies know she exists, they will search for her, and they will find her. No place will be safe. Nothing you or your uncle do can prevent that."

"In that you are wrong," Lian said. "I can put your daughter far beyond the reach of any of your enemies, and at the same time save her life."

Daiyu's eyes narrowed. "There is no place . . ."

"Not on Earth, you are right. But I can send her to the Moon, and put her on a Colonizer ship. Huiling will have a chance to have a normal life, without any fear of her mother's name or enemies. All you need to do is help me. And at the same time, you will be helping your daughter and yourself."

Her shoulders sagged even lower for a moment. Then Daiyu straightened up. "What must I do?"

Lian accepted Daiyu's agreement. "You will be allowed to return to your former life. Money will be provided, as you need it. Once you are beyond the reach of the police, you can resume your former activities. But at the same time you will establish a network of spies who will have only one function – to search out any possible threats against Delano and myself, and the PDF. As you know, many who want someone killed turn to the Triads and other gangs for weapons and assassins."

"But where come these plots?" Daiyu looked puzzled. "How would I discover . . ."

"All over the world, in every country, are people who hate and fear Colonel Delano and me. If we die, the aliens may not support Earth in its fight against the Ktarran invaders. You once had vast resources and connections into every criminal gang throughout the world. Once you reestablish those links, you need only to search and listen for any hint of conspiracies against the PDF. And report them to me."

Daiyu's eyes, now intense, stared at Lian. "You think this is important enough to save my life?"

"We, the PDF, are trying to save the planet. That includes you and your daughter. If we fail, your daughter might endure a worse fate than that waiting for her from your enemies. For that reason alone, you should want to join us."

"If you guarantee my daughter's safety, then I will serve you, Dr. Duan. I swear it."

"Then Huiling will be on the Moon in a few days. Once she is there, you can speak to her."

"What can I tell her?"

"The truth. That you are working with the PDF to help defend Earth. That should be more than enough for any young girl to know about her mother."

"And this prison? How will I leave this place?'

Lian smiled. "I brought clothes for you. You'll leave with us. Tomorrow, the warden will announce that Daiyu Shan bribed some guards and escaped. That should help you regain the trust of your former associates."

"You seem to have thought of everything, Dr. Duan."

"No, not everything. But since I cannot search for the evil that wants to destroy Delano or me, you must do it for us. As the Americans say, set a thief to catch a thief. Only this time, the prize will be your daughter's life."

Chapter 22
391 BKA

Grass and small leafy trees, mostly box elders and Fremont cottonwoods, opened up into a children's playground, empty now, in Quail Run Park. Major Barbara Blackstone drummed her fingers on the concrete table. The square surface had a chess board notched into its top, but she knew checkers, pinochle and bridge players used it, too. But not today. Today the park was closed to visitors.

Blackstone hated waiting. It gave her too much time to think, to remember the pain and the loss that had ripped all joy from her life. Her husband of less than three months had died, burned alive by the Ktarran beam weapons. Jeff had been stationed at Fort Hunter Army Base, about 250 miles north of Los Angeles. A newly-promoted major, he'd been organizing Army Reserve forces to help defend against the Ktarrans. Instead, the military facility had been leveled by the aliens. Jeff had lived for three days after the attack, before succumbing to his injuries. He died in her arms without ever regaining consciousness.

Grief stricken, Barbara resigned her US Army commission and joined the PDF the day after her husband's passing. Colonel Delano had issued a call to arms to save the planet. She had a much more personal and pragmatic reason for joining – revenge. The Ktarrans had killed Jeff, taken his life as callously as any mass murderer. Barbara decided she would make them pay for that. Now fools wanted to resist the PDF, to make deals with the Ktarrans, even sell out their fellow humans, all to save their own skins or fatten their own bank accounts. That folly would not be permitted to interfere with her plans.

Like many battle-hardened soldiers, she grew edgy waiting for the fighting to start. Her three lieutenants also sat at the table, trying their best to ignore her signs of irritation. Only one of her lieutenants had served with Barbara Blackstone in a combat role. But that one had assured the others it was only her way of handling simple frustration at continued inaction.

With the operation in place, Barbara hated any unnecessary delays, especially after nearly thirty hours of mission preparation.

But one of the two old National Guard helicopters transferred to the PDF yesterday had failed its pre-flight checklist. The bad news came from the former cop, now a captain in the same PDF, who'd piloted the bird from Santa Barbara to Riverside. Another thirty minutes, he said. Since functioning aircraft of any age or type were scarce after the Ktarran attack, there was nothing to do but wait.

The choppers, armed and fueled on the tarmac at March AFB, were key to the upcoming action. The University of California at Riverside sprawled over a large area, with countless structures of various sizes scattered haphazardly around the Student Center, which lay roughly in the middle of the campus. Entry and exit would be difficult.

Without the helicopters, there would be no way to monitor the rooftops, a natural place for bad guys with guns. The choppers could also spot possible enemy reinforcements on the move utilizing the many walkways and common areas. Not to mention that the old but upgraded Apaches each mounted a 30mm chain gun and 1,200 rounds of ammunition.

The angry activists – latest estimates placed their number at over 800 – had seized the Student Center three days ago and turned it into their base of operations. So far four small businesses in Riverside, ones that had contracted work with the PDF, had suffered, burned to the ground. At least seven people had died at the hands of the armed and rioting students.

Already outraged with the extension of martial law three weeks ago, the passage of the War Powers Act had tipped them over the edge and into outright violence and rebellion. To these students, the PDF represented everything wrong with the corrupt government and the powerful military-industrial complex. They claimed the alien Ktarrans were merely the excuse used by the military to seize power.

Students my ass. Barbara knew the student leaders were long-time political and professional agitators. Many were older than her twenty-nine years. Probably most hadn't attended a class in a decade, except those taught by teachers and guest lecturers more radical than themselves.

Now the protest movement threatened to grow even larger. Another university, this one in Missouri, planned to join with the Riverside faction. Close to 100 armed students would be arriving sometime in the next two hours. Their plan, such as it was, involved spreading the resistance to Los Angeles and closing down anyone who supported the PDF. That the PDF's goals were the salvation of mankind meant nothing to the radicals, intent only on their own growing political power.

Barbara smiled at that thought. The Missouri plane, already in the air, thought it would be landing at the Riverside airport. Instead it would be diverted, by force if necessary, at the last minute and directed to land at March Air Force Base. All nearby cell towers had already been locked down. Unable to communicate, the student agitators would be deplaned and interred before they could join the movement. Barbara didn't care about them. They were somebody else's problem.

She glanced down at the table and ordered her fingers to stop moving. If any of the others had a case of nerves, it didn't show. Thank God her three lieutenants had seen some combat, even if they weren't veterans like herself. Fortunately, they'd worked and trained together for the last ten days, and by now they knew and trusted her.

Another 20 newly-recruited PDF soldiers were scattered around nearby tables, weapons on the ground or empty benches. Most of these troops were former National Guard or Army Reserve trained, but without any combat experience. How well they would perform under pressure depended on her example.

The good news was that Barbara had developed a very simple plan, one that should be easy enough to implement. The bad news was that they were greatly outnumbered, and had no real idea of how many of the so-called students were armed and willing to fight.

She'd asked for more troops, but the newly-formed PDF was stretched thin. It would have taken several days before more could be brought in. That meant more civilian deaths and property destruction. If the mission went south, the repercussions could provide a morale boost to other radical groups unwilling to support the Alliance, the US government, or the PDF.

Taking everything into consideration, PDF Major Barbara Blackstone had considerable weight on her shoulders.

Her encrypted phone rang. Barbara made herself pick up the device casually. "Blackstone. Go ahead."

"The birds are in the air, Major. ETA five minutes."

"Roger that," she answered, and ended the call. Without close air support, they might all end up dead. Thank God the waiting was over. She stood. "We've got a green light. Check your comm links," she ordered the lieutenants. That didn't take long. "OK, let's move out."

The twenty-four person detachment squeezed themselves and their gear into the four minivans, and pulled out of the parking lot. Barbara, in the lead vehicle, told the driver to take it nice and slow. The birds had only a short flight from March AFB to the Riverside Campus, but they would want to take a good look from up high before swooping in.

Barbara commanded Squad 1. Her comm sergeant, Lily Miller, had already established the uplink to the choppers. What the pilots recorded on their cameras would be sent directly to Miller's tablet and displayed on the split screen.

"Got the feed, Major," Miller said. "Looking good."

By now the little caravan was on Interstate 215, the Escondido Freeway, which went right past the campus. Barbara glanced up at the sky, but couldn't see the choppers, which was reassuring. The students might be alerted if they saw a couple of helicopters hovering overhead. Assuming these thugs were alert enough to notice. Not many would have any real military training. By two o'clock in the afternoon, plenty of beer, weed, or other drugs would have been consumed.

The ride didn't take long, and soon they exited the freeway and moved onto West Campus Drive. The four minivans remained a 100 yards apart, to attract as little attention as possible. Campus Drive turned into Canyon Crest, and then they made the right turn onto Linden Street, which took them to the Student Recreational Center.

The minivan turned into the parking lot, and moved slowly toward the main entrance. The impressive glass and aluminum building was fronted by two large brick shrubbery enclosures which would provide suitable defensive positions for her troops, if they needed them. Barbara used her binoculars and saw two armed guards lounging outside the building, both with the usual AK-74s slung over their shoulders. By the time they looked up, the other vans had closed the gap and moved right behind the lead vehicle.

"Go!" Barbara got out on the passenger side, while the driver, Lieutenant Garcia, and four of his squad jumped from the sliding door. Before the surprised guards could react, five rifles were aimed at them. Mouths agape, they raised their hands. One started to reach for his phone, but Garcia ominously waved his rifle, and the man thought better of it.

The other vans had disgorged the rest of her team, and all were on the move. Squad 2 moved down the side of the building, to secure a secondary entrance just around the corner. What little intel they had suggested that their primary target, a former professor named Farrell, would be in the first floor conference room. Squad 3 took up position near the front entrance, while Squad 4 headed to the building's rear, to make sure no one got away.

So far, so good, Barbara thought. Not a shot fired or alarm given. Within moments the two sentries, disarmed, bound, and gagged with military-grade duct tape, lay helpless on the ground.

"Miller, notify the choppers we're going in," Barbara ordered her comm sergeant. She swung her own rifle around to the front of her body, and stepped through the oversized glass doors and into the shaded lobby.

Moving quickly away from the large, glass entrance, Barbara headed straight for the information desk, 25 feet inside the building. Three girls, dressed in fashionable terrorist chic, lounged behind the counter, with rifles lying atop the polished marble surface. Barbara's squad followed close behind her, then fanned out to either side.

Other men and women were scattered about the lobby, looking as surprised as the girls behind the counter. They stared at the soldiers, rifles at the ready, who had suddenly appeared in the building. Barbara knew the suppressors on half her team's weapons would intimidate anyone.

By the time they reacted, it was already too late. Barbara reached across the counter, grabbed the nearest girl by the hair, and pulled her close enough to jamb the rifle barrel against her throat.

"Everyone stay quiet and nobody move." Barbara used her command voice, harsh and threatening. "Where is Simon Farrell? Don't try to bullshit me or you're dead."

The girl shrank away from the rifle, moving her head as far back as Barbara's grip allowed. "They're on the first floor," she gasped.

"Mezzanine or the floor above?" Wide steps led upward to a lounge area in what the administration's website called the Mezzanine. "What office are they in?" Barbara jabbed the rifle harder, and the girl's eyes went wide.

"Conference room 104. It's on the Mezzanine . . ."

Automatic rifle fire exploded from above, striking the counter. The spray of bullets probably meant for Barbara killed two of the women behind the counter, including the one still in her grasp. Many of the rounds went high, shattering the glass entrance doors. Her squad returned fire almost at once, and the building erupted into a cacophony of screams and gunfire.

Barbara never hesitated, dashing across the lobby and racing up the steps to the Mezzanine two at a time. More rifle fire came from above, but nothing came her way and her team continued putting down cover fire. She heard Garcia's boots pounding up the stairs behind her. He fired at something, but she never saw his target.

She reached the top and darted across an open area to arrive at a second, narrower flight of stairs. This one was shorter than the first. She'd climbed halfway up when a man appeared above her, a rifle in his hands. Before he could take aim, Barbara squeezed off a quick burst, and the man staggered back with three holes in his chest, dead before he hit the floor.

Heads were popping up. Barbara threw herself down when she got to the top, landing hard on her elbows. Her rifle seemed to take on a life of its own, firing short bursts of 2-3 rounds the length of the corridor. A woman with an AK went down without getting off a shot, and two more ducked back into offices.

"I've got eyes on target, Garcia," she shouted. "Go!"

The lieutenant never hesitated. He bounded up the last few steps, moved across Barbara's field of fire, and ducked into an office on her right. She heard a quick eruption of gunfire from inside, but knew it came from Garcia's unsuppressed rifle. Two more of his men followed right behind him. The last one was barely out of sight before Garcia leaned out the doorway, covering the corridor. Barbara ignored the sound of shooting from the lobby as she scrambled up and darted down the hall, her rifle still ready to spit bullets at anyone that showed itself.

She reached a doorway and snapped her head around the jamb for a quick look. At least two shooters fired their weapons at her head, but she was already ducking back and throwing herself to the floor. Garcia opened up to give her some cover fire, but it was Lily, staying right behind her commander, who tapped Barbara's arm and handed her a grenade.

"It's live!"

Snatching it with one hand, Barbara stretched out and tossed the grenade inside the open doorway. She barely got her arm out of the device's hit zone before it exploded, the sound deafening in the hall. She heard glass shatter and someone screamed in pain. Instantly Garcia burst from his office, crossed the hall and into the smoke and dust-filled chamber. More sounds of gunfire, but Barbara ignored it as she scrambled to her feet, covered by Garcia's two men, who'd taken up positions behind her.

She trotted another twelve steps down the hall, eyes sweeping the corridor, alert to anyone coming into view. The next door, Room 104, remained closed, and so far no one had emerged from it. It probably had a second exit, but that would be around the far corner from where Barbara crouched. Hopefully Squad 2 had gotten up there fast enough to secure that escape route.

"Garcia, where's Squad 4? Did they seal the rear exit?"

Her lieutenant muttered into his comm device, while Barbara and her squad kept their weapons aimed at the door and corridor.

"Not sure, Major," Garcia said. "They've got eyes on the rear door, but it's closed and no one's tried to get out."

Nobody running for their lives bothered to close a door behind them. She took a deep breath. "Farrell, this is Major Blackstone of the PDF. I'm ordering you to put down your weapons and surrender. If we have to blow the door, you won't get out alive."

A muffled laugh sounded through the door. "You're the one that better surrender, bitch. 300 students, all of them armed, are already on the way. You won't get off the campus alive if you don't put down your guns."

"That's not going to . . ."

The corridor wall a foot in front of Barbara's face exploded in a spray of plasterboard dust. She threw herself back and saw more bullets tearing holes in the wall above her head.

Coughing, she spit out dust. "Damn those AK's." The bullets had been a little high, but if she hadn't been crouched over, she might have been hit.

"Save your breath, Major," Garcia said. "Next time they may get you."

An AK-74 might be an old weapon, but it had impressive penetration power, and still ranked high when you really, really needed to clear a room in a few seconds.

"Fuck 'em," Barbara said, spitting out plaster dust. "We'll use the explosives. Set it up." She glanced at her comm sergeant. "Miller, what's happening out there?"

A crackle of static. "Lobby is secure, Major, but a crowd is gathering outside, about 100 meters down the street. We've taken some fire. Another mob has already blocked the street we came in on."

"How many?"

"At least a 100, and most of them are carrying rifles. Looks like more are on the way."

"Damn these idiots. All right, cue the choppers. Looks like we're going to need them." Barbara turned toward the two men stringing the explosives. "Garcia, are we . . ."

"Almost there, Major. You'd better pull back while I plant the charge."

With a hand signal, Barbara retreated down the hall, covering Garcia, who had started crawling along the floor, pushing the black plastic box of explosives. He used his rifle to shove it to the center of the door, then squirmed away from the deadly device.

Since most of the explosive force would be in the hallway, they had to be out of any direct path of the blast. She reached down and grasped Garcia by the shoulder, and half-dragged him into the empty office he'd cleared before.

"Get ready," she ordered the squad, then turned to Garcia. "Blow it."

Garcia climbed to his feet, checked his rifle, and then thumbed the detonator.

The blast shook the building. Ceiling tiles and gray insulation dust fell from the suddenly-shaken overhead. Barbara ignored that, and stumbled into the corridor. Her ears rang from what must have been far more explosives than necessary, and she had trouble focusing. Damn, the building might come down. The door, when she bumped into the splintered jamb, had disappeared, blown off its hinges. Plenty of furniture must have been stacked up against the door, but the explosion had shoved all of that back, leaving a clear entry way for about two meters into the room.

Inside, still-swirling dust blotted out the afternoon sun from the now exposed window frames, the shattered glass fragments having been blown to the grounds below. She saw something moving, heard a hoarse voice mumbling something, but she didn't hesitate. Her assault rifle, on full auto now, swept the room. In three seconds, she emptied the magazine into the debris. Before the weapon locked open, Garcia was beside her, spraying the room while she dropped to one knee, coughing from the dust, and shoved a fresh magazine into the weapon.

"Fall back!"

Someone gave the command, and Barbara lunged for the corridor, Garcia's arm around her waist. The moment they were out of the wrecked conference room, two squad members tossed grenades into the room, aiming for the corners where survivors might be trying to recover from the shock of the blast.

The grenades exploded less than two seconds apart, creating new shock waves inside the room and bringing down more plaster dust.

"Clear the room, Garcia," she said, and moved back down the corridor. If Farrell and his henchmen were in the room, dead or wounded, Garcia would take care of them.

Even so, she needed to hold onto the aluminum banister to navigated the steps to the lobby. By the time she reached the front desk, her head had cleared enough to face the next crisis.

Gunfire had erupted outside the Student Center. The five soldiers in Squad 3 were firing into two directions. Barbara went to the main entrance with two of her team. "Get inside! Hurry."

She and the others began laying down cover fire, shooting toward the slowly advancing mob of men and women firing rifles and determined to destroy the soldiers.

"Choppers are inbound, Major!" Miller's voice in her ear sounded extra loud after the explosions. Meanwhile, the rest of the squad scrambled up the steps and into the Center, but one soldier went down on the last step, his skull split open by a bullet to the head.

"Damn!" Barbara pulled the last one in, and they both flung themselves down on the carpeted floor. Then the choppers swooped in, spraying 30 mm rounds from their miniguns directly into the advancing crowd. For what seemed like minutes, but probably wasn't more than ten or fifteen seconds, the choppers blasted away. Then their guns went silent. The helos disappeared, gone until they could reverse direction, reload the guns, and prepare for a second run.

The brutal and deadly aerial attack caught the mob by surprise. No one had expected machine gun fire from above. The strafing run left twenty or thirty dead or dying, and an equal number wounded. Whatever the body count, the will to fight had vanished. Throwing away their weapons, the attackers fled, disappearing into the paths and buildings, anywhere that promised them shelter from another airborne assault.

Barbara moved to the desk, pulled a water bottle from her belt, and drank until her throat cleared. When she emptied the bottle, Garcia was there. He and another soldier dragged a bloody and half-conscious man between them.

She smiled at Garcia. "You found one still alive? Who do we have here?"

Garcia laughed. "Farrell is one lucky bastard, Major. A couple of bodies were on top of him, and must have taken most of the blast."

Barbara's hand snapped out and grabbed Farrell by the neck. "One of my men died digging your ass out of the rubble, you bastard. If I didn't know what was waiting for you in Washington, I'd kill you right now."

She turned to Lily. "What's the count?"

"Two dead, two wounded, Major."

"OK, time to go," Barbara said. "Tell the choppers to cover us, and take out anyone on a roof. We'll grab the SUVs and head back to the base."

"What about the rest of Farrell's followers?"

She laughed. "Don't worry about them. After they see what happens to him, they'll disappear as fast and as far as possible." Barbara already knew Farrell's fate. If he'd surrendered, he'd have been sent to the work camp. But Colonel Delano had said that if anyone died taking him in, Farrell would be sentenced and hanged the next day.

In two minutes, with the roaring choppers still looping and swooping overhead, they were back in the vehicles and on the move. No one even took a shot at them. The threat of bullets spraying from the helicopters would scare anyone. Garcia stomped on the accelerator and with a squeal of tires, yanked the vehicle around in a tight turn and headed back toward the freeway.

Farrell, his face bleeding, was in the back seat, on the floor, with Lily's boots on his chest. The sooner they could get back to the base, the better. Barbara needed a shower and a drink, not necessarily in that order.

She and her troop had done their part and proven their worth.

The so-called students in the rest of the country would get the message. The fate of Farrell and the high body count of his people showed just how serious the PDF was. Now students and teachers across the country knew they would be held to the same standards. No more free passes to so-called students or revolutionary professors. The cushy sanctuary of this and every other university had disappeared. No one, repeat, no one, would be permitted to interfere with the PDF, not while it was trying to save the planet.

Major Barbara Blackstone sagged back against the seat. The first mission always proved to be the toughest. Now her team knew what it could do, and they would be even better prepared for the next operation. Whatever she needed to do in the future, she would be only too glad to play the role of avenging angel.

Chapter 23
344 BKA

Delano stretched out on the still warm bed, relaxing in the low lunar gravity. Lian snuggled against him, pulling the blue bedsheet up to her chin. He wrapped his arm around her shoulders, enjoying the feel of her smooth skin. Satisfying her gave him more pleasure than he'd thought possible, probably because Lian was the first woman he'd ever really loved.

Yes, lunar sex is the best. So many more possibilities. Much better than zero gravity, where you had to strap yourself in or climb into a onesie suit.

"Almost time for dinner," he said.

"Not hungry, my love."

He'd heard that before but didn't take it seriously. She could chow down with the best of them and yet keep her figure. Lian didn't have an ounce of fat on her deliciously slender body. He still couldn't figure how that worked.

For the two most powerful individuals in the PDF and the world, intimacy and privacy had become almost impossible. Four months had passed since the founding of the PDF and the initiation of the plans for Earth's defense, and they had worked non-stop during that time. To their surprise, Lian's uncle had suggested they might need some time to relax and recuperate.

He didn't have to ask twice. Taking advantage of an upcoming trip to the Moon, they decided to mix business with pleasure. Four the last four days, they'd disappeared from public sight, taking their mini-vacation at the JovCo executive facility on the Moon.

They spent as much time as they could in the tiny hotel's corporate luxury suite, talking quietly and making love. Their relationship, created hurriedly by the attack on the planet, remained strong. Facing death together several times over did have a habit of making a person focus on what really mattered.

Now their brief vacation had nearly ended. Officially they were inspecting the lunar facilities being constructed. They did do a few hours of inspections each day. Since the Moon wasn't all that large, they could cover quite a bit of lunar ground using a

Jumper. But mostly they spent quiet time with each other, phones and other communication devices turned off. Best of all was when they could lie in each other's arms, whispering to each other after making love.

They both had good back ups to cover the usual problems and resolve the issues that cropped up almost steadily, day after day. For this vacation, communications with the PDF were limited to an hour each day.

"What do we have to do tomorrow?" She reached out and took his hand.

"Not much, really," he said. "Go to New Beijing and visit the assembly yard. Or we could just blow it off and stay here. In bed."

"I've seen enough factories," she said. "Tomorrow is our last day before we have to get back. My uncle needs me to host another people's rally."

Though they had initially created the PDF to be a joint project, the serious problems that had developed from the Ktarran attack on China, Japan, and the Koreas required constant, hands-on attention. For Lian, the backlash against her uncle's rule continued to threaten his power base, and her presence at his side helped maintain a lid on the unrest simmering within the Chinese nation.

Chinese resistance against the PDF had faded somewhat, but Lian knew that it would take only a single misstep for it to reemerge. So she toured the bases and facilities that PDF had established in China, spoke with the common people across the land, and helped maintain the orderly flow of everyday life.

"Sounds about as exciting as what's waiting for me," Delano said. "Meeting with dignitaries from the eastern bloc in St. Petersburg." He held her tight. "God, I wish we could stay right here for at least a month."

Delano, too, had similar duties in the United States. Former President Clark's evil work continued to outlive his demise. The country's citizens took heart knowing that the PDF's leader, despite the hard policies of martial law, was one of their own. The fact that nations on three continents had proclaimed Delano the planet's savior also helped to ease the suffering.

His work with Russia as well as the United States kept him in public view. Lian's efforts remained more in the shadows. The Chinese people acknowledged her authority, but most believed that her lover Delano was making most of the decisions. The situation wasn't fair to her, but fitted her personality. She preferred working through others and staying in the background as much as possible.

For Delano, his brief interludes with Lian were what kept him going. Only when they were together could he really unwind, let him be himself without having to project the persona of the most powerful man in the world. But he didn't want to lean too much on Lian. She had her own problems to deal with. He felt grateful that Lian allowed herself to forget her country's woes while she cared for her lover's psyche.

"I wish we had more time," Delano said. "Two or three days a month isn't very much."

"We still have almost a year to go," Lian said. "In a few months, even a three-day vacation may be out of the question."

"Hard to believe five months have passed since the speech in Moscow."

"We have to survive another year," Lian said. "After that, once the Ktarrans come, nothing else will matter."

"Yes, at least it will be over." He straightened up in the bed, and as usual didn't compensate for the low gravity. It took a moment before he positioned himself on his side, facing her. "We've never talked about what we'll do after the Ktarrans come. Do you think we'll ever be able to have a normal life, get married, maybe even raise some kids?"

She touched his lips with her finger. "It would be nice to believe that, assuming we drive the Ktarrans off. But even if we do, the demands on our time will never let up. The people will need their high priest and priestess. I don't know how we can ever get away from that."

"It will get ugly for us even if we win," he said. "We've both made too many enemies, killed too many people. If we can't stop the Ktarrans, none of that really matters. But if we win, I'd bet the PDF gets disbanded within six months."

"Leaving us out in the cold," Lian said. "You're right, we've made too many enemies. Someone will blame us for something bad and even the PDF won't be able to protect us."

"So there's no hope for us. God, how did we get involved in this whole mess?"

Lian didn't answer. Instead she twisted around in the bed so she could meet his eyes. "I've been thinking about this for some time. I might have an idea about how we could get out from under."

Delano met her gaze. She was always thinking. He knew she was a much better planner and organizer. His skill set, if he had any, was in getting people to cooperate and get things done. *Man of action, woman of brains*. Still, it had worked for other leaders in the planet's history. They'd already proved they did well as a team.

But she had come up with something. "OK, I'll bite. What's your idea?"

She told him. When Lian finished, he saw the doubt in her eyes, wondering if he could bring himself to make the leap. If he loved her that much.

He kissed her softly. "It won't be easy, but I'm in. All in. Of course you'll have to promise to make love to me every day for the rest of our lives."

She snuggled against him. "That should be no problem. In fact, I think I can start building up some credits right now."

He had one last thought about her plan before his body took over. *Oh, yeah. It's gonna be real easy.*

Chapter 24

338 BKA

Spaceport, New Mexico

"Are you excited?" Colonel William Welsh couldn't hide his own eagerness.

Delano turned away from the observation window in Camp Sillman's tower. Two hundred yards away, technicians in white coveralls were finishing up the final pre-flight for Jumper 1.

"I was starting to think this day would never come," Delano said.

"Well, you wanted a miracle, and that takes a little longer." Welsh, seated at the table, winked at Gunny Stecker, the only other person in the room. "Don't forget, more than eight thousand people in five countries have worked on this ship, and I swear I've shaken hands with each and every one of them."

Colonel Welsh remained Delano's primary technical advisor regarding space ship development. A tall black man, Welsh had a long, thin face that matched his slender frame. A former fighter pilot, he'd been a science specialist on the Space Station when Delano and the aliens showed up. Welsh had helped develop the plan for the destruction of the third Ktarran battleship.

Since the creation of the PDF, Welsh split his time between Jiuquan and NASA. Other experts managed the flow of materials, construction, and design, but Welsh had the job of making sure everyone and everything did what Delano and Lian expected – build a spaceship that would help prepare for a space battle against the Ktarrans.

For their first task, each major country in the Alliance had been directed to construct two prototype ships. The first was to match precisely the actual specifications of the Starman's space vessel, those specs being obtained by de-constructing the two-seated scout craft discovered on Io. Reverse engineering the design hadn't proceeded smoothly. Theorists demanded the engineers justify their views in a more reasonable and scientific way than by mere demonstration that they worked.

When constructing their second ship, engineers from all three countries made minor modifications to the design, tweaks intended to improve performance or add useful features. Some of those changes included new computer software, as well as trifling physical changes to the control system and power train.

The results had been remarkable. In all three cases where the engineers faithfully copied the Starman design, the ships' engines not only functioned, but produced plenty of power, more than sufficient for a small scout ship. And in each case of the supposed enhancements, the power plants didn't even light up.

So much for tinkering with a proven concept. Clearly the Ancients knew a thing or two that Earth's engineers still hadn't figured out. Back to the drawing boards. Earth's engineers had several major enhancements they wanted to install, but for now they began working within the existing design parameters. While the power specialists studied the engines, teams started sketching out concepts. After a month of heated bickering in six languages, a compromise blueprint emerged and gradually achieved consensus.

Delano smiled and took a seat across from Welsh. "You've done a heck of a job, Bill. Lian and I appreciate it. And you think this thing will fly?"

"I know it will. You saw the last test flight figures?"

"Oh, yes. The one where you disobeyed orders and risked your ass riding along."

Welsh grinned. "Couldn't resist. It was a hoot. Like flying a Winnebago. I kept thinking we were about to roll over and just fall out of the sky."

More than six months had passed since the inception of the Planetary Defense Force, and at last a real operational test was ready to begin. About time. The Tarlons and Halkins had grown beyond impatience. They wanted to see results.

Two weeks ago, Delano watched as two prototypes arrived from Jiuquan, and a day later, another two were flown in from Russia. The Americans, despite their vaunted reputation in construction and engineering, needed another two days before their ships reached Camp Stillman.

Welsh's phone rang. He grunted into the speaker, muttered OK, and ended the call. "Ten minutes to lift off. Everything is on schedule. Now, let me go over the final specs with you."

To Delano's surprise, the layout looked remarkably like the old NASA Space Shuttle, retired in 2011. That craft had been designed in the 1970s, obsolete before it ever flew. It had resembled a prehistoric dinosaur that depended on booster rockets and enormous external fuel tanks. The new Jumper was a pure aircraft, but one with outer atmosphere capabilities. It was also quite a bit longer. Where the old shuttle measured a little over 120 feet in length, with a payload bay of 60 feet, the Jumper stretched nearly 150 feet from end to end, with a payload bay of 85 feet.

The payload bay length was design specific. The new Jumper could accommodate two standard 40 foot shipping containers, laid end-to-end.

When he first saw the specs, Delano couldn't believe what he was reading. Cargo containers that size had been in use for over seventy years. These new containers of course would not be made of the heavy steel used for transport on land and sea. Instead they would be constructed of lightweight #6069 aluminum alloy, which had been utilized in aircraft and aerospace for years. The freighters that made the Moon to Io run routinely transported eighty to a hundred such containers, each capable of holding twenty-five tons or more. Machine shops in China, working round the clock, could punch out these specialized containers at a rate of twelve a day.

Nor would any of the empty containers go to waste. They'd been designed to be disassembled and re-purposed for housing and storage beneath the lunar surface. Doomsday fanatics all over the planet had used similar shipping containers for air-tight underground bunkers for years. These new containers were standardized and manufactured with specialty parts that allowed them to be disassembled and reassembled into any construction project, for that matter. The massive development of sub-surface Moon facilities, already underway, would soon be dependent on their quick delivery.

"The really exciting part of the Jumpers are the engines," Welsh said. "Four engines at the rear provide more than enough lifting power, and a single reverse-thrust engine in the nose provides for an easy reentry. With that much power, the Jumper can take off like a big cargo aircraft, and climb slowly and safely to low earth orbit. No more rockets or boosters blasting away at top power and stressing the airframe! As long as the Jumper keeps accelerating, it will keep climbing. No need to rush the ascent phase."

Delano closed his eyes, remembering his first trip into space.

He'd figured the odds were fifty-fifty that the tiny rocket ship, powered by external boosters, would explode and turn him into molecules of dust.

Welsh couldn't keep the excitement out of his voice. "And for the return, the large wingspan allows the Jumper to glide easily through the atmosphere. The nose engine will provide more than enough braking power to allow a nice, steady glide back to Spaceport. No more flying backward, or worrying about heating or insulation problems."

That had been the design goal for the first generation of Space Shuttles, but the engineers had failed miserably. Extra power, Delano decided, solved a lot of problems in spacecraft design.

"Then the containers get unloaded in LEO?" Tired as he was, Delano could manage a smile.

"The Jumper's bay panels swing open, and a gentle puff of compressed air lifts each cargo container out of the payload bay. Or the freighter can use a crane, just like they did on Io. The space jockeys then move them to the freighters, and secure them, exactly as they do today when they load or unload an ore freighter. When they have a full complement, they light up the fusion engine and head for the Moon."

Delano studied the drawings. He hated to sound stupid, but he needed to know. "Could the Jumper make it to the Moon by itself?"

"Yes, I suppose," Welsh said. "But that's not what you wanted. To take the Jumper to the moon would require all kinds of design modifications and additions. More crew, more food, more supplies, more safety equipment. No, your original idea was the best. Just get the cargo containers into orbit as fast as possible, with everything reusable."

"What's the turn-around time?"

"If a Jumper takes off at 8 in the morning," Welsh said, "it can be back at Spaceport by six p.m. Then it can be serviced and ready for another flight the following day. But realistically, I expect a one to two day turnaround."

"That fast?" Delano was impressed.

"Yes. Just refuel the fusion pellets and oxygen and whatever else is essential, and you're good to go. The main reason for the quick turnaround time is the low acceleration, which means less wear and tear on the ship, its hull, or its pilot. We've also eliminated a lot of safety features. If something fails, the pilots just eject and hope for the best." He grinned. "For the first time, we have a spacecraft where power generation and acceleration are not the major issues."

Delano remembered the difficulty of building effective battleship in the first part of the last century. Speed, armor, firepower – pick any two.

"Will the engines hold up to multiple trips?" Delano tended to worry about things he didn't fully understand. "The engine design is that good, that stable?"

"Hell, yes. They had one running on a bench right here at Stillman for over fifty hours without a hitch or a hiccup." Welsh's excitement was catching. "For these Jumpers, the biggest stress is going to be the tires."

Delano hadn't understood that problem at first. An expert from Boeing had spent almost an hour with him, explaining the difficulties and technical issues with landing gear. Delano realized a lot of work had gone into correcting the problem. Since the fully loaded Jumper would require a long runway – needed to get the heavy vehicle up to airspeed – the tires had to withstand the load and heat for the time it took to get airborne. Landing would present no problem, with the extra-long runways, slower speed, and minimum weight.

For Jumpers used on the Moon, the gravity-well problems didn't exist. The wings could be detached, and the Jumper had plenty of power to climb into lunar orbit. The low gravity there would simplify landings and takeoffs. For lunar activity, the Jumper really would resemble a Winnebago.

Welsh's phone buzzed. He gave it a quick glance. "Jumper One is ready. Let's watch the show."

They stood and moved to the observation window. Jumper One was on the move, traveling slowly to the main runway. It turned onto the tarmac, then stopped beside the large crane. Engineers and ground crew checked to make sure both Jumper and crane were in position. In less than a minute, the crane began to lift a cargo container in the air.

Delano saw the crane operator take his hands off the controls and let the payload computer take over. The computer took its time. Five minutes passed until the first cargo container settled into its position in the open bay.

"For today, these containers are only half full, twelve tons of cargo each," Welsh offered. "We don't put them on the Jumper until it's ready to go. That keeps the stress off the tires as much as possible. No sense risking a full load on the first flight."

Some of the safety engineers wanted the first flight to fly empty, but Welsh had overruled them. Time, he reminded them, was of the essence. An empty flight would prove little, and if anything went wrong, they had two more shuttles ready.

The second container loaded almost as fast as the first. Delano saw the chief engineer give the signal. One at a time, the ponderous bay doors moved up to the vertical and then folded flat. That took another ten minutes, and the latches had to be checked.

Meanwhile, others in the ground crew checked the tires one final time. Then the last of the support team moved away. Delano scarcely noticed when the Jumper began to move, so slowly did the wheels begin to turn. Speed, he reminded himself, didn't matter here.

But gradually the Jumper picked up speed, accelerating until Delano and Welsh had to lean forward and to the side to follow the ship racing down the runway. It was almost out of sight before it lifted off the tarmac.

Welsh was staring at his phone, where an app tracked the Jumper's progress. "Two hundred ten miles an hour is liftoff speed."

The Jumper had traveled over a mile and a quarter before it reached that target and began to lift. Delano followed the craft until it disappeared in the sky.

He realized he'd been holding his breath. "That's impressive. How long until it reaches orbit?"

"The rendezvous point is optimized," Welsh said, "so it should be where it's supposed to be in just over two hours. A nice, slow ascent." He looked as proud as a new father.

"That's pretty good," Delano admitted.

"We planned this launch very carefully. Normally I'd expect a Jumper to get to low earth orbit and the rendezvous point in three to four hours. But there's no rush, and the pilot can take as long as he wants."

"What's next?"

"Now the hard part," Welsh said. "The freighter will use its crane to unload the containers. If all goes well, the pilot will return here in about six hours. If no hitches develop, Jumper Two will lift off tomorrow, this time with a full payload. If everything is still good, then we launch Jumpers Three and One the next day."

Delano knew the freighter waiting in low Earth orbit held its position and stood ready for cargo. The lunar construction team needed those containers and their contents as soon as possible. "Bill, you've done a great job. What's next?"

"If nothing goes wrong, I'll stay here for another ten days, until the program is deemed operational. Then it's back to Jiuquan. The first Dart is just about ready for testing, and I intend to fly one of those myself."

Delano had originally called these small, two-person fighters PT boats, but some test pilot started calling them Darts, probably because of the slender nose section that housed the rail gun. The name had stuck.

"Jeez, just don't get yourself killed," Delano said. "I want you in command of something a lot bigger than a . . . Dart."

Welsh nodded. "It's like anything else, Delano. If you plan to lead men into battle, you'd better have flown every type of aircraft, or in this case, space ship, before you give the first order. That way all the men under your command will believe in you, because they'll know you've flown what they're flying and know what it's like."

"OK, Bill, you're in charge. Get those Jumpers and containers up into orbit ASAP. We have a lot of construction to do on the Moon." *And not a lot of time.*

Chapter 25

278 BKA

West Virginia, USA

Another day, another two months had passed, and each of Delano's mornings, after his hour of PT, started with the usual hot black coffee and the printed list of the day's agenda. His staff, now numbering fifteen, prepared the same activity sheet every night, usually long after Delano and Lian had turned in. Not that he and Lian were spending much time together. The demands upon their time had simply grown too large, forcing them to work in separate locations.

Lian had already been in China for more than three weeks. The problems there had ballooned out of all proportion. Delano and General Klegg were keeping a lid on things in the United States, and President Demidov and Minister Borodin had imposed an iron grip on the Russian people and their new-found European allies. Even so, Delano had made two trips to Moscow and another to Berlin in the last six weeks, helping out when things became difficult there.

But the crisis in China, the world's largest country, remained acute. The terrible infrastructure destruction caused by the Ktarrans still lingered, and in some areas actually worsened. Diseases from the resulting poor sanitation and lack of fresh water had caused political unrest, a calamity that not even the Chinese Army could completely control. Two breakaway provinces had rebelled against central authority, requiring military force to end the nascent insurrections. Even the Jiuquan region needed the presence of heavily armed troops to protect the facility.

Civil instability also threatened the leadership of Lian's uncle. Two attempted coups had already weakened his power. One challenge had come from the Army itself. Lian had barely escaped an assassination attempt, and several threats to her life had already been neutralized. Meanwhile millions of Chinese, a number that Delano found staggering, demanded safe passage on the yet unconstructed Lifeboats. One political group insisted that nothing but escape ships be constructed, and that it was foolish to attempt to resist the Ktarrans. They believed safety lay only in fleeing the planet.

During all this, Delano could do little, except exhort the people of the world to support the PDF resistance effort. Europe, Africa, and South America all seethed with turmoil. Fortunately Russia set a hard example. Disturbances to its provincial regions were harshly repressed, and both China and the United States followed Russia's example.

While the planet roiled with discontent, Delano spent his days in meetings, hoping to get the defenses of Earth ready in time to withstand the Ktarrans. Not much satisfaction, but all that Delano could achieve.

Despite all the strife, the never-ending procession of daily meetings and briefings remained the same – Delano reviewing a list of the day's activities, agenda topics, and key attendees while he sat in his underwear drinking his first two cups of coffee. By now he'd grown numb to the interminable dreary sessions, each one a crisis of one kind or another that required resolution from the High Command of the PDF. His days were spent dealing with schedules, production problems, and partisan unrest. Worst of all were the almost daily decisions to punish people or sentence some to death for crimes against the PDF.

He knew that too much of this could send a man over the edge, a slip into insanity or blind rage. Delano had come close to losing it more than once, but thankfully each time Lian or the Gunny had been there to soothe his spirit and calm him down. Even General Klegg now felt sorry for Delano. He wondered what would happen if he lost it when Lian wasn't around, off on one of her frequent trips to Beijing.

Occasionally something actually useful appeared on the day's agenda. One of today's meetings appeared significant, a productive use of his time. And so at nine a.m. Delano, dressed in his new PDF uniform, strode briskly into the large conference chamber to attend a special planning session with a pretentious title – *Review and Signoff on Proposed Dart Capabilities and Mission Protocol*. By now Delano translated the formal language easily enough. The final design of the short-range space fighter, his original PT boat concept, would be presented to him and Lian for approval.

When Delano entered the conference room, he expected the

usual briefing – ten or so individuals sitting around the table, awaiting the leaders of the PDF to arrive. Right away he saw that today's meeting would be different. At least forty people, most of them men, crowded into the large conference room, everyone trying to get seated. About a third of those present were Chinese, with the remainder divided between Russian and American engineers, with a sprinkling of Japanese and Germans. The last seven or eight couldn't squeeze in at the table, so they'd pulled chairs as close as possible behind those already seated.

Lian, appearing tired and affected by the late hour in China, attended via the teleconference link established by Steve Macey.

Everyone continued talking and nobody seemed to care much about the arrival of the leader of the PDF, as if Delano were merely another distraction. He had to pull his chair out so that he could squeeze his body at the table.

He waited a full three minutes before the last discussion ended. At the far end of the table sat the chairman of today's meeting, Colonel Kosloff, with Colonel Mironov on one side, and Colonel Welsh on the other. Another Russian, a civilian, was hunched up right behind Kosloff. Clearing his throat, Kosloff rapped on the wood surface to bring the meeting to order.

"Doctor Duan, Colonel Delano," Kosloff began, "we are ready to present the initial design for the Dart two-seat fighter. Many issues remain to be resolved, but a preliminary build plan has been agreed upon." He glanced around the table, as if expecting one more challenge.

"Good morning, Colonel Kosloff, I'm glad to hear that," Delano said, before anyone could object. "Our thanks to all of you."

Kosloff nodded. "It has been a herculean effort, and an international one at that. Colonel Welsh provided much input from the Jumper program, and Colonel Mironov headed up the team of physicists. But I must stress the contribution of Chief Engineer Vano Mikoyan. He led the international team of fighter pilots, and provided a different approach to the final design. His efforts must be noted."

Delano studied the heavyset Russian just behind Kosloff, and wished he had allocated more time to study the briefing notes and attendee bios.

"Then we are grateful, Mr. Mikoyan," Lian said. As usual, she'd read the bios of all those present before every meeting.

"Your grandfather and great-grandfather would be proud."

Delano had glanced at the list of attendees, but hadn't picked up on that. Now he remembered. Arteem Mikoyan had developed the original MiG fighter, and his descendants had carried on his aircraft design traditions. Now that Delano's mind had been jostled, he remember the "Mi" in MiG stood for the name of one of the founders – Mikoyan.

"It has been an honor," Mikoyan replied, "to serve Russia and our planet."

"With his help, we have finished our preliminary design, which I can pass out for the first time today." Kosloff glanced at one of his assistants, who moved to the head of the table and gave a single sheet of paper to Delano, then passed out the rest of the sheets in bunches. "Thanks to Arteem Mikoyan, these ships will be as rugged and sturdy as all Russian weapons. They should even withstand a brief exposure to an alien beam weapon."

Delano stared at the image of the Dart space fighter (Design 1) on the page. The fighter was squat, ugly, and unimpressive on paper. It had short, stubby wings with pods attached at the outer end, and room for a crew of two sitting side-by-side. A long slender tube projected out from the nose.

"The Dart will be powered by three engines," Kosloff went on. "The primary thruster is at the rear, as in any normal aircraft design. This drive is essentially a copy of the Starman's Drive, its performance upgraded by at least twenty percent. We plan to incorporate our own computer controls. That effort is proceeding well. The two secondary engines are located at the outboard ends of the lateral booms, and each will generate about half the thrust of the main engine. An anti-matter engine will also be installed, but used only to generate the plasma screens."

Not really wings after all, Delano realized. But why on the wings, and not on the spacecraft's main thrust line?

"The two secondary thrusters are the idea of Chief Engineer Mikoyan," Kosloff said. "They will be attached by ball joints which will permit the engines to rotate 360 degrees and produce thrust in any position or direction. They will also accommodate up to 45 degrees of lateral rotation. With computer control synchronization of all three engines, the Dart should be able to maneuver much like a fighter aircraft even in the airless void of space."

"Assuming the software can be written." That comment came

from a glum-looking NASA engineer slumped a few chairs away from Delano.

"The software will be developed," Kosloff said firmly. "The initial design team of Chinese software engineers is already working on that. And remember, I was aboard the Space Station when the Halkins fought the first Ktarran cruiser. At the time, studying the readouts, we were amazed at the ability of the Halkin ships to change direction. We now know that the forces absorbed by those ships were quite severe. Our Dart should be faster and far more maneuverable than such larger vessels."

Colonel Welsh held up his hand, and got a nod from Kosloff.

"I want to add that I spent several days with Chief Engineer Mikoyan," Welsh said. "The types of maneuvers the Dart should be able to perform will greatly reduce our pilot training time. If the Dart can fly in space in much the same way as a fighter aircraft performs within the atmosphere, we will have a large pool of experienced aviators who will have a leg up on training. Of course, the sooner we get the men into the Darts, the more experience we'll obtain."

"Like all Alliance fighters, the Darts will rely on special software to fly," Kosloff went on. "Teams of software developers are already in place with more being assembled. If we had more time, it might be possible to operate the Darts remotely, but I doubt we can achieve that level of sophistication in the time we have left. Therefore human pilots and weapons specialists will be required. Pilot and spacecraft risk will be high, but we can manage for that."

Manage for that, Delano knew, meant accepting high casualty rates during testing.

"How will these ships be armed?" That was Delano's primary concern. He had no doubt the engineers could make the damn thing space-worthy. After all, they'd been handed a working engine on a platter. But it had to fight and deliver a powerful counterpunch to the Ktarrans, just like the PT boats he'd envisioned when they began to strategize about Earth's defense.

Welsh answered that one. "The primary weapon will be a beam weapon, the same design as the ones the Halkins and Tarlons use. That's in the turret behind the cockpit. Beneath the hull the Dart has a missile rack that can carry two tactical missiles, which can be a nuclear or conventional-shaped charge. The Dart will also be designed around a rail gun which will form the ship's primary axis. We think the Dart can carry about 100 copper-coated projectiles, each about 30 inches . . . 75 centimeters long and weighing 36 pounds or roughly sixteen kilograms. Given the length of the Dart's rail gun, the projectile should be able to achieve speeds of 2.4 kilometers per second (8,600 km/h), or about Mach 7, yielding 34-megajoules of kinetic energy at impact. We think we can handle that much recoil. That's more than enough power to punch through the Ktarran shields, and any hit on something solid should take one out of action."

Delano glanced at Lian on the screen. She appeared as impressed as he was. "Can you hit an enemy vessel with these . . . projectiles? Can't the Ktarrans just move out of their way?"

"I doubt if they'll even see them coming, they're so small and traveling so rapidly," Kosloff said. "And if the Ktarrans are moving about, their gunners will not be able to shoot as effectively. And if they're relatively stationary, our computer controlled beams should inflict plenty of damage."

"What about the recoil?" Lian asked. "Will that be a problem in space?"

That impressed Delano. He hadn't considered that recoil from the rail gun might be an issue in zero gravity.

"Yes, but with the proper software, we believe we can counter-thrust the main engine for each firing," Kosloff replied. "That way the recoil is negated by the engine. The effect on the ship and crew should be negligible."

OK, not understanding that, Delano decided, but he'd ask about it later. "Any other weapons?"

"No, but the missiles should provide a kill shot, if we can get them close enough. We're already working on several experimental coatings that should be stealthy and hardened enough to withstand a brief brush with the beam weapons. We'll also have a dozen or so decoys that should look just like the Dart to the Ktarran sensors. Taken together, the Dart should deliver a solid punch to their battleships, while retaining the ability to avoid Ktarran beam weapons. Of course the Darts' hull will be ruggedly constructed of the latest titanium alloys covered by a layer of tungsten carbide to withstand the heat of a beam weapon. Then everything is further coated with both stealth and energy reflecting materials."

"How effective will the missiles be?" Delano asked. "And why only two? I thought you'd want to cram as many onto each

Dart as possible." The room went silent, and he sensed he'd touched a nerve.

Kosloff glanced at Welsh, who cleared his throat.

"Colonel Delano," Welsh said, "in the last few months we've had many discussions regarding whether we should use nuclear missiles at all. During that time, our physicists and engineering teams have struggled with the inherent difficulties of using such weapons in space."

Delano didn't get it. "Why wouldn't we want to use nuclear weapons? We have hundreds and hundreds of such missiles throughout the Alliance."

"Yes, Colonel, that is true, but they are all designed for use against specific targets on the planet or in the atmosphere. In space they would be far less effective." Kosloff paused. He observed the blank look on Delano's face, and decided he'd better explain.

"On Earth, nuclear explosions produce their destructive effects in three ways," Kosloff said. "First, thermal energy, a heating of the air that has deadly effects. Second, there is the blast over-pressure effect, propagating energy through air or ground, depending on the detonation. The third effect, and the least destructive, is through the release of radiation. It's true that sufficient exposures kill living matter in hours or days. But in fact, the atmosphere attenuates the radiation rapidly within short distances."

"OK, why is that a problem?"

"Because in space, there is no air or material to increase the destructive effect of the explosion," Kosloff explained. "All the bomb material is destroyed, so the only deadly effect is from radiation, which unfortunately decreases its lethality according to the inverse square law."

Delano remembered the long and boring preliminary reports that he had skimmed. He'd skipped over one document labeled "nuclear weapons in space," figuring he knew enough about that topic. Obviously he had failed to grasp something basic. "Please tell me that you found a way to utilize them?"

"Yes, we did," Kosloff said. "We actually referenced work done in the 1950s. Your US Air Force researched what they call Project Orion, and also the Casaba Howitzer. The Soviet Union conducted similar studies. What we have done is develop a way to maximize the radiation effect, and direct most of it toward the target in a sixty degree cone."

Delano had never heard of either project. "I thought you said that radiation decreased rapidly with distance>"

"Yes, but we're modifying our nuclear mix to create maximum radiation. And by using a package case reinforced with beryllium oxide and backed by three centimeters of tungsten, we predict that we can increase the production of X-rays and neutrons by almost another sixty percent. That is enough to create a death zone almost a kilometer wide."

"Won't the Ktarran shields deflect the radiation?"

"Only to some extent," Kosloff said. "Their plasma screens are designed to stop beam radiation. Neutrons and X-rays can still get through."

"Then what will kill the crew? I thought it took hours or days to kill by radiation."

Kosloff smiled. "Ah, but we are not trying to kill the crew. We want to kill the ships, and these new warheads will do just that. The sudden increase in radiation will affect the matter and anti-matter chambers, creating instability which will cause the energy creation to fail. And by fail I mean explode."

Colonel Welsh cleared his throat. "We went over this with the Tarlon scientists. If we can detonate a specific type of nuclear missile within close enough range, they agreed that the ship's anti-matter drive will be overloaded, resulting in an catastrophic explosion.

Delano knew first hand what happened to anti-matter engines that overloaded. The explosive force exceeded a small nuclear explosion.

"If I get this right, enemy ships won't be destroyed by the missiles, but by their own anti-matter devices."

"Correct," Welsh said. "Naturally there are a lot of factors to consider. But any missile that can get within a kilometer or so should generate enough radiation to trigger the reaction."

"Sorry to be so ill-prepared, gentlemen," Delano said. "As long as you say it will work, that is good enough for me."

"Yes, the warheads will work," Kosloff said. "The theory predicts this, and we will begin testing live devices next week."

"OK, then, enough about missiles," Delano said. "Let's get back to the Darts. Will they be large enough to generate plasma screens strong enough to protect themselves?" One of the Chinese missile experts raised the question to Lian a few days earlier. "If they do not possess screens, they will be very vulnerable to Ktarran weapons."

Kosloff nodded. "Yes, of necessity they will possess screens for protection. Without a minimum level of plasma defense, they would be too fragile to risk combat with any Ktarran ship."

Delano had wondered about defensive screens as well, since the Darts wouldn't be using the antimatter generators for power. What he thought of as a force field was in reality a highly complex combination of separate plasma energy fields, each designed to protect against a particular type of radiation. The Ktarrans as well as their enemies utilized the same four types of screens, in the same combination. The outermost layer was a highly-charged plasma window, superheated to vaporize metals or small meteors.

This layer allowed the ships to travel at very high speed in normal space. Otherwise even a pebble or small rock might inflict a fatal collision. The Star Rider pilot's ship had encountered such a meteor, and it killed the Ancient pilot.

The second plasma screen consisted of many high energy laser beams, all bouncing off reflectors and crisscrossing many times to create a lattice of energy. Anything passing through the lattice was instantly heated to vapor and rendered harmless.

Those first two screens allowed light and other wavelengths of energy to pass through, so the third screen consisted of a single layer of tightly packed latticed atoms that were photochromatic. These atoms turned dark when struck by light or lasers or particle beams, and any incoming energy was dissipated.

Delano knew that during combat, power to the first and second screens could be reduced to minimal, and increased energy directed to the photochromatic layer. In anticipated fighting conditions, that third screen could withstand a Ktarran beam weapon for a second or two, depending on distance and power.

The fourth screen wasn't really an energy screen per se, but a physical lattice of single carbon atoms strong enough to resist anything that might penetrate through the first three layers. It also served as a means of strengthening the hull, allowing for the use of less material.

The whole topic of energy screens was relatively new to Earth's engineers. Delano remembered the difficulty he'd had trying to grasp the exotic concepts. Even some of Earth's finest physicists had blanched upon learning about the physics. But no one could argue with the fact that they worked, and that the enormous energy to power them could be obtained by scooping up anti-matter particles in space and using them to create almost limitless power.

The Halkins and Tarlons had provided the alien equivalent of blueprints on how to manufacture and integrate these energy systems. Without the effective use of plasma screens, there could be no possible defense against the Ktarrans.

Lian rose from her chair. "I must leave now to attend to another matter. Please carry on without me. Thank you all for your efforts. And remember that these small ships may be Earth's only line of defense if the Ktarrans get past Jupiter's gate. All our lives may depend on your work." She nodded to someone off camera, and the connection went dark.

Her words received the proper attention. This audience knew exactly what was at stake. Once again, Delano remembered Klegg's words – people are going to die.

Colonel Kosloff glanced around the table. "Are we ready to continue?"

Delano nodded. "Yes, let's resume. I'd like to know as much as possible about these weapons and defensive systems. Dr. Duan is correct. Without these Darts, we are not going to make it."

Chapter 26
250 BKA

Field Marshal Shuvalov woke with a start, the overhead light glaring into his eyes, bright enough to illuminate the entrance to hell. The buzzer was almost as bad, a jarring sound guaranteed to roust a man out of a drunken stupor. Without conscious thought, his hand went to the Makarov pistol that always rested on the bed beside his pillow. He heard the voice of his aide Demitri on the intercom, and knew it must have been he who triggered the crisis alarm.

Shuvalov silenced the buzzer by hitting it with the pistol's butt. "What is it?" His words sounded thick as he pushed his body upright. Advancing age prevented him from getting to his feet without first sitting upright.

"There's been an attack! A nuclear attack on Moscow!"

With a curse, Shuvalov hit another button on his nightstand that unlocked the door. The click of the mechanism opening sounded loud in the bedchamber. He reached out and turned out the overhead light even as his aide entered the room.

Dressed in pajamas, Demitri looked as disheveled as his superior. He waved a piece of paper in his hand. "A nuclear device has exploded outside Moscow."

Thank god for some good news, Shuvalov thought. At least it hadn't gone off in Red Square. Unless there were more than one. Plenty of time before daylight. He tossed the pistol onto the nightstand.

Shuvalov snatched up his robe from the foot of the bed and wrapped it around his body. He kept the room temperature at 16 degrees Celsius, to help him sleep. The down side of that practice meant when he needed to get up to pee, usually two or three times a night, he ended up struggling with the robe to keep from shivering. He hated the weaknesses that advancing age brought to his body.

"Read the message, Demitri."

"Yes sir. Right now the information is sketchy." He cleared his throat. "At 4:15 a.m. Moscow time, two men on a train from

Kaluga to Moscow were being questioned. The men, identified as being from Turkmenistan, had aroused the suspicions of the guards. Apparently the two panicked and attacked the security guards. One man broke away from the security officers and ran to his compartment. The other man had a gun, and managed to wound one of the guards. He was then shot and killed. Two minutes later, while the security people were trying to get into the men's compartment, a nuclear device exploded. The train was midway between Chekhov and Podolsk."

Shuvalov grunted. After all these years of peace, the dreaded nightmare had come true again.

"Chyort!" The simple curse couldn't convey a fraction of the anger Shuvalov felt. The train had been only forty or fifty kilometers from Moscow. He felt a moment of sorrow for the security police on the train, men and women who had done their jobs all too well and were now dead. They would probably be dead anyway, when the train reached Moscow. But he thanked the gods he no longer believed in for one thing – the always-live feed of current video and audio transmissions installed in every railcar on every train and station in Russia. Without that, no one would know what had happened.

Shuvalov took a deep breath. "I'll get dressed. Make sure the car is ready. We'll leave the dacha in fifteen minutes and return to Moscow. Contact President Demidov and Minister Borodin, to make sure they have received the news. Arrange for us to meet at Demidov's office. Oreshkin, too. I think we will definitely need his services."

The President and the other ministers should have received the same information, probably about the same time. They would all be heading for the Kremlin and Demidov's special conference room, located two hundred meters beneath the Kremlin. Meanwhile information would continue to flow in, but Shuvalov could monitor that from his government SUV.

"Yes, Field Marshal. Anything else?" Demitri couldn't keep the worry out of his voice.

"Yes. Contact the local police and find out all you can. I'll pull the response files from the office myself." His safe held contingency plans for any and every possible event, and contained several that might be applicable to this crisis. "Go, damn you. Go!"

*   *   *

President Demidov looked as haggard as his ministers. Like them, he'd been sleeping when the alarm sounded. The first data had come from the Russian satellite orbiting the motherland. It detected the nuclear double flash, pinpointed the location, and sounded the nationwide alarm of an attack. The mushroom cloud hadn't reached its peak before the staff in Minister Borodin's security services, located deep beneath Lubyanka Square, received the first data burst.

Minister Oreshkin arrived at the Kremlin a few moments after Shuvalov. Oreshkin must have been sleeping at his mistress's apartment, almost as far away as Shuvalov's dacha.

Demidov waited until Shuvalov took his seat, an aide bringing a glass of tea for the Field Marshal.

"Well," Demidov snapped. "What's the latest?"

That question, directed at Minister Borodin, made the man look up from his tablet. "A dirty bomb, lots of cesium," he said. "Not a fusion device. Low yield, initial estimate perhaps forty to fifty kilotons. Too big for a suitcase. Must have been loaded aboard with the baggage, with a remote detonator in the sleeping compartment. Wind is blowing to the southeast, away from Moscow."

The Hiroshima bomb only had the power of sixteen kilotons, and it destroyed a city. But at that time Japan had mostly flimsy housing. Structures in Russia were almost always sturdy, to deal with harsh winters. Still, progress in bomb making had improved the efficiency and destructiveness since then. Demidov felt sorry for those in the blast range or in the cloud's path. "How many dead?"

Oreshkin didn't look up from his tablet. "Low population at the site. Podolsk was closer to the blast. It has over two hundred thousand population. Perhaps thirty thousand dead from the blast. Maybe another twenty thousand from the fallout. More when the cesium enters the food chain or the dust is inhaled. Much depends on the wind patterns, and we won't know that for several hours."

"The two men on the train were from Turkmenistan," Borodin said. "Their papers, if legitimate, show them to be from the Kara Kala region. My men are already checking the facial recognition database against the names on the train. But probably those are the right names."

Travel, always restricted in Russia, had for years required DNA and fingerprint matching to the visual facial images. It had become very difficult to create false identity or travel papers.

"Kara Kala. How convenient," Demidov said. "Right across the border from Iran. I thought the Alliance had finished with those bastards."

Twenty years earlier, the Alliance of the United States, Russia, and China had seized all nuclear weapons and material from a dozen countries across the globe. Ruthless force – Shuvalov played a significant role in that process – had confiscated and collected thousands of pounds of nuclear material from Iran, India, Pakistan, North Korea, and South Africa. Facilities for the manufacture of weapons were destroyed, and the leaders of those countries warned not to start up such programs again.

The process had been ugly, but each of the three Alliance nations had been attacked, within a two-year period, by nuclear or dirty bombs. The Alliance decided to make certain such a thing could never happen again. Large rewards and guarantees of security were publicly offered for any information about attempts to use or conceal nuclear bombs or materials.

Iran had been the country that resisted the most, and Russia had dropped tactical nuclear devices on three sites known to have nuclear manufacturing capability. After that, and facing the combined might of the three Alliance countries, Iran grudgingly surrendered its weapons. But some of their scientists, mostly religious fanatics who believed in holy war against the infidels, had disappeared, and more than a few had crossed the mountains into Turkmenistan.

"Iran will claim to know nothing about this," Oreshkin said. "It may even be true."

Shuvalov snorted. "They know. They always know, especially if their own people are involved."

"I agree," Demidov said. "What should our response be? No, let me ask how harsh should our response be?"

"Kara Kala is where they boarded the train, no doubt with the best wishes of their friends," Borodin said. "So that city, and at least three more closest to the border."

"And Iran?" Shuvalov's voice showed no concern for Turkmenistan cities, though destroying four of them would devastate the nation. If the bomb had exploded within Moscow, the death toll would have been five or six times as high, and might even have crippled the government for critical months. More important, the PDF schedules and production levels might have been irreparably damaged. The entire effort to withstand the Ktarrans might have been compromised.

"The three largest cities closest to the border," Borodin said. "And we warn their leaders that if there is another incident, the next four bombs will be on Teheran, Karaj, Bakhtaran, and Qom."

Demidov nodded. "That should encourage the leaders in both countries to do a better job discovering such plots in the future."

"Do we need to speak with the Alliance?" Oreshkin asked.

"No, they will concur," Demidov said. "I will call them and let them know what we are doing. They may need to step up their own security efforts."

"What about Delano?" Oreshkin glanced at Shuvalov. "Everyone knows Americans are squeamish about such things."

Shuvalov had worked more closely with Colonel Delano than anyone in the Alliance. "If the bomb had gone off in Red Square," Shuvalov said, "the impact to the PDF would have been considerable. He may not like it, but he will understand."

"I agree," Demidov said. "Then all that needs to be done is for Marshal Shuvalov and Minister Oreshkin to set the launch codes for the missile attack. After the message is delivered, the Alliance will contact the governments in Turkmenistan and Iran. They can explain to their citizens the loss of life, and the amounts of currency that will be paid in restitution. If they complain, I'll tell them the compensation will be doubled."

"After this," Demidov continued, "we should have no more trouble from hotheads against the Alliance. The fools should have known better." He took a breath. "Then we are all in agreement with the response?"

Heads nodded.

Less than two hours after the detonation, the Russian response had been determined, and in the next hour, seven cities in two countries would be destroyed. Over a million people, most of whom knew nothing about the plot, would die. But the fifty thousand Russians had been innocent, too, and most of them were working for the PDF's goal of saving the planet.

An attack on Mother Russia could not be tolerated. No country, no terrorist group, nothing could be permitted to interrupt the PDF or harm the Russian people.

Chapter 27
240 BKA

Delano studied the simplified blueprints on the table. Day after day, meeting after meeting, decision after decision. He found it harder and harder to concentrate as the weeks merged into months. The defense of Earth rested on his shoulders, and they were starting to sag under the responsibility.

The last two weeks had been the worst of all. The attack on Moscow and the massive retaliation by Russia had shaken the world. Horrified people across the globe had condemned the brutal and swift Russian counterattack. Privately, Delano reacted in much the same manner, but then he considered the consequences.

If the bomb had not been discovered, the detonation would have been at noon in central Moscow. It might easily have killed President Demidov and his advisors. Indeed, they must have been the primary targets. More important, Moscow was the PDF's headquarters for planning and production in Europe. Irreplaceable valuable men and women, as well as data and production capabilities, would have been lost.

That might have jeopardized the entire Ktarran defense. So Delano said nothing, letting Demidov and Borodin be the public face of the Russian response to the terrorist attack. Threats to the PDF could not be tolerated. As General Klegg had so succinctly pointed out, people were going to die.

Soon enough, however, blame for the destruction fell upon the PDF. Since Delano had worked so closely with the Russians, Earth's disaffected millions pointed their fingers at him. As the cries against the PDF rose, Delano had been forced to speak out, warning the people of the world that the PDF would act resolutely to any threats to its existence or policies.

In the beginning he'd been little more than a figurehead, a symbol of Earth's hope for survival. The Alliance powers, each for their own purpose, had given him and Dr. Duan "authority" for the defense of Earth. But somewhere over the last six months, the symbolic authority had evolved into something real, metamorphizing into actual power.

Part of the change evolved from the non-Alliance nations. Without a seat at the big table, the countries of the world had gradually placed first their trust, then their support into Delano and Lian's Planetary Defense Force. The Russian "incident" threatened to change all that.

Of necessity, the PDF ignored the clamor, just or unjust, against its rule. The work of defending the planet continued. The very people complaining against Delano needed to be protected in spite of themselves.

Today brought another milestone to Earth's defense. The Destroyer Class ship awaited his approval. If he accepted the designers' proposal, millions of men and women throughout the world would begin constructing the primary weapon for Earth's defense. Once started down this road, there would be no turning back. Vast construction projects, many already under way, would commence or move to full production. No time or resources would remain for new ideas. Once approved, the Destroyer would represent the primary weapon against the Ktarrans.

Though the ship might be much larger than the Dart, the staff presenting the design today was small, only Colonel Kosloff, Dr. Mironov, and Colonel Welsh. Attending via teleconferencing was General Jang of China, and General Klegg of the US.

"It's basically a stripped-down version of the Tarlon ship," Kosloff began. "About a third smaller, since it won't need to carry the supplies and equipment necessary for wormhole travel, extended voyages, or cargo transport. Or crew comfort, for that matter. A two deck design, with the lower deck for propulsion, equipment, life support and storage. The main deck for crew quarters, command and control, and weapons. Crew size should be 10 to 12."

Delano lifted his eyes. "That small a crew?"

"Yes, that should be enough. Remember, the fewer crewmembers, the less life support and supplies needed. We're talking bare necessities – no fancy sleeping racks, food, quarters, esthetics, or comforts. We can get by with a small crew because we're overlaying computer controls for many of the functions that Tarlons and Ktarrans use people . . . I mean, their own kind. So we're figuring three engineers for propulsion and weapons, three for weapons control systems, two pilots, one comm and computer specialist, and one electronics specialist. That's ten, so we have capability for two more specialties if we need them. Plus the four crew for the Darts. It's going to be as cramped as a German U-Boat from World War II."

Delano knew the German submarine designers had no resources to waste on amenities for the crew, since they were all expected to be sunk after two or three missions. "Only three beam weapons?"

"Correct, we didn't want to modify the basic configuration, one that we know works. In fact, we should even have a bit more firepower than the Tarlons, since we'll be able to direct more power to the weapons. Plus we've added a missile launcher rack that can hold four tactical nuclear missiles. One Destroyer won't be able to slug it out with a Ktarran battleship, but two or three should be able to hold their own. And if they get help from a few Darts we should be evenly matched."

"No rail gun?"

Kosloff shook his head. "No, too much recoil for the design, and it would slow the Destroyer's speed and maneuverability. We want to keep the Destroyers moving, agile. It's just beams and missiles."

"At any rate, that's the game plan, Colonel Delano," General Klegg said. "We're figuring two Darts to accompany every Destroyer."

"How many Destroyers do you think we'll have ready when they return?" No need to say who "they" were.

"Destroyers? Well, we're hoping to have a hundred or more constructed and in operation by then. The choke point for production is the installation and testing of the software systems."

Delano already knew the estimates for the Darts – three hundred. But Darts also represented the final line of defense around Earth and the Moon. If the Ktarrans got past Jupiter's orbit, they could be striking Earth within hours. "So it's Darts and Destroyers for planetary defense."

"Yes, that's about it," Klegg said. "But hopefully we'll have some drones as well. They'll be used for reconnaissance and as decoys. They will mimic the signature of a Destroyer. Hopefully they'll attract attention from the Ktarrans."

"If more than a few Ktarran battleships reach Earth orbit," Delano said, "we're going to be in trouble."

"Look, the only thing that will save us are the computers," Colonel Welsh said. "We need hardware and software to fly the Destroyers and the Darts, and to direct the weapons. For the drones and rail gun platforms, we'll need self-flying birds that can react far faster than any human, or alien, for that matter."

"The hardware we have is more than adequate," General Jang said. He'd flown in specifically to attend this conference. "Our engineers have created the basic platforms. Chips for the software are coming from the United States, and the Russians are building the housing boxes. Everything must operate flawlessly under violent acceleration and decelerations. Shielding must be adequate to resist all types of radiation and physical shock. It will be close, but I believe the computers will be ready."

"At least we will not have to include code to resist hacks," Colonel Kosloff said. "That should reduce the coding effort by a third."

Everyone smiled at the feeble joke. For once the Alliance powers wouldn't be trying to purloin plans from each other, and the rest of the nations wouldn't bother to steal something they couldn't use. For more than forty years, military software had to be hack-proof and jam-proof. Eliminating those concerns would greatly simplify the programmers' task.

The coding effort would be enormous, but the finest military software developers in the world were already huddled together. The software teams were in St. Petersburg, Austin, Texas, and Shenzhen. Engineers from India, Israel, Japan, and many other places had already dispatched their top developers to one of the three sites.

Every line of code would be checked and rechecked by a dozen different teams, all eager to find any flaw in the software. If the systems crashed under stress, the defense of the planet might fail. Russians had taken the lead in the hardening process. Since they'd always produced smaller numbers of aircraft and weapons than the other Alliance members, they made sure their designs could resist as much physical stress as possible.

Delano remembered stories of MiG jet fighters belly-landing on runways, and not only surviving but ready to fly again the next day. That was exactly what Delano wanted from every piece of hardware and software delivered to the PDF. Rugged and reliable.

"So all of you are in agreement with these designs?" Delano let his gaze travel around the table. Everyone looked tired, and he knew how much effort had gone into this brief presentation.

"Yes, Colonel, we are," Welsh answered. "These Destroyers will get the job done. Losses will be heavy, but the birds will fly and they'll fight."

The others nodded agreement.

"Then let's get started," Delano said. "We're still behind schedule for the lunar assembly and construction facilities. It won't matter how many components we build if we can't assemble and test them on the Moon."

Chapter 28

169 BKA

Lian took her seat at the head of the conference table. Her PDF uniform enhanced her figure, and the somber colors lent authority to her persona. Beneath the open jacket, the well-worn brown leather holster attached to her belt held her personal Glock. The green and white globe emblem on her shoulders announced her rank in the PDF – Full Colonel, the highest rank. Only Delano wore the same emblem.

Her already short hair emphasized the military look. In the last few months the aura of command had touched both her appearance and her words. Especially in China, Lian had taken the reins of power more fully and forcefully than anyone expected, and she had not hesitated to use force against those who opposed her. But by now the people of her nation had grudgingly come to trust and respect her. Dr. Duan Lian looked, acted, and spoke as a leader, a leader concerned only with the safety of her country and her planet.

Lieutenant Shen took his position behind Lian. As her bodyguard and assistant, Shen attended all meetings and rarely left her side. He, too, wore a brown holster, though his contained a larger version of Lian's pistol. Not that he would need the weapon. As a Tiger soldier, Shen had reached the pinnacle as one of the Chinese Army's most dangerous fighters in hand-to-hand combat.

As co-leader of the PDF, Lian had attended many such meetings in the last few months, both with Delano at her side and without. However this meeting would be something quite different. She and Delano had decided that the establishment of a Defense Grid required special, almost full-time attention. The concept had not been included in their initial planetary defense plans, but it soon became clear that not enough fighting ships could be built or quality crews trained. So the need for a backup system to protect Earth became apparent. After the PDF leaders perceived that China would be the best country to lead in any defense grid construction, Lian had accepted responsibility.

Preliminary sessions had identified twenty key military and

scientific fields needed to launch the project. Propulsion, stealth, energy screens, computer systems, and many more now needed to be combined into a single weapon system. The project would construct a grid of automated satellites placed in orbit around the planet – mankind's last best hope to defend the Earth.

To initiate the project, the newly constituted team had journeyed to Beijing. Most of the members were Chinese, plus three Russians and three Americans.

"Good morning, everyone," Lian began, speaking in Chinese. "As you may know, Colonel Delano and I are already working with those teams who will build the fighting ships necessary to defend Earth. But General Zeng and others in the PDF have decided that we will also need a Planetary Defense Grid to provide the final line of protection for the planet. Today we, all of us in this room, will begin that effort. This team will design, build, and test the most complex automated weapons system since the Manhattan Project created the world's first atomic bomb. General Zeng and I will lead this effort." She nodded respectfully to Zeng.

The general, regarded as the second most powerful man in China, after Lian's uncle, bowed politely. Zeng was China's most senior contact with the PDF, and the entire might of China's armed services obeyed his commands.

"We have discussed the need for such a defense grid," Lian continued, "and have already drafted some preliminary designs. We expect the grid to be completely automated and controlled from three stations that will be constructed deep underground. The design envisions several anti-matter powered platforms each capable of carrying ten tactical nuclear missiles. If possible we would like to incorporate a rail gun as well, should the missiles be depleted."

She paused long enough to invite the first question. A Chinese missile specialist from the Peoples Liberation Army Rocket Force, Colonel Wang, spoke first.

"Colonel Duan, General Zeng, how many of these . . . platforms will be needed?"

The question wasn't an idle one. The available supply of nuclear tipped missiles had dropped, and inventory within the Alliance, already committed to arming the Destroyers and Darts, was rapidly becoming depleted. A major effort across the globe had developed to speed up the processing of more nuclear material. Unfortunately, creating nuclear fuel and turning it into weapons grade material required months of painstaking labor.

Zeng answered the question. "We believe that eight stations orbiting the planet in a low-to-medium orbit should be sufficient to ring the planet with a missile shield, Colonel Wang. That will give us eighty missiles ready to deploy. If more are needed, and we have the time and material, then we will build more."

A Russian general cleared his throat. "General Zeng, I understand that these platforms are to be built primarily in China. Are there any reasons for that decision?"

"Yes, there are," Lian said. "China still has a surplus of nuclear warhead and extensive missile construction capabilities, more than Russia or the United States possess. Therefore most of the physical assembly will be done here. In fact, twenty-five years ago, China initiated some preliminary designs for an orbiting missile platform. That project was shelved when the Alliance took shape. Some of that material may prove useful now."

The senior American officer raised his hand, and received Lian's acknowledgement.

"The United States also has some plans from the same time period regarding orbiting killer satellites. I'll have them brought over."

"Thank you," Lian said. "We will need every bit of help to implement an effective and reliable defense system. If specialty items are needed, our Russian and US team members will make those arrangements. Everyone in this room will devote their full time to this project. Of course complete cooperation with our Alliance team members will be mandatory. I hope no further examples will be required for that understanding."

Six weeks earlier Lian had ordered the death sentence for three engineers who had dragged their heels and given incorrect information to the PDF. Delano and she had agreed upon that policy almost as soon as they took command of the planet's resources. Total and open cooperation would be ruthlessly enforced, lest some might be tempted to advance an individual nation's interest over their Alliance partners.

"General Zeng and I have developed the initial list of technologies that will be required. Each of you in this room will take charge of one area of the weapon system. He and I will manage your efforts, and should anyone fall behind their schedule, they will be replaced."

The word "replaced" as Lian spoke it, could mean much more than a simple demotion or removal from the project. It could also be interpreted as being assigned to a "reeducation center," not a pleasant future.

"Here is our preliminary list of project tasks," Lian went on. "She touched a button on her tablet, and the following list appeared on the wall display screen:

1. Computer automation
2. Stealth
3. Missile collection and design
4. Missile control (target acquisition)
5. Missile modification
6. Missile launch
7. Rail gun design, installation, and targeting
8. Power generation
9. Energy screens
10. Supplies
11. Personnel staffing
12. Structural integrity (hardening)
13. Remote operation
14. Environmental control
15. Testing
16. Assembly
17. Decoy drones
18. Transportation
19. Logistics
20. Daily project management

She gave everyone time to read the list. "We have all the resources of the Alliance and the rest of the nations to draw upon. One item you may not be familiar with is Number 3. This refers to the search and collection of nuclear material. The Alliance's supply of fissionable material is running low. Destroyers and Darts will need at least 300 tactical nuclear missiles, and the Defense Grid will require another 80. That demand may possibly exhaust the planet's total supply of nuclear material."

Lian noted that several of her audience didn't quite understand the problem. "So Item Number three will refer to the collection and possible re-manufacturing of warhead mass, so that we can attain our goal of 80 missiles. I expect it will be quite a challenge. I will be lending my assistance to that effort as much as I can."

She saw heads nod in agreement. They all understood what was at stake.

"This project begins today." Lian glanced around the table. "Your past records of accomplishment means that most of the sub-projects are already familiar. Some of you may have to learn new skills as we proceed. Under normal conditions, it might take five years to build such a defense grid. We have less than six months to create a fully operational system to protect Earth."

"I know you have many questions." She turned to General Zeng. "Now it's time to begin."

He nodded agreement. "Yes, before it is too late."

Chapter 29

131 BKA

Delano took his seat in the small conference room next to his office. Waiting were Mark Tilman and Jim Bedford, along with General Klegg. Gunny Stecker followed the leader of the PDF, and took a seat against the far wall, where he could watch both the door and those in attendance. By now the Gunny had become practically invisible, and most people who saw Delano on a regular basis scarcely noticed him. Two PDF sergeants, both former Marines and friends of the Gunny, stood guard outside the room.

"Sorry I'm late," Delano apologized. He hated to keep people waiting, but a chance to talk to Lian didn't happen often enough. Sometimes days would pass without an opportunity for them to speak. For the last six months, she'd kept him sane by reminding him that the entire effort was coming to an end. *One way or another*, he always thought, but never said the words. Lian would have the same doubts.

"Understand," General Klegg said

Delano detected the hint of annoyance beneath the word. Fortunately, those types of hostility or condescension no longer affected him. Early on, a few politicians and military types had tried to push Delano around. That had turned into a career ender for an American senator. A Russian army general also got a little too aggressive, and was now in charge of a training camp in Siberia.

Word spread. Anyone trying to lean on Delano quickly found himself or herself out of the loop. For some reason, Lian didn't have as much of a problem with such things. Her uncle's status kept the naysayers off her back.

One lesson Delano learned as a Marine had proved especially helpful – never let anyone forget the chain of command. Another of his drill instructor's rules came to mind: if you've got the power and want to keep it, you've got to use it.

Still, Klegg had turned out to be a decent enough guy, working as hard and for the same goals. Mark Tilman and Jim Bedford fit into that category. In fact, Bedford had done wonders setting up inspection protocols for every single part of each and every ship and weapon manufactured for the PDF. Triple checks by Alliance teams at every step verified the manufacturing and delivery process.

Delano liked both men, and they'd done great work on a task that Hercules would have stepped away from. But as top-echelon business men, they were not accustomed to sitting around waiting.

After a brief greeting to the two men, everyone got right down to business. The Silicon Valley crowd of mega-millionaires, Tilman had warned him, and tree huggers were making trouble. Klegg had called the meeting to discuss the emergency.

"You've reviewed the briefing paper?" Jim Bedford's soft voice asked the question.

"Yes." Delano had not liked what he'd read. The paper had no suggestions for resolving the problem, always a bad sign. "Anything changed since yesterday?"

"Only that they've increased their resistance," Tilman said. "They want even more concessions. They know we have to have the hardware and software, and they're insisting on more control. They don't like the long hours, and they want more money. Hell, they don't like anything about this, especially taking orders from me or Jim. They didn't say it in so many words, but the scenario they presented is nothing more than an unofficial slowdown. If we don't accept their terms, what should take a week will take a month, and so on."

"What they really want is an end to the War Powers Act and a return to business as usual," Bedford added.

"Now? With the Ktarrans only a few months away?" *How stupid do they think I am*? Delano drummed his fingers on the polished walnut table. "And you want me to tell you how to handle the situation? Is that what I'm hearing? Isn't this an internal production problem?"

That last went to Klegg, who looked uncomfortable. "The trio running the show are the three richest men in the States. Each has a security force of at least a hundred well-equipped, professionally-trained staff. Hell, Tom Jackson's headquarters is already like a fortress, with hardened entry points and deep bomb shelters. Since the Ktarran attack, he's added even more physical and staff security. He pays them serious money and they follow orders."

Tom Jackson was CEO and majority stockholder in

WideVistas, the successor to Facebook and Google. The company was less than ten years old and already the biggest enterprise in world-wide social media and advertising.

"Plus they're major players in the news," Tilman added, "and they control a lot of the social reporting and blogs. The unspoken threat is to hit us in the media, which they've gotten very good at manipulating." He took a breath. "We can't just push them around like some union thugs."

"What do you suggest, Mark?" Delano's voice had softened, his usual prelude to an outburst. "Any ideas? Comments?"

"If the slowdown continues, we'll miss our target dates," Tilman said. "And there's not much time left to make it up."

"I don't think we can use force," Bedford joined in. "They're prepared for that, and the pics will be all over the vids in three minutes."

Delano sent his eyes back to Klegg.

"It would be bloody," the general agreed. "We'd have to be prepared for a major outcry against the War Powers Act and the PDF. Half the population already hates us."

And the other half doesn't like us very much. Delano knew the same situations existed in China and Europe. In fact, less than two months ago China had put down a bloody uprising in Quinghai province. When the PDF instituted the WPA, the US population had mostly accepted the draconian new order, but sentiment had shifted so much that the resistance in the US now exceeded that in the rest of the Alliance. A slight majority of people still gave Delano the benefit of the doubt, but if the Ktarrans didn't show up on schedule, his head would be on the chopping block.

"If we go soft," Bedford said, "our counterparts in China and Russia will not be happy."

"Maybe we could offer Jackson and the others more seats on the colony ships," Tilman suggested. "There must be something we can give them."

"That's it? That's all you've go?"

No one spoke. Delano sat quietly for a moment, staring at the table. "Gunny, where's the closest Marine battalion?"

Everyone's eyes went wide.

"There's a battalion at San Diego," Gunny Stecker said, "still trying to regroup. Probably not ready yet for serious action. But there are two first-class battalions at Camp Lejeune. One of them is always on 24 hour standby."

Tilman looked confused. "What's a battalion? I mean, how many men are we talking about?"

Gunny glanced at Delano, who nodded. "The 1st Battalion, 2nd Marines is a reinforced infantry force," Gunny said, "with about 800 men and a big selection of specialized equipment, tanks, artillery, and fighting vehicles. The 2nd Battalion is a Raider force, smaller, about 350 men, mostly light infantry."

The hammer or the knife. "Which would you advise, Gunny?"

Gunny Stecker didn't take long to decide. "The Raider force should be more than enough, if they have the right air support. Besides, Jackson will be keeping his eye on forces in California, National Guard and such. He may not expect troops from back east."

"You're not thinking of sending in the military," Klegg said. "My god, using the PDF against hotheaded individuals and radical groups is bad enough, but if you send in regular troops into Silicon Valley, there will be riots in the streets. I won't authorize it."

Delano ignored Klegg's protest. "Here's what I want. I intend to use overwhelming force, so that no other idiots get the same idea. Jackson and the other two ringleaders are to be arrested for crimes against the PDF. Let's start with Jackson. He's probably the one calling the shots. We'll mobilize the Raiders, keep the other battalion on standby, and the Air Force will provide air support and transport. If Jackson doesn't surrender fifteen minutes after the Marines arrive, I want his headquarters building destroyed. Then we'll do the same to every other building in that complex, one by one, until there's nothing left. After he and the others surrender, the PDF will confiscate 90% of each man's wealth."

"I won't order it," Klegg said.

"Fine. But I remember you told me that people were going to die when we started this. Now you're afraid of getting your hands dirty." Delano touched his tablet. "Steve, get in here."

"Steve will set up a call to General Zeng and Marshal Shuvalov." Delano pointed to the communication gear at the rear of the room. "You can tell them you won't authorize use of military forces to stop a slowdown for critical components, equipment that we promised to deliver and that they need. Let's hear what they have to say about that."

The Chinese had put down two full-scale rebellions and several smaller resistance movements. The Russians had crushed a revolt in Chechnya that involved the use of two army divisions totaling over eight thousand soldiers. In that one, total casualties on both sides exceeded thirty thousand.

The door opened and PDF Lieutenant Steve Macey sauntered in. No matter what uniform he wore, he never quite succeeded in looking military.

"Slowdowns," Delano said, addressing General Klegg, "will not be tolerated. Nor will sabotage. Is this a real problem, Tilman?"

Tilman looked uneasy, but he took a breath and met Delano's gaze. "Yeah, it's real. We're already a week behind schedule and still slipping."

That information hadn't been in the briefing memo. Delano turned to Bedford. "Real or not?

"It's real." Bedford looked as shocked as his boss. "I've already received a half dozen texts and two calls from my counterparts overseas."

"Steve, set up a call to Zeng and Shuvalov."

Steve glanced at his tablet. "It's after one in the morning in Beijing."

"Do it." Delano didn't care. Both men would take his call at any time, day or night.

"I don't like threats, Delano." Klegg glared at Steve as he went to the end of the room. "You're talking about killing hundreds of Americans."

Delano's eyes narrowed. "We all knew when this started that situations like this would arise, and that force would be needed. Suppose this slowdown causes us to produce a few less Destroyers or Darts, and because of that we lose the planet? To prevent that, I'm willing to kill anyone who gets in the way of the PDF."

"Even if they're innocent," Klegg said. "You've turned into a cold bastard."

"Maybe," Delano said. "You may be willing to take that chance but I'm not. If we let this bad behavior spread, billions may die."

"Find another way," Klegg said.

"The minute we start negotiating with these idiots, the PDF is finished. So if you won't give the orders, then you're out. I'll explain the situation to Shuvalov. He's got two Destroyer prototypes training in lunar orbit right now. They can be overhead in hours and their beam weapons will fix the problem."

"You'd use beam weapons on our own people? That isn't going to help our delivery dates."

"It'll be messy," Delano said, "but there's no time to waste. This kind of opposition is like cancer. Once it gets going, it's quick to spread and hard to stop. Call Dr. Spencer and tell her you've resigned. She'll take it from there. I'll ask for the Commandant of the Marines to take your place. And you won't need your seats on the colonizer."

Delano knew that Klegg had already booked four of his family members on a colonizer.

"Ready in two minutes," Steve called out. "Their aides are coming online now."

"Stop the call, goddamnit!" Klegg bellowed the words at Steve.

"Hold up, Steve." Delano didn't raise his voice, but directed his words to General Klegg "You'll take care of this? Arrest the three ringleaders, using whatever force necessary?"

"Yes, damn you," Klegg said.

"Good. Gunny, how fast can the Raider battalion mobilize and get to Silicon Valley?"

"The Raiders are always ready to go, Colonel," Gunny said. "No one is allowed to be more than fifty miles from the camp. Say twelve hours to mobilize, and four to get everyone to California. Will they provide their own air cover?"

"No, the Air Force can handle that," Delano said, glancing at Klegg. "Full air support?"

"When this is over, Delano, I'm going to beat the crap out of you." Klegg's tone would have scared most men.

Delano shrugged. "You'll have to get in line, General Klegg. Now hear this. Nobody outside this room is to talk about this. I'm sure Jackson will learn about the mobilization sooner or later, but I want to postpone that as long as possible. Except for the COs, don't tell the Marines anything."

Delano turned to Bedford. "Jim, wait two hours and then handle the communications with Jackson. Call them every three or four hours. Talk tough, threaten them with arrest, confiscation of property, whatever you can think of. Tell them if they don't cooperate, then too bad for them. Let them think we're bluffing. Can you handle that?"

"Can do, Colonel. It's what I've been saying so far. I'll just up the volume a little."

"General Klegg, I want this to land on them like the hammer of hell." Delano's voice was hard. "No more Mister Nice Guy because they're rich and famous. Don't forget that we've plenty of regular people busting their asses to help defend the planet. Do you understand?"

"Yes, Sir," Klegg said, his voice barely under control.

Delano ignored that. "Get satellites overhead, and start tracking their aircraft, vehicles, anything. I don't want Jackson and the others to slip away to some off-shore hideaway and make us waste time tracking them down."

"Yes, sir," Klegg repeated, biting off the words.

"Give Steve the names of the Marine commanders as soon as you have them. Meanwhile Gunny and I will go over some ideas we kicked around before, in case this situation ever came up. And I want to speak to the commanders in one hour, but kick off the mobilization right now. Any questions, gentlemen?"

No doubt they all had plenty, but no one said a word.

"Thank you," Delano said, rising to signal the end of the meeting. "See you then."

Chapter 30
129 BKA

Marine General Chester M. Pollock strode briskly down the steps of the Air Force Gulfstream executive transport, wearing combat fatigues and smoking a thick black cigar. He'd flown into Castle Air Force Base with less than an hour's notice to the local base commander. Nevertheless, the mystified CO had followed orders and arranged for the three large electric SUVs, now waiting only a few steps from the plane's stairway.

Pollock didn't look like the typical Marine Corps general. Tall and thin, he had a long, narrow face that always seemed ready to burst out into a big grin. In fact, he tended to laugh more than most of his somber counterparts. Out of uniform, his cheerful blue eyes added to the image of a successful car salesman or prosperous advertising agent. People had underestimated him all his life, including his enemies on the battlefields of Yemen and Afghanistan, to their later sorrow.

His entourage was small, only two aides and six security SFs to drive the vehicles, two SFs for each SUV. Pollock climbed into the lead SUV with his aides and guards, just as the first of the air transport aircraft, the latest in the Globemaster series, touched down on Castle's main runway. Six more transports would be landing at three-minute intervals. A thirteenth had been grounded due to mechanical trouble, but that didn't matter, since Pollock had more than enough transport to take care of business. Sufficient force, in fact, to topple any Central American country.

Settling into his seat within the SUV, Pollock pulled out his phone. The general who commanded Castle AFB was still in shock at the urgency and surprise arrival of the incoming aircraft. He'd been pulled off the golf course early this morning and ordered to report to the base, keep his mouth shut, and follow all orders from General Pollock or his men, at once and without question.

"Here come the trucks," Pollock's aide said, pointing to the line of six large freight haulers that had just cleared the main gate and driven directly to the main runway. They would transport all the Marine Raiders to the target, except for those in the fighting vehicles. "Right on schedule, General."

General Pollock grunted at the news and took a deep drag on the cigar. Normally he didn't inhale, but the excitement of getting into action had pumped up his adrenaline and he needed something to take his mind off the operation.

Privately briefed by Colonel Delano and General Klegg 12 hours ago, Pollock figured out soon enough why Delano chose him to lead the mission. Pollock's parents had lived with his wife in Camp Pendleton, and all three had died in the Ktarran attack. Delano had asked Pollock if he wanted payback.

"Damn right I do," Pollock answered.

"OK, you'll get it," Delano said. "But first you've got to take care of a problem we're having. You're temporarily transferred to the PDF and you're being placed in command of the 2nd Raider Battalion, 2nd Marines."

Pollock hadn't stopped smiling since getting the assignment. He leaned back in the comfortable seat and began making calls to his subordinates still aboard the Globemasters, the first of which had just touched down. The calls completed, he relaxed and watched a Sikorsky X-4 Raider combat helicopter being off-loaded from the first Globemaster. Each of the big aircraft could carry three X-4s, but the Battalion S-4 preferred to load only two, but with the crew and ample ordnance for each helo. Four more Globemasters, each carrying eighty-plus men and one armored fighting vehicle would be landing soon. The last big cargo carrier would provide the rear support and coordination needed.

Pollock had decided he didn't need anything heavier. If he had to use tanks to blast his way in, he'd already be in trouble. Besides, the twin-rotor X-4s carried plenty of missiles. Fast, agile, and with a low acoustic signature and minimum vibration, the helos could be in and out before most militaries could get a bead on them. The latest iteration of the Armored Fighting Vehicle came in many variations, but Pollock had chosen only three variants. One Commander's vehicle – he'd command the action from that – one mortar vehicle, and two anti-tank guided missile carriers.

In addition to carrying twenty-four Marines, all four vehicles bristled with guns and provided great psychological support. One look at the monsters barreling toward them and people tended to wet their pants. Jackson might have plenty of security guards, but Pollock doubted the businessman would have anything capable of stopping a AFV. An RPG wouldn't even dent the armor.

In less than twenty minutes, the blades on the first chopper started turning, while the air crew rechecked the helo and loaded the ordnance. Within the hour, all four birds would be fueled and in the air. Capable of low level flight at 260 miles per hour, the helos initially would be positioned just out of radar range of San Jose.

By now the last Globemaster had landed. Pollock turned to his aide. "Run down the list for me."

"Yes, sir," his aide replied, grinning despite his best effort to remain serious. Pollock had reviewed the same list only an hour ago. "Four X-4 helos, four Armored Fighting Vehicles, and 325 Marines."

Pollock returned the grin. Those Boeing Globemasters could haul a lot of military cargo and personnel, up to 81 tons. That capacity came in handy, if you needed to transport an AFV weighing 44 tons. Pollock would transfer to one of the command vehicles at San Jose. He already had use of a dedicated satellite for communications and observation.

Pollock had to admit his respect for General Klegg. The man had pulled the Globemasters from every facility on the eastern seaboard and packed them with every piece of hardware needed by a Marine battalion in the field, and done it all in less than twenty hours.

Colonel Delano had said he wanted a show of force, to set an example and send a message. Well, when Pollock got through with Tom Jackson's fancy and fortified headquarters, the mother of all demonstrations would have been delivered.

*   *   *

Tom Jackson, CEO and majority owner of WideVistas, took a sip from the forty-year-old Elgin Irish Whiskey in its Bohemian Czech cut-crystal goblet and waved aside his visitor's concerns. Joel Peccia had already finished his first drink, gulping the $10,000 dollar-a-bottle alcohol as if it were chilled beer from a keg on the Fourth of July.

"Stop worrying, Joel," Jackson said. "No PDF team is going to show up and force their way in here. I've got more men onsite than the PDF has west of the Mississippi. Besides, I've people watching every PDF site and monitoring their comm channels. If they even think about trying anything, I'll know about it."

Joel shook his head. "Maybe this wasn't such a good idea. Delano has a lot of serious firepower at his fingertips. Remember what he did to those gangs and cartels. Think about all those ships he's building on the moon."

Jackson sipped his drink. He'd been over all this before. Joel had turned out to be a weak sister, constantly in danger of losing his nerve. "We're watching them, too. Look, this whole invasion fairy tale is just a way for Delano and his cronies to seize power. In a few months, when the aliens don't arrive, the Alliance and Delano will have another story ready to string us along. That's why we've got to act now, to solidify our position and lock up all those contracts."

"Jeez, I hope you're right, Tom." Joel took another swig of whiskey, emptying his glass.

"Don't worry, I am. Delano can run the country any way he wants, just as long as we get our share. In fact, there's . . ." Jackson's phone rang. It wasn't his regular communications device, but the private one he used for serious matters, like talking to his mistress or a few bank presidents in New York or Zurich.

Fishing the device from his pocket, he glanced at the screen. A strange face wearing what Jackson guessed was army fatigues stared at him, a cigar clenched jauntily between his teeth. The man was obviously in some kind of moving vehicle, since he seemed to be bouncing around. Jackson didn't recognize the face, so he decided to break the connection. But before he could do that, a voice came through the phone.

"You'd better take this call, Jackson. I'm General Chester Pollock, United States Marine Corps and temporarily assigned to the PDF. I've got a message for you from Colonel Delano."

Jackson's top of the line, specially configured communication cellphone was supposed to block any incoming call, even from the police. "Who is this?" Jackson snarled as he activated the speaker. "How did you get this number?"

The General's face smiled as he exhaled a cloud of smoke. "Oh, we have our ways, Jackson. Not all the super techs in the country work in Silicon Valley." The smile vanished. "But let's get right down to business. I'm about two minutes from your main entrance, and I've come to place you and Joel Peccia under arrest for sabotage against the PDF. If you both surrender peacefully, I won't have to destroy your headquarters. Or yours either, Mr. Peccia. And nobody's gets hurt."

Jackson's face turned red. "Are you threatening me? I'm linked in to every news outlet in the country, and my legal team is standing by. If Delano tries any bullshit he'll be sorry."

"Well, no doubt you're right, but Colonel Delano or his legal problems don't concern me. If you're not going to cooperate, we can do it the hard way." Pollock turned away for a moment and said something that Jackson couldn't hear.

When Pollock finished, he held the phone close to his face. When he spoke, he sounded hard and cold. "You'll be receiving our first invitation to surrender in about twenty seconds, so I suggest you stay on the line."

"Tom, maybe we should rethink this," Joel said. "Everyone knows Delano likes killing people. Maybe we should . . ."

"Fuck, no!" Jackson's rage had only grown. He moved to his desk and started pushing buttons. "Alert security. Full armed response. Close and seal all entrances. We may have unauthorized visitors trying to enter the grounds. And be ready for . . ."

The explosion shook the building. The roof overhead was 30 inches of reinforced concrete, but the first missile, the latest in the Hellfire series, packed quite a punch. Designed to destroy tanks or hardened targets, it blasted Jackson's unarmored personal helicopter into flaming fragments. Five seconds later, the second and smaller chopper used to ferry the senior executives around, also turned into vapor.

The force of the explosions, aided by a secondary blast of the fuel storage tanks, cracked the concrete and soundproofing that protected Jackson's executive offices. A cloud of cement dust and plaster board drifted down, as fire and earthquake alarms went off throughout the building.

The phone, still clutched in Jackson's hand, came to life. "That takes care of one of your escape routes," Pollock said. "I'm approaching your main entrance, and I see the gate is closing. You have thirty seconds to get it open, or I'll blast it apart for you. And if you don't surrender in the next two minutes, the tenth floor will be targeted. Sixty seconds after that, the entire building will be leveled. Sixty seconds after that, all your subterranean tunnels will be turned into rubble."

Joel, his face white with fear, leaned over the desk. "Wait, I'll surrender. This is Joel Peccia."

"Better get out of the building fast, Peccia. My APC is

targeting the main entrance right now."

200 yards from the main gate, the APC slowed down. "Closing in on the gate, General," the driver called out, "and ready to fire."

Pollock glanced at his watch, and gave the gate operators an extra fifteen seconds. But nothing moved, and he could see security forces lining up behind a five foot reinforced barrier that had slid into place. Some carried what appeared to be RPGs. Rocket Propelled Grenades were illegal in the United States, and mere possession meant at least five years in prison. "Chopper One, do you have the gate targeted?"

The pilot's voice crackled in the tiny speaker. "Yes, sir. Hellfire locked on target."

"Open the gate, Chopper One. We'll take care of the security structure alongside." Pollock didn't want to use the Hellfire against the adjacent security structures. The powerful missile would kill everything inside a building. Meanwhile the smaller shells from the AFV could easily blast open the security structures, and using them might save a few lives.

"Missile away!"

Pollock turned to his driver. "Put a few shells into the guard structure."

A moment later, the AFV main gunner, manning his perch above and behind the crew, opened up with the 20 mm automatic cannon. The large slugs tore into the left-side security structure just as the Hellfire arrived, detonating behind the barrier and blasting it and those defenders into fragments.

After about twenty rounds, the guard station on the left looked like Swiss cheese. The AFV gunner shifted his aim to the right-side guardhouse, but already Pollock could see men scrambling from the structure, running away from the main entrance.

"Good. That got their attention. Send in the Marines." Pollock switched channels. "Chopper One and Two, make sure no one leaves the complex. You are authorized to fire on any vehicle attempting to leave. Fire a warning burst if possible, but no vehicle gets out. Understood?"

"Roger, General. On the move."

By that time, two AFVs, each carrying twenty-four Marines, had roared past Pollock's command vehicle. "Follow them in. Head for the main building. Let's go find our Mr. Jackson."

That turned out to be a time-consuming process. Pollock found Joel Peccia, his face white and hands high in the air, stumbling over the rubble outside the Headquarters Complex main entrance. Debris and bodies from the roof were scattered about, many of them burned beyond recognition. Shattered glass also littered the ground. A hundred yards away a growing crowd of employees stood trembling in the warm air. The Marines, shouting aggressively and waving their rifles, were emptying every building on the campus, and would photograph and tag every person. Machine gunners on the AFVs covered the crowd, another show of force in case anyone wanted to complain.

Jackson had tried to escape through the subterranean tunnels beneath the headquarters building. One passage led to a second building, and Pollock's troops arrived at that exit point before anyone could escape that way.

Jackson then tried a second tunnel, nearly half a mile long, which exited beyond the grounds into the basement of a nearby small house. Fortunately, the PDF had extracted that information from the CEO's chief architect, who the PDF had "persuaded" into revealing the escape tunnels and their exit points.

After they picked up Jackson, the Marines blew up the house and tunnel, sealing that exit route.

The entire operation had lasted less than twenty minutes. But fifty-one people were dead, most of them security personnel at the main gate or those manning the heliport on the roof. And twelve innocent people, all employees, died.

Pollock felt bad about that, and knew Delano would, too. Still, many of those dead would have known about the slowdown, and either greed or cowardice had kept them silent. But the General felt certain that Jackson would pay for each of those deaths, probably by handing over tens of millions of dollars to each victim. Delano would likely confiscate all the rest of his wealth before sentencing Jackson to hang. The other CEOs might get off, but they'd be on notice if anything like that happened again.

"Everything under control, General," his aide reported. "Looks like we can maintain this operation with a hundred or so Marines. The rest of the men can get back to Camp Lejeune."

"Not yet. Keep them here for a week or so, until you're certain. After that, you'll probably be here for a few months, so make your plans accordingly. This is one less headache the PDF will have to deal with. I doubt anyone else in corporate America will try to sabotage the PDF's efforts."

Silicon Valley had plenty of power and influence, but not the kind needed to stop determined men with rifles, or a missile on approach. Pollock glanced around at the wreckage covering the grounds in front of Jackson's fancy headquarters. Satisfied with what he saw, he lit a fresh cigar.

He'd delivered exactly what Colonel Delano wanted – a hammer blow that would send the PDF's message – don't mess around with the planet's future.

Chapter 31
87 BKA

The Halkin shuttle descended onto the lunar landing pad, directed to a blinking reception zone close to the main building as befitted its most important cargo. A scattering of gray powder whirled about the alien craft as it touched down, but the moon dust settled quickly enough even in the low gravity.

In two minutes, Delano and the Gunny descended from the portal with care, still not proficient in the new, lightweight pressure suits. In the Halkin dialect, Delano said goodbye to the shuttle's pilot and thanked him for a smooth touchdown. Delano accepted the adage that any landing you could walk away from was a good one.

The flight suits worked even better than advertised. Developed by a Korean company specifically for use by PDF pilots in the coming war, the orange and red semi-rigid outfits could sustain a man in a vacuum for a few hours. The president of the firm had lost his family in the Ktarran attack and volunteered his resources and support to the PDF. His company, in conjunction with pilots in Moscow, produced a high-quality pressure suit that would provide extra protection for the pilots of the Dart spacecraft.

After strenuous testing by the crews taking the Jumpers into Earth orbit, the suits were accepted by the PDF. Delano knew they would save lives in combat, and help reassure pilots and crews that they might survive even if their ship were damaged by a slight brush from a Ktarran particle beam.

Before Delano had stepped more than a few meters from the shuttle, an orange-colored, six-wheeled transport rolled out of the hangar and slid to a stop beside the two travelers. The driver opened the side hatch and beckoned them inside, reaching out a hand to help guide the new arrivals in.

Once inside, the driver secured the door, then greeted his passengers. The man wore a different type of suit, and Delano couldn't see much of his face. But he noticed the PDF patch on the man's shoulder, and thanked him for his service. Every person serving in the Planetary Defense Force was a valuable volunteer who understood what was at stake.

Even before the buggy started toward the hangar, the shuttle lifted off, to return to its mother ship, waiting in low orbit over the Moon.

The taxi made a tight turn and rolled fifty meters across the landing area, and into what had formerly been the JovCo Mining arrival facility. Except for some key personnel, all the JovCo staff had long since been shipped back to Earth. The PDF had appropriated (for the duration) the entire complex. JovCo's headquarters would now provide a similar function for the PDF.

"Thank God we're on the ground again." The words sounded natural enough through the suit's speakers. Gunny did not like any part of traveling through space, even though the trip from Earth orbit to the Moon's surface had lasted only eight hours, courtesy of Halkin Captain Horath and his ship.

"I'm just grateful we're off the planet," Delano agreed. "The last few weeks have been . . . exciting." *Yeah, that's the word, exciting. Šilený.* The Czech word for "insane" might be a better choice. The shambles of his own life over the last year made him eager to fight the Ktarrans, no matter what the odds.

He'd done things once unimaginable, accomplished deeds that might save humanity, or just as easily destroy it. Delano had also sent people to their deaths, and those weighed heavily on him, especially at night when sleep refused to come. Only when he had Lian at his side did the demons withdraw into darkness.

One of Delano's first directives establishing the PDF required that every applicant had lost a relative or close friend in the Ktarran bombardment. He wanted only men and women loyal to Earth and eager to fight the coming invasion in the PDF. Anyone without that qualification went through a strict background check, their motives scrutinized. In some cases Delano himself became the final authority for acceptance.

That decision included a large pool of potential members from the US West Coast and China. In the case of Russia and other nations untouched by the Ktarrans, he made sure that everyone who applied was carefully screened for loyalty to Earth and the PDF first, then to their own country.

President Demidov had protested the extra scrutiny given his military, but Delano and Lian held firm. For the PDF, the first allegiance had to be to the planet. "Earth First" became the rallying and recruitment cry.

A year later, the PDF had become a household name. Everyone on the planet knew what the organization stood for. It had taken more than six months before the protests against them had dwindled to a trickle. Everyone – from individuals to governments – had learned the lesson Delano and Lian had espoused in their first speech. The PDF would be extreme in its measures to protect the planet.

By now half the planet's population hated the PDF and its leaders. Fortunately, the other half stood resolute in their support of Delano and Lian's mission to save humanity.

The PDF might be familiar, but its leaders, Colonel Delano and Dr. Duan Lian, were even more well known. Known and hated. Too many people had been forced to sacrifice for the coming war, and they had no use for the PDF, no matter what its motives.

He didn't really care about them anymore. The Alliance and the PDF had all the nations of planet Earth firmly under control. Nearly three million people had died around the globe to achieve that status, most of those from Russian nukes after the attack on Moscow. Every country now knew the consequence of obstruction to the Alliance and the PDF. The once-distant future now drew close. In two or three short months, the bloodthirsty Ktarrans would arrive, or Delano would be out of a job.

But today a new phase in Earth's preparation for interstellar war began. The Moon would provide the primary shield for the planet, and Delano had decided to direct Earth's defense from here. Occupy the high ground. Soldiers had fought for that throughout history. That it made sense militarily meant little. The malcontents on Earth accused Delano of running away. Truth be told, there was something to that allegation. For better or worse, his days of living on Earth had come to an end. For his own protection and sanity, he needed to leave the doubters, haters, and troublemakers behind. Now he had to hope the Moon was far enough.

These thoughts and others whirled through Delano's head, and he had to force himself to set them aside. *Stop feeling sorry for yourself and focus*! A new challenge awaited, and he'd better prepare himself. Within a minute, the ungainly transport rolled into the nearest of the three main hangars. Delano glanced out a window and watched the heavy airlock door slide close. Another two minutes passed while the chamber re-pressurized.

The transport's radio blared something unintelligible, but the driver obviously understood it. "Welcome to the Moon, Colonel Delano," he said as he opened the hatch. "Watch your step getting out. It takes a few days before you get used to the low gravity."

"Thanks. It's good to be here." Delano meant it. Grateful didn't really convey the relief he felt. In the last six weeks, he'd survived two assassination attempts. One by a Mideast faction that believed Delano was the Koranic personification of the Angel of Death. A team of so-called true believers launched three Stinger type missiles at Delano's helicopter, and only his pilot's exceptionally skillful tactics brought them to a safe landing.

The other attempt had been a disturbed American from California, who blamed the loss of his family in the Ktarran bombardment on Delano. The man actually got close enough to take a shot before the PDF security took him down. Fortunately for Delano, the man's first shot missed, and Delano found himself hugging the concrete, pinned beneath a two-hundred-pound bodyguard, before the assassin got off his second bullet.

These events on Earth no longer mattered. Across the globe, intelligent and dedicated men worked around the clock to prepare the planet for war. But the final phase of Earth's deployment against the Ktarran Empire would commence here, on the moon. Even before the first mobilization plans were completed, the need for a strategic presence on the Moon became apparent. Soon it became the primary defense and construction site for Earth, and for the PDF's weapons of war.

Following the driver's example, Delano removed his helmet, feeling the hiss as the air pressure equalized. He took a deep breath, and the air seemed as fresh as a Rocky Mountain meadow. He let himself relax.

Both Delano and the Gunny wobbled a little in the low gravity that magnified every movement. They took a few cautious steps away from the buggy, just as a PDF major and her two aides arrived, joining the driver.

Major Mary Ann Bennet glided over, her short blond hair peeking out from beneath a black ball cap with the logo of the New York Yankees. She looked much younger than her thirty-two years, but Bennett had risen quickly through the ranks and functioned as the senior PDF officer in charge of the JovCo facility. She didn't bother to salute. Instead she grasped Delano's arm without asking, and steered him into an access tunnel. An aide assisted Gunny.

"Don't worry about being guided," Bennet said. "New arrivals get most of their injuries in the first twenty-four hours. Newbies think that since things fall so slowly you can't get hurt, that all you have to do is put out your hand. Our med-techs end up fixing their broken wrists and arms. Since you've spent time in zero gravity, Colonel, you should be all right in a few days."

Delano wasn't so sure, and the Gunny didn't look all that confident either. But the major's relaxed grip kept him balanced. With their escorts' assistance, Delano and the Gunny moved gingerly down a bright blue corridor. They passed through two air-tight doors, then entered the elevator.

At least that's what the major called it. A lunar adaptation, it looked more like a hole in the ground. Lunar surface, he corrected himself. A circular tunnel about five meters across had been bored straight down, with eight safety grips attached to tracks on the walls. Delano thought it looked more like a smooth-bored bottomless well.

"It looks dangerous, but it works just fine," Bennett said. "When you grasp one of the handholds, you either go down or up, depending on where you set your hand."

Delano saw that the tracks extended as far as he could see. Apparently you just held on until you reached the bottom, or top. It must feel odd to have nothing under your feet as you descended. Bennett grasped a handle with one hand, and used the other to keep a firm grip on Delano's arm. She pulled him into the opening, and Delano seized the same handle.

They slowly descended a little more than one hundred meters into the Moon's interior. The featureless walls were painted a bright white, to reduce the amount of illumination needed, Delano knew. "This primary access elevator goes directly to the Hotel. Other elevators go to different levels, and there's always an alternate pathway to the level you want, in case one of the tunnels loses integrity."

That sounded disturbing. "Does that happen much?"

"I've been here six months without a hitch," Bennett said. "One of my primary duties is safety inspections. In the event of a breach, an alarm sounds and the air-tight hatches close automatically. If someone's on the wrong side, they've got about five seconds to reach safety."

Delano figured out that losing integrity meant a breach in the tunnel and exposure to vacuum. He hadn't noticed any hatches, and decided they must be built into the walls. He found he was clutching the handle with all his strength. The sensation of falling was remarkable, like in a dream. They floated downward at a steady pace, and he had to work to keep his feet beneath him as they descended.

He noticed that Bennett was holding on with little more than her fingertips. Near the bottom of the tunnel she loosed her hold on the handle. The mechanism stopped, and they drifted slowly to the bottom. She pulled her human cargo into a corridor. A few meters later – and through another hatchway – they entered his new dwelling, the former VIP suite of the JovCo Hotel.

The unit consisted of four chambers – a small board room, a sitting room, and two bedroom suites, each with its own bathroom.

Bennett didn't let go of Delano's arm until she had him inside the board room and in a chair. Then she floated leisurely onto a sofa facing both men. Her actions appeared unhurried and deliberate, almost like a slow-motion ballet, but highly efficient, no wasted motion or thrashing about. Much the same as movement aboard the Space Station. "Please let me know if you need anything, Colonel. My two aides, Liam and Verda, are at your service."

Bennett introduced both aides, each a lieutenant. "Verda is from Tijuana. She crossed the border after the attack. Liam is from Santa Barbara." She didn't need to explain who they'd lost or why they'd joined. "And as you requested, there's a four person security detail that will report directly to Gunny Stecker."

"Thank you." Delano shook hands with Lian and Verda. He'd read Bennett's file, but not those of her aides. "Major, what's the schedule like?"

"Nothing for the next twelve hours," Bennet answered. "Gives you both a chance to eat and relax, and get a bit of rest. Then, if you're ready, the inspections start. We'll take you around to meet whomever you need to see. After that, you decide what you want to do."

Naturally the lunar PDF personnel would treat him as if he were made of glass, some delicate upper-echelon chair warmer. *Not bloody likely.*

"JovCo first?"

"Yes, sir." Bennet remained cool.

Delano shook his head. "No, Major. We'll go to New Beijing first, to see Senior Colonel Jang. I'll take the twelve hours, but I want to meet with him right after that. Please schedule it and arrange a full security team to accompany us."

Bennett looked a bit disappointed. Obviously she wanted to show off her own command first. "Yes, sir. My team was hoping to meet with you tomorrow. But no problem."

Colonel Jang had transferred to New Beijing within a month of the PDF getting started. He still reported directly to General Zeng, and both men had realized early how big a role the Moon would play. Jang had commanded the fighter pilots who defended Beijing and launched the missile strike that triggered the EMP pulse.

Delano had met with him several times, and liked the dour airman. Lian had turned her charms on Jang, and soon won him over to her side. By now Jang accepted Delano as a necessary player in the planet's defense, not some barbarian interloper who had captured a princess of China.

"Your people can wait a few days, Major Bennett," Delano said. "A major planning session will take place in New Beijing in the next thirty hours. You know how sensitive the Chinese are to the chain of command." He smiled. "You and your team will be there as well."

"Yes, sir." Bennett put her disappointment behind her. "Anything else you require?"

"No, Major. Just send the security team down. Gunny will want to talk to them before we turn in. We really do need the rest."

She took the dismissal gracefully. "Yes, Sir." She turned to Liam. "Bring them in."

Gunny wrapped up the security issues in fifteen minutes. Basically he just wanted the exterior door guarded by two soldiers at all times, with the other two on call nearby. He ended with a warning that anyone who entered the suite unannounced would be shot, and that there would be no warnings. A moment later, Delano and the Gunny were alone, the interior door closed. He didn't bother checking for bugs. Neither of them would be talking about anything critical in here.

After Gunny finished checking the video feeds, Delano poured them both a drink of Irish whiskey from the suite's private bar. With his plastic glass in hand, he leaned back in the chair, letting his body sag in the gentle gravity.

A large view screen showed images from the surface, and Delano found that he could use a remote to angle the camera in any direction he wanted, except toward the sun. An automatic safety kept the lens from overloading.

The board room was as far below ground as possible. Tycoons habitually preferred to rest at spots relatively immune to atom bombs. Or in this case, lunar quakes. The room did not seem like a bomb shelter. It appeared to be a chamber in a luxurious corporate office, as another view screen scrolled a steady stream of spectacular lunar views from behind the chairman's end of the table.

In the last year, the corporate offices and luxury hotel's accommodations had been heavily upgraded and extended. The tiny, six-room hotel remained intact, but a lounge area just down the corridor had been converted into a communications center, and all the rooms in the underground structure now boasted the latest in computer and telecommunications equipment. In anticipation of Delano's arrival, two more pressure doors protected the suite from any sudden loss of air. The thick doors would also resist any attempt to force a passage. Even on the Moon, assassins could still be lurking nearby.

During the renovation, the PDF had installed a connecting door between the Chairman's Suite and the adjacent room, converting the individual chambers into a large suite that would allow Delano and Lian the luxury of their own room, with the additional benefit of a private work area.

Not that Lian had traveled with him. Schedule permitting, she would join Delano in a week or so, as soon as she wrapped up some production problems in China with the Defense Grid. But Delano had left New Mexico early.

Already stressed to the max, the threats against his life had increased significantly. Urged on by General Klegg, he decided to get the hell out of Dodge before the next fool got lucky. On the Moon, he'd be surrounded by a hefty force of PDF personnel, pilots and engineers mostly, but with plenty of construction and manufacturing people as well. The odds of any personal attack would drop drastically.

The Moon had undergone major and minor expansion. Three more surface facilities had been constructed, making six major settlements. The new additions were spacecraft assembly sites.

Already rows of Darts occupied a specially constructed launching grid, parked in sealed revetments that allowed each Dart to be accessed by underground tunnels and take off at will. Main battle Destroyers were being assembled at another. The last facility, completed only a few months ago, contained the starships – the Colonizers – under construction.

Prior to the arrival of the aliens, fewer than twelve hundred people occupied the three lunar bases, with New Beijing the largest. JovCo's mining operations utilized almost three hundred workers. The US/UK settlement held less than two hundred scientists and support staff.

Now the Moon's population had swelled to over six thousand. Each day more and more people and supplies arrived. Early on, lunar operations had jumped to the top of the Planetary Defense Task Force list. Construction of every type went on non-stop, day after day, excavating and expanding every facility.

Not only did the Darts and other ships need to be assembled and tested there, but Delano and his staff quickly realized that the Moon had to transform into a fortified bastion for Earth's and its own defense.

Each day between forty to fifty Jumpers landed on the lunar surface, carrying supplies, construction workers, pilots, and electronic specialists. As with every major conflict, the war would be won or lost by logistics. Troops and equipment had to be at the proper place, at the right time, and in sufficient quantities.

On Earth, such facilities could never have accommodated such rapid construction. Fortunately, the Moon's regolith, the loose soil and debris that covered its surface, was both lightweight and easy to mine. Seismically active, the Moon acts like a hunk of soft iron under impact. As far back as the first lunar landings, NASA discovered that the lunar surface could easily be worked. Now miners had drilled deep into the soft surface, crushing the very regolith itself, then mixing it with a combination of bonding agents that created a rock-hard and airtight material used to line the walls and tunnels.

The sub-surface moon, however, is also dry, cool and mostly rigid, like a chunk of stone or iron. Tidal moonquakes, which set it vibrating like a tuning fork, were a perennial problem. Even shallow quakes lasted a remarkably long time, often as long as ten minutes, during which the moon rang like a bell. That persistence could be more significant than a moonquake's magnitude.

Therefore building materials had to be somewhat flexible, so no air-leaking cracks would develop. The new deep dwelling places had to be constructed thick enough to withstand repeated bending and shaking. And the explosive force generated by a Ktarran beam weapon.

The resulting new chambers, all at least a hundred meters below the regolith, provided the real lunar expansion. Like an iceberg, ninety percent of the new construction was buried well below the surface.

Living quarters, air and water supplies, food, weapons, and computers provided the building blocks of the Moon's defensive networks. The newly-established bases would act as an outlier defense position, and help protect Earth in the event of an attack.

Fortunately, the new excavations were very hard to detect, since the modified stone used in the construction showed up on a scan as just another lunar rock formation. During Ktarran assault, Delano and his experts – mostly the Halkins and Tarlons – had decided that enemy ships would not likely be performing deep interior scans. Or so everyone in the PDF hoped.

Construction on these and other projects continued round the clock. Crews worked ten hour shifts deepening, hardening, and hiding the underground caverns. Then follow-up teams modified each cavity, turning it into living quarters, weapons storage, and food supply depots.

By the time of the Ktarran arrival, approximately ten thousand men and women would be working on the Moon, including a full quota of fighter pilots for the Darts and crews for the Destroyers.

Plans for the Moon's defense had already been devised. The existing and new surface sites would be defended by automated weapons, controlled by computers and operators miles away and buried deep in the interior. The hidden sites would be protected by nearby bases that would provide a sublunar escape route. Rail guns and missiles and beam weapons, all operated remotely, would fight the Ktarrans.

In case of alien destruction of all weapons, those underground facilities would be supplied with enough food and water to last the survivors many years. The Moon had become a stronghold for Earth's security and the human race.

The massive lunar development had worried the Tarlons and Halkins. They had suggested that only ship assembly facilities be constructed. They didn't believe that so much construction and fortification could be completed before the Ktarrans arrived.

Lately they had softened their opposition, as the scale and speed of the construction impressed even the strongest Halkin doubter. Earth's alien allies had never witnessed manufacturing and development on such a major scale. No one on Earth had ever seen such a thing either, but that was beside the point. With every resource on Earth dedicated to fighting the Ktarrans, progress proceeded rapidly. Political posturing, manufacturing delays, supply bottlenecks, all were addressed immediately and with whatever resource or force required.

Computers and robots made everything possible. Both worked 24/7, and needed little maintenance. With well trained and highly motivated operators, construction increased rapidly. More computers now controlled the transport and arrival of needed supplies, following the "Just In Time" manufacturing processes.

The Ktarrans, when they arrived, were going to be surprised. Whatever reports they'd received about the Moon would have described a mostly-barren satellite, one that had little value or defensive worth. Instead, they would find it bristling with short-range missiles and rail guns, and hundreds of Darts ready to engage.

Now Delano just worried that it wasn't going to be enough. He kept that doubt to himself, however. He had to appear strong, no matter what the truth might be. Too many people were depending on his decisions. Sighing, he wished Lian were with him, giving him reassurance. Sometimes he felt her belief in the future of the planet was far greater than his own.

Chapter 32
86 BKA

At least today it's a little different – a low gravity conference room – as Delano eased himself into a seat. The simple plastic chair with its thin black cushion looked uncomfortable, but in one-sixth gravity the sensation proved otherwise. New Beijing's largest conference chamber lacked the size and amenities of JovCo's, but it accommodated a white duralast table and eight chairs.

Video conferencing equipment and cameras took up most of one wall, wires dangling from several boxes. Nobody on the Moon, it seemed, wasted much time on aesthetics. With space at a premium in every lunar facility, larger meetings utilized video as much as possible.

No one remarked that oversized gatherings of any kind were shunned, on the off-chance of some dome failure or destructive moonquake. No sense risking too many valuable eggs in one basket.

Delano had arrived early, to make sure he could be among the first to enter the chamber. This way he could take a seat anywhere, leaving the head of the table for Senior Colonel Jang. As Lian often reminded her partner, Chinese sensitivities could hinge on the slightest breach of protocol. Better safe than sorry. In the last year Delano had learned many lessons, some the hard way, about keeping people under control while minimizing friction.

Major Mary Ann Bennett sat beside him, looking relaxed in her spotless PDF uniform. No baseball cap today. The Gunny dragged a chair away from the table and sat with his back against the wall, where he could watch the door and the assembled staff. He wore a holster under his left arm. It contained the same customized Glock he and Delano had carried on the Space Station. A duplicate weapon and a spare magazine rested inside Delano's carry bag.

Delano had just flipped on his tablet when Jang entered the chamber and stopped in his tracks, surprised at finding the leader of the PDF already present and not seated at the head of the table.

The cortège following in Jang's footsteps also halted.

Mindful of the low gravity, Delano rose and bowed slightly. "Good morning, Senior Colonel Jang." He spoke in English, that being the language that the pilots would use in combat.

The Chinese colonel took the room in with a quick glance, then returned the bow. "Good afternoon, Colonel Delano. Welcome to New Beijing. Your early arrival caught everyone by surprise."

Jang took his place across from Delano. Both men had eschewed the large chair at the head of the table. They would face each other as equals. Behind Jang his two aides entered and took seats on either side. The last member of Jang's team, Major Peng Qilang, took the seat at the foot of the table. Peng's uniform was the standard Chinese lunar garb, light green cargo shorts and a matching T-shirt. The shirt had a collar and two breast pockets. Peng wore the emblem of a fighter pilot on his right shoulder and the PDF patch on his left. Senior Colonel Jang wore only his Chinese military emblem of rank.

Captain Chiew Chuntao and Lieutenant Chenguang Lee stared across the table at Delano, this being their first direct meeting with the leader of the PDF. Chiew, short and full figured, had cut her dark hair even shorter than she'd worn it on Earth. Both aides were more than competent. Chenguang looked more western, tall and slender with a ready and pleasant smile. According to Delano's file, she provided more than just official help to her superior, not that there was anything wrong with that. Interestingly, her name meant "morning light," which seemed appropriate. He'd met both before on conference calls.

"I do not believe you have met Major Peng," Jang said.

"That is correct," Delano said, "but I've read his impressive file. On behalf of all of us who were on the Space Station, I thank you for your daring missile launch during the Ktarran attack. We could not have survived without it."

Peng had flown his Strike fighter far beyond its operating altitude, the better to launch the specially-modified missiles that generated a massive EMP blast, temporarily blinding the Ktarrans for a few key minutes at the height of the battle. Without that, the Tarlon and Halkin ships could never have gotten close enough to the enemy battleships to launch their attack. Seconds after releasing those two missiles, the aircraft stalled, and fell out of control almost sixty thousand feet. Peng had escaped death by mere moments.

"It was my honor," Peng replied. "Fortune favored us that day."

Thirty million dead didn't seem so fortunate, but Delano knew the man meant well. "And now you command the Planetary Fleet of Darts."

"Yes, under Colonel Jang. I will lead them into battle against the Ktarrans."

Just like Commander Mitsuo Fuchida, the Japanese pilot who led the first wave of aircraft on the Pearl Harbor raid. The comparison stopped there, because Pearl had been caught by surprise, while the Ktarrans would be prepared for anything. Just how ready Peng really was remained to be seen, but that meeting was not today. Dart operational status and policy headed the agenda for this meeting.

"Will you and your men be ready?" Delano had read the status reports, but there remained no substitute for looking in the man's eyes.

Peng glanced at Jang, who nodded. "Tell him your status," Jang said.

"Our first training phase is almost ended," Peng said, leaning forward. His English was good, with only a trace of an accent. "In three weeks we will initiate deep space training and weapons testing. The first production run of Darts, almost two hundred, is nearly complete. Components continue to arrive each day, and are being printed or assembled and tested here. If not for the new gyroscopes, we would already be aloft."

The Darts had turned out to be the most sophisticated and complicated of the PDF weapons. Neither the Ktarrans nor the Tarlons and their allies had developed any small fighters, something Earth's modern military history demanded. Unlike the larger cruisers, which were relatively simple modifications of the Tarlon vessels, the Darts were pure Earth-based technology. Ever since Delano, Colonel Welsh, and the others had proposed that concept, the design had undergone almost continual modification. Each enhancement, of course, made the Dart stronger, faster, more powerful, or smarter. And took longer to build, test, train, and required more men to support.

Delano and General Zeng had finally put a halt to all upgrades. The temptation to add one more weapon or system remained strong. What the designers had now would have to do the job. Otherwise combat training would be held up indefinitely.

"How many competent pilots?"

Major Peng never hesitated. "As of now we have what I consider just over a hundred first-class pilots. The training simulators confirm my assessment, and many of them have flown combat missions for the Alliance."

"What's the breakdown?"

Peng didn't need to consult his notes. "Thirty-two Chinese, forty-one Russian, twenty-six Americans. The rest are French, British, and Israeli. Most of the support teams are American and Chinese."

American fighter pilots, Delano knew, had always relied on electronic cockpit superiority. What the PDF needed now were pure pilots, men and women who could fly a kitchen table if it possessed a seat belt and a large enough power supply.

"And how many of these pilots are good enough to be your wingman, Major Peng?"

"All of them," Peng answered. "These are the best of the best, physically and mentally. I have trained with each one. They know how to fly and how to fight. More important, they want to fight."

In Earth's air combat history, the records proved that a small percentage of top pilots accounted for the majority of kills. That ratio would not work against the Ktarrans, since a Dart might be destroyed by any of several Ktarrans.

Peng seemed to read Delano's mind. "These pilots will continue to train until the enemy's arrival. If those who follow cannot match up to this first wave of pilots, they will still be more than competent for routine combat. Not every fighter pilot can be an ace."

Delano gazed at Peng, and the moment of silence stretched out. But Major Peng held Delano's eyes.

"Then, Major Peng, I am satisfied that our fleet of Darts is in good hands. But I have one major request. We do not believe the design has been tested sufficiently. I want a few Darts tested to failure." Delano saw that Peng did not understand. "I want you to take a Dart and stress it and its pilot to the max, until something fails. Rotate your pilots every hour, no less. Then move a new crew in and continue testing for another hour, until something else fails or the pilot blacks out."

Peng's face registered shock, but Delano ignored it. "One of our programmers developed a simulator, based on the Dart's final specs." He reached into his bag, and drew out a memory stick. "The programmer will be here in a few days, and will help your software team install the program, then customize it as the test proceeds. He knows what we want, and I expect you will give him your support and everything he requires."

"I'm not sure I understand, Colonel Delano." Peng's doubts showed on his face.

"We, and by that I mean myself, Field Marshal Shuvalov, and others in the PDF command want the Dart tested to failure. For example, the rail gun must be fired at its maximum rate and as often as possible. The same with the beam weapon, both under every conceivable condition. We want to know where their weak points are. A few hours constant stress and random movements at high acceleration should produce conditions similar to actual combat."

Delano's "random movements" constituted a major understatement. He'd seen the computer simulation. Crews would be stressed well past the average blackout response under heavy acceleration. But he knew that was the best way to train. As the saying went, amateurs train until they get it right, professionals train until they can't possibly do it wrong.

"And if the Dart explodes or crashes? If the pilot is killed?" Peng sounded angry now. "If you stress any aircraft or pilot beyond their limits, you will have deadly accidents."

"I understand. But recorders and instruments will tell us what happened," Delano said. "I realize this is very dangerous, and there may be casualties. But when our pilots go out to fight against the Ktarrans, they must know all the weak points of their ships and themselves. That may help a lot more of them survive the battle."

"This is most unusual," Jang said. "All systems were stress tested on Earth. To propose such a test so late in the program . . ."

"We always knew we could not test the Darts properly on Earth," Delano said. "It has to be done in zero gravity, and until now, we have not had that environment. And the knowledge gained may enable us to correct potential problems before the battle."

Peng sagged back in the chair, the low gravity enhancing the motion. "Then I should be the one testing the Dart. Otherwise . . ."

"No, you are specifically ordered to not take part in this phase," Delano said. "I need you and your expertise to evaluate the people and the equipment, and to lead the Darts into battle. Unless you want to give up your command?"

"Colonel Delano is right." Jang cut in before Peng said something foolish. "Better to have men and equipment fail now than in battle. I agree Major Peng is too valuable to risk as a test pilot."

"Good," Delano said. "I've studied the records of every pilot in the command. The evaluation board on Earth agrees as well. They all rate highly, so create a list randomly. We may only get one shot against the Ktarrans, and nothing must be left to chance."

Peng glanced at Jang, and saw that his Colonel had already accepted the order. "Very well. I will support the test."

"Thank you, Major Peng. I expected no less." Delano nodded at Jang. "With backup firepower from the Destroyers, your Darts should be able to strike a heavy blow, one the Ktarrans may not expect." Delano hesitated. "Please tell your pilots . . . I'll tell them the same thing, they are not being asked to sacrifice their lives. They'll take no more risks than the Destroyers, perhaps even fewer."

"Yes, sir."

Bullshit alert! Delano grinned. "And inform your people that I'll be standing on the lead Destroyer. If I had the skill to fly anything, I'd be driving a Dart right beside you."

Even Colonel Jang raised an eyebrow at that. "I have already requested command of a Destroyer, Colonel Delano. I cannot perform sufficiently in a Dart, but I believe I can be of use in a Destroyer. If so, you will be welcome on my ship."

"Your request has already been approved, Colonel Jang. General Zeng will be talking with you about that. Assuming that you can find someone to run things while you complete the training."

"Captain Chiew already has taken control of much of the construction and training." Jang appeared relaxed for the first time since the meeting started. "If you have no other issues, perhaps she can now begin the briefing?"

Delano nodded. "Of course. Please proceed, Captain Chiew."

Chiew adjusted her tablet, showing no interest or concern either for what she'd just heard or in her possible new responsibilities. She launched into a full status report.

For the next hour, without once cracking a smile or letting her emotions show, Chiew detailed every facet of New Beijing's war effort. Supplies, facilities expansion, Dart construction schedules, deliveries, assembly schedules, training, medical issues, morale, and of course, the political motivation sessions. Delano had tried to get those cut out of the curriculum but to no avail. Political propaganda was too much infused into the Chinese and Russian cultures to be completely eliminated in so short a time. Well, Delano had a plan for that, too.

At least Jang's staff modified and reduced the political material, shifting emphasis to the PDF and the people of the entire planet. Delano hoped some of the discussions would help change the occasional nationalism that still threatened the PDF's efforts even now.

For the last year, Delano had spent every minute of his spare time studying naval and air combat warfare. Every moment he spent traveling he dedicated to learning as much as he could. His Marine background provided him combat experience, but he'd fought on the ground, and that wasn't the same as what was coming. The fight aboard the Space Station didn't count, as it involved small numbers in what was euphemistically described as CQB, Close Quarter Battle.

After the first conference in Moscow, he decided to make himself an expert on military history. So Delano read and studied one or two books a week, watched actual combat footage, and had arranged many conferences and one-on-one sessions with those who had physically fought or planned such conflicts. By achieving a broad grasp of military operations, he hoped to find some analogous situations to the coming conflict.

To his surprise, the person who provided the most insight and support was Russian Minister and Field Marshal Shuvalov. The Russian general quickly figured out what Delano wanted, and joined in the research. Shuvalov had studied warfare for almost sixty years, and had a huge library of unpublished and secret material available, including private diaries that encompassed every rank.

That data proved useful. While many military types in the Alliance and the rest of the world might criticize Delano's conclusions or ideas, few dared to raise any objections when Shuvalov stood behind him, nodding approval.

Delano and Shuvalov jumped right in. Every major military

figure, from Alexander the Great to Julius Caesar, Genghis Khan to Napoleon, was examined, their campaigns studied. Soon the studies included the more recent past. Leaders like Erwin Rommel, Hans Guderian, and the greatest German general of them all – Eric Von Manstein – were examined in detail. Nor were the Russians and Americans forgotten. Marshalls Zukov and Rokossovsky, and Generals Patton and Eisenhower.

The navy received even more study. Men like Nimitz, Yamamoto, Doenitz, and many others who contributed greatly to the art of war. Marshall Shuvalov and Delano studied all of them and many more. With Shuvalov's support, Delano helped expedite the development of the Moon as a major defensive base. Intelligence, scouting, probing attacks, surprise, fake withdrawals, any aspect that might be useful in space was researched. As often happened in warfare, the past was prelude to the future.

The great campaigns in Earth's history received the same scrutiny. The American Civil War, World Wars I and II, especially Hitler's invasions of France and Russia provided valuable knowledge. Even guerrilla wars in Vietnam, Afghanistan, and Iraq provided some insights. The material available seemed endless, but Shuvalov, with help from his staff and a few aides from the American military colleges, filtered out the unnecessary and unimportant.

The closest analogy Delano and Shuvalov found turned out to be World War II in the Pacific, a mixture of air and sea combat that pitted the Empire of Japan against the United States. The similarities between the Pacific Campaign and the coming Ktarran War proved striking. Like the Japanese, the Ktarrans would be operating at the end of a long supply line. They would seek a quick victory, if for no other reason than that they had a large number of restive worlds to rule.

In the Pacific conflict, the Japanese initially had the edge. They possessed the largest battleships, the most aircraft carriers, plus the best planes and pilots, all with extensive combat experience. They were masters of the weapons they possessed, and used them with ruthless precision. Their main opponents, the United States and England, had inferior naval aircraft and pilots, poor destroyers and faulty torpedoes, and many other weapons needed for the conflict. They also lacked the critical skills of night fighting and surprise attack, all of which Japan used to increase their advantage.

The Ktarrans had large and powerful ships, and crews who had served on them for many years. According to the Tarlons, Ktarran crews were lifetime commitments, and they trained constantly. Their commanders knew the capabilities of their ships, crews and weapons. They preferred to attack, and showed no fear at greater numbers, believing themselves the superior warriors. Their history of expansion confirmed it.

Of course they had weaknesses. Their arrogance made them careless, as when they attacked Earth. As soon as the Ktarrans discovered their enemy had no ships or beam weapons, they became overconfident, and let themselves be lured down into range of Alliance nuclear missiles. Their leader, too, had brushed aside any doubts about capturing Delano and his team aboard the Space Station. That blunder had allowed Delano and his team to come up with a Trojan Horse that blasted the largest battleship apart from within.

Unfortunately, one Ktarran ship had observed all this from Jupiter's orbit, and departed with the knowledge that Earth was indeed a formidable foe. When the enemy returned, they would not make those same slipups.

But Planet Earth, like the United States in the Pacific War, also had some advantages. The PDF forces would be operating close to their supply bases. Their logistics and construction capabilities continued to amaze and impress the Tarlons and Halkins. Earth's computers were far beyond anything the Ktarrans possessed or imagined. Perhaps the most stunning reaction to a piece of Earth technology came from the Tarlons when they saw computer controlled printers that could create large mechanisms, hulls, even repair equipment without the need for machine shops or hand finishing.

The idea that robots and computers could build precisely what was required was a technology practically unknown to the Ktarrans or even the Tarlons. Each Destroyer would contain a small computer printer capable of manufacturing any of a thousand different components. That would enable the vessels to carry fewer parts, saving valuable storage and reducing weight.

In the Pacific war, the Americans utilized and deployed advanced radar and improved sonar equipment that soon gave them an edge. The PDF's computer-controlled firing systems would be a new concept for the Ktarrans, and the use of Darts as weapons would also surprise them.

At least in the first encounter. What Delano wanted was to make sure there wasn't a second time, at least not until Earth and its solar system could be properly protected. The Ktarrans understood nuclear weapons, and in the seventeen months they would have more than enough time to construct as many of the devices as they wanted. Fifty nukes striking Earth's major cities would probably cripple the planet and leave it helpless against a second strike.

No, the Ktarrans needed to be beaten so strongly that they would fall back, and abandon any expansion plans into this quadrant of the galaxy, at least for a time. Given another year, Earth could surround itself with a ring of steel and weapons that would render it impregnable. Once that was achieved, Earth and its alien allies could take the offensive and begin launching counterstrikes that would attack supply bases and possibly lead to rebellion throughout the Ktarran Empire.

To achieve that, all Delano and the PDF had to do was direct Earth's planetary defense. Since there were no experts on space warfare, he decided to become one himself. With Marshal Shuvalov's guidance and the support of flexible thinkers, the PDF High Command team was created, and a strategic plan was developed.

That team, led by Generals Klegg, Zeng, and Shuvalov, included Colonel Welsh, six naval captains or admirals, and four senior fighter pilots. They were supported by all the computer resources necessary, with an entire war gaming staff numbering over a hundred military historians and data modeling programmers.

Using the battle records of the Tarlons and Halkins, combined with the specifications for the Darts and Destroyers, the High Command developed what was expected to be the defense plan for Earth.

In the Pacific War, the US Navy went up against the better trained and more experienced Japanese counterparts. Initial American losses had been staggering, almost fatal. It had taken almost two years before American ships, planes, and their pilots first equaled, then surpassed, the resource-deprived Japanese.

The PDF did not have the luxury of two years. An untrained and inexperienced space force had to win its first battle with the Ktarrans. A serious loss would be devastating to Earth, and even a draw might doom the planet. Nothing critical could be left to chance.

Delano hadn't liked telling Peng and Jang to test the Darts to destruction, but that hard decision needed to be made. Better to lose a few pilots and their Darts now, when mistakes and problems could be corrected, than have such failures in the first encounter, where many more lives would be at stake.

The decision might be logical, might even be the right one under the circumstances. But in the last year Delano had given far too many such orders for the rationalization to mean as much anymore. *People are going to die.* General Klegg had proven prophetic. Men and women had died, were dying, because Delano and Lian asked them to, or ruthlessly ordered it to happen.

During the day, the weight on his shoulders didn't bother him quite so much. At night it was different. Only Lian's calm presence when they were together banished the demons of doubt and fear. As long as she believed in him, believed in what they were doing, he could carry on. Delano wished she were at his side right now, the touch of her body against his, even her reassuring smile.

Soon, he told himself. *Soon.*

* * *

At last Chiew ended her presentation, her report thorough and professional. She had deftly fielded at least a dozen questions from Delano and a few from Major Bennett. Delano had recorded everything, but he accepted the memory stick she gave him. He turned to Major Bennett, who had remained mostly silent during the presentation. Of course she was in touch with Chiew daily, as the facilities exchanged data or services.

"Major Bennett will now brief us on the Transports' status."

The JovCo facility had been assigned the construction of the Colonizer Transports. Like the other spacecraft required, the parts had been manufactured and assembled on Earth, at two different sites, one in Russia and the other in the United States, near the Spaceport facility. Every part had to be certified by both locations, to ensure that the items were fully interchangeable, and teams had regularly transported personnel and parts back and forth.

Bennett linked her tablet to the presentation computer, and began. "As you know, the original plan called for ten Transports to be built. To achieve that estimate would have required too many construction specialists and resources. We would basically have been building ships for their construction crews."

"Then it is official that we will have only five Transports for the colonists?" Jang didn't sound too disappointed. He would have seen the preliminary reports.

"Possibly six," Bennett said. "Depending on how much time we can compress, we might be able to manage that. After all, we don't know how long the battle will last. If it drags on for a few weeks, we may be able to launch more." She sighed. "But six would be the maximum. Because of other priorities, we will not have sufficient logistics for any more. For the timeline, we will have only five."

The carefully planned pipeline of materials needed by the Lunar staff and the three kinds of spacecraft being assembled had been precisely calculated and planned by the best just-in-time manufacturing experts. And not just parts. People, too, had to arrive and be housed and fed until they could board the Transports. Logistics had turned out to be a ruthless political dictator, making decisions on life and death based on what schedule the PDF wanted to follow.

After limited testing of internal systems on Earth – they couldn't test the drives within the atmosphere – the Colonizers were broken down, and parts were packed and shipped to the Moon for reassembly and final testing. Two thousand American and Russian engineers and construction staff had been assigned to the JovCo site, and had begun construction on the expanded facilities. The first batch of ship parts hadn't arrived until six months ago, and work had been a frenzy since.

Six of the largest computer printers ever constructed operated round the clock at JovCo's construction site, creating and assembling the very steel fabric of the Colonizer hulls. Every possible replacement part for those machines had been stocked in quantity, so that the machines could work their magic without pause.

"The last change to the Darts design necessitated a modification to the Colonizer docking bays. Fortunately, that was the final major construction modification allowed."

The basic plan called for the Colonizer, after lunar launch, to return to Earth orbit. There each would take on final supplies and the colonists, all ferried by the Jumpers directly from the planet.

Some livestock and live plants would be loaded at that time. Performing this phase in Earth orbit would reduce logistical pressure on the Moon.

The intention was for both people and stock aboard the Colonizers to spend part of their stay in hibernation. Long Duration Sleep technology had advanced sufficiently so that a human body could "sleep" for forty to sixty days at a time without any adverse effects. The medical staffs had decided that time might even be extended under lower gravity conditions. At any rate, the colonists would rotate through their transport's sleep center, which would reduce the drain on life support by twenty percent or so throughout the voyage.

The Tarlons had provided possible destination points, star locations where wormholes seemed likely. But the closest of those would still require more than three years to reach. Each vessel had a different destination sector assigned. There had been discussions about sending the Colonizer Transports out in pairs, but that really didn't provide any advantages. In the event of a major failure in one ship, resources on the other would not be available to assist. So every effort was made to ensure the transports could repair themselves on route.

The destinations were all within the same galactic vector, but the specifics of that were one of Earth's most closely guarded secrets. If the defense of Earth failed, Delano and the PDF High Command did not want the Ktarrans coming after the colonists.

Each Colonizer would carry four fully-armed Darts in hull-mounted bays. The small fighting ships could be used as scouts or a defensive screen if necessary. A fifth could be assembled from ship stores if needed. But the main defensive power of the Colonizer would be its five beam weapons. Not enough to turn them into fighting ships, given their size, but hopefully at least enough to defend themselves should they encounter Ktarrans or some new hostile alien race.

While Major Bennett droned on, Delano thought about the Colonizers. Nearly everyone on the Moon had family or relatives assigned a berth on a Transport. But most workers on the Moon would have to stay behind, to support the fight against the Ktarrans. PDF Marines were already making provisions to prevent stowaways and deal with last minute arrivals.

The stowaway issue, just one more critical problem, reached Delano's desk after two construction workers created a concealed closet just large enough to accommodate the men and a few days' supply of food and water. Delano agreed with the High Command that the potential stowaways would be executed immediately, with no exceptions. Each Colonizer captain had to agree to that in advance. Otherwise critical resources would be consumed by people who might not have the required skills.

"So the Colonizer departure schedule can now be finalized," Bennet concluded. "We'll launch them five days apart, and the last will depart just before the expected arrival date of the Ktarrans."

We hope. That event continued to create confusion. The Tarlons couldn't pinpoint the exact date when the wormhole would be stable enough to provide access to Earth's solar system. Even now monitors – half a dozen drones with gravity wave detectors – had been positioned near Jupiter to search for the first clues that the wormhole would become active. Delano hoped to have at least forty to fifty hours of advance warning.

Nevertheless, the departure schedule was tight. Delano wanted the last Colonizer gone before the Ktarrans arrived, so as to leave no trail for them to follow. If all the ships could not launch before the Ktarrans came, a different sector of space would be utilized for the escape. If Earth were defeated, the best possible scenario would be that the Ktarrans wouldn't learn about the transports until it was too late to track them.

"Good work, Major Bennett, Captain Chiew. I'd like to speak with you again before I return to Earth."

"When would that be?" General Jang couldn't keep the curiosity out of his voice.

Delano smiled. His trip to the Moon had been practically unannounced, and no doubt people were wondering why he came. "I expect to go back in a week or ten days, after I've finished my tour on a Destroyer. I'm heading out to Jupiter space for a week of maneuvers and testing. The Halkin ship will be accompanying me."

"Any specific purpose in mind?"

"No, I just wanted to get a feel for what's coming," Delano answered. With luck, he'd do a lot more than just visit Jupiter.

Chapter 33
85 BKA

The great ship rested on the lunar surface, its gunmetal gray hull protected from the sun's heat by a canopy of mylar sheets stretched above it. But nothing draped over its body could conceal the nature of the craft – a deep space Colonizer vessel. Two hundred ten meters long, one hundred ten wide, and almost thirty-five meters high, the ship that would eventually lift off from the Moon would be more sophisticated than any aircraft carrier or ocean liner ever built. If mankind's destiny was to perish under the Ktarran invasion, this ship, and four others like it, would be humanity's last best hope for the future.

Its name was *Aurora*. A beautiful name for a ship as ugly as they come, with blunt lines and hard edges. At first glance, she appeared a dubious choice for her task of saving the human race.

The other four Colonizers, in various stages of assembly, had their own places nearby, each connected by a 75 meter access tube to a centrally located massive construction facility. Like eight spokes on a wheel, the five ships connected to the central hub. Where spokes number six, seven, and eight would be, lay a seemingly endless landing field for the shuttles, transports, and cargo movers that carried people and parts to the site, Lunar Construction Facility Seven. No one called it that. Everyone who took one look at the place, and simply called it The Dockyard.

Another site a hundred kilometers away, with similar dimensions provided assembly and testing for the Darts and Destroyers. In less than sixteen months, the two sites had transformed the Moon into a true space-faring port.

A few days earlier, the Dockyard construction officer had certified the hull as airtight. After that, the *Aurora* was physically connected, via a pair of airlocks, to the lunar construction barn where the individual sections, shipped up from Earth, were assembled. The barn, ten meters high and one hundred and twenty meters long, seemed huge.

Delano and Lian had waited impatiently for this day, and when they received word of *Aurora's* progress, they scheduled their visit.

Hand in hand, they glided down Access Tube #1 and stepped aboard the still-unfinished Colonizer ship. From the outside, the *Aurora* appeared finished, its exterior gleaming in the reflected lunar sunlight and displaying a dizzying array of antennae and sensors protruding from the shiny metal. The ship's interior revealed another story, with wires and cables trailing everywhere, insulation dangling from the bare steel hull, and shipping boxes and tools scattered about. More instruments and devices had yet to be added.

"It's much bigger than I expected," Lian said. "I know what the specs say, but it seems . . ."

Delano grinned. Lian seldom had trouble finding the right word. "Gargantuan? Titanic? Colossal?" He squeezed her hand. "It's all of those, all right. What do you call it, Dockmaster?"

Today the only person accompanying them, by Delano's firm request, was the Dockyard's master engineer, Ira Mankowitz. Well over six feet tall, the Brooklyn-born Mankowitz was built like a bull, with thick arms and legs that did not seem out of place on his powerful frame. Many people had manufactured the thousands of parts that went into the *Aurora*, but Mankowitz and his teams had assembled them into a finished product. The ships were as much a part of him as anything ever made.

"It's been an honor to build them, Colonel Delano, Dr. Duan. All my life I worked on dozens of projects, each one larger than the last. But this is the end of the rainbow for me."

"So you think they will fly?" Lian's question wasn't an idle one. There wouldn't be time for a lot of testing.

"They'll fly, Dr. Duan," Mankowitz said. "Like any new ship, they'll have a few problems to work out. But these ships are intended to be self-maintaining, with the design and equipment to repair any implementation issues that may crop up. Every system and component has been thoroughly computer modeled and stress tested on Earth."

That requirement had been one of the main specifications, Delano knew. These ships had to work. There was no room for error. "You've done a great job. Now give us the private tour."

"We just finished pressurizing the hull a few days ago," Mankowitz said. "The *Aurora* will hold 900 passengers and 70 crewmen, and carry enough supplies for five years. Of course, about a third of the passengers will be in LDS at any given time."

Delano shook his head. The *Aurora* possessed nearly 300

Long Duration Sleep modules. Keeping roughly a third of the ship's complement in suspended animation on a two-months rotation would greatly reduce the demand for food, oxygen, and other consumables. LDS would also ease the crowding. Troublemakers could be isolated as well.

"Is there any danger from such heavy use of the LDS?" Lian reached out her hand and touched part of the hull, almost in awe of the vast structure.

"The docs say no," Mankowitz said, "but I wouldn't be surprised if a few turn into vegetables or lose portions of their memory. Four or five years is a long time, even with frequent rotations."

"How crowded will it be?" Delano knew the numbers, but Mankowitz was the man on the ground, or as the Marines used to say, "he knew the real scoop."

"Well, *Aurora's* got six levels. Think of her as five pizza boxes stacked on top of each other, with a smaller box up top. Not graceful by any means, but it's the best configuration for a deep space voyage or for traveling in a wormhole."

If the *Aurora* or any of the other Colonizers discovered a useful wormhole, the plan was to take advantage of it. That meant the ship couldn't be too long, and not much wider than it was. The Ktarrans maximized their massive ships by building them into a roughly spherical shape, but the construction timetable of the PDF necessitated a more squarish structure.

The *Aurora's* double hull had been constructed from forty foot panels and lifted up from Earth's surface by a fleet of Jumpers. A cargo container could hold sixty panels, each one forty feet long and eight feet high. Thickness of a panel would be two inches of tough but lightweight #6060 aluminum alloy.

The Dockyard workers utilized robot welders to fit every panel together, and other robots measured and verified the work. A final coating of steel epoxy a quarter inch thick added strength to each panel. This process was applied at the Dockyard. The end result was a strong hull easily capable of surviving in space for ten years. The hull was also tough enough to filter most adverse radiation even without the shields.

"With all the food and supplies necessary for everyone," Lian asked, "will people be able to stand being so crowded?"

Mankowitz smiled. "It will be very cozy. Like living in a low-end high-rise in New York or Shanghai. Up close and personal. Individual quarters for married people, each with four bunks. Single folks will stay in one of the barracks, eight to a cabin. One locker the size of a suitcase allocated to each person. Any other personal goods approved by the pre-loading committee go into the cargo hold. And don't forget the docs. They'll be pumping soothing aromas into the air and handing out plenty of happy pills. If everyone minds their own business, it shouldn't be too bad."

Not everyone would. Especially those chosen more for their political connections than practical skills. "Anyone who causes problems," Delano said, "will be tossed into LDS and kept there as long as possible. Serious threats will be dealt with by the Captain."

Ira smiled. "I know there are special quarters for twenty Space Marines. I'm sure they'll be able to handle any trouble."

Delano wondered about that. The Space Marines, as they were called, were trained men and women who had joined the PDF early and worked hard to support its goals. They would operate *Aurora's* defenses in case they ran into Ktarrans or some other species looking for trouble. And maintain shipboard discipline during the voyage. But a crew of highly intelligent scientists and technicians could be a greater danger on a long voyage, and some idiots would always find a way to make trouble.

In fact, Delano had worked with the men chosen to captain each Colonizer, and together they had created a handbook for policy and decision making. He advised the captains to incarcerate without hesitation. If necessary, space anyone who might become a problem. One thing the PDF had learned was that some people would simply resist any program, even one obviously for the common good. Those dangerous people would have to be restrained. Permanently, if needed. *Very Machiavellian.*

By now the trio had progressed their way deep into the *Aurora*. Mankowitz guided the way, warning them to watch their step.

"So we entered at Level 1, which is mostly storage and supplies. Empty storerooms right now. Let's move on."

They pulled themselves up the main access tube to reach Level 2. "This will hold the LDS units," Mankowitz said, "plus a hospital, medical research, physical fitness chambers, some labs, things like that."

They wasted only a few moments on Level 2. "Level 3, that's engineering and auxiliary control."

Mankowitz guided them onto the engineering level. "Supplies and maintenance equipment for the engines, antigravity and screen generators, weapons maintenance, and computer control systems are all right here on this single level."

That design had been deliberate, Delano knew. In the event the crew had to make repairs, every critical component needed to be close at hand. Repairs in space would likely be time dependent.

"How do you know what you'll need," Lian asked? "Can you fit everything on this level?"

"Not quite," Mankowitz said. "Some bulky replacement equipment, secondary repairs, things like that will have to be stored on Level 1. But hopefully we've identified the key components to fix 90% of potential problems. Naturally we'll have our printers to manufacture any part we need."

"It's always the part you don't have that's the one you want," Delano said. He knew the designers had done their best, despite the unknown potential problems.

It was Level 4 that interested Delano.

"Level 4 has a Med Lab, and some crew living quarters," Mankowitz explained. "But it's the main entrance to the Command and Control room, which is in the forward part of the ship. C&C is a multilevel configuration that can be sealed off from the rest of the ship in the event of alien contact or a space fight. Other than that, this level is almost entirely dedicated to living quarters and a few laboratories."

They spent quite some time on Level 4, with Mankowitz describing where the various control systems would be placed. There was even a large panel of ballistic glass in the forward section, but nothing to see outside but a few containers.

Delano knew quite a bit about control rooms, and this one in particular. For example, the hull plating on the forward section was even thicker than that of the rest of the ship. From this center, weapons, screens, propulsion, navigation, power generation, communications, computer management, and life support would be controlled and maintained. It was the fighting heart of the *Aurora*. In time of crisis, most of the crew and all the Marines would be in C&C.

"Level 5 is mostly living quarters, shops, and the mess hall.

They'll have to eat in shifts, cafeteria style, two hundred at a time. That will keep the cooks busy all day. Everybody will take a turn at mess duty, cleaning tables and serving food. No exceptions, I understand, except there is a small mess for the crew and Marines. They say it's going to be two meals a day, with protein bars for snacks in between. Most of the food carried aboard will be down below, in long-term storage."

Delano had endorsed those decisions, too. Plus, you couldn't have key staff waiting on a food line. As for everyone else, the motto was simple – everyone works, if they want to eat. Complaints would be resolved by a Captain's Mast, where people would be judged and sentenced. Or spaced, if the crime were serious enough. Throughout the PDF, hard justice was the rule, and it would be carried out on board each of the Colonizers. Every potential colonist had been warned about the consequences of shirking duties or causing trouble.

They didn't spend much time on Level 5. Delano and Lian wanted to see Level 6, which was a slightly smaller unit perched on top of the other levels. Level 6 had two weapons stations already installed, and some other technical labs, but almost two thirds of Level 6 would be devoted to a hydroponics lab, where additional food and specialty items could be grown. And a chicken coop, to provide fresh meat and eggs.

Four-inch-thick metallic glass, itself as strong as any of the hull panels, would permit the use of actual sunlight when available. Otherwise light could be generated by the anti-matter engines and routed via fiber optic cables to the Solarium.

"Well, that's the tour," Ira said.

Over an hour had passed. "Not quite," Delano said. "I'd like to see the docking bays."

Mankowitz nodded. "Sorry, nearly forgot. Docking bays, Level Four, next stop on the tour."

They descended via the main access corridor, dropping slowly in the lunar gravity, and using their hands to regulate their descent. Once they reached Level 4, they went to the rear of the ship, the section farthest from the control room.

"This area isn't quite finished yet," Mankowitz said. He led them over to a thick window, where they could see into the Docking Bay. "There's no pressure in there, so we can't go in without a suit. The two Darts will be launched and retrieved here, and screens will provide the primary protection from open space.

But whenever needed, the forward and rear doors can be closed and the entire compartment pressurized. Two Jumpers will be stored in each bay as well, shuttles if you will, in case suitable planets are found and you need an away team for exploration."

Delano, like most of those who'd been in space with the Tarlons and Halkins, always felt a little nervous when the only thing keeping empty space from killing you was an unseen plasma screen. He remember the fear he'd felt the first time he stepped through one.

But the two docking bays, one on each side of the Aurora, could each carry and support two Dart fighters. If necessary, a fifth Dart could be constructed from spare parts. These four fighting ships would give the *Aurora* a real chance in the event they encountered any Ktarrans.

If the Ktarrans conquered Earth, they would almost certainly learn about the departure of the five Colonizer ships, and might even attempt to pursue them. So both the *Aurora* and her Darts carried a full complement of tactical nuclear and conventional warheads. One other provision for protection was the plan to have at least one Destroyer, specially modified, to accompany the *Aurora* and the other Colonizers.

The tour ended back in the Dockyard, and Delano and Lian shook hands with Mankowitz. "Thank you so much for your effort, Ira," Delano said. "You may turn out to be the man who built the ships that saved humanity. And for that, Lian and I are truly grateful."

"No thanks required, Colonel Delano, Dr. Duan. Just make sure I'm on the last ship leaving Earth. I've always wanted to travel in space, and this way I'll get to see more wonders than most people."

"You are booked on the *Centauri*," Lian said. "You'll be the Master Engineer, and they'll be lucky to have you aboard."

The engineer seemed embarrassed by her words. "Dr. Duan, I understand you named the *Aurora*, and the others?"

"Yes, I helped select the names," she said. "Let's hope they bring each ship luck."

The five Colonizer ships were the *Aurora, Orion, Serenity, Pegasus, and Centauri*. If Earth had more time, two more ships were nearly through the pre-construction phase on Earth: the *Perseus* and *Aquila*. The first to depart Earth's environs would be the *Aurora*. The *Centauri* would be last, departing right before the

Ktarrans were scheduled to arrive.

The names chosen had been picked from Earth's constellations. Except for *Aurora* and *Serenity*, which Lian had liked. Each Alliance nation wanted to name a ship, but with mixed crews of Chinese, Americans, Russians, and others, the squabble over names had started to heat up. Delano and Lian decided it was better to have nation-neutral, uplifting names. He hoped it would be the first act of unity for a ship of mixed backgrounds and ethnicities.

"If you can keep a secret, Ira," Delano said, "you may be seeing both of us again."

He didn't give him time to answer, leaving the surprised engineer with a blank look on his face. Delano pulled Lian along as they headed back toward the Dockyard. "Show's over, time to get back to work."

Mankowitz escorted the two leaders of the PDF back to the warehouse and their anxiously awaiting security staffs. Then he headed back to his office, a small windowless cubicle in a corner of the big structure. It held a desk and five tables, each one covered with an inch-thick stack of drawings.

The final blueprints – computer generated and printed on specialized devices – for each of the Colonizers were laid out here, a table for each ship. Mankowitz glided over to the smallest pile, the one that depicted the *Centauri*. He rifled through the diagrams for the ship until he found the sector he wanted, one that contained the senior crew quarters on level four.

He studied the structure for the quarters that would house the ship's captain and his senior crew. Prime real estate, he knew. There were ten cubicles in a single row, with the captain's closest to the portal that led back into the control room. All the cubicles had the same specifications. Mankowitz noted the exact same diagram had been used for the first four ships.

Using a stylus, he made a notation on the blueprint, then went to his computer. By shaving 30 centimeters off each room, he added an eleventh cubicle to the *Centauri*. This new chamber would be small, but private and adequate for two. Located at the dead end portion of the corridor, it would be adjacent to the room where Mankowitz, as Chief Engineer, and his wife would live.

Of course, he wasn't allowed to make changes to the final designs without committee approval, but no one had ever questioned any of his decisions, nor would they now. The entire process took only minutes, and when he finished a broad smile of satisfaction crossed his face.

Yes, he and his wife would enjoy living next to the two leaders of the PDF.

Chapter 34
85 BKA

Aboard the Halkin ship, Delano and Lian stood side by side, gazing through the thick slab of transparent aluminum that the ships' officers used for its forward viewport. The viewing quality wasn't as good as the hardened glass used by the Earth ships, but the aluminum material was far stronger, and the Halkin designers apparently decided the need for optical quality ranked lower than the critical need to keep the hull strong.

If one needed precision, high-quality cameras relayed an even sharper image onto the bridge's monitors, and the image could be enhanced as well as shifted by wavelength. Still, like almost all living creatures, the need to actually "see" their surroundings remained ever-present, no doubt recreated from the genetic material of the Ancients.

At present, the need for quality was negligible. The enormity of Jupiter, even at the distance of three hundred thousand kilometers from the outer magnetosphere, still pumped out enough radiation to dazzle the eyes. Human eyes, that is. Captain Horath, the commander of the only alien ship still in the solar system, could tolerate much higher radiation levels than the puny humans.

We're not so hot. Delano remembered when the initial genetic analysis of Tarlon and Halkin material indicated earthlings had less advanced optics, hearing, taste, physical strength, and even touch. Humans basically had no physical advantages over either race, a sobering thought that did much to silence the Earth-firsters who complained about aliens at every opportunity.

Apparently humans were the genetic equivalent of the great compromise, excelling at nothing but mentally flexible. As often before in history, weakness could become strength. Puny muscles helped mankind develop strong machines. Limited eyesight range spurred the invention of optical glasses and telescopes.

"We may not be great at anything," Delano muttered, "but we still get the job done."

"What was that?" Lian looked at him with surprise.

"Oh, nothing," he said, giving her an extra hug. "Just thinking out loud."

"And in English."

"Sorry." It probably didn't matter any longer, but they still had the urge to keep their thoughts to themselves. In the sixteen months since they first learned the Halkin language, Delano and Lian had worked their way through several Chinese dialects, Japanese, Spanish, Korean, and a half dozen other vernaculars. If the aliens wanted to eavesdrop on their private thoughts, they would have to learn a lot of different languages. Currently Delano and Lian discussed private matters only in French.

A flare of light on the viewport brought them back to the examination of Jupiter. For several seconds, a river of flowing electrons – electricity to the non-scientists – had appeared, connecting Jupiter's ionosphere with its closest moon, Io. The spectacular and frightening sight – visible energy flowing from a planet to its nearest moon – might be the greatest wonder in the solar system.

The Tarlon scientist, Jarendo, had explained that, after the proper conversions, that perhaps as much as five million amps might transfer between the two bodies, producing not only a dazzling display, but tremendous radio bursts. Those occasional surges had been a major problem for Io's miners, as the moon actually could become electrically charged, negative on one side and positive on the other. One such field had measured 400,000 amps across the satellite.

Quite a few JovCo miners had died before they learned that everything needed to be well insulated.

"I hope we don't get any closer," Lian said. "This is scary enough."

Delano felt the same, but didn't want to increase her worries. "Horath says the shields can handle far more radiation."

Captain Horath interrupted their discussion. "It is time to begin the first test, Delano and Lian."

Which meant take your seats and buckle in, because it's going to be a bumpy ride.

"Yes, Captain," Delano said.

He and Lian grabbed their respective seats and fastened the odd-shaped belts around them. A single pull snugged all the straps down, leaving only Delano's hands free. The *Meseka* had plenty of unoccupied stations in its command center. Most of Horath's original crew had departed the solar system after the Ktarran encounter. Even the presence of three Tarlons didn't fill the bridge.

The *Meseka's* bridge differed from most Earth designs for a control center. All the primary systems were operated and maintained from this single chamber, which helped explain its large dimensions, almost forty percent of the spacecraft's interior space. Captain Horath was now about to go into battle, simulated, against some PDF warships.

Today even Delano, otherwise a mere observer, had a function to fulfill. He checked in on his comm link with the Earth ship, then reported. "Captain Horath, the first Destroyer is ready."

"Acknowledged," the Halkin grunted. He shifted to the Halkin language. "Commencing attack. Weapons at ten percent. Prepare for acceleration."

Those commands were for Horath's crew. In seconds the ship was moving, the acceleration force pressing Delano into his control chair. The ship's speed continued to increase. The force, which he estimated at about four gravities, continued, as the *Meseka* hurled itself toward the approaching Earth destroyer.

On the simulated target, PDF Captain Higgins had command of the *Resolute* – its specific name was D28 – a standard vessel of Earth's new and untested space force. He seemed willing to fight head on, and he fired his energy weapons first, taking only a few seconds to locate and latch on to the approaching Halkin ship.

Horath held his course steady, absorbing the energy beam for a few clicks. Delano understood the tactic. The Halkin allowed the Earth ship's beams, also set to ten percent, to strike the *Meseka*, but before they could concentrate their power long enough to penetrate the shields, Horath issued the next command.

"Launch flare. Pitch down twenty degrees, right twenty."

The flare was an Earth tactic. Its burning magnesium would temporarily increase the *Meseka's* image on the attacking ship's screens, simulating a hit. Meanwhile, Horath's ship would be moving off its previous course trajectory – this time below and shifting to the right of its original course.

"Reacquire target. Fire!"

While the Earth Destroyer continued to concentrate its three energy beams on a block of burning magnesium coated with a cobalt alloy, the *Meseka* had shifted its position and fired its own weapons. Since the range had closed, the weapons' effective power had increased. The Earth ship, struck by the *Meseka's* beams and its sensors temporarily blinded, couldn't locate its attacker. The Destroyer tried to evade, but by then the powerful Halkin beams had been concentrated long enough to register if not a kill, at least a seriously damaged opponent.

"Damn!" The word blasted into Delano's ear piece, as Captain Higgins acknowledged the defeat.

"Cease fire, Captain Horath," Delano said. "The Destroyer acknowledges your success."

The Halkin, as aware as any on the Earth ship, had already given the cease-fire order. Captain Higgins, despite the best training by his instructors and peers, had lost his vessel within twenty seconds of the attack. It was, Delano knew, the difference between classroom training and field combat. The tactic itself was as old as the Sumerians. Feint here, attack there. Distract your opponent. Let him think he is winning until he is destroyed. Alexander had used a similar attack plan at the Battle of Gaugamela, almost twenty five hundred years earlier.

Delano recalled what his drill instructor said during his training. "Nothing like a few rounds hissing over your head to keep you focused." *Focused, yeah, that's the word. All while trying to control your bowels.*

The "battle" had lasted less than twenty seconds. For the next three hours, the two ships tested different attack and defense tactics. High speed thrusts from unexpected quarters, simulated loss of a beam weapon or two, inability to achieve maximum thrust, and a dozen more scenarios.

When the time expired, Higgins and his Destroyer had been obliterated eight times, while defeating the Halkin ship only twice, with two draws. That translated into really bad results, especially against a ship only a third the size of the average Ktarran behemoth.

He thought of the joke that swept through Spaceport a few days back. "What would a PDF-designed rifle look like? A beautiful American stock, a flimsy Russian-made stamped receiver and bolt, and a Chinese barrel that was too heavy and tends to burst." Delano hadn't laughed when he first heard it.

Well, we won't be attacking them one on one. I hope.

When the exercise ended, a weary Delano and Lian attended the after-action debriefing aboard the *Meseka*. Delano found it hard to concentrate, as the technicians and weapons experts from both sides exchanged information and argued over the evaluation team's results. His body was stiff, and he could feel the bruises on his shoulders and hips from the violent gyrations. The Halkins seemed immune to the stresses, and the PDF officers and men of the *Resolute* had grown used to violent acceleration and deceleration as part of their training.

Lian appeared to have handled the bone-jarring changes in velocity better than Delano. Which didn't surprise him. He knew Lian had buffed up into a soldier's physique, while all of Delano's exercises had barely kept him in shape. *Too much sitting on my ass and drinking coffee. Yeah, that was it.*

When the debrief concluded, he and Lian had nearly thirty minutes before the next conference call. This was the second in a series of planned strategy meetings. Time was running out for Earth and its defense preparations. The Tarlon scientists had declared that the worm hole might reopen any time after the next twenty to thirty days. By now Earth had launched three Colonizers into deep space, another one was in Earth orbit topping off, and the last, the *Centauri*, would lift off the Moon in ten days.

No matter how much Earth trusted the aliens' estimate, the PDF didn't dare take a chance cutting the window too closely. In fifteen days, all ships would be on station, fully armed and ready for the Ktarrans' arrival. Supply would maintain their deliveries and training would continue, but soon every vessel and its weapons would be locked and loaded.

In one sense, Delano felt glad the waiting had nearly ended. The stress had gotten to him in the last few weeks. The constant worrying had worn him down, set him on edge. One way or another, he needed this to end.

Of course if the Ktarrans didn't bother to show up, Delano would look like a major fool who'd cried the sky was falling. No doubt every country in the world would be looking to separate his head from his shoulders. He'd killed or imprisoned thousands and thousands of people across the globe, and if the invasion turned out to be a dud, Delano's would be the first name on the list of those taking the fall. Lian at least could hope for protection from her uncle, though even that might not be enough.

Not that Delano cared about personal threats any longer. *Win or lose, I just want it to be over.*

Chapter 35
9 BKA

The edge of the Ktarran empire . . .

In the vast emptiness of space, far from the nearest Ktarran-controlled planet. Commander Veloreck found the interminable waiting hard on his ships and their crews. Nevertheless, the discipline remained strict and absolute. Once a ship joined the Earth attack force, it stayed on station. No exceptions, even for senior commanders.

He dared not disobey the Pannoch, so the ships trained and fine-tuned their weapons. Maneuvers of every possibility were studied, planned for, and executed. Then the process repeated.

The Pannoch expected nothing less. He wanted the invasion force, ships and crews, to be at the peak of their capabilities. Their anger at the harsh treatment would on only serve to increase their hated of the planet Earth.

The rigorous training applied to both Ktarrans and the slave crews. If any of the crew complained, punishments were handed out liberally, and several Ktarrans found themselves chained to the eating table for errors in judgment or laxity in the performance of their duties.

Only the arrival of the supply ships bringing fresh meat broke the monotony. Tempers up and down the ranks grew frayed, but no one dared disobey the Pannoch's orders. Eventually even the slowest-witted among the captains and crews got the message – this assault was going to be different.

The Ktarran fleet had never in its history prepared for a fleet battle. Other than a few ships working together, the idea that fifty or a hundred vessels could combine their firepower had not existed.

Even so, Veloreck wondered about the waste of time and resources. Food, water, and other vital supplies were being consumed as fast as the supply fleet could deliver them. The Ktarran crews resented the long stay in space, something unheard of in their history. Deprived of the usual hunts, the confined crews seethed against the tough restrictions.

Some of the slave crews died as well, driven to desperation by the long periods of work and the brutality of the training. Fortunately, slaves were plentiful and readily replaced.

Of course none of these problems mattered to the remote Pannoch, who would have ignored them if anyone mentioned them. Veloreck's sub-commanders had wanted him to complain to Ktarra, but Veloreck knew better than that. Instead he ordered even more discipline.

By this stage of the invasion preparation, every Ktarran and slave crewman hated the animals of Earth. Now their hostility would be directed at any inhabitants of the planet.

Nevertheless, the long period of training and preparation was drawing to an end. The wormhole to the planet known as Earth would reopen soon. The last supply ships had delivered their cargoes, and one by one, crews and vessels reported themselves ready.

Despite the rigors of the extended training, the crews now took pride in themselves, as their expertise and capabilities with their weapons increased. After all, they reasoned, what could a planet that didn't have beam weapon or inter-stellar travel capabilities do to resist this mighty Ktarran armada?

The expedition to Earth promised to turn into an extended hunt. After the cities were destroyed, hunts would be organized for food and sport. After that, the once-defiant planet would be burned to ash from orbit. Between their energy beams and the new atomic weapons, nothing would ever grow again.

Even Veloreck had occasional thoughts about such things. But first he had to crush whatever resistance the humans might offer. He felt in his bones that Earth would resist, and it might even be able to inflict serious damage to his vast Ktarran fleet.

Earth had atomic missiles and might have other unknown weapons as well. Something whispered in his ear that this conflict would not be an easy one.

The day before the wormhole opened, Veloreck summoned his sub-commanders, Teeg and Jothe, for one last conference before the departure for Earth.

When they arrived on Veloreck's ship, he dispensed with any ceremony. "I know you have prepared your crews and ships. for every possible encounter. In that you have done well, and I have already informed the Pannoch of your efforts. But I want you both to prepare for the unexpected. These humans may be weak in terms of ships and weapons, but they may also have capabilities of which we are unaware. So I want you both to be ready for any new tactics. This is a battle we must win, and the planet Earth must be destroyed."

"It will be done," Teeg declared. "We have the mightiest fleet ever assembled in the galaxy. Nothing can stand before us."

"Every Ktarran and slave is ready," Jothe said. "All are eager to put an end to this training and waiting. Even thoughts of a hard fight do not trouble them."

"Perhaps," Veloreck said. "But I worry about these animals. In their encounter with Turhan's ships, they reacted quickly, organizing their forces and developing a plan that succeeded in destroying his three ships. And don't forget, that happened without the use of true space craft, aside from their puny air vessels."

"We will not fall for such tricks again," Jothe said.

"The best defense against such animals is overwhelming force, and we have that," Teeg agreed. "As long as we advance with care, nothing they possess can threaten us."

"Nothing they *possessed*," Veloreck said. "But I feel certain that they will have both ships and plans to resist us. The Tarlons and Halkins have given them plenty of warning about our ships and numbers. They will be ready for both. We would be fools if we did not expect stubborn resistance, and I feel certain that we will take heavy casualties."

He took a moment, studying both Ktarrans. "I have one final thought, one final order for you both. Whatever we encounter, you will commit your forces totally. No favorites are to be withheld, no pouch brothers or cousins to be protected. Each of you must be prepared to sacrifice your entire command without hesitation. Delays in implementing orders, requests for clarifications, or any of the usual methods of delaying action will be considered cowardice. You know the punishment for that."

Teeg and Jothe exchanged glances.

"Yes, Commander," they said in unison.

"Good," Veloreck said. "Then we are agreed. Convey my orders to your crews, and impress upon them the need for victory at all costs."

Veloreck rose, ending the meeting. "Return to your ships. We depart for Earth as soon as the wormhole stabilizes."

Part II - Confrontation

Chapter 36
1 BKA

"Wake up, Colonel Delano. You need to wake up now! You can do it, sweetie. Come on!"

The insistent voice kept repeating the words, until Delano floated his way back to consciousness. When he finally managed to open his gummy eyes, harsh light almost directly overhead prohibited him from seeing much of anything. He tried to raise his hand to shield his face, but the effort took more energy than he had, leaving him squinting against the brightness.

"What . . . what's happening." His tongue felt thick, and Delano knew he'd slurred the words. Not that it mattered. Nothing mattered, except that he wanted to go back to sleep.

"Stay with me, Colonel. Stay awake." The voice sounded soothing now. "You'll feel better in a few minutes. Just lie there and relax. The corrective meds should be flushing out the last of the benzodiazepine from your system. It won't take long."

By now Delano determined that the vaguely familiar voice belonged to a woman. But he obediently closed his eyes and tried to relax. He must have dozed off, because when his eyes next opened, he came fully alert, almost the way he'd trained his body to respond when he'd fought in the deserts of Yemen.

This time he knew who he was, and where. The floating sensation had a basis in reality. Delano was aboard a PDF Destroyer, orbiting the Moon. No, not the Moon. By this time the vessel would be out beyond Mars' orbit. And the Ktarrans . . . he tried to sit up, but the bunk's harness restrained him.

"Just a sec, Colonel," Linda said. "Do you know where you are? And who I am?"

The questions sounded innocuous, but he knew the protocol. One of the hazards of Long Duration Sleep was temporary memory loss. Another was poor muscular coordination that might last several days. His questioner might have checked all his read-outs, but she still had to examine him physically for any after effects. Anything serious and he'd be taken off active duty.

He recognized the short blond hair, blue eyes and the wide smile. "Linda Tasco." Delano's tongue felt thick, his lips rubbery. "You're med-tech for the . . . *Defiant*." He managed a smile.

"That's Senior Med-Tech to you." She laughed, as much with her eyes as her mouth. "Very good, but in case you've forgotten, I prefer to use my maiden name, Grayson."

He nodded in remembrance. His voice lowered. "Any sign of the Ktarrans?"

The cheerful smile vanished. "Possible. While you were in LDS, the Tarlons and Halkins detected a . . . twinge, that's what they called it, out past Elara's orbit. The location isn't where they expected the wormhole to materialize, but they're watching it. Our own instruments spotted the same . . . twinges a few hours later."

So now we have twinges, a new fucking word. And off Elara? What the hell was that? He needed a moment to recall Elara was one of Jupiter's moons. "How long have I been out?"

She glanced down at her tablet. "102 hours."

It took a few seconds, but his brain managed to process the data. "Wasn't I supposed to be out for 150 hours?"

Linda checked another instrument. "Yes, but all your life signs are well in the green. You've been nourished, exercised, dosed with vitamins, and your brain, such as it is, stimulated. The extra time in LDS isn't that important at your age. In a few hours you'll be at the top of your game."

Delano unhooked the restraints, pushing aside the thin blanket. Specially made in Germany with Egyptian cotton, the lightweight material weighed only a few ounces. But it had kept his naked body warm enough during the LDS. Fresh adhesive bandages showed where tubes and monitors had been placed on his chest, legs, and arms.

His coordination felt off, but that would pass. He knew the drugs that Linda had pumped into him were effective enough. And probably safe, unless she included some of her own "special" concoctions. One caution in her fitness file mentioned that she liked to experiment.

Linda helped him sit up. "Thirsty? I've got a great pick-me-up that I created . . ."

"No, thanks. I'll get something from the kitchen."

She read his mind. "Coward! Afraid of a little extra

stimulant?" She waved a plastic bottle in front of him.

"Yes." He made the word firm. "You're the last person who should be prescribing drugs. Where are my clothes?" Delano climbed off the bunk with care, adjusting to the low gravity maintained by the *Defiant*.

"Better not let the crew see you like that."

He glanced down at his naked body, spotted with white blotches from the bandages. Yes, definite shrinkage had occurred. Another by-product of LDS that tended to last a few days. *Or so they said.*

She laughed again, and this time Delano joined in. Linda could say and do anything as far as he was concerned. Without her stimulants, the Ktarrans might have captured the Space Station and killed everyone onboard, including Delano and Lian. The med-tech had been wounded in the gun fight, shooting alongside the Gunny.

She probably hadn't hit anything in that battle, but Linda had determined to rectify that failure. After three months of training, she had qualified as an expert in small arms and Close Quarters Combat.

Linda handed him his tablet. "Don't forget this. And drink plenty of water. You need to keep hydrating."

"Thanks."

"If you need any help with the . . . shrinkage, I've got something for that, too. Peter swears by it."

Too much information. He shook his head. "Take care, Linda."

Putting on his clothes took only a moment, though he had trouble with the lightweight deck shoes, more like padded yoga socks, specifically designed for low or no gravity environments.

The Med-Lab was near the rear of the ship, opposite the Cardio Room, which would be available in the case of multiple injured. Work space was tight, barely more than that aboard a submarine, and even less than on the freighters that made the run from the Moon to Io.

Delano glided along to the Kitchen/Lounge where he drank a bottle of water, then helped himself to a cup of black coffee. A few sips of the strong brew cleared his thoughts. Whatever the Tarlons and the brainy boys on Earth believed, these "twinges" were pretty much on the wormhole arrival schedule. Not to mention that if nothing serious had happened, Linda would have let him remain asleep for at least another twenty-four hours. Delano felt certain the Ktarrans were coming.

The *Defiant's* galley didn't have much room for lounging, but could feed eight people at a time, if you called microwaving your own food and sitting elbow-to-elbow gourmet dining. Eating in shifts was the solution. Each Destroyer class ship had design capacity for 18, four of whom were the crews for the two Darts attached to the hull. However the *Defiant*, as Delano's flagship, required an additional six passengers – Delano and his "staff" of five specialists.

To avoid overloading the ship's life support, three of Delano's staff were also assigned to the ship's regular duties. That included the positions for navigator, med-tech, and senior engineer. To accommodate Delano and his two battle-control assistants, the already crowded Control Room had received an additional three-person console to provide tactical control and communications for the fleet. It was a solution that pleased no one in the already crowded vessel.

He took another sip of coffee, this time enjoying the flavor. While he had the time, Delano decided to review the ship's roster. Flipping open his ever-present tablet, he selected the Table of Organization and Equipment (TOE) for this trip, which fit on a single screen.

Defiant Crew Roster & TOE (18)

Ship Captain	Captain Kai Chan
Executive Officer (Pilot)	Captain Seanna O'Shaughnessy
Navigator*	Acting Lt. Peter Tasco**
Senior Engineer*	Acting Lt. Nikolai Kosloff
Communications	Sergeant Jerome Cowan
Med-Tech*	Senior Tech Linda Grayson**
Flight Engineer	James Cook
Power Engineer	Wang Chen
#1 Gun Commander	Liam Astor
#1 Gun Specialist	Jacques (Jock) Barton
#2 Gun Commander	Hou Jingjing
#2 Gun Specialist	Tina Gutman
#3 Gun Commander	Manuel (Manny) Ortega
#3 Gun Specialist	Chelsea Wexton
Alpha Dart Captain	Chuck Hollingsworth
Alpha Dart Gunner	Roman Abramovich
Beta Dart Captain	Arkady Volozh
Beta Dart Gunner	Ruben Vardanayan

*   Member of Admiral Delano's staff, duty permitting
** Spouses

Supercargo (3)

Admiral, Forward Fleet	PDF Colonel Joseph Delano
Fleet Comm Officer	Lieutenant Steve Macey
Fleet Movement Spec.	Lt. Jack (Gunny) Stecker

Delano defined "supercargo" as useless to the functioning of the ship, which was certainly true in one sense. An eclectic crew, he decided. Three Chinese, four Russians, one Brit, one Frenchman, one Irish, and eight North Americans. Despite the mix, most of the crew had worked together for months. The previous navigator, senior engineer, and med-tech had complained bitterly about being bumped in the last few weeks, but Delano had insisted. The navigator and med-tech slots were considered critical, and the husband and wife team of Peter Tasco and Linda Grayson were certainly well qualified.

As for the senior engineer position, Kosloff had spent more time in space than anyone, and had participated in the design of the ship and its myriad of components. More important, he had alien contact experience, and could deal directly with the Tarlons and Halkins. All in all, Delano knew he had the best crew in the fleet.

He'd started on his second cup when a yawning Gunny Stecker joined him in the lounge. Since he'd stayed at Delano's side for over a year, he usually got less sleep than his boss, turning in only after Delano went to sleep, but always rising earlier. Gunny looked refreshed, and even less affected by the enforced LDS treatment. Delano shook his head. The man was made of iron. Neither hardship nor deprivation seemed to affect him. He had, after all, killed a Ktarran and five of the slave species practically by himself.

Neither man said anything for awhile. After eighteen months of working and fighting together, they knew each other too well to need to waste words. Gunny drained his cup and leaned back. "So, Colonel, do you think this is it? These twinges?"

Delano looked up from his tablet. "Afraid so, Gunny. The Tarlons have never seen these twinges before, so something unusual is going on. Maybe the Ktarrans know more about wormholes than we all thought."

"Yeah, that's what I figured. More bad intel. You feeling ready?"

"Marines are always ready." Delano shrugged at the obvious platitude. "Anyway, it's too late now to worry. *Muy tarde ahora.* We arrived at the rendezvous point six hours ago, and the rest of the task force is already here. We were the last to arrive." He changed the topic. "Is there anything you need? Data? Equipment?"

"No, nothing. I can work the board in my sleep. You've got the hard job."

Yeah, pick a military strategy and maybe get your ship and the planet destroyed. No stress there. Still, he'd trained for this encounter, and so had the Gunny.

"Keep an eye on the crew for me, Gunny. Just in case anyone gets a case of nerves."

Stecker shook his head. "Not this crew. They're more afraid of Captain Chan than any Ktarran, let alone me or you. Just tell him what you want, and he'll do the rest."

Delano grinned. Major Kai Chan, taller than most Americans, made the Gunny's physique look slight. A block of solid muscle, Chan had withstood more Gs during training than anyone else in the fleet. More important, he could think fast under pressure. Delano had selected him to command the *Defiant* over two Russians and a senior US Naval pilot, and nobody raised the slightest objection.

Always go with the best. Delano knew he had the fastest ship and the best crew in the PDF assault force. They would follow his orders because they trusted each other and respected him. For this conflict, the commander in chief would be at the tip of the spear, not safe in some underground command bunker in the rear echelon. *Which right now didn't seem like such a bad idea.*

"What's happening?" Steve Macey bounced his way into the lounge, hands clutching at every safety bar along the way.

"The last of the sleepers awakes," Gunny said. "It's about time, slacker. We thought you were going to sack out for another week."

Steve eased himself into a chair with a sigh of relief. "I don't feel so good."

Delano didn't like that. Almost everyone came out of LDS happy and calm, their bodies full of endorphins – dopamine and serotonin. "Did Linda give you something to drink?"

"Yeah, she said it would help . . ."

Yeah, right. "Keep an eye on him, Gunny, until whatever she gave him wears off," Delano said. "I think it's time for me to go to the Control Center."

Leaving the lounge, Delano followed the main corridor, moving past the sleeping quarters and storage areas until he reached the forward section of the ship. He passed through the open safety door, and took a quick glance around. Every console was manned, even though the *Defiant* wasn't on alert. Only the command stations where Delano, Gunny, and Steve would occupy were empty.

Delano glided down the aisle until he reached his command station, a trio of outsized combat chairs surrounded by consoles and controls. He squeezed into the gap between his position and the captain's control, which consisted of another console and three chairs. Captain Chan occupied the leftmost chair. The center station - Power Engineering – belonged to Wang Chen. The rightmost chair belonged to the XO, Chief Pilot Seanna

O'Shaughnessy.

The unusual seating arrangement allowed both the ship's captain and pilot to monitor the power settings at a glance. They could also look down at Delano's console with ease.

"Admiral on the Bridge!" Captain Chan waited until Delano had settled himself, rather than announce his arrival as he struggled his way into his chair.

"At ease," Delano answered. "Good morning, Captain Chan, and good morning to all." Of course it wasn't really morning, or night for that matter, except for Delano. *Idiot*!

No one commented, of course. He might be the Admiral of the Fleet, but on the *Defiant* Delano was just a passenger. Nevertheless, everyone took time to gaze at their newly arrived Admiral. As soon as he boarded, an exhausted Delano had been placed into the LDS, and the crew hadn't much chance to see him, let alone get to know him.

PDF Captain Kai Chan, turned to Delano. "Welcome back, Sir. We've detected two more fluctuations in the last four hours, both just outside of Elara's orbit, each one stronger than the one before. Command thinks the wormhole will materialize near there."

"So they're coming." A statement this time, not a question. At least his shipmates had awakened him at the first sign of activity.

"Yes, Admiral," Chan said. "We received a message from Lunar command. They're pretty sure the Ktarrans are on their way. Apparently they've figured out a way to manipulate the wormhole parameters, to make it appear much further away or closer to Earth. At least our brainy boys think it's a possibility."

Probably the Ktarrans didn't want to walk into an ambush by showing up where they were expected. Well, the enemy learns and adapts just as we do. Nobody expected the Ktarrans to be stupid a second time. "Everyone in place?"

Captain Chan nodded. "Just spoke with C-and-C. Senior Colonel Welsh has the Main Defense Force at Battle One Status, ready to go. The Defense Grid also reports all systems go."

Earth's defenses, after endless days of arguing and planning, had been divided into two parts.

The MDF was the largest – 87 Destroyers – split into two groups. Both followed the same orbit as Earth, one preceding the planet by five thousand kilometers, and the second following at the same distance. Theoretically, either could respond to an assault from any direction within minutes. Otherwise the entire PDF force would be used to protect Earth from any beam or nuclear or biological attack.

Delano's Initial Contact Force, or ICF, was the tip of the spear. It would initiate combat, but its main purpose was to offer one last chance for peace. If that failed, as everyone expected, the ICF would endeavor to sow confusion within the attacking enemy forces, and hopefully provide feedback to Earth as to the strength and tactics of the Ktarrans. *If we don't get blown to bits.*

In the event the Ktarrans sent only a small force of ships, the ICF would initiate contact, then attempt to blockade the wormhole to prevent any of the enemy from escaping.

The simplistic plan, such as it was, still remained a strategic guess. Nobody really knew what was going to happen. Even the Tarlons and Halkins had never fought a battle on this scale. The Ktarrans, too, could have new weapons and tactics of their own.

In the final analysis, only Earth's computer-controlled beams and missiles gave the defense any chance of success. Still, the Tarlons and Halkins had looked in awe at Earth's computers and fire control units.

Delano scanned his primary console, divided into multiple virtual panels. Gunny Stecker arrived to take the chair on the left. Lieutenant Steve Macey eased himself into position on the right. Steve didn't look much better now than in the lounge, but he brought up his comm station efficiently enough.

Macey's assignment was to maintain communications between the *Defiant* and Delano and the rest of the PDF forces. Two large displays and three smaller ones faced the comm expert. These would provide him with a steady stream of data and visuals. A large VR helmet would enable him to coordinate the incoming streams, and transfer images of whatever he deemed critical to Delano's position.

The Gunny had a similar but more specific task. As the battle action intensified, his mission was to identify and track Ktarran ships that appeared to be in command, either overall or of specific segments of the enemy force. That data would be entered into the ship's computer, which would attempt to analyze and predict the Ktarran battle plan.

When the early plans for defense began to evolve six months earlier, Steve had trained the Gunny on the complex system, which required calculated and precise review of enemy attack data. To everyone's surprise, the Gunny had proved quite adept at interpreting the data streams. That skill, combined with long hours of daily practice, would now assist him in the analysis. Secondarily, he would back up Delano and help spot any potential attacks on the *Defiant*.

As Delano tested his gear, he saw the med-tech standing at the hatch, speaking with Captain Chan. They exchanged a few quiet words, and then Chan returned to his command chair and plugged himself in.

Delano grunted. He could guess what that conversation had been about. Linda had been certifying his fitness for duty, and Captain Chan would be confirming it with Main Force HQ.

Not that it mattered. Unless Delano started drooling, no one was going to ask him to step aside. To that end, he plugged in his headset and opened his tablet.

"Admiral, Field Marshal Shuvalov has requested that you contact him at your convenience," Captain Chan said. As per orders, everyone on the ships of the fleet spoke English, the language they had used since training started.

"Thank you, Captain," Delano said, nodding first to Chan and then letting his gaze take in the others of the crew at their stations. Delano would have preferred boarding the *Defiant* a few days earlier, so he could get to meet the crew individually, but there'd been no time for that.

Delano decided to review the activities of the past one hundred hours, to see what he'd missed. He connected his tablet to the console, and brought up the ship's correspondence. A quick scan revealed nothing much had happened since the Mini-Fleet departed lunar orbit, except that two resupply ships, long- range Jumpers, had come and gone, topping off the vessels with fuel, air, water, and other supplies. The second vessel had departed twenty hours ago, so the *Defiant* and her sister ships were fully stocked.

The *Defiant* had been the last vessel to join the ICF mini-fleet, arriving only three days ago. The other ships had waited anxiously for the *Defiant*, since only she possessed the specialized equipment needed to fulfill her role as fleet command.

By the time Delano finished his review, the Gunny and Steve settled in and reported all systems green.

"Steve, connect me to Marshal Shuvalov."

That simple command took some work. The ship's regular radio communications between the Mini-Fleet and Lunar Command, what the techies called the OWLT (One Way Light Time), at this moment was about eight minutes, which meant a round trip of sixteen minutes (TWLT). That didn't include the actual conversation, or the recipient's time to think and reply. All in all, a cumbersome process, but until recently, the only method available.

But Steve knew that Delano and the field marshal needed to talk, not send messages back and forth. So he activated the QuantC, the quantum communication system. This still very experimental technology allowed communication in real time, utilizing quantum physics.

Delano watched Steve set up the sophisticated power supply, getting the Power Engineer seated behind and above Delano involved. A special antenna had to be lowered through the force fields and directly into an active vacuum scoop. The transmitter then converted the sound waves from the ship into Super Symmetrical quantum units. These were injected into the sea of ever-present particles – neutrinos, cosmic rays, gravity waves, and other bits of flotsam and jetsam that briefly flashed into and out of existence – the soup of sub-atomic matter that filled every cubic meter of vacuum space.

The high-power magnets of the power scoops separated the particles into matter and anti-matter chambers, from which they were recombined, via mutual annihilation, to produce the power needed to operate the ship and its force fields.

Or so Delano understood. He could repeat the words, but they made as little sense today as when he'd first heard them seventeen months ago. To really comprehend the concepts required very high level mathematical training. The Earth scientists had done their best to explain, but the conversion into something a non-technical person could understand turned out to be not very helpful.

The addition of the Super Symmetry particles – what the physicists and hi-brows called SUSY – added another wrinkle to the concept. When the lecturer started explaining how SUSY particles were exact opposites of regular sub-atomic particles, Delano gave up. He managed to take away the concept that quantum particles could be inserted into the space-time mix of matter and anti-matter which allowed the quanta to flow into subspace. These "quanta" could then be instantly retrieved, by a matching receiver and paired quanta, anywhere in the solar system. Some scientists claimed anywhere in the galaxy, but that fanciful theory remained to be tested.

Once the quanta were in subspace, an identical receiver could extract the anti-quanta particles that corresponded to the original transmitter, instantaneously. The devices had to be physically paired before being separated, and the smallest change in one could defeat the attempt to communicate. As far as Delano knew, no one had the slightest idea how one transmitter could pick out the quanta from another device millions of kilometers away. The theory had barely passed out of the experimental stage, and only a few units had managed to function properly. Politely, it remained a work in progress.

Even the Tarlons and Halkins did not have such a capability. The Tarlon Jarendo implied that the Ancients must have possessed such devices, allowing them to communicate across galactic space, and possibly even to other galaxies.

Delano's *Defiant* had one such instrument, and Marshal Shuvalov had access to another, this one in his command vessel, the *Enterprise*, orbiting the Moon. Bottom line, the two could converse as if they were in the same room. Delano had tested the device in lunar environs, and it had worked. Now it would be utilized for real, across a distance of millions of miles, not thousands.

"Colonel, the link is established," Steve said. He flipped a switch on his board, and a green light activated on Delano's console.

"Got it," Delano said. He pushed the talk button. "Marshal Shuvalov, can you hear me?"

"Da, I hear you Colonel Delano, though you sound like you are underwater."

Delano got the same impression. The voice synthesizers still needed better alignment to recombine and rearrange the quanta particles back into normal speech wavelengths. But he didn't notice any delay, just a bit more static than on the usual satellite call or radio transmission.

"At least this QuantC device seems to work at this distance," Delano said. "You'll be kept up to date. What news do you have for us?"

"Ah, yes, the so-called twitches have increased in frequency.

Jarendo thinks a wormhole will be forming soon. But he believes this is not the regular process. He thinks perhaps the Ktarrans have found a way to modify the wormhole, possibly enlarge or relocate it. The Tarlons suspect it will appear on the far side of Jupiter, somewhere near Elara's orbital space."

Something new from the Ktarrans, and they hadn't even arrived. "Copy that, Marshal Shuvalov. We'll be on the alert."

"Are you fully ready for the encounter, Colonel Delano?"

He glanced over his shoulder at Captain Chan, who nodded. "The *Defiant* is ready. We'll link up again as soon as our instruments detect anything."

"Good. By the way, the *Centauri* departed Earth orbit a few hours ago. Shuvalov out."

Delano heard the background hiss as the link was cut. Steve heard it too, and he broke the connection at his end as well. No one wanted to burn out the delicate equipment.

"Not much of a call," Steve said.

"Just wanted to hear my voice," Delano said. "It's the same with all the REMFs. But glad to hear the *Centauri* is on its way." The fifth and last Colonizer carried almost a thousand souls aboard, colonists who would try to plant the human seed on new worlds, hopefully ones safe from the Ktarrans' deadly reach.

"Always sounds funnier when the shoe is on the other foot," Gunny commented. "Now we are the REMFs."

Delano laughed. "Yeah. But enough BS. Let's start running through the plans. We may not have much time."

Part III - Conflict

Chapter 37
0 BKA

The PDF leaders had spent months preparing for the coming encounter with the Ktarrans. The Destroyer and Dart commanders had worked not only with the squadron fighter pilots, but also with the handful of qualified pilots and navigators from the Jupiter-to-Lunar run. Peter Tasco belonged to that group. Preparations included the Halkin and Tarlon leaders, who had real world experience fighting the Ktarrans.

Earth's military leaders then developed more than thirty different operational plans. These were tested by the squadrons, modified as needed, and then fed into every ship's tactical computer.

While no one expected a precise match in actual combat, a selected program could still be useful in quickly resolving some tactical issues and opportunities.

That program, installed on Delano's and the Gunny's consoles, as well as Captain Chan's and Captain O'Shaughnessy's, would guide the fleet during the coming encounter. Even if the *Defiant* were out of action or unable to communicate, the remaining ships would know exactly what maneuvers would be optimal for the given situation.

The shipboard computers were, as Delano knew, as good as Earth's military and private industry could build and program. In fact, the computers and guidance systems had proven to be the most complicated part of the development of Earth's fleet. All the systems had to be tested, integrated, and hardened to perform under intense and ever-changing battle conditions. In other words, the software had to function properly the first time.

The Fleet Command Console provided state-of-the-art instruments and viewscreens to manage Earth's first major space battle. The three-dimensional display, a forty-five-inch curved surface, could be moved, adjusted, enhanced, and enlarged at any point by a mere touch of Delano's finger. Feeds from two other ships transmitted their data directly into this console, where they were integrated with the *Defiant's* screens. The end result was that Delano could view a sector of space thousands of miles across, and hundreds of miles in height.

The Tarlons and Halkins had blinked in surprise at the visual representation, and declared that neither they nor the Ktarrans had anything close to such an information display. With an unparalleled view of the battle, Earth would have a significant advantage.

The fire-control systems for the beams and missiles constituted another significant edge for Earth's forces. Delano's ships would be smaller, faster, and deliver more energy from each of their beam weapons. Whether those advantages would be enough to compensate for overwhelming enemy firepower remained to be seen.

As he had a dozen times before, Delano wished he had Earth's combined forces behind him. But if the Ktarrans appeared suddenly in lunar orbit, the planet would be defenseless. That possibility meant Delano's smaller force would meet the Ktarrans, try to engage them, and slow them down. No matter what the cost, the first battle would provide Earth with extended knowledge of Ktarran weapons and tactics. That intelligence might prove crucial in any subsequent battles, or perhaps even the final encounter.

Three hours later, Delano leaned back and let himself relax. The ship was ready, the crew was ready, and he felt as well prepared as possible.

Steve agreed. "Green lights across all the boards."

"Same here, Colonel," Gunny said.

"OK, let's take a break and get some coffee."

Delano asked Captain Chan if he'd like to accompany them, but the ship master declined. However, the three friends had scarcely tasted their coffee when the ship's intercom jolted them into action.

"Admiral Delano, report to the Control Center."

The message repeated once, all that was needed on such a small ship. Delano started moving, dumping his coffee in the trash before racing down the corridor to the Control Center.

This time Chan didn't wait for his admiral to take his seat. "Our gravity wave detector has registered some unusual readings in the Elara area."

But it was Colonel Kosloff who provided the information.

"We registered a brief but intense fluctuation near Elara's orbit. The moon is almost directly opposite the other side of Jupiter, so we get a good reading."

"A wormhole?"

"No, not that, I think," Kosloff said. "Too powerful a reading at this distance. We should contact Moon Base."

Both the Space Station and Moon Base had more powerful gravity wave detectors. Such instruments reacted instantaneously to fluctuations in gravity. Steve restarted the QuantC connection, but before he could initiate transmission from his end, a message came in.

"*Defiant*, this is Moon Base Command. We've just detected a disruption near Elara space. General Jang says to stand by for more information."

Delano activated his own mike. "We saw it, too, Moon Base. Any idea what it was?"

"Not yet, *Defiant*. Need some time to check our instruments. Will take a few minutes."

Changes in gravity waves, unlike visible light or normal radiation, could be detected instantly, but the most sensitive detection devices were on the Moon or in Earth orbit. In fact, the Space Station's high energy pack had detected the first wormhole appearance seventeen months ago. The other long-range sensors operated under restrictions of the speed of light. These included the spectrometer, cosmic ray detectors, and the ultraviolet and infrared sensors.

At Earth's current distance from Jupiter, that meant about thirty minutes would pass before the other instruments received any data, which then had to be studied. Even so, Delano had to wait patiently for almost forty minutes before the QuantC mechanical voice came to life again.

"*Defiant*. We confirm that a nuclear device has been detonated in Elara space. About ninety seconds later, a small ship, about the size of a Halkin vessel, appeared in the same location. We're guessing the wormhole exit point is now in Elara space and active. Over."

"Just the one ship?"

"So far, *Defiant*. We've got every instrument locked onto the area, including the telescopes on the Station and in Lunar orbit. We'll advise you if anything else comes through."

The Space Station maintained a 1.5 meter telescope. The one

in orbit around the Moon was even larger, about 2.5 meters, and its six cameras saw visible, infrared, and ultraviolet light. A large radio telescope in lunar orbit could hear anything whispered throughout the solar system.

"Kosloff, can you confirm the nuclear explosion?" Delano tried to keep the excitement out of his voice.

"No. Not with these instruments. But it makes sense. A large blast could certainly disrupt the local gravity, at least for a few seconds. I'm almost finished getting our telescope and interferometer properly aimed."

Unlike the rest of Earth's Destroyer fleet, the *Defiant* had a sizable scope of its own, only .9 meters, so it was no match against the big boys. But the ship was quite a bit closer to Jupiter, only 290,000,000 kilometers, more than half the distance from Earth, and it might be almost as capable as the ones circling the home world. Light and other energies from a nuclear explosion would reach the *Defiant* in about sixteen minutes.

Seventeen minutes passed. "I'm reading a Ktarran ship, Admiral," Kosloff announced. He didn't bother to look up from his console. "Got its energy signature. Estimate its bulk as approximately that of the Halkin vessel."

The Halkins preferred small, agile ships. The Tarlon ship that had briefly visited Earth space had been about thirty percent larger. But the smallest Ktarran ship had been almost three times the size of the Tarlon vessel.

A confirming message came through the QuantC, but Delano didn't bother to reply. Steve would respond if necessary.

"Another ship just arrived," Kosloff said. Thirty seconds later, he reported a third vessel had appeared. A full ninety seconds after that, another ship appeared, this one at least three or four times larger than the first three.

"That last one is bigger than the one you destroyed at the Station," Kosloff added.

Yeah, here come the heavies. "Acknowledged, Colonel Kosloff," Delano said.

Not much happened after that, and minutes passed with no visible movement by any of the alien ships. Delano reminded himself that what his instruments displayed took place almost fifteen minutes earlier. He stared at the simulation image on one of his screens. The large battleship and its three escorts moved approximately two thousand kilometers from the wormhole. The three smaller craft took position circling around what had to be a command vessel.

Kosloff took readings, while the observers in Earth orbit did the same. The QuantC came alive for the third time, and this time Field Marshal Shuvalov was on the line.

"Colonel Delano," Shuvalov began, "what do you think?"

"Probably an advance scouting party," Delano replied. "Just checking everything out to make sure they're not walking into an ambush."

The last time Ktarran ships came through the wormhole they'd scarcely paused before moving toward the inner planets.

"Yes, very cautious. That is our conclusion also," Shuvalov said. "Which means they have made their plans and are probably ready for us. Are you prepared to make contact with them?"

"Yes, but I intend to wait until they start moving toward us. If this is all they're sending through, we should be able to handle them."

Neither man believed these were all the Ktarrans were sending. You don't send a large nuclear bomb through a wormhole just for a handful of ships. And if it were merely a scouting party, one ship would be more than sufficient.

"Very well. Perhaps we should maintain contact using this device."

The QuantC had only been tested sparingly, and nobody really knew how long it could maintain a connection.

"Yes, Marshal Shuvalov, I agree. We should . . ."

"Something coming in on the interferometer," Kosloff sang out. "I think it's perhaps another ship."

No one spoke while Kosloff studied the read outs. Delano wanted to ask, but Captain Chan wasn't showing any interest, and Delano didn't want to look impatient in front of him and the rest of the crew.

"Ships! Multiple ships exiting from the wormhole!" Kosloff's excitement echoed through the bridge.

"How many?" Delano asked the question mechanically.

"I'm . . . not sure. They're still coming through."

"Make sure you get an accurate count."

Captain Chan gave that order, which Delano should have done. The minutes dragged by, and by now Delano could see them appearing out of the wormhole on the telescope's display. A ship appeared every twenty or thirty seconds.

When the count passed one hundred, Delano grunted. His first contact scenarios were dwindling rapidly. The silence on the bridge was total, except for Kosloff's voice as he intoned the count, updating it every ten ships or so. Nor did the QuantC have anything to say. No doubt the command post on the Moon didn't expect these numbers either.

Delano ignored the count. One, a hundred, two hundred, didn't make much difference. Even at the low estimate of ten beam weapons per ship, there would be over a thousand energy beams attacking Earth's fleet. He started considering his remaining attack options.

The number of ships entering the solar system ceased at 156. As they arrived, the Ktarran ships kept moving, arranging themselves into a rectangular grid pattern. When the invasion fleet completed its arrangement, the ships began to increase speed, heading right for Delano's position.

"OK, they see us," Delano said.

"Grid is 12 ships wide stacked by 11 high," Kosloff said. "200 kilometers behind are 15 ships spread in a single line behind the grid, probably a reserve force or support vessels."

Delano did the numbers in his head. "What about the remaining nine ships? Are they guarding the wormhole."

"Yes, they are almost stationary," Kosloff said. "Main force is on course toward us and steadily increasing speed."

"Let me know when they stop accelerating."

A big concern of the PDF was that the Ktarrans might try to create a short wormhole, something that would enable them to reach Earth's outskirts in minutes, not days. That possibility kept the main Earth fleet close to the mother world. The Tarlons had doubted that tactic would be employed, since the Ktarran ships were much larger and required higher speeds to open a wormhole. Such extremes tended to weaken the subspace field, thus creating a temporary but often fatal wormhole for such large ships.

But you didn't develop your defense plans based on what you expected the enemy to do. You had to prepare for whatever he was capable of doing. None of the over-confident US Admirals had ever imagined the Japanese Fleet would bomb Pearl Harbor, though the Imperial Japanese Navy was quite capable of such an operation.

The Ktarran grid had stabilized, and was now moving steadily toward Delano's advance fleet. That was slightly off the direct course to Earth. That meant the enemy ships had detected his little flotilla and decided to deal with it first. Perhaps they, too, wanted to feel out the opposing forces.

Delano found himself strangely relaxed. A massive armada of enemy ships had arrived in the solar system, and that event had justified every action undertaken by the PDF in the last seventeen months. If Delano and the leaders of the Alliance hadn't acted as ruthlessly and efficiently as possible, the forces defending Earth would have been much smaller, if they even existed at all. He still might not be popular on Earth, but now the naysayers had to admit they were wrong.

He leaned back in his chair. "OK, how long before they reach us?"

Kosloff didn't need much time to calculate that. "If they continue accelerating until they reach 0.008 lightspeed, and assuming an equal time to decelerate before they reach us, they'll be here in about seven or eight hours."

The Ktarran ships might be traveling at incredible speeds, but the speed of light remained infinitely faster.

Taking a deep breath, Delano made his voice crisp. "Captain Chan, put me on the link to the rest of the fleet. For the first time in months, we have hard data to share. Meanwhile, start calculating an encounter point. I want our squadron at full attack speed when we meet. We'll assume they'll begin decelerating early, to come to grips with us."

As the Tarlons and Halkins had explained, space combat usually takes place within certain speed ranges. Too fast, and you can't maintain a lock on your target. Too slow, and you're a sitting duck. The sweet spot for optimum beam weapon efficiency and survivability was between 200 and 280 kilometers per second.

The standard beam weapons could deliver maximum burn up to a distance of 400 kilometers for a stationary target, and about 300 kilometers for a moving vessel. Those numbers came from the Tarlons and Halkins, based on space battles with the Ktarrans. Delano's ships carried slightly improved versions of the beam weapons, which extended the range to almost 450 kilometers. Earth's scientists had also managed to increase both the speed and power of the space drives.

That would be a significant advantage. But the biggest advancement came from linking the weapons to computer controlled firing systems. The weapon operator could lock onto a target, and a high-speed quantum computer, analyzing hundreds of inputs per millisecond, would keep the beam focused despite evasive maneuvers by the enemy vessel.

Delano expected that to provide a real shock to the Ktarrans. In their last encounter they'd learned that Earth had possessed no beam weapon technology. The idea that humans could adopt such weapons and improve on them would be a nasty surprise.

With the fleet-wide comm link established, Delano took charge. "Attention all ships. In about six hours, we'll begin closing on the Ktarran fleet. I want everyone to get at least four hours sleep. That will still provide sufficient time for preparation. Steve, notify all captains that we will be using Attack Plan 9B. Any changes will depend on enemy responses or movements prior to actual contact. That's all for now. Delano out."

He turned toward Steve. "Did Shuvalov get that?"

"Yes, Colonel."

Shuvalov wouldn't respond unless he heard something he didn't like. The plans had been war-gamed months ago, and would be modified as feedback on the enemy ships came in. Whatever plan was utilized likely wouldn't make much difference. Delano doubted if the Ktarrans had any experience with such a large-scale, coordinated operation. Any Earth attack plan would be a surprise to them.

This would be the first major fleet combat in space for both sides. Still, Delano wondered what new tactics would be used by the Ktarrans. *Dear Lord, don't let me screw up!*

Chapter 38
0 BKA

Six hours later Delano zipped up the last seal on his flight suit, then settled into his command chair, helmet resting on his lap. He turned to Captain Chan, who now had assumed his primary function – operational control of the Advance Fleet. Delano would still give the orders, but Chan would be in tactical control of the squadron.

"All ships report full readiness, Admiral," Chan said. "Captain Tanaka is ready to assume command and control should that be necessary."

Tanaka would take command if the *Defiant* were lost or incapacitated. "Good. Then we're as ready as we can be. Decrease speed to three hundred kilometers."

The two fleets were closing on each other at close to 800 kilometers per second. The Ktarrans had been reducing speed for several hours. Both forces would converge at roughly the same velocity.

The *Defiant* stood ready. Every crewmember had managed to get some rest, either on their own or with help from Linda's happy/sleepy dispensary. Now belted into their seats and wearing flight suits, this crew would be the first Earth force to face the Ktarrans.

The crew wore the suits as a protective measure. The Ktarrans didn't use them. Apparently their ships were compartmented more than Earth's, and a hull breach wouldn't necessarily disable them. The biggest chamber on the *Defiant* was the Command Center, usually referred to as the Bridge, and if that lost integrity, the suits would keep the crew alive until repairs were made.

Everyone on the Bridge waited at their assigned station. Only Med-Tech Linda Grayson had no official duties here, but she sat on a small jump seat near the hatch, ready with her medical kit or to drag wounded off the bridge and down to the Med Lab.

Missing were the four crewmen for the Darts. They were already aboard their ships, buttoned up, waiting to add their contribution to Plan 9B.

Delano glanced behind him. Chan was ready, and Captain Seanna O'Shaughnessy continued testing her controls. She would be the one actually flying the ship during the fighting. Peter Tasco, officially the navigator, would be her backup.

On his wide angle screen, Delano watched the two fleets hurtling toward each other. His special display enabled him to see from one side of the Ktarran position to the other. As he watched, the enemy wings began to speed up and curve toward the *Defiant*. Delano grunted in approval. They would try to envelop him at the moment of attack, hitting him from the flanks as well as the center.

"Shifting too soon . . . mistake number one," Gunny muttered. "Right on schedule."

Show time. The enemy had arrived. Neither side bothered to try any further communications. Three hours earlier Delano had sent a message to the Ktarran fleet in their own language, but that had been ignored. So screw them.

Gunny's screen flashed, and he gave the thumbs up. Delano took one last check, then had to swallow to moisten his throat. *Must be the dry air. Yeah, that's it.* "Captain Chan, initiate Attack Plan 9B."

The battle to save Earth had begun.

All twenty of the Advance Fleet increased speed to maximum power. The artificial gravity generators had already been switched off, as had all other non-essential systems. Almost all power generated now went to weapons and defensive screens. In moments they had passed the optimum velocity for effective beam combat, but Plan 9B didn't call for any initial use of beam weapons.

"Launch all missiles." Captain Chan's voice remained calm, the same tone he'd used during months of training.

Twenty missiles, one from each ship, blasted from their tubes. The flash of their rocket exhaust momentarily blinded the forward sensors. Five seconds after the launch, the *Defiant* shuddered as she released her second missile.

In less than seven seconds, twenty Destroyers launched forty tactical nuclear-tipped missiles toward the Ktarran fleet. The weapons had some capability to adjust their course, so as to keep the EMP warhead directed toward the target. Each missile had a specific grid area for its initial target. Anything within that area would attract the warhead, and even if the targeted vessel should try to maneuver, the computer-guided seeker head would compensate as needed to stay on target.

The moment the rocket fumes cleared the sensors, Chan's next command came. "Launch all Darts!"

Within fifteen seconds forty Darts were tearing away from their respective ships, their thrusters adding to their initial velocity.

The Darts constituted the main weapon right now. While the Ktarran ships sought to destroy the missiles coming right at them, the Darts could lock on and fire their beam weapons and rail guns. A skilled operator could find and lock onto a target within seconds. After that, the computer kept track of calculations of speed and angle, and a possible impact point. Each Dart managed to fire off at least three or four rail gun projectiles before the next order came.

"Shift to flank attack!" Captain Chan must have felt some excitement, because he repeated the order. "Shift to flank attack now. Reduce speed to attack speed."

The twenty ships of the Advance Fleet, including *Defiant*, began turning, ten ships altering course to attack the leading edge of the Ktarran right flank, and ten angling toward the Ktarran left. The forty Darts also split into two forces. And launched their own missiles at the intended targets, this time on the flanks.

The leading edge of each Ktarran wing, which had necessarily extended the spacing as part of the attempted envelopment, now found themselves under intensive attack by ten Destroyers and twenty Darts. With the chaos in the Ktarran center from the initial wave of missiles, blossoms of nuclear bombs exploding kept the enemy busy and dulled their sensors. Ktarran ships fired at missiles, Darts, anything that moved. That chaos meant the enemy ships on the wing edges were momentarily and locally outnumbered.

With gut-wrenching G-forces, the *Defiant* had turned to the left, and now Captain Seanna came into her own. Jerking the ship up, down, left, right, she remained on course toward her selected target. At maximum range, the *Defiant's* beam weapons flashed into existence, columns of reddish fire that reached out and touched the closest Ktarran vessel.

Delano found himself clutching onto his seat belt, reacting to the ever-changing G-forces. Within seconds, the Ktarrans beams lashed out in return. But once again, the Earth forces had struck first. Now their beam weapons continued to burn, draining massive amounts of energy from the *Defiant*, but keeping their deadly particle beams focused on the enemy.

Space seemed to explode with energy rays, varying in color from red to orange to yellow, and flashing across the ever-dwindling distance between forces. The usual blackness of space now resembled a massive array of twinkling Christmas lights, where slashing energy made flaring contact with defense screens. The *Defiant* twisted and turned, trying to avoid the enemy energy beams. Suddenly the *Defiant* staggered, as if struck by a giant hammer. For an instant Delano remembered the violent shaking of the Space Station when the Ktarran beam sliced off the rear section.

But that had been a carefully controlled and precisely aimed burst of energy. What hit the *Defiant* was the full force of one or more energy beam weapons from what seemed like a thousand projectors. Before the shields could fail, Captain Seanna slipped away from the deadly beam, only to be re-acquired or caught by another within seconds.

This time the ship did more than just shudder. The shield failed momentarily, then recovered as Seanna accelerated away from the deadly energy flow. But alarms went off on the bridge. A hole the size of a basketball appeared on the upper surface of the inner hull, blasted open by the last millisecond of energy from a Ktarran beam weapon.

Heart racing, Delano stared at the hull in shock, as air rushed out of the ship, taking anything loose or unfastened with it. The beam had passed about two feet over his head before dissipating into the hull on the opposite site. The interior panels there had melted, but the tough metal hull beneath had resisted.

Air still rushed through the hull opening. He forced his eyes back to the screen, trying to evaluate the attack. But his brain kept reminding him that a double hole would have seriously damaged the *Defiant*, perhaps even crippled it. Not to mention that if the beam had touched his head, helmet or not, he'd be a dead man.

At the first alarm, Kosloff disengaged his seat belt, snatched up an emergency patch, and redirected himself to the hole. He crashed into the hull alongside the opening, but the pressure had already dropped enough so that he didn't get sucked up against it. Ignoring the *Defiant's* constant maneuvers, Kosloff adjusted the patch with one hand and slapped it over the opening. The flexible sealant, one meter square, bent outward, but temporarily sealed the opening, stopping the outrush of the last few air molecules from the chamber.

By then the flight engineer, Jim Cook, had joined Kosloff. Together they managed to seal the hole with some flex aluminum, a composite material more permanent than the emergency patch. If the hole had been any larger, even the plasma shield might not have been able to maintain hull integrity. But before the engineers completed the seal, almost all the air had dissipated into space.

Back at his console, Cook adjusted the air flow coming into the chamber. It would take a minute or two to get back to normal pressure. Thanks to their flight suits, the crew continued functioning. A cloud of black smoke wafted in the returning air, no doubt a sign of some harsh chemical compound that the air scrubbers would have to eliminate before anyone could safely remove their helmets.

While the two engineers worked to restore the compartment's integrity, the rest of the crew had simply switched over to their internal air supply. Belted into their chairs, the crews' flight suits kept them alive and in the fight.

More important, the crew continued to operate their consoles, never halting for an instant. The *Defiant's* three beam weapons never stopped firing. They'd opened fire the instant the enemy ships came within range. Each two-person man gun crew guided the beam onto an enemy ship, or even a sector of space expected to hold a target, and adjusted the power and focus of the beam. Gun control computers then tracked the enemy ship and reacted to every movement, faster and more accurately than any human. They kept the high-energy particle stream on target until the enemy ship escaped the beam or its shield collapsed.

Then the *Defiant* swept through the Ktarran line, and a few moments later, out of range of the Ktarran beam weapons. The battle had lasted a little over a minute. Gunny had already adjusted the view screen sensors, and Delano had a good look at the enemy's formation. Or lack of it, he decided. The orderly grid had vanished, turned into a snowfall of sparkling lights and random movement. His screens changed and adjusted to their new input.

"Alpha force lost three destroyers and five Darts," Gunny announced, his head still bent over his screen.

Damn. Time for the casualty count. "What about Beta?"

Delano hoped they had fared no worse. *Defiant* had been part of the Alpha group, while Beta, under Captain Tanaka, had gone against the Ktarran left flank.

It took a moment to get that figure. "Beta reports two destroyers lost, and three Darts. Minor damage to other ships, but nothing to stop them from fighting. Captain Tanaka is already recovering his Darts."

Delano grimaced. He'd lost twenty-five percent of his force, a grim statistic for a new commander. But Beta still had eight ships, just about enough for the next phase. "Good news. Tell Tanaka to proceed to the wormhole as planned."

Delano felt the ship shudder, and a moment later, shake again. He turned to Captain Chan.

"Both Darts recovered, Admiral. Commander Volozh reports damage, extent unknown."

So the *Defiant* hadn't lost either of its Darts, a good omen. Hopefully the damaged Dart would fly and fight again.

"What is *Defiant's* damage? Can we still fight? Any sign of pursuit?"

"Kosloff and Cook are assessing our structure and plasma screens. Just the single hole. No sign of pursuit," Chan said. "All energy units functioning normally."

"Main Ktarran fleet is regrouping, Admiral," Gunny said. "They took some serious damage. I think we caught them by surprise."

New ships, new weapons, and new tactics. *Welcome to Earth, you bastards.* Still, the Ktarran admiral would learn fast enough. And now he had to worry about a force of humans behind him. He would likely modify his planned course of action. The enemy commander didn't have many choices. He could return to the wormhole with all or part of his fleet, or he could continue to Earth space. Whatever he decided, he would need time to make his decision.

Time was what the Advance Fleet needed, too.

"Patch me through to Tanaka," Delano said. In a moment Steve gave him the OK.

"Captain Tanaka, this is Colonel . . . Admiral Delano. Can you still take Beta Group to the wormhole? The Ktarrans have eight or nine ships there, including at least two capital ships."

"Already on course, Admiral, at full boost." Tanaka's precise English had a Boston accent. "We have some minor damage, but we'll make repairs along the way."

"Do what you can with the wormhole without getting yourself killed. If we can cut their communications for a few days, we'll be ahead. Give my thanks to everyone in Beta."

"Good luck to you, Admiral," Tanaka said. "Tanaka out."

Steve cut the connection.

"I've got the first pass at the Ktarran BDA," Gunny announced. One of his duties was bomb damage assessment.

Everyone stopped what they were doing, every eye turned toward the Gunny.

"Looks like thirteen ships destroyed, with eleven damaged, maybe more" he said. "I'd put that against our losses of five Destroyers and eight Darts."

Delano did the rough calculation. "For their big battleships, that's almost three to one. And remember each Ktarran ship has the firepower of three of our Destroyers."

Nobody cheered, but the crew's faces reflected satisfaction. They'd taken losses, but they also attacked a force almost ten times their size in number of ships alone. That made their own losses bearable.

"OK, we've given the bully a bloody nose, and stopped him in his tracks," Delano said. "But he still outnumbers us and he'll be better prepared next time. Now it's time to get back home. Captain Chan, Lieutenant Tasco, plot us a course back to Earth. With luck maybe we can slip past these guys while they're still pulling up their pants."

The Earth ships were fast for their size, faster than the Tarlon or Halkin equivalents, but the Ktarran ships were big, with massive power drives. Delano didn't want to arrive in Earth orbit with the enemy ships breathing down his neck.

Chapter 39

Grand Commander Veloreck had given the order to halt the Ktarran fleet. Despite protests from some of his captains who wanted to pursue the fleeing Earthlings, or at least go after those now headed for the wormhole. Veloreck, however, had no intention of dispersing his forces. Instead he merely summoned his two sub-commanders, Jothe and Teeg, to his flagship.

Each of the three Ktarrans commanded roughly one-third of the fleet that now remained motionless in space, just inside of this system's asteroid belt. But by the order of Pannoch Staleeck, the Almighty ruler of Ktarra, Veloreck led the fleet. That meant he gave the orders and enforced them.

Veloreck met his two sub commanders in his conference chamber, then ordered the usual servants and recorders to depart. When the door closed, he growled at his commanders. "What do you think?"

Neither Ktarran needed to ask what he meant.

"Their nuclear weapons," Jothe began, "they were very powerful. There were no direct hits, but the radiation bursts apparently overloaded the some anti-matter engines. At the same time, the electro-magnetic waves overwhelmed our sensors, blinded us in many cases. It was difficult for our weapons slaves to track and destroy the missiles while trying to attack the enemy."

"How is it even possible that weapons of such explosive force can be utilized in a missile that can travel so rapidly?" Teeg asked. "And can even adjust its course?"

"We know that the humans used nuclear weapons against Turhan's ships in his attack on Earth," Veloreck said. "But we have never been able to use such weapons in space combat. Our nuclear bombs are more powerful, but that doesn't help us."

"The humans launched more than eighty missiles against us," Jothe said. "It is difficult to stop so many. Ships they targeted needed to use all their beam weapons to defeat the missiles. Fortunately only six detonated close enough to destroy a ship."

"But many exploded near enough to cause damage or destroy sensors," Teeg argued. "Who knows how many of these missiles the humans have? They must have many more, to waste that many in their first encounter with our ships. Eighty nuclear missiles – that number is greater than our entire supply of atomic bombs."

"And the enemy missiles were hard to destroy. Aboard my ship," Jothe said, "it took eight beam weapons several seconds to explode one. Every weapon had to be utilized in destroying them."

Veloreck thought about that. Their beam weapons were unable to accomplish much in the way of counter-fire against the Earth ships. No wonder the humans were able to escape with so many ships intact.

"What about the projectile weapons?" Teeg asked. "One of my ships was struck by something that blasted through the screens and the hull. The projectile carried no explosives, but was traveling at such speed that we could not record its velocity. It ripped completely through the ship without slowing. The ship was lucky to escape without any serious damage."

At least four ships had been struck and destroyed by these projectiles. "This is a new weapon, unlike anything we've seen before," Veloreck admitted. "How can a projectile be accelerated to such speed without recoil? How can it be aimed so accurately as to actually strike a ship, even one that is taking evasive action?"

No one had an answer to that question. Veloreck looked from one to another. "What about these small ships? They maneuver as if flying in an atmosphere. They seemed to be armed with missiles, a beam weapon, and this projectile device. They operate their weapons at high speeds, scoring hits against us while we are still trying to pinpoint them with a beam."

"Their beam weapons are an improvement as well," Jothe said. "Our sensors recorded that they produced almost six percent more output than ours."

"More power, and they stayed on target for longer periods," Veloreck said. "Yes, this is an entirely new enemy that we face. They were primitive when the Halkins arrived. Now they dare to face us in battle. Look how many more such ships await us at the planet, more than we have ever seen any world produce before. Pannoch Staleeck was right to insist on such a large force." He looked at each in turn. "Now we have to see if it will be large enough."

Blank expressions greeted his words. "If we engage their main fleet, and suffer the same ratio of losses, we'll be lucky to have a ship or two still functioning after the battle. And that is assuming that the ships we see guarding Earth are the only ones they have."

"We must attack," Teeg said. "Otherwise . . ."

"Yes, we must attack," Veloreck agreed. "But first we must ask for reinforcements. We must also modify our tactics. We cannot merely travel to Earth and face them as we just did. We need a new plan."

"To ask Pannoch Staleeck for more ships," Jothe said, "will send him into a rage. We'll all lose our heads."

"We'll lose them if we fail to destroy the humans," Veloreck said. "Better to risk his rage at a distance than when we're groveling at his feet."

Jothe and Teeg looked at each other. They really had no choice.

"I will transmit a message to Ktarra, describing the battle, and say that we are asking for more ships." Veloreck emphasized the *we*. "While we are waiting for home world's response, we will repair our ships and modify our tactics." He leaned forward.

"First, we must increase the strength of our shields. Any power not critical to ship operations is to be disabled. Cut the gravity fields to fifteen percent. We need to increase the protection and screening surrounding the anti-matter chambers. Second, I want more sensors installed, and provisions made to replace damaged ones as soon as possible. Third, we will widen our formation and break into three separate groups."

"Teeg, you have the most ships and the greatest number of bombs under your command. When I give the order, you will proceed at high speed to the human planet. You will not respond or initiate any ship-to-ship actions unless they directly block your path. You will accelerate as fast as possible straight to the planet, ignoring the enemy or the planet's moon bases. Then you will unleash your missiles on any targets of value, preferably military ones. By utilizing all your energy to power the shields, you should be able to withstand any counter attacks long enough to empty your supply of bombs."

"But how will . . ."

Veloreck ignored him. "Jothe, you and I will follow behind Teeg, but slightly slower. We will plan to arrive right after Teeg completes his attack. When the humans turn to pursue him, as they must unless they want to see their planet destroyed, they will have to abandon their formations. Then we will fall upon them from behind and destroy as many as possible. Oh, and Jothe, you will transfer your supply of nuclear weapons to Commander Teeg, as will I. Our mission will be to engage and destroy the Earth fleet. My ships have only a few bombs, but we will utilize them to destroy the planet's population centers, once the human fleet is eliminated.

"As soon as the humans concentrate on Jothe's forces," Veloreck said, "I will lead my command to deliver a second strike against the planet. As Teeg launches his missiles, he will also identify targets of value on the surface, then radio them to me, so that I can launch my bombs without having to waste time searching for sites worthy of destruction."

"The humans will concentrate on my ships," Teeg said. "I'll be destroyed."

"No, *you* will not," Veloreck said. "Yes, most of your ships will be destroyed, but you and your flagship will survive. Once you launch your missiles against the planet, you will divert all your power to the shields, and that should keep you alive until you're out of range of the planet's defenses. Meanwhile Jothe and I will arrive to deliver the finishing blows. As fast as you can turn your ships around, you will return to the planet with whatever ships you have left, to join in the killing."

"My ships, my cousins," Teeg said, "they'll be killed!"

"Their sacrifice will be remembered. But you will survive," Veloreck said. "If we destroy the humans, Ktarra will find more ships for a hero such as you to command. Remember, more ships can always be built, but reattaching your head will be much more difficult.

Silence greeted his words, but both nodded in acceptance of their new orders.

"Now you will both prepare your ships for our new mission, while I must contact Pannoch Staleeck and inform him of our changed plan. If he has no useful suggestions, we will attack as I described as soon as the ships are ready. Hopefully Pannoch will not demand my immediate return to feast upon my body."

*   *   *

Back on Ktarra, Staleeck reviewed the gloomy transmission from Veloreck. The connection hadn't worked smoothly, probably from so much radiation affecting the fleet's sensors. But the bad news came through well enough. Veloreck related the details of the attack, even mentioning the human Delano, who had broadcast an appeal for peace as the fleet regrouped outside the wormhole.

Of course Veloreck hadn't bothered to reply to the human transmission. But then Delano and a mere twenty ships – design and configuration unknown – had attacked the much larger Ktarran force. Weighing the results, Veloreck stated that should the full force of Earth ships attack, the Ktarran fleet might achieve victory, but the cost would be an estimated ninety percent of the fleet.

For a single planet, that would be a horrendous price to pay. It might take fifty cycles to recover from such a loss. Veloreck expressed a willingness to do battle, but would prefer to wait for more reinforcements if possible.

Staleeck had resisted the urge to order his fleet commander to attack at once whatever the cost. He merely acknowledged receipt of the message and ordered Veloreck to hold his position. Alone, Staleeck considered his options. A costly victory might weaken the Empire, but defeat would be unthinkable.

Unfortunately, Staleeck had only a small reserve force available, less than thirty ships, and only two of them top of the line battleships. Nor did he have any more atomic missiles. It would take several cycles before any sizable quantity could be assembled. That meant the reserve force would have only beam weapons. Nevertheless, he decided to order the reserve force dispatched to Earth at once. In the event of a close battle, those thirty ships might be enough to finish off any of the surviving human ships and destroy the planet.

That would leave him only a handful of fighting ships for the entire Empire. Diverting so many vessels at the same time would be all too noticeable to the slave planets and those still fighting the Empire. The remnants of the Tarlons, Halkins, and Arcanans yet waged war against Ktarra, and might decide to counterattack.

He would have to gamble there. The option of allowing Earth to survive was unacceptable. Staleeck growled. He turned to one of his servants. "Send a message to Veloreck. Tell him the reserve force will be sent as soon as possible, but that it will not arrive in time to help him. Tell him that he must attack at once with what forces he has. No more delays will be tolerated. The reserve force will be used to clean up whatever Earth ships survive and, if necessary, destroy the planet."

Veloreck's attack had to succeed, or at least destroy the planet's fleet. If a victorious Earth and its forces managed to transmit any messages through the wormhole, the Empire's slaves might rise in revolt. Even Ktarra might be in danger. Whatever the cost in ships, Veloreck had to destroy Earth's ability to resist the Empire.

Because if he didn't, Veloreck might survive the battle, only to die at the emperor's hand on Ktarra.

Chapter 40
000 BKA

The primary home of the National Security Agency of the United States is located on the Fort Meade Army base, fifteen miles southwest of Baltimore. From the outside, several large office buildings appear to constitute the Agency, but most of the computer and high tech equipment are deep underground. In 2028 the cavernous facilities had been enlarged and hardened, increasing from fifteen to twenty-eight acres.

Working so far below the surface tended to induce claustrophobia in the permanent staff. Therefore facilities were often larger than what might be found on the surface, with pastel-painted surfaces utilizing bright and breezy tones, while soothing aromas floated invisibly in the recirculated air. But bright colors and floral wall art didn't do much to counter the grim atmosphere that now permeated the facility.

Thirteen months after the first attack by the Ktarrans and the rise of the PDF, a large conference room seventy feet below the earth had been modified and turned over to a special group of cryptographers. Like others fighting the alien enemy, this group had little to be cheerful about.

The purpose of this new and secure facility within the NSA was to monitor and research any Ktarran communications. During the first attack on Earth several messages between the three attacking vessels were intercepted. A few months after the assault, Colonel Delano of the PDF learned that the Tarlons and Halkins also possessed some snippets of radio traffic between the Ktarran ships. These transmissions were combined and distributed among the Alliance for analysis, but the bulk of the decoding effort centered at the NSA.

Unfortunately, the intercepted Ktarran messages were brief and in code, and neither alien race had ever managed to read any of the communications. Nevertheless, Delano insisted on establishing a single counter intelligence group dedicated to cracking the Ktarran code. Soon close to a hundred Alliance scientists, linguists, computer specialists, and military communication experts were hard at work, deep beneath the surface of Fort Meade.

The core team consisted of six Chinese, nine Americans, and four Russians. Some progress occurred, but nothing like a major breakthrough. In desperation, two months before the expected arrival of the Ktarrans, the PDF added two additional members.

Sir Nigel Bahara from the UK joined the team and quickly assumed the role of team leader. From the neck down, Sir Nigel appeared to be the epitome of British culture. His Savile Row bespoke tweed suits, Marmaduke silk ties, and Berluti Italian shoes contrasted sharply with the relaxed business casual of the others at the NSA. From the neck up, Bahara was the living expression of one of India's desert bandits, with a thick beard, heavy eyebrows, and large dark eyes set beneath a broad forehead jutting over a long-bladed nose.

Five generations earlier, his ancestors had abandoned their historical banditry in the Thar Desert outside the city of Jodhpur and emigrated to a slum in London. But in less than twenty years, the family fortune had grown sufficiently to send the subsequent generations to Oxford and Eaton. Sir Nigel had first come to the attention of the British government at age eleven, when he won first prize by solving a specially created crossword puzzle from the London Times. Not only did Nigel Bahara solve the puzzle, he did it in record time, eclipsing the other and much older entrants.

At age twenty-five, Sir Nigel received his knighthood for "exemplary services rendered to the Crown." No one knew exactly what those services were. Those who dared to ask Sir Nigel received a cold stare that brought the family's desert raider origins to the fore. Those in the know assumed that some country's top secret diplomatic codes had been broken.

Sir Nigel's arrival at the NSA facility coincided with that of another, Ahvin of the Halkin. The second wife to Captain Horath thus became the first alien to set foot on the Planet Earth. Thanks to the NSA's paranoia about security and the medical community's irrational fears of off-world infection, no one outside those working directly on the Ktarran code breaking effort knew an alien had landed on Earth.

Ahvin had made the first contact with Delano and Lian, teaching them the rudiments of the Ktarran trade language, the lingua franca of the stellar quadrant. While her primary responsibility in the Halkin crew translated as cook's assistant, her secondary function was language translation. That included any First Contact situations. By now this task had eclipsed her meal provider duties. She had been present at every major discussion with Delano and Lian, and now spoke excellent English, Russian, and two dialects of Chinese.

Like Delano and Lian, Ahvin learned languages easily, often just by listening and observing. But code breaking was another story. Like the many other species fighting the Ktarrans, none of the Halkins had ever figured out their coded messages.

Ahvin made quite a stir when she first arrived. She had appeared small in comparison to her husband Horath or to the other males on the Halkin ship. But compared to the average human she looked large enough to play professional football. Powerful muscles rippled under her soft tan fur. Humans, it turned out, possessed an almost irresistible urge to stroke her shoulders.

She showed no concern at mixing with humans, declaring that earthly diseases would have little or no effect on her own physiology. That fact was grudgingly confirmed by Earth's best doctors after three weeks of intensive studies. Nor did any pathogens appear to leap from her body into humans. Nevertheless, reasonable precautions were taken. Some of the always-cautious Chinese contingent continued to wear face masks to reduce any chance of infection.

Now the Ktarrans had entered Earth's solar system, and radio messages had once again been detected. Working with Sir Nigel, who had quickly assumed the unofficial leadership of the crypto team, they began their real work the day of PDF Admiral Delano's attack on the main Ktarran fleet.

"I think it a bit odd that the Ktarran ships halt after the battle," Sir Nigel began, his upper class voice recapping the newest messages. Meeting with his team leaders, he stared at a large projection screen that displayed all the intercepted radio traffic. "This Ktarran message was broadcast on a narrow band. Two ships acknowledge. About fifteen minutes later, two small shuttles leave those respective battleships and rendezvous with another, even larger ship."

"High Commander orders his sub-commanders to report to his ship," Ahvin said. "Must have only two."

"Then that particular battleship is the command carrier? The *Zelbinion*?" Sir Nigel made it a question, but no one challenged his assertion.

"Must be," Ahvin had translated the ship's name for them. "Now we know where High Commander directs the battle."

"Our understanding is getting better," Sir Nigel agreed. "We can deduce the names of the two subordinate ships, or their respective captains, which is even better. Both messages from the shuttles to the leading battleship used a modification of the same phrase."

"Then we have the alert word, ship's name, and order to report," one of the Chinese specialists said. "A few more words and the computers can get to work."

"If this High Commander is reassessing his options, there will be plenty of new orders once the sub-commanders return to their own ships." Sir Nigel glanced at his notes. "We're getting close. I agree. A few more words and we should have enough to provide at least a partial decryption."

"I will transmit the information about the three command ships to Marshal Shuvalov," one of the Russian cryptologists said. The site had a direct link to the field marshal. "That is valuable targeting information."

"Yes, it is," Sir Nigel agreed. "Just a little more and we'll have them."

Chapter 41
1 Day After Ktarran Arrival (AKA)

The Advance Fleet had split into two parts. While Captain Raizo Tanaka's eight ships headed for the wormhole, Delano's seven remaining ships raced above the orbital plane of the planets. Their furious dash through the Ktarran fleet had left them farther from Earth orbit than the enemy. To get back, Delano had to avoid the Ktarrans now between them and Earth. Traveling at max speed, the *Defiant* and its six accompanying Destroyers hoped to fly around the enemy. If they could keep enough distance between themselves and the Ktarran fleet, they should be able to get back to Earth space. Hopefully in time to join in the defense of the planet.

Fortunately, the Ktarrans didn't bother to chase or try to intercept Delano. An hour after the battle, and with no sign of the Ktarrans doing anything, Captain Chan adjusted his course and headed for Moon Base, where they could refuel and rearm.

As soon as they were on their way, Delano let himself sag back in his chair. *Damn! Survived another one.* He'd dodged death in the deserts of Yemen, and on the Space Station. This time, however, the list of lost ships and crews preyed on his mind. Delano had led men and women into battle, people who trusted him. They had fought and died still trusting their commander. But bottom line, his soldiers had lost their lives, and that was not a good thing.

Delano ignored Captain Chan, busy inspecting the repairs to the hull before he would allow the crew to remove their flight suits. Theoretically, the regenerated shields could contain the air within the ship, but not even aliens, friendly or not, trusted the screens that much. Instead, Delano brooded on the lost ships and crews. He knew their names and could see their faces. They had been alive, and now were dead, blasted into debris.

He'd dreaded the day these decisions would confront him. Delano had tried to focus on the fact that people would die no matter what choice he made. He could only hope to choose the path that would save the most.

For I myself am a man under authority, with soldiers under me. I tell this one, 'Go,' and he goes; and that one, 'Come,' and he comes. I say to my servant, 'Do this,' and he does it.

The Bible verse popped unexpectedly into Delano's head, a relic from his Catholic education in Brooklyn. But the truth of that unknown centurion's words, spoken more than two thousand years earlier, was never more evident than now. Delano had ordered his soldiers into battle. They had gone without question and many had died. He had dispatched Tanaka's force to the wormhole hoping for a tactical stroke of good luck, and many of them would die, too.

Delano put aside his black thoughts, though he had no time for any festivity. Captain Tanaka's eight ships were heading for a real fight, one with the enemy on full alert and now aware of Earth's weapons. Tanaka would be outgunned as well. Those ships might be heading to their destruction, and Delano had sent them there.

Snap out of it, Marine! Delano forced his thoughts back to the present and the problem at hand. The chance to take out the wormhole, even briefly, would be worth the risk. On the plus side, the Ktarrans would wonder about Earth's audacity, and whether or not there were more surprises awaiting them.

At last Captain Chan gave the OK on the repairs. The crew shed their helmets and flight suits and spent a few moments quietly celebrating their victory, despite the acrid smell in the chamber. The long months of training and preparations had paid off in a near-flawless performance. Nevertheless, the loss of three ships affected everyone.

Right after they made the turn for Earth, a radio signal arrived from Shuvalov. Communications with the main Fleet had become intermittent since before the battle. The QuantC link remained out of order, and no one seemed to know where the problem was. The *Defiant* and the other ships had been subjected to plenty of radiation, and any of a hundred parts might have burned out.

For all Delano knew, the quanta particles had run off with the SUSY g-strings, or some such bullshit.

Steve and Kosloff, however, swore the fault was at the other end. Whatever the problem, the *Defiant* was back to relying on regular radio links and slow transmission times. It also meant the Ktarrans could listen in, though whether they could make any sense of the encrypted messages remained doubtful.

Shuvalov wanted to hear a recap of the attack and Delano gave him the highlights. "I think we caught them by surprise. They were probably expecting us to run, and the Ktarrans were a little slow when we launched our attack. It took them a few seconds to get their act together, but then they were damned efficient. Even a handful of these battleships pack some heavy firepower. Over."

"They are still regrouping," Shuvalov said. At this distance, the radio transmissions took almost five minutes to reach Earth. "We picked up messages between ships, and a much longer one that was directed toward the wormhole. The Ktarran commander must be reporting or asking for reinforcements. Over."

More ships! Just what we need. "The Ktarrans will attack soon enough," Delano said, refusing to consider the idea of Ktarran reinforcements. "They didn't come here with over 100 ships just to turn back. They must know that if they give us a few more months, we'll outnumber and outgun them. Over."

Earth's production capacity had just reached optimum construction levels. Ships of all types would continue to roll off assembly lines. The most critical resource now was qualified pilots and crews. But that need was also being addressed.

"Da, if we have the time." Shuvalov didn't believe it either. "Hurry back, Colonel Delano. Out."

Delano felt himself go limp. The battle adrenalin had faded. He now had time to study and comprehend the list of the dead. He climbed out of his seat and headed for the break room. Better to drink the coffee now, so he could get it out of his system. In nine or ten hours, the *Defiant* would reach Earth, and a new battle would begin. He wondered how many would die in this next conflict. He might be rushing to his own destruction.

He remembered another grim Marine Corps saying: "The Corps taught me how to kill, but it didn't teach me how to deal with killing." Delano shook off the gloomy thoughts. This was no time to appear weak in front of his crew. He still had duties to perform, and so did they. The responsibilities weren't going to get off his back anytime soon.

As Delano got back to work, he recalled what his drill instructor claimed was the most important fact to learn in Officer Candidate School: "Marines die. That's what we're here for. To make sure that the civilians at home stay alive."

Chapter 42
1 AKA

Activity at the NSA decryption center in Maryland had climbed to a frenetic level. More than sixty analysts, hunched over their data terminals, fed information to the massive supercomputers located in the bunker far below. Each intercepted phrase went through a computer scan which compared it to every other message captured. The output went to review by the human analysts. They added their own interpretations and re-entered the data for a second or third or fourth review by the parallel analytic processors, based on IBM's Watson technology, which processed the modified data yet again.

The looping process was never-ending, with a separate team for each message. The best cryptographers from the Alliance and half a dozen other countries tried to combine the individual phrases or words, attempting to break the Ktarran code. The work had to be completed within hours, instead of the days or weeks normally required for such an effort. But Earth had no more time. If they couldn't crack the Ktarran code before the enemy fleet arrived at Earth, the information would be useless.

The teams kept working, drinking coffee and praying the computers wouldn't go down. And each team leader, when he felt he had something solid, hand delivered the results to Sir Nigel's office. There the odd Brit and a few others examined the data and tried to find the hidden algorithm that would make sense of the message.

"These are the latest decrypt on one of the larger battleships, Nigel. This looks solid."

Sir Nigel Bahara lifted his eyes from his own terminal, and saw a team leader from Shanghai standing in front of his desk. The man, whose name was Li Wei, wore a black T-shirt with white English lettering declaring 'Alice loves Bob who loves Carlos.'

The odd phrase identified the wearer as someone in the cryptology field, meaning "A sends a message to B who transmits it to C." A very old and very in joke, Nigel knew it wouldn't translate well into Cantonese.

"What do you have?"

"We've identified the leader of the first wave of ships. According to Ahvin, she translates the battleship's name as the *Brenick,* and the fleet commander's name is Teeg. Commander Teeg. She thinks."

The team automatically delivered any solid information to the Halkin language specialist. That way no time was lost going through the normal chain of command. Ahvin reviewed both the raw data and the computer-suggested translation. She had left the base a few hours ago, to rejoin her husband aboard Horath's ship. She was, after all, a member of his crew with her own duties to perform. Nevertheless, she continued working with Nigel and his teams from the ship in orbit. That let Ahvin continue her work descrambling the Ktarran coded messages.

"Let me see it," Nigel said.

Li moved to the side chair at Nigel's desk, so he could operate the tablet.

Nigel needed only a moment to verify the accuracy of the information. But while it might be interesting to identify the name of the commanding ship, it didn't really tell him what he wanted to know. The first few messages hadn't done much to help Nigel and his team. Then had come a longer message, this directed for the ships at the wormhole. Captain Tanaka had intercepted that, and transmitted it back to Earth.

The message, obviously from the Ktarran fleet commander, must have reported the encounter with Delano's mini-fleet and asked for a clarification of orders. Ship-to-ship traffic had ended after that for nearly two hours, until another message came through the wormhole.

Tanaka captured that one, too, and forwarded it on. The Ktarrans had done nothing for another fifteen minutes, then a flurry of transmissions began to flow from the *Zelbinion* and Grand Commander Veloreck. For the next two hours, radio traffic remained near-constant between the Ktarran ships. Then some vessels, according to the long-range telescopes and energy detectors, began exchanging cargo.

After that activity ceased, with a single phrase transmitted from the *Zelbinion*, the Ktarran fleet once again headed for Earth. In less than an hour, a significant gap opened up between the ships, with about a third of the ships configuring themselves around the *Brenick,* while the rest of the fleet gradually fell behind. At current estimated speeds, the first wave of Ktarrans would be here in approximately ten hours, possibly less.

Nigel punched a button on his phone. Ten seconds later, he had Ahvin on the link.

"Any idea what the *Brenick* is doing?"

"They must have transferred some special weapons to the lead ships," Ahvin said. "Captain Horath agrees."

That didn't sound promising. "Can you guess what type of weapon?"

"No, we have no idea," Ahvin said. "We have only seen them use beam weapons."

After he broke the connection, Nigel leaned back in his chair and closed his eyes. What type of weapon was it? If he could figure that out, Earth might be able to mount the best possible defense. But if the Ktarrans had developed a biological weapon and were using these ships to deliver it, that might be very bad news. A few airbursts could spread a virus or other type of human killer throughout the world in less than twenty-four hours, and there was no way to stop that.

Still, engineering bio-weapons didn't seem to fit the Ktarran profile, and neither the Halkins nor the Tarlons had any record of such a weapon. Nor did the Ktarrans have a stock of humans to test it on. What could kill a Halkin might not even make a human sick.

But after the Ktarrans started moving again, a flurry of messages resumed between the *Brenick* and the ships under its command. In the last few hours, almost every ship in the approaching first wave had communicated with the *Brenick*, many of them multiple times. Every one of those messages was being captured and analyzed.

Logic had helped decipher many of those transmissions, with the help of the massive computers located a few hundred feet below Nigel's office. Three captured transmissions turned out to be unencrypted. These were either equipment failures or simply carelessness or haste on the operator's part.

Whatever the reason, command and routine phrases were becoming clear. The list of decrypted words continued to grow, and several terms that referred to changes in speed and course were computer-rated at 90+ percent accuracy.

The commander of the *Brenick* apparently had some information disease and could not stop talking. Compared to the nearly silent *Zelbinion*, the *Brenick* sounded like a talk-show host. Requests for follow ups or confirmations to the ships in the advance wave seemed almost incessant.

Fortunately, many of these commands were often repeated, and in the hurry to reply, more uncoded transmissions were being used.

Nigel knew that another day or two would crack the entire Ktarran code, but he had only hours to provide useful information.

Two Chinese linguists entered his office, both men breathing hard. "We have a major breakthrough," the first man said. "It's definitely a missile attack, to be launched at a specific time."

"We even have the deceleration command, Nigel," the other man said. "If we could get the launch command, we might have something useful."

The order to launch missiles would be given some time after the *Brenick's* ships began deceleration. The attack would depend on all of Teeg's ships arriving in near-Earth space at approximately the same time. It couldn't be timed precisely, as some vessels would decelerate more efficiently than others. That meant there had to be coordination instructions so the Ktarrans could release their missiles within moments of each other.

With that information, Earth's defending ships could ready themselves for the defense as much as they could.

Nigel leaned back in his chair, eyes closed for a moment. None of the analysts said anything, letting the man think. Suddenly his eyes opened and he straightened up. "We are never going to crack this encryption in the time we have. Perhaps we should just ask the Ktarrans what time the deceleration begins?"

For a moment, there was nothing but silence. Then the man in the black T-shirt started waving his hands. "Yes! We have their clock time. We could build a message."

Each alien transmission consisted of a ship's name, the current time, and the actual message. The team had a dozen ship names, and the internal clock used by the Ktarrans had been easy to calculate.

Nigel smiled. "And send it to the *Brenick*. Its comms operators must be overloaded by now. They might not even bother to check the source of the message."

Fifteen minutes later, with Ahvin's help, Nigel's team had constructed a brief message. They had cracked about sixteen words with certainty, and another ten or so with a high degree of confidence. Hopefully that would be more than sufficient. The brief message, with an appropriate header from one of the ships under the *Brenick's* command, read as follows: Repeat attack launch time.

Ahvin didn't like it. "I suggest you change it to: Confirm attack start time." She sounded confident in that choice of words.

Nigel nodded. "Very good, that should work just as well. Encrypt it and send the message up to Colonel Welsh. Tell his comms officer to get it out on a narrow beam, aimed directly for the *Brenick*. Then get every dish we have ready to catch the reply."

The final encrypted message read as follows: *Tismer* to *Brenick* confirm attack start time. EOT.

"Now we just have to hope that the *Tismer* doesn't catch the transmission," Nigel said. *And hope we didn't just ask them about their schedule for lunch.*

Chapter 43
2 AKA

In Earth orbit, the remaining 87 ships of the PDF waited. Crews and support personnel had completed their preparations, and all non-essential people had departed for Earth or the Moon. Fully stocked with food, weapons, and supplies, the fleet waited, some crews impatiently, for the Ktarrans to arrive.

The command centers on the Moon and Earth had seen and reviewed the data of Colonel Delano's attack against the enemy host. That success boosted morale. Everyone praised his performance against such uneven odds. Even his worst enemies had to admit his courage. The number of PDF-haters had dropped drastically in the last few weeks, and the space battle had virtually eliminated any adverse PDF sentiment on the planet. The anti-war factions, still bitter over what they called Delano's dictatorship, admitted that a friendly alien race would not need to initiate contact with over a hundred warships.

Now fear gripped the planet. The thought of the Ktarrans arriving in orbit to resume their rain of destruction terrified the people of Earth. New religions sprang up overnight, prophesying the end of times and blaming mankind's sins for the coming destruction. Cities emptied as fast as possible. Anyone who could abandoned their homes and headed for the countryside. But huge numbers remained behind, unable to flee. The old and infirm had no choice but to stay.

Those unfortunates who couldn't get out started digging, trying to get as far below ground as possible. Panic gripped the masses. Looting broke out, and the police forces of the world, despite preparations for this situation, were unable to contain all the chaos. Nor were the military forces of much use. They remained too busy fortifying their defensive positions, preparing to resist the invaders as long as possible.

Aboard the PDF Command Destroyer *Enterprise*, Field Marshal Shuvalov and PDF Colonel William Welsh sat side by side watching the six meter, three-dimensional display that plotted the Ktarran advance. Right now, the two men controlled Earth's fleet in orbit, while General Jang commanded all forces on the

Moon.

With Delano temporarily out of the picture, Shuvalov and Welsh took active command of the PDF forces. Shuvalov had insisted on going into space to help coordinate the battle, despite the warnings of his doctor. For the last several years, his health had been declining. Now the rigors of space travel and low or zero gravity only added to his medical danger. But he had refused all advice to remain on Earth, or at least the Moon.

Shuvalov's iron will had prevailed against everyone's better judgment, and so now he sat beside Colonel Welsh, directing the fleet. Welsh's expertise had gone into each craft's design. He knew the vessels, knew what they could do, and had the trust of their pilots and crews.

Seventeen months ago, Welsh had fought beside Delano on the Space Station. A former USAF fighter and drone pilot, Welsh had worked since then with the engineers to build the new ships needed for planetary defense. He'd flown and qualified on the Jumper, Dart, Destroyer, and Transport. He'd flown the first Destroyer off the assembly line for several weeks during its shakedown trials. Welsh had hundreds of flight hours on the new vessels, and nobody knew more about the PDF ships and their capabilities.

Shuvalov's military experience helped him grasp the complexities of the battle plans. More significant, he'd worked with Delano for the last year and a half developing tactics. With Delano absent, Shuvalov had no problem assuming operational control of the fleet.

For the coming encounter, he and Welsh positioned the remaining Destroyers on both sides of the planet. They could then reposition them to match whatever vector the enemy chose to attack Earth.

A few hundred meters away from the *Enterprise*, the Halkin ship *Meseka*, commanded by Captain Horath, tracked the Ktarran approach using a smaller version of the same display utilized by Welsh and Shuvalov. The leaders of both ships studied the projected encounter with the enemy.

If both the *Enterprise* and the Moon base were destroyed, command would fall to General Klegg, now bunkered beneath the rolling hills of West Virginia, with General Feng and Minister Borodin at his side. But until Delano returned, Shuvalov monitored the overall strategy, while Welsh commanded the fleet waiting to defend Earth.

Four hours had passed since the Ktarran ships halted after Delano's attack. But now they were on the move, accelerating and heading directly toward Earth. Before long, the deep space sensors on the Moon detected a change in the enemy formation. Roughly a third of the ships were drawing ahead, separating the enemy force into two distinct units.

Welsh and Shuvalov continued tracking the Ktarrans, and it didn't take long to figure out the change in tactics.

"The strategy looks plain enough," Welsh said. "The first wave is traveling at what looks like full power, and moving in advance of the rest of the Ktarrans. They will probably time their deceleration so as to arrive at the optimum point where they can launch missiles."

"For the initial wave, it has to be a missile attack on the planet," Shuvalov agreed. "The first group is heading directly toward us under maximum power. At that speed, they won't have time to attack us or Earth's cities with beam weapons."

Welsh didn't like what he was seeing. "Yeah, but if they're just launching missiles, speed may be an advantage. Our Destroyers probably won't be able to stop them before they launch, and the Defense Grid cannot handle so many."

"I agree," Shuvalov said. "That means missiles will get through to Earth. We must hope that they carry only nuclear bombs. If they have biological or chemical weapons, even a few may be too much for survival."

Alien germs or nerve agents might linger in Earth's atmosphere for years, spreading death.

"Let's hope they don't," Welsh said. "I'll notify Klegg. He needs to know what's coming."

The Ktarrans probably intended to destroy enough of Earth and its support structure so that the human fleet couldn't be sustained. Then the Ktarrans would clean up the Earth ships at their leisure.

The first wave of 60 enemy ships appeared to be coming straight in. At their speed of approach, the Earth fleet would be unable to target anything until the ships were only a few hundred kilometers above the atmosphere.

"But how many missiles do they have?" Shuvalov knew that was the real question. "And how many megatons for each one?" If each Ktarran ship launched three or four large missiles, Earth would not survive.

"They'll probably launch and disperse in every direction," Welsh said, thinking out loud. "We'd waste a lot of time chasing after them. But they'll be going too fast to slow down and properly target the major population centers."

"If we try to stop them, we'd leave our forces scattered when the rest of the Ktarrans arrive," Shuvalov said. "Unacceptable."

"Then we need to let this first wave through," Welsh said. "The Defense Grid will have to try and take them out." He didn't like the option. It meant that Earth cities would be attacked again, this time by an unknown number of nuclear missiles, each one almost certainly capable of destroying a city and much of its surroundings.

"It will depend on how many missiles they have," Shuvalov said. "They can't have too many, or they would not be using this attack pattern. If every ship carried a few missiles, they would arrive and launch together."

"They wouldn't put too many missiles on one ship," Welsh continued, thinking out loud. "If we took out the ship, they'd lose all those missiles."

"Therefore we assume one or two missiles per ship," Shuvalov said. "At these speeds, that's all the time they will have to launch. Is safe assumption?"

Welsh considered that. "Yes, I think so. They have to locate a target and program the missile. Otherwise all they're likely to hit is ocean or miss the planet altogether. Bad for the fish, but the planet is seven-tenths water."

"Then we will have some time, not much, to plot an intercept course," Shuvalov agreed. "But at the speeds the missiles will be traveling, our beam weapons may not have enough time to destroy them or their ships before they launch or get out of range."

"We have to find a way to help the Defense Grid," Welsh said. "Too bad we don't know when they will start their deceleration. We can calculate approximations from their speed, but I'm not sure how accurate that will be."

"Or divert them," Shuvalov said. "How well do you think the Ktarrans have hardened their missiles against an EMP?"

"They know we created such pulses when they attacked last time," Welsh said. "But that was against ships. They may not expect such a tactic against their missiles. They'll probably have some shielding, but likely not as solid as ours."

"Then we might pull our ships away at the last moment." Shuvalov reached out and touched the screen. "Explode several EMP-generating missiles. Meanwhile, our ships can maximize their shields for protection from any resulting EMP pulses."

"If we detonate enough missiles above Earth, the Ktarran missiles might lose their lock on targets," Welsh said. "We'll have to hope the Defense Grid doesn't go down. It will have to take care of this first wave of ships."

Shuvalov shook his head. "No, that will be too many ships for the Grid. We need to divert some ships to drive off this first group, and make sure they don't return to Earth space too quickly after they complete their attack run."

"I don't like that idea either." Welsh studied the screen. "All our tactics are based on our ships working together. If we get into individual ship actions, we'll be at a disadvantage."

"Is true. We need to meet them with a united front," Shuvalov said. The brave words didn't conceal the truth to either man. They would have no real reserves, and the odds were truly against them.

"We need more information," Welsh said. "Maybe we can get some help from Sir Nigel, and his message to that Ktarran ship, the *Brenick*. I'll check with the communication guys and see how they're doing."

*   *   *

Almost four hours earlier, the comms operators aboard the *Enterprise* had taken 40 minutes to prep the transmission units, adjust the power, align the transmitter, and send Sir Nigel's message. The message had to appear as if coming from a nearby ship. Another hour passed while the message traveled toward the *Brenick*.

The reply returned just over a hundred minutes later. The Ktarran ships continued to close the distance to Earth, and more important, the comms operator aboard the *Brenick* didn't seem to care about security. He re-transmitted the arrival time without even a comment.

Welsh needed only a moment to see the importance of the reply. He headed back to the command center, where he found Shuvalov still staring at the console and watching the approaching ships.

"We have to get this to Delano at once," Welsh said, handing a copy of the translated arrival time to Shuvalov. "It may change his plans. If Delano knows when they're going to begin deceleration, he might be able to time his own arrival. Maybe hit them from the rear."

Shuvalov studied the display and shrugged. "It may not be possible, but if it is, then he could disrupt their attack, at least partially. Anything to help the Defense Grid. For now, the Ktarrans are not concerned with Delano's seven ships. As long as they believe he is simply returning to Earth, a few more ships won't affect their strike plan."

"This could give him a good chance for a surprise attack," Welsh said. "I'm sure he can rough up a plan to do some damage."

"He only has seven ships," Shuvalov said. "Not nearly enough."

"Yes, but he has all his Darts," Welsh argued. "And his position would be behind the Ktarrans, and traveling at the same speed. Most of their beam weapons are directed forward. An assault on their rear could give the Defense Grid some help."

"And the rest of the Ktarran fleet will be right behind him."

Both men went silent. Putting Delano's tiny squadron between the two Ktarran forces probably meant he wouldn't survive the encounter.

Their connection to the Halkin ship came to life. Usually the Halkins didn't have much to say, but they always listened in to understand what was happening. "This is Horath. Ktarran ships are weakest from behind." The Halkin Captain's heavy accent didn't detract from his message. "Right now, only Delano can match speed and trajectories to attack from rear. If it is possible."

"Thank you, Captain Horath," Welsh said. "We will ask him to make the attempt."

Shuvalov considered the possibilities, one of which was that he was sending Delano and his crews to their deaths on a suicide mission. "Very well. I'll contact Delano and give him these new orders. He may not have a moment to waste. Colonel Welsh, please notify the Defense Grid and prepare the EMP bursts. Then we will position our ships for the main assault. We need to notify General Klegg. Earth's cities will be under bombardment once again."

Both men knew that if the Ktarrans figured out Delano's plan, to strike the *Brenick's* rear, the main part of their fleet would close the gap and blast Delano's ships and crews into atoms. War was indeed hell, especially when you had to send people you knew to almost certain death.

Earth's defense might now depend on just how well Colonel Delano could disrupt the enemy's missile attack.

Chapter 44
+001 BKA

Delano and his squadron were returning to Earth space at optimum speed when the call from Shuvalov came in over the QuantC. Apparently the earlier communication problems had been on the *Enterprise's* end. The call was marked private, so Delano picked up his headset to hear the Marshal's words. As the call dragged on, those crewmembers at their stations turned to stare at Delano. His side of the conversation remained limited, with Shuvalov doing most of the talking.

When the call ended, Delano sat there lost in thought. The Gunny glanced at Steve, who had broken the connection. The rest of the crew took their cue from Delano and his assistants. The news almost certainly had to be bad. The air of euphoria from their small victory evaporated, and the ship's command center went quiet.

Finally Delano straightened up, and swiveled his chair to face Captain Chan. "The Ktarrans have split into two groups." Delano raised his voice so that everyone could hear. "The first wave, about 60 ships, is accelerating at top speed toward Earth. Shuvalov doesn't believe they intend to slow down enough to use their beam weapons, but will instead launch missiles at Earth as they blow by. A few minutes later, the second wave will arrive, to destroy our disorganized fleet and then finish off Earth."

Delano paused. "The bad news is that at those speeds, the first wave of Ktarrans won't be easy to target, either with our ships' missiles or beams. It's likely the Ktarrans' velocity will carry them well past Earth, and it will take those ships some time before they can return to the fight. So the Defense Grid will have to take them out, with a little help from an EMP or two launched from Earth and the Moon."

Most of the other crew members nodded grimly. Earth would be plastered by a missile attack.

"But here's what Earth wants us to do. Shuvalov hopes we can match speeds with the first group, follow them as they begin their attack run, and hit them from behind. To do that we'll have to drop between the two groups of Ktarrans, which means everyone will be targeting us. Possibly our own Defense Grid as well, since it may not be able to tell us apart."

Chan's mouth fell open, but before he could get in a word, XO Seanna started in. "They want us to do what? Are they crazy? Position ourselves between the two fleets?"

Delano shrugged. "Apparently. Shuvalov doesn't believe the Defense Grid can stop that many incoming ships and missiles by itself, not at those speeds. If we can get behind them, we should be able to knock off a few, and maybe disrupt a few more. Otherwise we'll just have sixty ships coming back at Earth as soon as they can launch their missiles and turn around."

"Can we even make the attempt?" Chan had regained his usual calm demeanor. "We would have to arrive just before they launch missiles, and at the proper positioning for a rear attack."

"That's what we need to know," Delano agreed. "Peter, can you can plot us a course?"

Peter Tasco had originally been a navigator on the Moon to Io run. Since then, he worked non-stop for the PDF and Delano from Day One. He and his wife, Linda, had also played a key role in the fight at the International Space Station. He knew the capabilities of the *Defiant* and nobody in the fleet would be better at calculating an intercept course.

Peter looked up from his plot screen. "I'll run the calculations," he said. "From where we are, and depending on their speed, it may not be possible."

"Do it," Delano said. "The sooner we know the better." He turned toward the still frowning Executive Officer. "Captain O'Shaughnessy, can you thread the needle? We'd have to drop in right behind the first wave, just before they complete their slowdown. And launch our Darts. It will take some flying."

Seanna's eyes darted at Captain Chan, a "see what you've got us into" look. But she spoke calmly enough. "I'll work with Peter. Maybe we can come up with something."

Delano knew Peter Tasco had managed the only high speed arrival at the lunar facility, using the Moon's gravity to slow down his runaway escape shuttle. If anyone could plot the necessary trajectories, it was Peter.

"All right people," Delano said. "We know what we have to do, so everyone make ready. Captains Volozh and Hollingsworth, you need to prepare the Darts. And remember, we need time to broadcast the plan to the rest of the squadron."

Delano turned to Steve. "Notify the other ships to get ready for a new course and a new plan of engagement. If it's a go, they won't have much time to prepare."

He didn't bother to add that the battle they were heading into might not last very long for any of them, not with the main Ktarran fleet coming up right behind them. Everyone on board could figure out those odds for themselves.

*   *   *

Three hours later, the high speed rendezvous still remained only a possibility. Peter and Seanna had come up with a course, several of them in fact, but a lot of factors remained up in the air. Nevertheless, the *Defiant* and the other ships had already initiated a course change, and increased their speed from optimum to full power.

Delano knew the *Defiant* could travel for days at optimum power, but full power put far more strain on the ship. First, power to the plasma shields had to be reduced to the minimum. Then gravity, life support, and all other non-essential systems had to be turned off or scaled down. The antimatter drive could then be fed more power, but no one really knew how long you could run the scoops at that speed.

The ship builders and engineers, in discussions with the Halkins, declared that a point of diminishing returns could be reached. At that instant, the overloaded engines could fail. All it would take were a few atoms of antimatter to combine with regular matter, such as the scoops themselves, to create a fireball that would instantly destroy the ship.

So how fast could the ship go? Until it exploded seemed to be the answer. According to the Halkins, each variant of the antimatter drive had a slightly different theoretical maximum speed. The problem was that you couldn't quite calculate the number until it was too late.

The Halkins and Tarlons aboard the *Meseka* had only vague suggestions. They and the Earth engineers recommended as much caution as possible. Blowing the ship to atoms wouldn't help stop the Ktarran fleet.

But a maximum safe speed came up a little short to achieve the rendezvous. Delano studied the display screen. They might be able to make it. They also might blow themselves up.

Another challenge was the angle of approach. If the squadron appeared to be heading for the rear of the first wave of Ktarrans, Delano's ships would be revealing their plan. Therefore they had to continue toward Earth, with a last minute course correction to bring them in the rear of Commander Teeg's advance force.

Finally Peter developed a series of course corrections that *might*, he emphasized *might*, get them into the proper position. Assuming the *Defiant* didn't disintegrate or vaporize.

"Thanks, Peter," Delano said. He knew what pressure the navigator worked under. His wife was aboard the ship. It would have been all too human for him to have said that it simply couldn't be done.

Delano, Chan, Seanna, Peter, and the Gunny talked it over while still at their stations. No need to hide anything from the rest of the crew. But in the end, Delano made the final decision.

"Peter, you and Seanna start prepping for the run. Coordinate with the best speed Chan can give us. I want a shot at Teeg's ships. Make sure we arrive at a tangent, right behind the left edge of the first wave. If we can position ourselves there, we won't be hopelessly outnumbered at the point of attack."

He met the eyes of everyone in the command center. No one showed any fear or unwillingness to follow the order. They were here, after all, for the opportunity to fight the Ktarrans. And just as Delano had, each one had considered the not unlikely possibility that they would not survive the mission.

"Chan, notify the rest of the squadron of what we're planning. I want everyone ready for the new course and at full power in ten minutes."

Chapter 45
2 BKA

Captain Raizo Tanaka studied the fuzzy outlines on his display screen that indicated the rear guard of the Ktarran fleet, left behind to guard the wormhole. His eight ships had reached the halfway point between the place of battle and the wormhole. Soon Tanaka would have to start making decisions about when to decelerate and how to conduct his attack.

The wormhole itself couldn't be seen at this distance, not with the human eye. You had to be within a few kilometers to notice the shifting patterns of warped space and time, and even then you might miss it. Only gravity wave detectors could reliably identify the everchanging fluctuations resulting from time and space distortions. But he knew it was there, an invisible opening and a highway to distant star systems.

In less than thirteen hours Tanaka would be in reach of the Ktarran rear guard. They had detected his small fleet of eight Destroyers approaching, but so far the enemy showed no inclination to come out and meet him. They seemed confident enough to wait for his arrival. Either that, or they had orders to stay where they were.

Tanaka had no idea of what plan of attack he would utilize when he arrived. Delano's orders, normally precise, left everything up to Tanaka.

"Just do something," Delano had said. "The Ktarrans will expect us to use every ship to defend Earth. I want their main force to worry about their escape route. If you can chase them away, so much the better. Just don't sacrifice your ships."

That meant Tanaka would have to attack a waiting enemy at a location at least two days of travel from Earth. The Ktarrans had left a sizable force behind to guard the wormhole, eleven ships in total. Figuring ten beam weapons per ship, that meant the enemy could direct at least one hundred and ten weapons at Tanaka's squadron. He would have only twenty-four such weapons on his eight Destroyers, so he would be outgunned at least four to one.

By now he could see that the enemy rear guard consisted of three large battleships and eight smaller ships. Even their smallest vessel was almost twice the size of any of Tanaka's destroyers.

The Darts would lessen that disadvantage. Each of his ships supported two Darts, so he would have another sixteen beam weapons there, plus the rail guns. The three Ktarran battleships, Tanaka knew, might have twelve or more beam weapons.

He also had his missiles. They were the only factor capable of equalizing the confrontation. Each of Delano's Destroyers had set forth from the lunar base with eight nuclear missiles, four of which were intended for the Darts. But each Destroyer could launch only two at a time. After that, both Destroyer and Dart needed to be manually reloaded, requiring a twenty minute EVA.

Each of Tanaka's vessels had already launched two at the Ktarran main force, so Tanaka had sixteen missiles left. Actually only fifteen, since one of his Destroyers had been damaged and its missile launch tube destroyed. Subtract another two for the *Naganami*, Tanaka's own ship – he had another use planned for those – so his Destroyers would have only thirteen missiles to initiate the attack, plus the sixteen carried by the Darts.

The Ktarrans wouldn't be surprised by the missiles this time. They'd seen the effect from Delano's attack. They would be ready for EMPs and their beam weapons would be optimized for destroying attacking missiles.

Tanaka sat, staring at the console. The rest of the crew in the command center left him alone, whispering their comments and wondering about how the oncoming fight would take shape, fully expecting their own ship, the *Naganami*, would be leading the attack no matter what the plan.

The ship's odd name – all the Destroyer captains were allowed to choose their ship's name – seemed a strange one. Marshal Shuvalov had planned, in typical Russian style, to number the ships as they came off the assembly line. The first Destroyer built would be D-1, the second D-2, and so on. Delano wanted real names, arguing that crews would fight harder for a ship with a personality, rather than a number. Even if that feature existed only in their minds.

Few of Tanaka's compatriots recognized either the word *Naganami* – the name could be translated as *Long Waves* – or the heritage of its captain. Colonel Delano, however, had recognized the name "Tanaka" immediately, thanks to his studies of the Pacific war with Marshal Shuvalov.

In World War II, Admiral Raizo Tanaka of the Imperial

Japanese Navy, led eight of his destroyers down the "slot," planning to attack the American base on Guadalcanal in a night raid. A much more powerful American force, five cruisers and four destroyers, spotted them on radar, and initiated an attack in the appropriately named "Iron Bottom Sound." Before the Guadalcanal campaign finished, over twenty ships and countless men and aircraft had gone to their watery grave there.

Despite being surprised by the Americans, Tanaka's great grandfather immediately counterattacked. He used his destroyers so skillfully that he sank or damaged almost all of the American ships. In so doing Admiral Tanaka inflicted the most severe defeat ever suffered by the US Navy in a surface encounter since the Pearl Harbor attack. The Admiral's flagship in that encounter was the *Naganami*. Even before that battle, American marines and sailors considered Admiral Tanaka a nemesis to the US Forces. They called him "Tenacious Tanaka."

At their first meeting, Delano had asked Tanaka if he were related to the famous admiral, and was happy to learn this Raizo Tanaka was his great-grandson. The fact that Delano knew all about the admiral's career and victories had greatly impressed Tanaka, leaving him determined not to disappoint the leader of the PDF.

Tanaka slumped down in his seat, closed his eyes, and tried to focus. The tactics Delano used wouldn't work a second time. The Ktarrans would be ready. But they would also be uneasy, knowing that a smaller force felt capable of challenging them. He guessed most of these ships would be second-rate. The Ktarrans wouldn't leave any of their best ships and crews behind on guard duty.

Perhaps they lacked combat experience as well. According to the Halkins, the Ktarrans had little or no experience with coordinated large-scale attacks. Just as important, the enemy now understood that even if they defeated Tanaka's ships, Ktarran losses would be high.

Their mixed-species crews wouldn't be well motivated. They served under duress and would fight only because they feared death, either from their masters or from their enemies. Nor would they like the idea of facing missiles, where a strike could blow them out of existence. Beam weapon damage could be repaired, but a nuclear bomb exploding close to your hull didn't improve your survival rate.

Maybe that was a way to exploit their fear. The missile hit ratio in Delano's attack was less than six or seven to one. What if he concentrated all his missiles on a few ships? If he made his attack initially look like a repeat of Delano's, but then shifted his focus.

Tanaka sat up with a start. Maybe he could still catch them by surprise, take advantage of their lack of combat experience.

He turned to his pilot. "Prepare to modify our course. I want to approach the wormhole directly, so that the Ktarrans have their backs to it. Do it gradually. I don't want them to figure out what we're doing for as long as possible." Tanaka nodded in satisfaction. Always let the enemy have a way to escape. If he could chase a few back into the wormhole, then the morale of those remaining would disappear.

"Comms, send a message to Earth Fleet, telling them why we're changing course. Then notify all our Destroyer captains. I want a conference call in . . ." he glanced at the clock, "in thirty minutes."

He thought about his great-grandfather once again. *Perhaps some of your spirit lives on, venerable ancestor.*

*   *   *

Twelve hours later, Captain Tanaka ordered his squadron to begin deceleration. His eight Destroyers and sixteen Darts had readied themselves an hour ago, and now the inter-ship chatter had ended. The last radio transmission from Earth Force stated that the battle there would begin almost at the same time as Tanaka attacked the wormhole.

The waiting Ktarran vessels had shifted position as well, forming a close-knit grid in a 3-5-3 arrangement, with each ship about a kilometer apart. Tanaka studied the ships on his console.

		1	**2**	3	
4	5	**6**	7	8
	9	**10**	11	

Each enemy vessel was assigned a number, with the larger battleships showing in bold.

The three large Ktarran ships occupied the center of each

line. No more widespread positions that created a weaker flank on either side. Each ship would provide some cover for adjacent vessels, and they could easily shift position to react to individual threats. An efficient arrangement.

Nevertheless, their commanders would be wondering about Tanaka's approaching force, moving confidently toward the wormhole. Nervous or frightened people make mistakes. If he could just give the Ktarrans a reason to run, hit them hard enough, maybe they'd decide retreat is a safer option than fighting an aggressive hostile force.

Tanaka's tactical plan gave his crew assurance, and he easily adapted it to the enemy's 3-5-3 formation. It differed from Delano's attack enough to give the Ktarrans a new look. Even if everything went to hell, any surviving Earth ships should still be able to get away. In that case the rendezvous point was Jupiter's moon, Io, where the crews might get some help from the miners still hiding beneath the volcanic surface.

Not that he worried about that. Tanaka had faith in his tactics and ships. Smaller forces had successfully engaged larger ones many times in Earth's military history, and what had been done once could be accomplished again. Numbers did not always guarantee victory. Surprise remained the ultimate goal of every attack.

Final preparations completed, the waiting began. Tanaka glanced at the countdown clock. Less than an hour remained before contact. By coincidence, the attack on Earth would start in about two or three hours. A solid blow here would give Earth Force a big boost.

Now everything depended on the Ktarrans.

*   *   *

Belted tightly into his command seat, Tanaka took one last look at his crew. Everyone manned their station, and the ship had been readied long ago. Interior doors and hatches were closed, and all non-critical systems shut down or minimized. Reports from the other ships in the squadron confirmed their preparations. With a soft chime, the countdown clock reached zero.

"Initiate braking," Tanaka ordered. His command went out to the other ships as well as the *Naganami*. His eight ships formed a double line, four by four, and half a kilometer apart. Tanaka's ship was in the upper line, second from the left. The center of Tanaka's vessels matched the center of the Ktarrans. He wanted them to believe he was planning a simple frontal assault.

He saw that the wormhole's defenders had tightened their defensive line, and now waited for the human attack, their screens flickering with increased power.

Tanaka made certain his voice remained calm. "Launch the Darts."

Aboard every Destroyer, the Darts released their clamping restraints, the clanking sound resonating throughout the hulls. The small ships drifted away from their mother ships, separating out and forming two new lines directly above that of the Destroyers. Each Dart carried its two missiles.

The Ktarrans waited, their screens at maximum strength. They were not moving toward Tanaka's ships, preferring to have a stable shooting platform. The Earth squadron continued decelerating, slowing the ships down rapidly, until maximum effective attack speed had been reached.

"Launch EMPs," Tanaka ordered.

Three Destroyers each launched a single missile, hurling itself toward the enemy line and each targeting one of the big battleships. The missiles accelerated at maximum speed, leaving the squadron behind. At five hundred and fifty kilometers, the Ktarran beam weapons opened up, at least sixty weapons hunting the incoming missiles. But by the time the Ktarrans found the range, the missiles had crossed the 450 kilometer point and all three detonated successfully, the nuclear blasts creating a broad EMP burst directed toward the enemy fleet.

Tanaka grunted, even as he fought the straps that held him fast against the deceleration. His ship's consoles went blank from the EMP radiation but that lasted only a few seconds. The Ktarrans would react quickly, too, but with most of the radiation directed forward, he expected them to be blind for at least ten seconds, perhaps twenty.

Tanaka, biting hard on his lower lip, ignored the G-forces assaulting his body. For almost ten seconds, nothing happened, as Tanaka's squadron crossed over the 450 kilometer line.

Twelve seconds after the EMP missiles exploded, Tanaka's ships had drawn to within 400 kilometers from the Ktarrans. "All Destroyers, launch missiles!" Seven missiles blasted off their rails, all aimed at the big Ktarran battleship (#6) in the center of the formation.

The moment the missiles were gone, Tanaka gave the next order. "Squadron, attack low! Darts, attack right!" He'd waited just long enough for the enormous energy output to diminish.

Eight Destroyers and sixteen Darts split apart and changed course. Ignoring the three Ktarran ships at the top of the grid, the Destroyers lowered their angle of attack, now targeting the battleship in the center bottom. "Launch missiles!"

Another seven missiles blasted free, and aimed at the Ktarran battleship (#10) in the center of the bottom row of the grid.

The Darts had a different set of targets, the three small vessels to the right of the enemy's center. The Darts launched sixteen missiles at three ships (# 7, 8, & 11), then shifted their course to the center of the grid. They opened fire with rail guns and beam weapons, focusing on their main target, the big battleship (#6) in the center of the Ktarran grid.

Using their maneuverability, the Darts kept up their fire, dodging and weaving as they drove toward the center of the enemy.

Tanaka's attack plan had concentrated his missiles on a small number of enemy ships. Instead of trying to attack them all, he'd selected his targets before the attack began, hoping to overwhelm the defenders and break their formation.

The missiles from the Destroyers, preprogrammed to their specific targets, flung themselves at two battleships (#6 & 10). The three ships targeted by the Darts were effectively out of the fight, as they tried to destroy the oncoming missiles.

Tanaka dismissed that part of the battle. With their missiles expended, the Darts would begin firing at the center battleship using their beams and rail guns. It might not have much effect, but the Darts merely needed to keep the center of the Ktarran line busy for a few moments, while Tanaka's Destroyers hammered the enemy right flank.

His ships now increased their speed, as their beam weapons targeted the smaller enemy ships, now less than a hundred kilometers distant.

To the Ktarran battleship (#10) directly in Tanaka's path, the missiles, still accelerating, appeared to be coming right down the big ship's throat. Traveling almost too fast to be destroyed at this range, most interception firing ceased on the battleship, as its defensive screens were set to maximum.

The three Ktarran escorts tried to take out the missiles, but stopping eight missiles aimed at a single target proved an impossible assignment at such close range. Still, the battleship and its escorts actually destroyed seven of the missiles. One got through, however, and exploded within a hundred meters of the big ship.

Well within the range of the particle radiation burst, the big ship's antimatter chambers immediately overloaded. The resulting blast turned the vessel into a thousand fiery fragments.

While trying to stop the missiles, the smaller escort ships (4, 5 & 9) were vulnerable to Tanaka's beam weapons. They lanced out, the computers controlling the beams more than capable of adjusting for any Ktarran movements.

Tanaka turned his eyes away from the battleships, and focused on the Ktarran left flank. The enemy had engaged the Darts' missiles, but they only had moments to destroy them, and in that short a time the Ktarrans couldn't target all of them. Multiple nuclear detonations sparkled on Tanaka's console, and he saw at least two missiles explode close enough to take out a pair of escorts.

He had no time for satisfaction. Tanaka's eyes shifted to the Darts, now furiously accelerating once again, aiming their rail guns at the still stationary battleship in what had been the Ktarran center.

The Dart pilots fired at anything in their path, and Tanaka had to shake his head at their courage. He saw two of them struck by beam weapons and dissolve in flames. But then the rest were too close, and moving too fast, for the Ktarrans to get a fix on them.

He swung his eyes back to the ships targeted by the Destroyers, the enemy right flank. Hopefully, he had created enough confusion and caused enough damage to let his squadron get past the remains of the enemy.

Then they were through, angling to the left of the wormhole and racing away at max speed until they were out of Ktarran range. The Destroyers had immediately set their defensive screens at maximum, while the Darts randomly shifted position to avoid the enemy beam weapons chasing after them.

Even before the squadron reached safety, Tanaka was taking stock of the action. His console showed the story – one battleship gone, another appeared damaged, and three support ships destroyed.

Other enemy ships would have minor damage as well, both from beam weapons and the hits from the rail guns. Tanaka, meanwhile, had lost two Darts and one Destroyer in his mad dash through the Ktarran line.

That would be a bitter but favorable trade-off, Tanaka knew. What he didn't know was that the biggest battleship, the one anchoring the center, had also been struck by a rail gun projectile. The depleted uranium slug had passed right through the control center of the Ktarran command ship. In fact, it penetrated the entire length of the ship, managing not to hit anything either too solid or explosive in its passage.

However, the commander of the damaged ship, his control room breached and losing atmosphere, had felt the heat from the projectile's passage only a meter above his head. The normally brave Ktarran had his wits frightened out of him by this unknown weapon. The moment his repair crew sealed the hole, he ordered his wounded ship back through the wormhole, shouting something about repairs.

Before Tanaka could regroup his ships for a second attack, the enemy command battleship had abandoned its position and moved toward the wormhole. Running for safety, though he saw no visible damage, only some venting air plumes.

Tanaka stared at the console in disbelief. A slightly damaged enemy ship, as far as he could tell, was withdrawing.

Suddenly an escort ship turned and followed the first toward the wormhole. The remaining battleship, which had not even been targeted, plus the five surviving escort ships now clustered around it, remained behind to guard the wormhole.

"Collect the Darts," he ordered. By the time his Destroyers could slow down enough to curve back toward the enemy, the Darts were starting to dock.

Tanaka had no intention of calling it a day. Though every missile in his command had launched their missiles, he still had the two on the *Naganami*. He would fire one to create another EMP, and use the last one for an experiment – sending it directly into the wormhole's opening.

No one knew what the result would be. Neither the Tarlons or Halkins had ever considered such a possibility. The nuclear detonation might seal the opening, transmit the energy to some other place or time, or it might do nothing at all. But if there were a way to trap the Ktarrans within Earth's solar system, it might be possible to finish all of them.

By now, Tanaka's squadron had killed their momentum and set a new course to return to the wormhole and attack the remaining Ktarran battleship. He guessed the single big ship had taken damage from the near-miss nuclear detonations. Just how weakened it might be remained to be seen.

Whatever the outcome, the odds had evened out considerably. Seven Ktarran ships against seven Destroyers and fourteen Darts. The Ktarrans still outgunned him, but if the Darts could utilize their mobility and rail guns, Tanaka's squadron might yet defeat them. It could turn into a brutal slugfest. If only he had a dozen missiles, Tanaka thought, he could really hurt them.

He issued new orders. In less than a minute, he guided the squadron back on a collision course, but this time traveling at a much slower speed.

"Four minutes to optimum launch of EMP missile," Tanaka's weapons officer called out.

Tanaka grunted again. He'd launch the Darts right after the missile.

"One of the escorts is moving away!" The comms officer sounded as excited as a kid.

A glance at the console showed one vessel, the smallest, heading for the wormhole. "Our odds are improving," Tanaka said. "They must believe we have more missiles."

If they did, the Ktarrans could expect to be destroyed. They would think that, with fewer ships for the Earth vessels to target, the nuclear missiles would be much more effective.

Tanaka studied the clock. The Ktarrans still had time to escape.

"Thirty seconds to optimum EMP launch."

"All Darts! Release five seconds after EMP launch," Tanaka said.

And then the clock went to zero, and the missile blasted off the *Naganami*, headed straight for the one remaining battleship.

Enemy beam weapons leapt into existence, attempting to destroy the missile, but though beams twice brushed the still-accelerating missile, it survived and kept on course.

"Detonation in five seconds!"

"Darts away!"

The initial flash overloaded the console's monitors for almost ten seconds, but when the images returned, they revealed an entirely new battle situation. Instead of engaging the Earth vessels, Tanaka saw the Ktarran ships turning about and lumbering toward the wormhole.

"In beam range in thirty seconds!"

But to escape, the Ktarrans had to get to the wormhole, and Tanaka's ships were closing the gap between the two forces fast.

"Fire at will!" At last the weapons officer shouted the command.

The Darts were closing just as fast, and beams and hardened projectiles were directed at the fleeing ships. The enemy's return fire, from the rear of their ships, was scanty, while every one of Tanaka's weapons was pouring out energy.

One escort ship exploded, a brief fireball of flaming metal. Another was venting atmosphere even as it vanished into the wormhole. Tanaka's squadron kept up the attack, until the last Ktarran ship, the battleship, plodded its way into the wormhole and disappeared. By then the remaining escorts had preceded their leader into the safety of the wormhole.

Or possibly not. Tanaka was right behind them heading for the same wormhole. "Launch missile!" he ordered. "Then get us out of here!"

He watched the missile roar off the rails. It reached the wormhole in seconds and passed from sight. And then nothing. No explosion, no radiation burst. The nuclear device must have affected something, somewhere, but Tanaka had no idea what.

All that mattered was that the enemy rear guard had been driven off. Whether the wormhole had collapsed, possibly destroying the escaping ships, remained unknown. All his information was negative. No energy surges were recorded on his instruments.

But the battle was over. Tanaka slumped in his seat, enjoying a brief moment of rest. "Comms, send a message to Earth Force. 'Rear guard destroyed or fled into wormhole. Missile launched into wormhole. No visible result. Tanaka.'"

Delano would be happy to receive the battle report. Tanaka undid the restraint that had kept him firmly in his seat, then opened his faceplate and leaned back with a contented sigh. Perhaps his great-grandfather would be pleased as well.

Chapter 46
2 AKA

The Almighty Ruler of Ktarra, Pannoch Staleeck, read the message delivered by a frightened Peltor aide. Staleeck resisted the urge to take out his anger on the hapless messenger. Good servants were hard to find, even on Ktarra.

The dispatch consisted of only a few words – even those seemed garbled – but Staleeck recognized the panic in the missive.

"Attacked by Earth ships, damaged need repairs. Returning to base. *Moordil.*"

The *Moordil* was an older battle cruiser assigned to guard the wormhole, ostensibly to prevent any Earth ships or their allies from escaping. Pressed into service at the last moment, it should have been on station relaying dispatches from Grand Commander Veloreck to Ktarra.

Something was wrong, Staleeck realized. Somehow the *Moordil* had been involved in a battle, not near the Earth planet, but at the wormhole. The message offered nothing more. Even if damaged, the *Moordil* might return to base, but surely the other ships would remain at the wormhole to maintain communications with the fleet. But there had been no follow-up reports for some time.

Veloreck's last transmission indicated that he was about to attack the Earth fleet and destroy it. Since then, nothing from Earth space and no acknowledgment of Staleeck's two requests for status updates.

Staleeck wondered where the humans had found ships to attack Veloreck's reserve and rear guard. And why hadn't further messages come from the *Moordil* the moment it exited the wormhole? For that matter, by now Veloreck would surely have sent more updates. He'd been ordered to remain in communication with Ktarra as much as possible.

Unless the wormhole reserve force had been destroyed, and the *Moordil* escaped into the wormhole to save itself. Staleeck noted the time on the message. The *Moordil* should have reached the Ktarran Support Base by now. Even if it had been unable to communicate during the transit of the wormhole, surely it would have sent a dispatch immediately upon reaching the Base.

Staleeck had a possible explanation for that failure to report. The *Moordil* and its ships had been defeated and driven back into the wormhole. The *Moordil's* captain might be waiting for reports of a victory by Veloreck before reporting his own defeat.

If that turned out to be the case, Staleeck would have the *Moordil's* captain chained to a feasting table and eaten alive.

By now the battle for planet Earth would be nearing completion. But somehow Veloreck's fleet couldn't communicate with the Ktarran home world.

Staleeck snapped his formidable jaws together, the grim sound making the trembling Peltor take a step back.

"Take this message and send it to the commander of the Support Base. 'Send one ship through the wormhole to human planet. Hold all other ships at Base until communications with Commander Veloreck re-established. *Moordil* to contact Ktarra upon receipt.'"

"Transmit that at once," Staleeck ordered. The Peltor servant, still fearful of being eaten, bowed low and ran off.

Staleeck struck his hand against his chest, the usual Ktarran reaction to frustration. He would not send the ships still gathering at Base Station to the planet Earth, not until he knew of Veloreck's progress. It could not be possible that Earth, in such short a period of time, had gone from no fighting ships to a fleet capable of defeating Grand Commander Veloreck.

Impossible, of course. But a lingering thought said that it might be possible. If the captain of the *Moordil* had turned and fled the battle, Staleeck would feed on the creature's flesh himself.

The next messenger had better bring good news, or there would be one less Peltor servant in the palace.

*   *   *

In the Command Center beneath the West Virginia hills, General Klegg took his seat at the command station. From there he could see the eight double consoles that controlled the defense grid satellites. Each satellite possessed ten nuclear-tipped missiles. Two soldiers manned every station, one to scan the space around the satellite and the other to operate the weapon.

"Soldiers" didn't seem to be the right word, Klegg decided, especially since most weren't wearing anything resembling a uniform. He doubted if anyone working the stations was older than twenty-one, and most probably quite a bit younger. Five were women. For this kind of remote warfare, you wanted gamers, kids really, who had worked with computers and game controllers all their lives. Their reactions, as well as their judgments, were far faster and superior to any adult you might train to work the equipment.

Every one of these kids came from the top ranks of professional gamers around the world. In fact, three of the sixteen were former champs, and the others had earned piles of cash playing in open events. To make it to the top of the gamer world you needed more than just skill and hand-eye coordination. You needed intuition, the ability to guess the future based on what you saw and felt.

Despite what he knew about their past, Klegg couldn't quite get over his feelings that these remained children playing games, only this time with live missiles and the fate of cities at their fingertips. But that didn't matter. He knew these were the best of the best at interpreting and acting upon computer and visual input at the same time.

Joining Klegg were several senior leaders of the PDF and Alliance militaries. The battle between the Ktarran and Earth fleets would soon erupt in space. If the aliens attacked Earth, Klegg would be calling the shots. Some in the Alliance had voiced concerns about Klegg's acting in their best interests.

Therefore General Zeng of China, Minister Borodin of Russia, and Vivian Spencer, the head of the NSA, were present, hovering around Klegg's station. Ostensibly, they were there to advise him. But even Vivian had orders from the President of the United States to make sure Klegg didn't sacrifice American cities. That she was also engaged to General Klegg didn't bother the President or stop her from giving Klegg what orders she felt relevant.

Zeng and Borodin each had a pair of aides, all of them hanging over Klegg's shoulder and getting in each other's way.

However, not even Klegg would make the final decisions today. Dr. Duan Lian was there as well. The Defense Grid had been her baby since they first started working on the plans, and she knew more about it than General Zeng, or anyone else, for that matter.

The kids were her idea. Lian had searched the world of video gamers, then recruited the most suitable ones into the PDF. Some of the brightest contributed to the software and control hardware development. In fact, the console controllers looked more like sophisticated gaming equipment than military control hardware. Eventually Lian brought the top operators here to West Virginia for their final training and preparation.

The Grid had to be coordinated from a single location, to minimize the chance of multiple satellites tracking the same enemy ship or missile. The bunker in West Virginia, the same one used during the first Ktarran attack, had the best and most well-protected worldwide communications equipment.

"Good evening, General Klegg," Lian said. She took the only empty seat in the room, the one right next to Klegg's. General Zeng sat behind her, with Borodin at his side. Lieutenant Shen, her ever-present bodyguard, watched from a few paces away.

"The Ktarrans are almost in range," Klegg said. "They're braking hard, have been for some time. Admiral Delano is about to fall in behind the first wave. Hopefully he'll be able to disrupt some of the ships and prevent them from firing their missiles."

"And Marshal Shuvalov and Colonel Welsh?"

"Already linked in," Klegg said. "Colonel Peng will have operational control over the fleet, under Shuvalov and Welsh."

Colonel Peng Qilang's promotion had taken effect only days ago. Peng had flown fighter jets for the Chinese Air Force. Thanks to some skillful and fancy flying, he'd been instrumental in stopping the first Ktarran attack. He'd spent the last six months on the Moon, training pilots and testing ships, especially the Destroyer Class. He knew the ships, and he knew the crews. More important, he wanted to fight. He, too, had lost relatives in the attack on China's cities.

No one was more surprised than Peng when Delano recommended him for tactical command of the Earth Alliance Fleet. Equally surprised were Generals Zeng and Jang at Peng's selection over many other possible candidates from the United States and Russia. But Delano wanted the best, and Lian had strongly recommended Peng.

The eighty-plus Destroyers and their accompanying Darts were waiting for the Ktarrans to arrive. Peng's orders had been short, but would probably prove difficult to achieve: stop as many of the enemy ships as possible from launching at Earth, then adjust to attack and defeat the following force of ships under Grand Commander Veloreck.

Welsh and Shuvalov remained aboard the *Enterprise*, orbiting a 1,000 kilometers above Earth. They would direct the overall defense from there, but Peng would lead the actual fighting.

The first blow in the battle for Earth would thus come from the Defense Grid. Lian watched as the Ktarran ships under Commander Teeg decelerated. Their approach speed had been high and now they had to pay the price. By the time they were ready to launch missiles at Earth, their crews would already have undergone serious deceleration forces and probably plenty of mental stress.

"Colonel Delano is generating an EMP, to blind the main portion of the Ktarran fleet behind him," Klegg said. He glanced toward Lian. "It's time."

She nodded. "Activate your stations." That command went to the young men and women waiting at their consoles. One by one, the stations ran a final software check. Then the systems unlocked, giving effective control of each Grid satellite to its operators.

"Delano's team is scoring some hits," Klegg said, keeping his gaze on his own monitoring station. "Two ships already destroyed, and he's got the Ktarrans looking over their shoulders."

Lian didn't say anything. Her lover had already survived a very dangerous confrontation with the Ktarrans, and now he was diving right into the midst of the attacking fleet. His foolish courage would probably get him killed, but that was the man he was, and Lian had known better than to try and change him. Delano's sense of honor demanded that he fight at the forefront of the battle. Lian would have preferred to be at his side, but her expertise with the Defense Grid was too valuable a resource to lose.

Not that there remained much to decide. Unless something unusual developed, the kids would be making most of the decisions. Until they ran out of missiles. Then the satellites would be nearly useless, with only a single rail gun to fight the Ktarran ships.

She glanced at the eight teams of operators. Everyone looked nervous, shifting and twisting in their seats, hands trembling in excitement. But she knew that would disappear the moment the "big game" started. An incredible amount of effort, time, and resources had gone into this project, and now it might all be over in minutes.

The Destroyer fleet circling Earth space would leave these first sixty Ktarran ships alone. They were moving too fast to target, and their actual time in Earth's skies would be only moments. Their momentum would carry them far beyond the planet, and it would probably take twenty minutes or longer for them to turn around and head back to the battle.

The Crypto Section had broken much of the Ktarran code, and would relay to General Klegg the missile launch command the instant they heard it. Klegg's mouth was dry, and he wanted to drink some water, but couldn't take his eyes off the console. Then a voice crackled in his ear.

"General Klegg, this is Nigel at Crypto. The slow-down order was just given. Estimate you have fifty seconds before they begin braking."

That alert went to the *Enterprise* as well. Colonel Welsh gave the next order. "Colonel Peng, break off your ships."

Peng acknowledged the order. In less than five seconds all of his ships were moving, separating into two groups and leaving a broad channel of empty space for the Ktarrans to occupy that led straight to the planet.

The PDF ships, under Colonel Peng, continued moving until they formed two lines of Destroyers and Darts. The Ktarran ships would pass between and slightly below them on their way to Earth. That way the beam weapons of both sides could fire at the passing Ktarrans and not worry about any stray beams reaching across to interfere with the Destroyers on the other side. Every ship in Earth's fleet would now have a few seconds of time to try and damage the Ktarrans before they launched their missiles. If nothing else, Peng's force would provide yet another distraction for the enemy captains.

The Destroyers had scarcely reached their positions when the first of Teeg's ships entered the kill zone.

"Lian, I think it's . . ." Klegg's voice trailed off.

"Yes, all grid control to consoles," Lian ordered. "Fire at will."

Less than a second later, the first missile left its satellite, launched by a sixteen-year-old girl from China named Yu Yan. She'd been given the responsibility of estimating the Ktarran approach, and delivering the EMP missile where it would do the most good.

Lian leaned back in her chair, her finger tapping nervously on the arm. Control had passed out of her hands. The Defense Grid would stop the attack or nothing would. The battle to save planet Earth had begun.

Chapter 47
2 AKA

"So they can be beaten," Delano said, when Tanaka's first message reached him. The *Defiant's* crew all had smiles on their faces. News of Tanaka's success provided a major boost to morale, and Delano guessed that Field Marshal Shuvalov with the Earth Fleet would soon be having the same reaction. The QuantC device had malfunctioned again, so the message would travel back to Earth at the snail-mail speed of light.

The news couldn't have come at a better time. The *Defiant* and her crew were getting ready to take on the Ktarrans, and the knowledge that they could be driven off by a smaller force gave everyone hope.

Forty minutes later, a follow-up message from Tanaka arrived, providing more details on the battle, some video files, and a two-page analysis of the encounter. By this time Steve had managed to get the QuantC back online, and passed Tanaka's second report back to Earth, saving almost twenty minutes of travel time.

Delano immediately called a meeting with Captain Chan, Pilot Seanna O'Shaughnessy, Navigator Peter Tasco, and his two aides, Steve Macey and the Gunny.

The senior team crowded together in the lounge while everyone read through Tanaka's notes. When they finished, Delano started in. "Those Ktarrans that Tanaka took out may have been second-rate troops, but I think his attack would have shaken even the most experienced fighters."

"From what we've seen," Captain Chan said, "they do not respond well to new tactics, or to unexpected challenges. According to the Halkins, the Ktarrans almost always have superior numbers or firepower on their side."

"Attacking and veering away seems to confuse them," Seanna said. "They appear to be unfamiliar with hit and run tactics. The more we can utilize movement, the better."

"I think our missiles are scaring the crap out of them," Gunny said. "They've probably never encountered smart weapons that can track and turn with them."

"The Ktarran commanders, Veloreck and Teeg, hesitate whenever something new confronts them," Delano said. "I think we need to keep doing what they don't expect."

"Attack when we should retreat," Chan agreed. "Or attack where they least expect it."

"That's what I want," Delano said. "Teeg certainly won't be expecting us to charge right into the rear of his formation. If we can manage that, we'll have a good shot at disrupting their strike on Earth. It may be good enough to give the Defense Grid a chance to stop their missiles."

"Will our IFF protect us if we get too close?" Peter Tasco's calculations had made the rendezvous possible.

The Identification Friend or Foe automatically identified friendly ships. None of the Ktarrans had anything like that. Theoretically, a missile, or another Earth ship for that matter, would not target a friendly vessel.

Delano turned to Chan. He'd been a pilot in China's air forces, and knew more about IFF than anyone there. "What do you think, Captain?"

"We're using your American software," Chan said. "It was chosen because it worked better with the computer hardware. According to the programming, if there is a twenty percent chance of error, the weapon will not detonate."

"Yeah, right," Steve scoffed. "The programming always works until it encounters something the designers didn't plan for. Those missiles will be coming right at us, after passing through sixty enemy ships. There won't be much time for communications. I'd say it's fifty-fifty."

No one challenged Steve's words, and Delano agreed with the higher estimate. "Whatever the odds, we'll have to take the chance. OK, we're going to attack Teeg's rear. We'll just have to hope for the best." He glanced around the table, then set his gaze on Seanna.

"Seanna, you've seen the attack plan. I'd like to make one change, if you're up for it. I want you to pilot us right through the Ktarrans so the *Defiant* can take out Teeg's command ship. I want these aliens to know that we can locate and identify their leaders, and come after them. If we can do that at the start of the fighting, we might shake up his captains, perhaps disrupt some of their attack plans."

Teeg, the leader of the first wave of Ktarran ships, had

already revealed much of his planned assault. His ship, the largest in the group, had by now taken position in the center rear of the force. Obviously, the alien commander had no plans to personally lead his ships into what looked to be a hard-fought battle. Teeg had grouped six ships around his own position for protection, with two smaller vessels trailing behind.

Seanna considered the idea. "That means we'll have to take out those two ships just to clear the way. The minute we start, they'll know what we're up to."

"We have to send these guys a message," Delano said. "I want their leaders to understand that we can find them. That way they'll keep looking over their shoulders."

"We're almost out of time," Peter Tasco said. "We need to make the final course correction in about thirty minutes. Once we do that, both the forward and rear battle groups will know exactly what we're planning. Veloreck's group will close up behind us faster than we can get to Teeg's command carrier."

"Perhaps we could get some help," Chan said. "If we could use our Quantum communication device to coordinate an EMP pulse from Earth Force, the interference might blind Veloreck's sensors just long enough for us to get into position."

"Shuvalov will be using EMPs against them anyway," Delano said, talking as much to himself as to the team. "I'll bet we're better protected against the pulses than the Ktarrans."

"I have an idea," Peter said. "Instead of trying to coordinate with Shuvalov, why don't we just drop one of our missiles behind us, and let Veloreck's force run into it."

"Almost like a mine," Chan said. "I like it. If we can rig the missile to detonate when they're right on top of it, we might buy ourselves some time."

Delano liked it, too. "A nuclear blast close up might really blow out their sensors, especially if they're not expecting an EMP. Those missiles are supposed to be stealthy, right?"

"Well, they're double coated," Gunny said. "First with a mix containing high concentrations of iron powders in a polymer matrix. Over that goes a coat of conductive fiber-filled composites. If we just dump the missile, there won't be any energy trail for them to track. I doubt their sensors will spot something as small as a missile."

Everyone stared at Gunny, surprised at his knowledge of missile technology.

"If we had more time, we could separate the warhead from the propulsion unit," Chan said. "But that would probably take a few hours."

"Meanwhile we have to jury-rig a detonator," Delano said. "Better get Kosloff and Chen working on that."

"How much time will that take?" Seanna asked. "I'll have to know where to position the *Defiant* so that the Ktarrans will be heading straight for it."

"Kosloff can give you an estimate." Delano glanced around the table. "OK, people, let's do it. Chan, you make sure the missile gets modified. Seanna and Peter will plot our course and figure out the drop point. Steve, get on the horn and notify the rest of the squadron of what we're doing, and that there's going to be some hard acceleration. Any questions?"

"We're going to try this?" Seanna didn't seem too confident. "Has anybody thought about how we're going to get away after we attack?"

"That's easy," Delano said. "You're going to fly us out of the furball right after we finish off Teeg's ship."

She stared at him. But all she said was, "yes, Admiral."

*   *   *

Twenty-seven minutes later, Delano again strapped himself into his station. The activity aboard the *Defiant* had been non-stop. Peter still couldn't confirm that the squadron could reach an appropriate spot to squeeze in between the two Ktarran fleets. The rest of the ships had received relatively simple orders – follow the *Defiant*, attack as many enemy vessels as possible, and break off when things got too ugly.

Colonel Kosloff supervised the most difficult task – prepping one of the *Defiant's* two remaining missiles for the EMP pulse. He had to suit up, along with Hollingsworth and Abramovich, then EVA out onto the hull. The missile had to be removed from its launcher, always a two-person job that the Alpha Dart team didn't trust anyone else aboard ship to do. Then Kosloff got to work, opening the casing and deactivating the propulsion connection.

By then the Power Engineer, Wang Chen, had jury-rigged a radio remote detonator and joined Kosloff outside the ship. They wired it into place. A three-meter length of copper wire would act as the receiving antenna. The missile was then returned to its original storage rack, where it normally would be attached by two metallic straps.

Instead Chen substituted a magnetic grip pad that should hold the missile in place, provided no sudden or extreme changes of course or velocity occurred. The last step required attaching a small oxygen cannister, usually used as an emergency air supply. Once the power to the magnetic pad was cut, the cannister would provide enough of an air blast to push the missile away from the *Defiant*.

The EVA team completed their work with no time to spare, and one by one climbed back into the ship. The last man in, Kosloff, had just enough time to close the hatch and get to his battle station. More than a little out of breath, he buckled himself in. "Admiral, the device is ready." He held up the two switches that would first release the mine, then detonate it. "I wouldn't trust the detonator more than a thousand kilometers."

From what Delano was seeing on his console, that distance would be more than needed. Peter and Seanna were both working their computers, calculating and recalculating the possible course changes. Finally Peter slumped back in his seat. "I think we're good to go, Admiral."

"Stand by to initiate course change," Seanna announced. "Fifteen seconds!"

Cutting this a little close. Delano's mouth felt dry, but the time for worrying had passed.

"Changing course . . . now!" Seanna's normally soft voice echoed through the command center.

"All ships, full speed ahead," Captain Chan ordered. "Change configuration . . . now!"

The *Defiant* would take the lead, the remaining six Destroyers following directly behind her at one kilometer intervals. As soon as the ships fell into their new formation, Chan had another order. "All ships, increase to flank speed!"

The ships were following US Navy conventions. "Full speed" called for the maximum recommended speed, around ninety percent of what the engines could reliably deliver. "Flank Speed" was the theoretical maximum of 100% power generation. That last ten percent would double the drain on the deuterium fuel that acted as a catalyst for the anti-matter engines.

No one could be certain how long a ship could maintain that

speed. But if Delano wanted his squadron to get into position, they needed all the velocity they could muster for at least fifteen minutes.

Now comes the hard part. Would the ship, all the ships for that matter, hold together? "Captain Chan, Lieutenant Chen, please cut power the moment you detect a possible overload." It would probably be too late, but Delano didn't want to go out in a blaze of exploding anti-matter.

The fifteen minutes crawled by, and another sixty seconds after that before Seanna overrode the controls. "All ships, return to full speed ahead," she shouted. Wang anticipated the command, and with a growl of lost power, the *Defiant* slowed its acceleration slightly.

So far, so good. Delano saw that he still had all six of the squadron ships trailing behind. If they could hold this speed, the *Defiant* might just squeeze in behind Teeg's ships. He realized he was holding his breath, and let it out. *Don't want to appear too nervous in front of your crew.*

"Power generation holding steady," Chen reported. "No damage detected in power channels."

"Thank you," Delano said. "Peter, are we still on course?"

"Affirmative, Admiral," he said. "In the pipe, five by five."

The response meant that the ship was exactly on its projected course, and in the center of the optimum track.

"Radio chatter from Ktarran flagship is increasing." Sergeant Jerome Cowan had been monitoring the Ktarran channels. "I think they've figured out what we're doing. The *Zelbinion* is broadcasting to all ships."

The *Defiant* continued accelerating, while Teeg's fleet continued to decelerate. They had to slow down enough to attack Earth, and there wasn't much they could do about the seven Earth vessels falling in behind them and closing fast.

Delano glanced at Seanna. She now controlled not only the *Defiant*, but the other ships following her lead. He knew she was a good pilot, but did she have the nerves to take the *Defiant* directly into the middle of Teeg's ships? He wanted to ask her, but Captain Chan caught his eye. Chan seemed at ease, watching Seanna with his hands folded on his lap.

Well, damn! If Chan didn't have any doubts, Delano didn't intend to ask any stupid questions.

"Veloreck's ships are picking up speed," Peter announced.

"He's closing in on our rear."

"How long?" Captain Chan still didn't seem concerned.

"Leading wave is only forty thousand kilometers back," Peter said. "They'll be in range in about fifty seconds."

"Closing rapidly with Teeg's ships," Seanna said. "Ninety seconds to deceleration."

"Kosloff, are you ready to release the missile?" Chan asked.

"Yes, Major."

Delano bit his lip. He wanted to give the orders, but the ship belonged to Chan, and the captain knew what needed to be done. Delano had one last worry, that Kosloff would activate the wrong switch and blow them all to atoms. *Yeah, that would solve the problem.*

"Release the missile," Chan said.

"Missile away," Kosloff answered. "Air cannister is pushing the missile away."

One less worry. Hopefully it would detonate.

The squadron didn't dare decelerate too early, or the missile might catch up to them.

"*Zelbinion* and leading Ktarran ships closing rapidly," Peter announced.

"Stand by to detonate missile," Chan ordered.

"*Zelbinion* still closing." This time Peter's voice sounded a little strained.

Captain Chan kept his eyes on the console, watching the display and waiting for the optimum moment.

"Deceleration in ten seconds," Seanna said.

That meant the *Defiant* was closing rapidly with the rear ships of Teeg's fleet.

"Detonate the missile, Colonel Kosloff," Chan said.

The radio wave took almost a second to reach the still-receding missile. The Ktarrans never saw it until it exploded less than ten kilometers from the foremost ships and only sixty from the *Zelbinion*.

Delano saw the bomb go off, the flare from the two- megaton warhead sending a blast of radiation that temporarily affected the *Defiant's* rear sensors.

"Decelerating now!" Seanna's voice had gained an octave as well.

"All ships," Chan said. "Attack at will. Attack!"

Chapter 48
2 AKA

Grand Commander Veloreck received the report that remnants of the small group of ships that attacked him previously had changed course. They had increased their speed as well and were heading straight for the rear of Teeg's forces. A second report soon followed, stating that the enemy ships would not be able to gain position on Teeg's rear before he attacked. Scarcely had that message been delivered when a third arrived, declaring the opposite.

Veloreck's jaws snapped, flinging a spray of drool into the air. These filthy human animals were not doing what they should be doing! If they were capable of offering a defense, he'd expected them to be waiting at the wormhole for his arrival. Time-consuming effort and energy had gone into forcing the wormhole to open a million kilometers from its natural exit. When he arrived, he found nothing! Nor had there been any ships stationed at the original exit point.

Instead, a small fleet of ships had waited for him to advance. The foolish human attack confused his captains long enough to cause some damage and escape. Now seven human ships were trying to get behind Teeg. They must have guessed his attack plan. Earlier he received the report about the Ktarran rear guard being attacked and then fleeing into the wormhole. Those cowards had fled the solar system, leaving Veloreck out of communication with Ktarra. He would need a ship able to transmit a message directly into the wormhole to have any chance of recalling those deserters back to their duty or even to re-establish a link with home world.

Now the human animals plotted a possible disrupting attack on Teeg's rear. These human ships needed to be destroyed. An attack from the rear was the most dangerous, since Teeg's ships would already be decelerating hard. If they spun around on their horizontal axis, they would be traveling practically blind. Besides, they would need all their beam weapons for the larger human fleet awaiting them.

Veloreck would have to speed up his own fleet to intercept

the seven human ships. He'd wanted time for Teeg's force to grind down the human defenses, but now Veloreck would have to get involved sooner. "Order the fleet to increase speed! I want those humans destroyed before they can attack Teeg."

It took awhile to get the message out to all the ships and receive their acknowledgements. The fleet then boosted its speed by nine percent, just enough to position the Ktarrans right behind the Earth ships if they continued with their intercept plan. Already he could see the human ships on his control screen.

"Notify Teeg! Tell him enemy ships are behind him! We will attack them."

Veloreck growled while his staff prepared the ships. Then the blips on the screen grew larger, and he could see the seven Earth ships falling in behind Teeg's force. In a few more moments, they would open fire. However before they got within range, Veloreck's leading ships would be there. Yes, this time the humans would pay for daring to stand up to his forces. In a few more microts he would . . .

The nuclear explosion sent out a wave of radiation that fully engulfed most of Veloreck's ships. The missile detonated about thirty kilometers from the leading vessels. The single blast didn't damage any of his ships, but its EMP pulse caught the Ktarrans by surprise and caused confusion in the closest ships.

Veloreck's main console went dark, as the hull sensors burned out from the EMP. His crews had been warned about this tactic, and spare sensors were at hand to replace any burned out or damaged devices. But the unexpected EMP caught the Ktarran crews off guard, and it took them almost thirty seconds to restore the Grand Commander's battle console, and probably even longer for most of the other ships.

At such close range, the EMP shock was far out of proportion to its size. Veloreck's leading ships had nearly been on top of it at detonation, less than a few kilometers away. Other ships, blind and thinking they were under attack, changed course or slowed down to avoid more unseen missiles. Two ships nearly collided, and had to make frantic maneuvers to avoid disaster. That forced other ships out of formation, and the tightly-knit fleet lost some of its cohesion.

Veloreck's bellow of anger rocked the command chamber. Ktarrans and slaves shivered at the sound, knowing it portended the death of some poor victim for incompetence. But that would have to wait. Despite his fury at friend and foe, Veloreck watched in frustration as the seven Earth ships, beams blazing energy, disappeared into the rear of Teeg's formation.

* * *

Yes! Delano clenched his fist at the nuclear blast behind him. The *Defiant* and her sister ships were prepared for the explosion, sensors drawn in and replacements ready if needed. But when the missile went off, Delano's squadron was almost six hundred kilometers away, and the EMP effect at that distance was not that powerful.

Its effect on Grand Commander Veloreck proved far more successful than Delano had expected. The Ktarran fleet slowed momentarily, its formation disrupted. He didn't really care. Half blind, they were now too far behind him to stop his squadron's penetration.

The seven Destroyers had shifted slightly into echelon formation, with the *Defiant* leading the way. Her sister ships had received different orders. They were to attack the enemy's rear left flank, destroying as many ships as possible. Staying slightly to the side of Teeg's ships would give them a good chance to avoid any Defense Grid missiles and reduce the number of beam weapons that could be aimed against them. Delano had given Seanna a much more difficult and dangerous assignment – disregard Earth's missiles and bore into the center rear of Teeg's ships, hunting for the commander himself.

Whatever doubts Delano might have had about Seanna's courage or flying skill disappeared. She maneuvered the *Defiant* almost as agilely as a Dart, alternating power to the main engines and thrusters. In fact, the *Defiant's* two Darts had trouble keeping their station, which was fifty meters above and a hundred meters behind their mother ship.

* * *

Commander Teeg had never experienced such gravity forces. The *Brenick* was decelerating at maximum speed, well above the rated engine power. The seldom-used restraining straps pulled at his massive chest, and throughout the ship's command center, he could hear the groans and wheezes of his crew.

His pain and that of his crew meant nothing now. Teeg intended to stay right in the middle of his forces, the safest location during the attack. All energy had been diverted to the engines for deceleration and to the screens, to increase their effectiveness. Gravity, life support, internal power, and almost all of his beam weapons, had been shut down. Another dozen non-essential systems were also offline.

Teeg's ships would be performing the same difficult maneuver. In their case, they also had to examine approximately a quarter of the Earth's surface and try to identify large population or military targets. Then the weapon masters would lock those coordinates into the missiles and fire. Only after that would they have power to divert to the weapons and make their escape.

Fortunately they were traveling so fast that it would be difficult for any Earth ship to target them. At least, that's what Teeg counted upon. He intended to survive this first encounter, fly past Earth until the fleet could slow down enough to turn, get back into formation, and return to the attack. Hopefully he would still have enough ships to make a difference.

The *Brenick* had no missiles to launch, but Teeg had twelve beam weapons, enough to destroy any Earth ship it encountered.

"Missile approaching from Earth," a voice shouted. "Multiple missiles being launched!"

"Prepare for EMP. Begin evasive maneuvers," Teeg ordered. There wasn't anything else he could do. Only his leading ships had their beam weapons powered up.

"Missiles still being launched," the weapons' controller said. "More missiles coming online!"

Teeg stared at his screens. The Earth ships waiting in his path were scrambling out of the way, parting like a curtain to his left and right. Thus leaving a clear path for the onrushing missiles.

Veloreck's plan hadn't included missiles launched from the planet's orbit. Somehow the enemy had constructed a missile platform above the planet. These filthy human animals had many ways of waging war. Teeg's ships would be blasted to dust.

The first missile detonated four hundred and forty kilometers in front of his lead ship. The powerful pulse blanked out half of Teeg's screens. It took almost 12 seconds, a lifetime in a close-fought battle, before the instruments recovered or were replaced. By then the missiles had locked onto their targets and begun exploding.

Teeg's ships occupied a rectangular box four hundred kilometers wide and three hundred deep. Teeg stared in horror as his ships flamed out of existence in nuclear flares. The missiles were closing too fast to be targeted. By now his ships were also under attack from the Earth ships. They had taken positions at right angles to his flight path, and beam weapons flashed along the hulls of his ships.

Despite the strong resistance, Teeg's ships started releasing their own missiles, aiming them at any target on Earth that seemed worthy of nuclear destruction. In a few more moments, Teeg and his remaining ships would be safe, hurtling past the planet. Losses would be high, but the plan was working.

*   *   *

Watching his console, Delano saw the chaos erupting in Teeg's formation, thanks to the Defense Grid missile attack. While the Ktarrans struggled to slow down enough to target and launch their missiles, all *Defiant* had to do was dodge the lumbering enemy ships. Seanna penetrated Teeg's rear guard, ignoring the few beam weapons aimed at her, weaving past two ships before the Ktarrans could lock their beam weapons on the *Defiant*.

Delano had never imagined such maneuvering, and likely the Destroyer's designers would have felt the same. Without taking a single hit, Seanna had guided the *Defiant* almost directly behind the *Brenick*, Teeg's command ship.

Up to now, neither the *Defiant* nor her two darts had fired a weapon, but that was about to change. The *Brenick's* beam weapons, those that could bear on the *Defiant*, fired first. Delano, staring at his console, saw that the *Brenick's* display had changed intensity. The usual dull reddish orange flickering screens had morphed into bright red, and Delano quickly realized Teeg had ordered maximum power to his defense screens.

But the *Brenick* still had to decelerate, or risk finding herself facing the brunt of Earth's missiles, already on their way. That left very little power for the beam weapons.

Captain Chan gave the order to fire even before Seanna had fully lined up behind the *Brenick*. *Defiant's* three beam weapons lashed out at the back of Teeg's flagship, trying to penetrate her screens. But the *Brenick's* defenses held, and though the three beams repeatedly struck the vessel, no damage resulted.

"Focus all weapons on rear drive pod," Chan ordered.

But that required some doing, and even the *Defiant's* beam computers couldn't maintain that level of accuracy. Not with Seanna juking and weaving unpredictably. Then Delano felt the ship lurch, struck by a beam weapon from some other Ktarran ship. Seanna managed to break the lock before the screen failed, but the maneuvers prevented the *Defiant's* three beam weapons from doing much damage.

Delano swore, meaningless words that merely vented his frustration. He'd gotten into position, but somehow the *Brenick* resisted his efforts.

*   *   *

Above and behind the *Defiant*, her two Darts joined in the attack, adding their beams to the endeavor. Each Dart had already been grazed by a hostile beam, and they were doing their best to keep a lock on the enemy target.

Beta Dart Captain Arkady Volozh felt the heat from another beam weapon flash across his fighter. It lasted only an instant, but apparently long enough to take out *Beta's* beam weapon.

"Chyort!" Forgetting English in his frustration, Volozh screamed the Russian obscenity loud enough for Delano to pick it out of the background noise. Volozh screamed his next order. "Ruben, the gun!"

But *Beta* Gunner Ruben Vardanayan had already abandoned the useless beam control to switch to the rail gun.

With an incoherent shout of rage, Volozh twisted the Dart onto a new course and applied full power. He shot ahead of the *Defiant*, closing rapidly on the *Brenick*. But this time he lined up the ship directly, and Ruben began firing.

The first three thirty-centimeter copper projectiles, one launched each second, missed the *Brenick*, but with the range closing so fast, the next three all struck the enemy flagship. But nothing happened. Ruben continued firing, sending slug after slug into the rear of Teeg's ship.

The *Brenick* was a large ship, and at this shortened range it became almost impossible to miss. Those projectiles bored right through the screens, penetrated the final hull barrier and tore into the ship's interior.

Suddenly the *Brenick's* screens died, the bright red haze vanishing into blackness in less than two seconds. "Jaitsa razbit!" With energy beams stabbing all around him, Volozh wrenched the steering control and blasted straight up at max thrust, above the enemy ships and out of the way of any incoming missiles.

*   *   *

Delano saw the *Brenick's* screens go dark. *Yes! Got him!*

"Defense Grid missiles closing," Steve Macey shouted. "We better get outta the way."

Captain Chan saw the danger as well. "All ships! Break off attack! Break off attack now!"

Seanna ignored him, still intent on closing the distance and aligning her ship. The three beam weapons on the *Defiant* again lashed out at the *Brenick*, and this time they focused in only a few seconds. It was long enough.

The *Brenick* exploded, the blast starting from deep inside her, and bursting through the thin hull, now not reinforced by the ship's screens. The damage wasn't immediately fatal, but one look told Seanna that the ship was finished. Without waiting for orders, she juked the *Defiant* straight up, following the Darts, and heading up and out of the fight as fast as possible.

*   *   *

"We've been hit!" The *Brenick's* attack officer screamed. "Attacked from the rear! Multiple hits. Shields ineffective. Damage to . . ."

Teeg didn't hear the rest. First the *Brenick's* shields had collapsed. Then the engines failed, and now he felt a shudder as the big ship took another hit. The sound of metal rupturing filled the command center. He had time for one last thought. The projectile weapons! We've been . . .

The *Brenick* exploded, blown apart by her ruptured containment fields that allowed matter and anti-matter to mix in a fireball of destruction.

*   *   *

Nuclear missiles were exploding all around Delano's *Defiant*.

They had reached the primary impact zone for the first wave of Earth's missiles.

Delano, his jaw clenched, watched the demise of the *Brenick*. Now all he could think of was telling Seanna to get them the fuck out of here. But he never said a word, though his brain kept screaming the words, *"Get us out of here!"*

He needn't have bothered. Seanna hadn't waited for either Delano or Chan to tell her what to do. She'd held on the attack well past the margin for safety, entering the zone where the Defense Grid missiles were targeting enemy ships. Now Seanna started climbing, her two Darts leading the way. With a curse she wrenched the control stick to its maximum position. She'd seen the missiles coming, and realized the *Defiant* was right in their path. Not the place to be, not this close to Earth.

Delano stared at the screen. Teeg's ships were blowing up, flashed to ash by nuclear fires or Earth's energy weapons. Space itself seemed filled with crisscrossing energy beams, and more than a few brushed over the *Defiant*. Now the G-forces pressed hard against Delano's chest. The ship had never been designed for this extreme maneuvering. He heard a strange noise, the tough metal of the hull starting to twist and buckle. Then he blacked out, as the blood drained from his eyes by the force.

How Seanna withstood the strain he would never know. Delano, Chan, and most of the male crew lost consciousness for at least a few seconds. Earth tests had suggested that women could withstand acceleration forces better than men, and Seanna had just proved them correct.

Somehow she stayed conscious and managed to ease off the climb. The G-forces dropped rapidly. Beside Delano, the Gunny regained consciousness and managed to re-center his screens, recovering far faster than his commander. By the time Delano could refocus his eyes, the *Defiant* was safe, away from the killing box. The remaining survivors of Teeg's ships had flashed past Earth.

"Decelerating and setting a course back toward Earth orbit." Seanna's voice had returned to normal.

A look at the screens showed that Teeg's surviving ships were also continuing their own deceleration.

At least we're not dead. Delano nodded in satisfaction. The *Defiant* was OK. Best of all, Teeg's vessel had been hit and destroyed, not just by a beam weapon or a missile, but by targeted hits from a rail gun. *Scratch one command ship, motherfucker.*

"OK, we survived that one, people. Let's get back into the fight."

*   *   *

From the Ktarran command battleship *Zelbinion*, Veloreck watched in anger as the seven ships charged into Teeg's rear. The unexpected EMP had slowed his arrival for only a few moments, but enough to let the human ships slip into the gap and attack Teeg from behind. One brave ship had actually penetrated into Teeg's formation, and fired its weapons against the command ship. Two of the Earth ships were obliterated, but incredibly five managed to escape.

Then, as the last ship was escaping, the *Brenick* exploded, turning into a fiery ball of flame that spread like a shooting star. The burning pyre left Commander Teeg dead. Veloreck suspected the guilty ship to be commanded by the human Delano, the one who first confronted the Ktarran forces and had demolished Turhan's command carrier more than a cycle ago.

Neither Teeg nor Delano mattered any longer. Teeg had fulfilled his mission, launching missiles at the helpless cities of the planet and breaking up the cohesion of the human ships waiting to defend the planet. The Earth ships had taken their toll on Teeg's force as it passed by, and the incredible missile attack from the planet had caught Veloreck by surprise.

Where had they obtained so many missiles? How could they fire them so accurately? Somehow the weapons appeared to lock onto a target, and maintain that lock even as the Ktarran ship performed evasive maneuvers. A brush from a beam weapon didn't harm the attacking missiles. It required at least two or three seconds from a weapon to destroy it.

Veloreck gave the final order to his fleet – attack and destroy all the Earth ships. He had time to send another message to the remains of Teeg's fleet – return and attack at utmost speed. Those twenty or so surviving ships should provide a deadly thrust to the humans, coming from what would be their rear.

He saw the human ships forming into two ragged lines, ready to oppose him. Ahead of the *Zelbinion*, energy beams from human and Ktarran ships flashed into existence, lashing out across the empty space between the two fleets.

The *Zelbinion* lurched violently, as the ship slowed down, reaching optimum attack velocity a moment before the two fleets fully engaged. Once again the Earth ships launched missiles, but Veloreck's fighters were ready for them. Pairs of beam weapons searched out the incoming rockets, blasting many to dust before they reached their targets.

Once the missiles were dealt with, the real fight began. The Ktarran ships moved slowly, almost leisurely, into optimum beam weapon range. Velocity no longer mattered. Power configurations were changed, allowing the screens and beam weapons to draw most of the available power, so as to both defend and destroy their attackers.

The battle for planet Earth had begun.

Chapter 49
2 BKA

Walter McEvily wiped the sweat from his face, but the gesture didn't interfere with his task. Rising temperatures inside the computer resources facility at New Beijing were about to crash the system. If these computers failed, the PDF forces might not be able to withstand the imminent Ktarran attack. Never in his life did so much depend on his preventing the disaster that now threatened him and the PDF.

The temperature continued rising rapidly inside the Lunar computer center. Walter yanked off his T-shirt and dropped it on the floor. Fingers flying over the keyboard, he shut down every system not critical. His singlet had gone five minutes earlier, preceded by the jacket he put on whenever he entered the chilly facility, where temperatures usually hovered around 62 degrees Fahrenheit.

Though only twenty-six years old, Walter had the beer belly of a man twenty years older. A software developer by trade, Walter had joined the PDF right after its formation. Like many others, he had a personal grudge against the Ktarrans. His parents had both died in South Korea, in the city of Incheon.

Walter's father had taught engineering at Manhattan College in New York, and during his long tenure had developed a friendship with another professor in the department, Dr. Daniel Cho, born in South Korea. Both men had retired years earlier, and Walter's parents were visiting their friends, now living in Incheon, on a holiday vacation.

The Ktarrans had leveled the Port of Incheon, before moving on to Seoul and Beijing. Walter McEvily, an only child, had watched the alien assault in horror on live TV from New York. His parents had never harmed anyone in their lives, let alone done anything worthy of being killed.

They had been delighted when Walter chose to study electrical engineering at Manhattan College. He had taken classes taught by both his father and Professor Cho, and graduated with a degree in electrical engineering. But it was Professor Cho who encouraged Walter to seek his second doctorate in computer design, marrying two skills that few attempted to master.

For all his mental abilities, Walter had been a lonesome adolescent, overweight and with a slight speech defect that not even his blue eyes and freckled face could overcome. Now in his mid-twenties, he remained thirty pounds above his recommended weight. Despite good grades that should have attracted plenty of serious college girls, he remained a deep introvert. Even on the Moon, women made him nervous and tongue-tied. Computers more than filled his life, however. All such concerns disappeared the day his parents died beneath the Ktarran energy beams.

Walter joined the PDF after he heard Delano and Lian's speech in Moscow. Too overweight for combat, his aptitudes had catapulted him to the uppermost of scientific experts working against the coming invaders. Within six months, he'd risen to the top of computer scientists, and had taken over a difficult task, establishing a data center beneath the lunar surface.

The most sophisticated hardware and software on the Moon had one primary function – to coordinate data from orbiting satellites, and process that data to determine the arrival times and approach speeds of the Ktarran fleet. That information went directly to the desk of General Jang, the senior officer in New Beijing, where he used it to coordinate the planetary defenses. It also went directly to the *Enterprise*, where Field Marshal Shuvalov and Colonel Welsh utilized the information to control the PDF fleet.

Walter had not only established the data center, but he wrote and tested the software controlling the telescopes and other scientific instruments needed to track the approaching ships.

When the system went online two months ago, everything worked flawlessly, and only minor problems had surfaced, a clear testament to Walter's design, planning, and testing skills. The Ktarrans had been tracked since they exited the wormhole, and Walter personally recalibrated the system after Delano's squadron attack. Now all Walter's efforts might be wasted. The room's air conditioning system, specifically the condenser, had failed. Heat, the computer's worst enemy, was climbing rapidly inside the normally cold data center.

That the air conditioning system had been vigorously tested, both on Earth before shipment and upon arrival at the Lunar site, no longer mattered. Walter's planning included a backup unit, and he'd inspected every component of consignment himself upon its arrival.

What he had not done was bother to test the backup unit, since that would be used mostly for spare parts in the unlikely event of a breakdown. Now the unlikely had happened. Almost an hour earlier, the main condenser failed. With the help of his team, Walter had the backup ready to go inside the refrigeration unit within thirty minutes.

Only then did they realize the backup unit was a slightly larger version, and could not be installed. The packaging indicated the proper size, but what was inside the box was not what the label and contents stated. Saboteurs might have deliberately mislabeled it, or it could have been simple incompetence. After cursing himself for not checking more closely, Walter kicked the useless backup condenser out of his way.

A glance at the large temperature readout confirmed his worst fears. The computer room was normally kept at 62 degrees Fahrenheit, to absorb the enormous heat generated by the equipment and computers. Walter had the capability to lower that to 58 degrees if needed. Now the display showed 78 degrees and climbing, despite his increasing the air conditioning to its maximum cooling setting. Excess heat would slow the processors down, until they eventually failed completely.

Almost every computer in the room needed to work at maximum capacity, calculating the thousands of various course corrections, movements, and possible arrival times for the individual ships in the Ktarran fleet. Those vessels were already on the way to Earth. General Jang and his commanders required the information right now. Walter had been compiling and transferring the data to the Lunar War Operations Center when the failure occurred.

Walter finished shutting down non-critical systems. He grabbed one of his staff. "Get a screwdriver and start removing the covers and side panels to all the equipment. We need to let the heat out and circulate the air as much as possible."

Two more operators arrived, and he had orders for them, too. "Search the entire complex for fans, any fans, I don't care what size. Get on the comm system and say we need every fan we can get, and we need it right now. Direct the air flow right into the cabinets. We've got to lower the temperature on the chips and circuit boards. And bring every extension cord you can find. Try to connect the fans to any available outlet in the corridor or other offices. Plugging them in here will only add to the heat buildup."

He grabbed a small power screwdriver from the toolbox and started opening up the nearest box. The covers, designed to protect the delicate electronics from dust, would hold in the heat. Within five minutes, every panel that could be opened lay bare, the circuit boards and chips exposed to the warm air already circulating within the large room. But at least the heat wasn't building up inside the component cases.

"What is going on here? Why isn't the arrival data being delivered?" The speaker's English was heavily accented, but Walter understood the words and recognized the voice of Captain Chiew Chuntao, General Jang's pit bull. Eyes wide, she glanced around, taking in the chaos of the normally orderly computer complex. Now parts and fans lay scattered everywhere, while power cables snaked haphazardly across the floor.

"We've had a failure in the air compressor," Walter said, wiping the sweat from his eyes, "and the backup isn't functional. The machine shop can't modify the unit in less than three hours. So we're trying to minimize the heat gain by turning off some less critical systems, slowing down the CPUs, and rigging fans to move the air around."

He looked at the temperature display mounted over the main control console – 82 degrees. As he watched, it changed to 83.

"Where is the data?" Chiew demanded, her foot tapping nervously on the flooring.

Walter's first instinct was to tell her to go to hell, but he managed to restrain himself. Jang wasn't a bad guy, even if Chiew was an asshole.

"Tell General Jang that the computer system is on the verge of failure. Data delivery may stop at any moment. Explain that we've turned every computer processor down as slow as it will clock. That means everything is going to take longer. At 90 degrees, maybe a little less, chips will start to fail. At 95 degrees most of them will burn out. Tell Jang that we hope to get him as much info as we can before that."

Chiew opened her mouth, but then she realized that this might be a good time to keep quiet. "Is there anything I can do to help?"

Walter was wondering the same thing. The catastrophic meltdown was only minutes away. He'd shut down every non-critical system, and opened up the hardware cabinets. What else could he do? His eyes wandered around the room, then focused on Captain Chiew's foot, nervously tapping on the floor tile.

The two-foot squares of high pressure laminate covered a raised floor. Beneath those tiles a maze of wires and cables moved power and data from one computer system to another. Suddenly he remembered his days in college, working part-time as a computer operator.

He grabbed the startled Chiew by the shoulders. "Yes! You can help. Search the building and bring me every fire extinguisher you can find. And hurry. These machines are gonna burn out any minute." He motioned toward the temperature display. As he looked it changed to 87 degrees.

He glanced around the room. Most of the cabinet panels were off, exposing the internals of the network racks and processor units. His four assistants, after positioning the fans, stood around, fear in their eyes. They knew the crash was only minutes away. Besides shutting down unneeded systems and ventilating the cabinets, there wasn't much else they could do.

Walter turned to his team. "Start ripping up the floor tiles. Get as many up as you can. Leave just enough so we can move around." He needed access, but walking through the jungle of wires and cables would do more harm than good. More than likely he'd trip and break his neck.

They went to work. Meanwhile, Walter grabbed a red fire extinguisher, one of two mounted on a support wall. The CO^2 wasn't meant for putting out computer fires. The Halotron gas system took care of that. But the ten-pound extinguisher was useful for any small fire that might break out. He pulled the safety ring off, aimed it at the exposed flooring, and pulled the trigger. A blast of carbon dioxide spewed out, a white cloud of rapidly moving gas.

Taking care not to aim directly at the delicate electronic innards, Walter swept the spray over the exposed flooring. When that had a fine coating of white carbon dioxide, he moved to another part of the room. By the time he emptied the extinguisher, he could feel a chill in the areas touched by the stream. With no fire to extinguish, the emerging carbon dioxide absorbed large amounts of heat from the air.

He started on the room's only other extinguisher, this time in a different area. By the time he emptied that, Chiew and one of her aides came back, each of them struggling with three extinguishers.

The other operators wanted to help, but Walter shook his head and ordered them to stay in the hall. One mistake and the blast of cold carbon dioxide could shatter the delicate circuit boards and chips. He would do it himself. The trick, he realized, was to spray as close to the open cabinets as possible, without letting the stream of carbon dioxide directly hit the equipment.

He emptied two more extinguishers, then glanced at the temperature display. It had risen to 89 degrees, but seemed to be holding steady at that temperature.

"I will inform General Jang that you have the situation under control," Captain Chiew shouted, trying to be heard over the escaping gas.

"Tell him to process the data as quickly as possible," Walter shouted back, starting on another extinguisher. "And we're going to need every fire extinguisher on the base."

Chiew turned to her aide, and barked something in Chinese, which Walter didn't follow. The aide nodded and darted off.

Walter took a deep breath. You had to be careful not to breathe the CO^2, as it was extremely cold and could damage your lungs. He had time for a quick thought. Maybe the most important thing he'd learned in college, during his long and boring night shifts working in the campus computer facility, was how to keep beer cold and make instant ice cream using a fire extinguisher.

He dropped another empty tank and kicked it under the floor. The tank itself was cold as ice from the escaping gas, and every little bit of heat absorption might help.

Now he just had to hope the Ktarran data got to General Jang before the base ran out of fire extinguishers.

Chapter 50
3 AKA

Shuvalov settled himself in his command chair with a sigh of satisfaction. For his medical condition, low gravity offered as many pluses as minuses. For one thing, he could sit for hours without straining his back. Of course if the ship had to make any sudden changes in direction or velocity, the stress might easily kill him. Not that he cared about that. He knew his last days were fast approaching, and even Russia's best doctors couldn't stave off the inevitable for much longer. Whatever the personal risk, Shuvalov intended to assist as much as possible in the defense of his country and planet.

He knew all the battle plans in detail. More important, he had worked with Delano for the last year and a half developing tactics. The two, alone and with other staffers, had spoken for months about Ktarran tactics and psychology. With Delano temporarily out of the picture, Shuvalov had no problem assuming command. In the unlikely event that Colonel Welsh or General Klegg opposed any of his orders, they would have to make a compelling case.

For the first encounter, Shuvalov and Welsh positioned their eighty-seven remaining Destroyers on both sides of the Ktarran flight path. That gave every single Earth ship, sitting motionlessly in space, a clear and steady shot at the enemy before and during any missile launch.

Now they waited. The Main Defense Fleet and the Defense Grid reported complete readiness. Shuvalov didn't even need to issue any further orders. The individual ships' gunners would fire the moment they had a viable target, and keep shooting until the enemy ships sped out of range or were destroyed.

Shuvalov thought about the orders he'd given to Colonel Delano. The odds for his survival were slim, especially if the main Ktarran force speeded up to catch Delano's few ships from behind. But Delano was a soldier, no, a Marine, and he would execute the order even if he ended up dead.

"Here they come!" Welsh called out, tapping on his console.

The Ktarrans, screens flaring bright red, were decelerating

violently. Their ships were stacked five high and spread out over a sixty kilometer front. Speed and shields would be their main tactic, with only a few beam weapons allocated for missile interception. For this first action, Shuvalov expected little if any damage to the PDF's Destroyer fleet from enemy weapons. Almost all Ktarran energy would be pumped into their screens.

"Defense Grid launching missiles," Welsh announced. "Missiles on track for enemy ships."

*   *   *

In the West Virginia Defense Grid bunker, Lian and her missile operators didn't have to wait long. Months of training and testing were exhausted in only seventy-five seconds. By then the Defense Grid, its launching racks empty, had fired seventy-nine missiles at the onrushing Ktarran advance force. One missile had failed to launch, causing its youthful controller to erupt in anger.

The Ktarran forces did better then expected. They managed to destroy at least thirty-six of Earth's missiles, but the spread of weapons had forced many ships to change course to avoid destruction. A few ships failed to lock onto any planetary target.

Lian stared at the screen, watching the Ktarran missiles hurl themselves at Earth from less than a hundred kilometers above the Exosphere. Traveling at very high speeds, they flew too fast for any interceptors or missile defenses, and only a few lucky shots from the Destroyers managed to damage any at all.

The Ktarran missiles plunged into Earth's atmosphere. The enemy ships had only moments to select a target and launch their missiles. But for most, that proved to be more than sufficient to lock onto a target. The Ktarrans had launched forty-six missiles at Earth. Twenty-two of those were intercepted and destroyed, but twenty-four missiles had avoided the Defense Grid.

Now all Lian could do was watch the devastation.

The missiles began to explode. The portion of the planet exposed to attack was a sector from the eastern Atlantic Ocean to Albania, including Europe and Africa. The destruction began with the first explosion above the UK, but the rain of nuclear weapons quickly spread south, across France, Spain and the western Mediterranean. Seventeen missiles struck North Africa, from Morocco and Algeria all the way south through Nigeria.

The large display showed more than just the cities destroyed.

Eleven missiles had detonated over the Atlantic and Mediterranean, wreaking havoc on any ships beneath them, but at least minimizing the loss of life.

Nineteen missiles exploded a few thousand meters above major cities. Two more impacted the ground but failed to detonate.

Lian watched at the list of cities destroyed grew: Bristol and Southampton in the UK, Nantes, Limoges, Caen, and Toulouse in France, Zaragosa and Valencia in Spain, then the cities of Palma, Tangier, Rabat, Tunis and Algiers. The last missile detonated over Bamako in Mali.

Satellites measured the energy release, and initial estimates assigned each Ktarran missile the equivalent of a twenty megaton bomb. The horrific devastation and resultant loss of life was severe, but it could have been much worse. By the luck of planetary rotation, London, Paris, and Madrid escaped destruction.

To deliver the attack, the Ktarran advance force under Commander Teeg had taken a beating – forty ships out of the sixty destroyed, either by the Defense Grid, beam weapons from the Earth fleet, or Delano's attack on their rear. Now the real assault would begin.

General Klegg left his seat and moved to stand beside Lian, her eyes still fixed on the control screens. He understood the pain and guilt that she felt. He had suffered through much the same experience during the last Ktarran attack. Then he'd been forced to watch helplessly as enemy beam weapons destroyed city after city, enduring the ongoing destruction until the enemy ships descended close enough for the counterstrike.

"We did . . . you did all we could," Klegg said. "The Grid's missiles kept a lot of Ktarrans from launching their weapons properly. Your team did better than I expected, better than anyone could hope for."

Objectively, Lian knew Klegg spoke the truth. But emotionally, she felt like she'd failed Earth, failed all the millions who died or were going to die. But the damage could have been much worse, had the missiles been able to target China or the United States. That fact, however, would not help the dead and dying in Europe and Africa. Nor did it help Lian, whose only thoughts now were for Delano's safety.

*   *   *

On his monitor, Shuvalov saw the first beams from the PDF weapons flash into existence. Then the screen turned into a sparkling display as the tactical missiles from the Defense Grid detonated.

Within seconds, almost every beam weapon in the Earth Force reached out to attack the passing Ktarran ships. Overloaded sensors burned out everywhere, and Shuvalov's command screen momentarily flickered to pure white. The gunners would be as affected as the command ship, but somehow they kept up their fire for the twenty seconds or so that the Ktarrans were in range.

Then the enemy survivors cleared the trap, still moving at a high speed past the planet. Between the Grid's missiles and the PDF beams, Shuvalov's first guess was that about forty of Teeg's ships had been destroyed. The Destroyers' beam weapons, while not actually effective, had definitely added to the confusion caused by the Defense Grid. No doubt many enemy ships never found a capital target. But plenty of missiles had been launched, and Earth was going to suffer a rain of nuclear bombs.

Nevertheless the first Ktarran wave had passed Earth, and now the major portion of the enemy fleet was bearing down on the Destroyers and Darts.

Colonel Welsh barked orders into his comms. "Peng, get your ships in position. You've got less than one minute before the main force arrives."

Colonel Peng had already given the order. The eighty remaining ships had quickly re-positioned themselves between Earth and the Ktarrans. The Destroyers formed two rough lines, one above the other, blocking the approach to the planet. For this first contact, they didn't have to worry about Ktarran flanking maneuvers. The enemy was moving much too fast for any finesse on their initial pass.

Welsh deployed the pitiful seven Destroyers and fifteen Darts of the reserve force behind Peng's lines. The *Enterprise* anchored the center of the reserve, the last PDF ship between the Ktarrans and Earth.

"All ships!" Welsh gave a quick glance at Shuvalov, who nodded. "All ships! Attack when ready. If they try to go through the line, pursue and destroy from behind."

"Command, this is Peng. Releasing the Darts. All Darts –

attack!"

The Darts, almost 160, blazed with energy as they accelerated at full power. They didn't need to travel for more than a few seconds before they began firing. Attacking in pairs, they picked a Ktarran vessel and focused their beam weapons on it. Meanwhile, the rail gunners fired projectile after projectile at the approaching ships.

"Destroyers, attack!" Peng gave the order, and his ships surged to meet the oncoming wave of Ktarran dreadnaughts.

In moments, the cohesive battle formations of both Earth and the Ktarrans disintegrated into a wild melee, a massive furball that filled the heavens, scarcely a hundred miles above the planet's atmosphere.

The Destroyers were far more mobile than the Ktarran battleships, and the Darts even more agile. They disappeared into the midst of the Ktarrans, weaving and dodging beam weapons as they sought to engage the middle and rear of the enemy. The goal of every Dart was to maneuver at high speed, to get behind a Ktarran ship where the rail gun and beam weapon would be most effective.

Months of planning and training would now be tested, with the fate of Earth hanging in the balance. The second phase of the Battle of the Line had begun.

Chapter 51
3 AKA

Deep beneath the ground in Maryland, the NSA code breakers continued their work, oblivious to the Ktarran threat rapidly approaching the planet. The effort to break the Ktarran code had speeded up, as the aliens drew closer and increased their communications traffic. While initially the analysts did not have enough usable words to decipher, now the intercept team had more snippets of words than they could handle.

Sir Nigel and his team kept working, searching for the key that would unlock the code. Certain key phrases could be of enormous import, but they had to be isolated and identified. Enemy ship to ship communications were being picked up by the massive net of lunar and orbital antennae and translated, with the NSA computers working at maximum speed.

Despite the hectic activity, time had almost run out, and the main enemy fleet was almost in Earth space. Meanwhile Nigel still couldn't be sure of when that arrival would take place.

So far nothing of importance had been learned. Of more interest were the orders emanating from the command ships, especially the *Zelbinion*. She kept broadcasting orders to the other vessels. Response to commands were tracked to the individual ships, and as the enemy drew closer, even the NSA's giant analytic processors could scarcely keep up with the traffic being downloaded from New Beijing.

Frustration grew, and Sir Nigel knew that time was running out. But he kept working, knowing that a break-through could occur at any time. A floor below him, sixty code-breakers continued feeding every intercepted message into the world's most powerful computers. Taking another sip of his cold coffee, he examined the latest list of intercepts. He tried not to think about the battle starting overhead.

Lee Wei burst into Nigel's office, waving his tablet in the air. "Sir Nigel, we got something!"

Nigel refused to let the young man's excitement affect him. "What is it, Lee?"

"A transmission from the *Zelbinion*. A priority message

ordering a damaged ship to return to the wormhole."

"Are you sure?"

"Yes, yes!" He shrugged. "Well, almost certainly."

"Show me." Nigel studied the tablet. The intercept was in Chinese, but Nigel had no trouble reading that. It only took a moment. "Indeed, you may have found something useful. Wait a moment."

Nigel wrote on his own tablet, then activated the translation into Ktarran. "Yes, it looks good." A few more seconds of rapid typing, then he handed it back to Lee.

Lee read the words, then comprehension swept over him. "Biǎo dá jí dà de xǐ yuè!" He actually jumped for joy.

Nigel translated his crude phrase as "Hell, yeah!"

"Send it at full power as soon as you can," Nigel said. "There's a great bloody battle already going on up there."

Lee was already out of the Sir Nigel's office, heading at a dead run for Broadcast Command just down the hall.

Nigel smiled, and glanced down at the words he'd just handed to Lee.

Zelbinion to all ships. Priority One. Return to wormhole immediate. Repeat, immediate.

Those words should cause plenty of confusion in the Ktarran ranks, Nigel knew. Especially the word "immediate." That Ktarran particular code word meant "at once and no questions." It might even slow the Ktarran assault.

Nigel picked up his phone and called Marshal Shuvalov aboard the *Enterprise*. The marshal needed to know to take the appropriate action. Hopefully something good would come out of their hard work.

*   *   *

Delano had time for a quick glance at Earth before the planet slipped from his viewscreen. He gave his squadron the order to rejoin the *Defiant*, and discovered that two of his seven ships had not survived the encounter with Teeg's ships. The surviving five needed almost six minutes of gut-twisting deceleration before they started regrouping around the *Defiant*. He used the time to reconsider his original plan – to return to the main fleet and join the fight there. That no longer looked like the best course of action. Too many Ktarran ships had survived the missile attack on

Earth.

Fortunately, his squadron had started decelerating as soon as possible. The much larger Ktarrans had blown past Earth and several minutes passed before they even began to slow down. They probably needed more time to reform into a new formation. That delay would consume more precious minutes since their commander, Teeg, was dead, his great ship destroyed. And Grand Commander Veloreck had too much on his hands to give the remnants of Teeg's ships any real direction or leadership.

By the time Delano's ships halted their movement away from Earth and prepared to reverse course, they had all gathered alongside the *Defiant*. Every ship had some damage to report, including the loss of four Darts.

They needn't have bothered to rush. The nineteen survivors of Teeg's fleet took far longer to slow down and change course so as to return to the furball. Their missile attack on the planet had met heavy resistance, and they'd lost more than two thirds of their ships in the initial assault wave.

That interval gave Captain Chan and the other captains a few minutes to gather themselves and prepare for the next orders. It also gave Delano a chance to communicate with Shuvalov, who didn't have time for more than a few words. What would come to be called The Battle of the Line had already started.

"Keep those ships away from Earth as long as you can," Shuvalov snapped. "We're already taking heavy losses. Out."

Clear enough. Sacrifice yourself to give us a little more time to hold the line.

Delano had one moment of temptation. He'd talked to Shuvalov on a private comm frequency, and no one else had heard the exchange. Delano could take the squadron back to Earth, where their chances of survival were much better than fighting against odds of four to one. No one would know, and even if they did, they would understand. *Yeah, sure.*

"Captain Chan, order all ships to form up on the *Defiant*. We have to stop these Ktarrans from returning to Earth. Steve, put me on the squadron's frequency."

"Yes, Admiral," Steve said. It took only seconds to broadcast the attention signal and receive the acknowledgements. "All Alpha Destroyers reporting standby. Awaiting your orders."

"Thanks, Comms," Delano said. "All ships, the Ktarrans we were chasing are returning to Earth orbit to join in the fight. We can't let nineteen Ktarran battleships attack our main fleet from behind, or even to stop and bombard Earth. I intend to slow them down as much as possible, to keep them out of the fight. We still have . . ." he glanced at the screen, "twelve Darts available. I want the Darts to initiate the attack, blast right through the enemy, then turn around and hit them from the rear."

That tactical decision was easy enough. They'd all trained for exactly that type of attack.

Delano turned to Gunny. "How long until the Ktarrans are within weapons range?"

"About two minutes, Admiral," Gunny said.

"All Darts are to begin the attack seventy-five seconds from now – Mark."

Silence greeted his order. *Damn, I have to say something*! This was one of those leadership moments when fighting men and women had to understand the reason they were ordered into battle, and possibly to their own death.

"I know we're outnumbered," Delano said, still on ship-wide communications, "but those are our people and cities back there, our friends and families. To give the rest of our ships a chance to hold the line, we must slow down these Ktarrans. The Defense Grid is out of missiles, and we're the only force around that can delay these ships."

He glanced at Captain Chan, who seemed unperturbed by the order that was almost certainly condemning them all to death. But there was no protest, no argument. Every captain, every man and woman aboard every Destroyer and Dart, could see the danger. Shuvalov had instinctively made the correct call.

"The *Defiant* will lead the way," Delano said. "Good luck to all of us. Delano out."

Everyone returned to their stations and belted in. Gunny gave the final countdown. "Darts to begin attack in 5 . . . 4 . . . 3 . . . 2 . . . 1. Attack!"

Ten Darts hurtled away from the mother ships, heading straight at the Ktarrans.

Delano studied the monitor. The Ktarrans had finally started back toward Earth. Now they seemed unsure. They actually reduced their speed a second time. The idea that an inferior force might dare to attack a larger one still wasn't part of their playbook. Nor did they have a real plan. Teeg was dead, his ship destroyed. No help there. Delano guessed they were wasting time deciding who was in charge.

"All ships. Attack." With Delano studying the Ktarrans, Captain Chan gave the order thirty seconds after the Darts started moving. "We are in your hands again, Seanna."

The *Defiant* started accelerating, but this time there wasn't any need for haste. The other four ships took their positions, two on each side of Delano's vessel. The *Defiant* would draw the heaviest fire.

Delano turned to the Gunny for a status check

"All systems in the green and ready, Admiral."

"Comms online, Admiral." Steve sounded unperturbed. "Let's go get 'em."

We're all a bunch of crazy fools. Delano turned back to his screen. Time to get to work.

*   *   *

In orbit above Earth, Colonel Peng watched the Ktarran battleships approach, looming large even at a thousand kilometers. The moment had arrived.

"This is Peng to all Darts! Attack! Attack!"

One hundred and sixty Darts blasted away, accelerating at max speed toward the oncoming ships. The Ktarran beam weapons opened fire, hundreds of beams crossing over each other as they struggled to light up the ships rushing at them. But the Darts were small targets, and they wove and changed their angle of attack with a rapidity that the Ktarrans had never seen and could not expect. Each Dart had only a single beam weapon, but after the pilot selected a target, the software took over. The pilot then concentrated on flying the Dart while the gunner opened up with the rail gun.

Within seconds, hundreds of projectiles were launched. For this phase of the battle plan, onboard computers aimed and fired the rail gun, compensating as much as possible for the Darts' erratic maneuvers. Enemy beam weapons swept around and over the Darts, but holding a beam on such a small craft traveling at high speed required both Ktarran skill and luck.

A handful of Darts, struck by enemy beam weapons, exploded in a blaze of energy. But most got through, weaving and dodging through space toward the approaching Ktarran battleships.

In the first attack by Delano's squadron, the Darts had operated in conjunction with his Destroyers. Peng doubted if the Ktarrans even considered the idea that the small ships could operate independently. Yet a single Dart with a lucky or very accurate shot could potentially destroy any Ktarran vessel. The Darts unexpected ability to nimbly change course and direction added to their effectiveness. Their violent counterattack caught the Ktarrans off-guard,

Peng watched the last of the Darts disappear into the enemy formation. If their confusion lasted long enough, the Darts would have time to return to the battle. The Darts themselves couldn't defeat the Ktarrans, but thanks to their incredible maneuverability and high speed, they could blow right by them, then get into position to deliver a nasty counterattack from the rear.

Peng watched the seconds tick by on his chronometer. Fifteen seconds after the last Dart disappeared, he issued the next order. "All Destroyers, attack. Plan Beta. Plan Beta."

The eighty Destroyers flung themselves after the Darts, but at a slightly slower speed. The Beta Attack Plan required coordination of force, with Destroyers operating in pairs. A target was selected, the two ships' computers linked up, and then the software coordinated six beam weapons onto the enemy ship.

Shuvalov and Welsh had decided not to attack the Ktarran battleships one on one, though at this point in the battle the PDF had almost as many Destroyers as the enemy had ships. Instead Peng's pilots attacked one enemy battleship with two Destroyers. The theory was that this would cause more damage to a battleship from the concentrated firepower – six beam weapons against ten – and that beam weapons from other nearby battleships would not be as accurate at a greater distance.

Theory clashed with reality almost at once. Ktarran beam weapons coupled with fully powered screens held off most of the Destroyers. The targeted enemy vessels took damage, but most kept their screens intact. Peng's ships couldn't remain stationary long enough to get a good lock on their targets. Without maneuvering, the Destroyers were too vulnerable to enemy weapons.

The Peng's Destroyers fought tenaciously, but the Ktarrans slowed their advance enough to engage the Earth ships. Meanwhile at least ten alien battleships pushed through the original line of battle. These were immediately engaged by the six

Destroyers and twelve Darts of the reserve. But more enemy ships broke through, and some began to take up positions over Earth.

The PDF ships heard only one thing, that the reserve had entered the fight. That told every Destroyer captain and crew how grave the situation was. Nothing would be held back. There would be no tactical retreat. This was one fight they had to win.

Peng's ships were taking heavy damage, and losses mounted. In a few more seconds, the entire line would be broken in so many places. Then the enemy could push through and choose their Earth targets.

As the entire defense was about to collapse, the Darts returned with a fury. It had taken them just over a minute to decelerate and turn around after their high-speed attack run. Now they resumed their attack, beams and rail guns firing at point blank range into the rear of Ktarran ships.

Those rail guns quickly proved their worth. While it still took beam weapons several seconds to burn through an enemy's screens, the high speed projectile weighing over twenty-five pounds made its presence felt immediately. The depleted uranium slug coated with carbon tungsten went right through the energy screens and past the inner carbon web. The thinner hulls of the Ktarran ships couldn't stop them either, and the projectiles inflicted considerable damage inside the vessels.

With luck, even a single shot might hit something vital, knocking an enemy ship out of the fight temporarily or permanently. Occasionally the projectiles passed through the hull a second time without causing major damage, but even that passage vented the ship's atmosphere.

Before the Ktarrans could react to this new tactic, the Darts had inflicted major damage. Suddenly the enemy captains had to look in every direction, their ships being attacked by two different types of vessels with differing attack modes. Nothing had ever prepared the Ktarrans for this type of warfare. No species hitherto encountered utilized such tactics. The movement toward the planet slowed. Ktarran gunners now needed to target these small ships, a threat that seemed more immediate than the Destroyers.

Aboard the flagship, Colonel Welsh snapped an order into the comm unit. "All Darts, continue high speed attacks. Do not engage at long range. Do not try to stay in formation. Get in close and keep hitting enemy ships from the rear."

Shuvalov nodded agreement while he kept his eyes on the

screen. The Ktarrans were gradually pushing the Earth ships back toward the planet. Destroyers were taking hits, and many of them had lost power or been driven out of the fight. Enemy ships were breaking through whatever remained of the line, and there were no more forces in reserve.

Welsh ordered the *Enterprise* to join the fighting. Shuvalov could do nothing but hold on, the shifting acceleration forces punishing his body and preventing his mind from working. He looked at Welsh. "You'll have to take over, Colonel. I'm afraid I'm unable to continue."

"Yes, Sir." Welsh reached over and touched the Field Marshal's shoulder for a moment. Welsh scanned the consoles, but there was little he could add. The battle had passed the point where he or anyone had central control.

*   *   *

Four thousand kilometers from the Battle of the Line, Delano eyed the nineteen Ktarran ships moving slowly toward him. No doubt they expected to be greeted by a wave of missiles, but the *Defiant* and her four sister ships had exhausted their supply. The new Ktarran commander would figure that out soon enough, and then nothing would hold them back.

"Captain Chan," Delano ordered. "Let's make them think we still have missiles."

Chan nodded. "All Darts, simulate missile attack, then get behind them and attack from all directions. Now!"

The Darts flashed onto Delano's screen, heading for the enemy ships. The Ktarrans immediately began evasive maneuvers, anticipating a flight of missiles. Halfway to their targets, just as the Ktarran beams lashed out, the Darts changed their attack vectors, moving at random and firing their rail guns.

"All Destroyers, attack!" ordered Chan. "Attack in pairs!"

The *Defiant* surged forward, pushing Delano back into his seat. Within seconds they were in range, and the ship's three beam weapons activated. At long range, this was more of a distraction, its purpose to give the Darts time to slip past the enemy and return.

By now the Ktarrans had figured out that there would not be a missile attack. They surged forward, determined to attack the five puny Destroyers blocking their path to Earth.

Seanna piloted the *Defiant* with gut-wrenching skill. The ship twisted and changed course with such rapidity that the seat restraints dug into Delano's body. Somehow the three beam stations managed to keep firing, and they were scoring hits. On the screen Delano watched a Ktarran ship explode, but that was followed seconds later by the destruction of a Destroyer.

Then the Darts were back, attacking from all directions, sometimes maneuvering to such close range that they were in danger of collision with the Ktarran vessels. Their attack became continuous, and after a pass at one enemy ship, they simply shifted to the next closest one. As one Dart was driven off, another arrived from a different direction.

Delano kept his eyes on the monitor, observing the flashing beams of energy.

Commanding or piloting the *Defiant* were both out of his hands, and he felt the helplessness of a non-combatant surrounded by a platoon of active fighters. The brutal close-quarter fighting caused plenty of damage to the Ktarrans, unused to such tactics. Six of the enemy ships had been obliterated, but another Destroyer was blasted apart. At least six Darts had also fallen off the view screen.

The savage fighting continued. Then the *Defiant* took a hit. Seanna had dodged one beam only to run into another. Before she could recover, the ship's plasma screen failed. Delano nearly blacked out from the gyrations she made.

But even Seanna's skill couldn't overcome the multiple beams. The ship took another hit, and without defensive screens, the energy beam blasted right through the hull, burning everything in its path. Power was lost, and the force of the escaping air twisted the *Defiant*, sending it tumbling and spinning end-over-end, out of control.

Shaking his head, Delano saw that the Command Center had been blasted open. About a third of the ship had turned into molten steel by the enemy's weapon. Two of the gun crews were dead, flash-burned by the passage of the beam. The *Defiant* was open to space. Only their pressure suits kept the survivors alive.

Emergency power kicked in, and Delano's console came back to life.

The Gunny recovered faster than Delano. "Six enemy battleships destroyed, another two damaged."

Steve, his voice sounding strangely high, was sending out a

Mayday, calling for help.

Delano did another count of his own. Three of the Destroyers were gone, a fourth limping away trailing smoke. The thirteen surviving Ktarran ships, having broken through Delano's squadron, had resumed course for Earth.

Then he realized that only twelve ships were departing. One Ktarran had turned and was coming toward the *Defiant*. *Oh, shit! Not good!*

The Ktarrans must have recognized the *Defiant* as the leader of the ships challenging their progress, and now intended to make sure they finished it off. Or maybe they hoped to take some prisoners alive.

Delano swung his head around, fighting against the dizzying motion of the out-of-control *Defiant*. Through Captain Chan's faceplate, Delano saw a trickle of blood oozing from the man's forehead. Some debris must have struck him in the helmet, putting him out of commission, at least temporarily. Seanna looked woozy, but didn't appear to have any injury.

"Seanna," Delano shouted in the suit's microphone. "Can you get us out of here? A Ktarran is coming after us!"

She took a moment, then glanced down at her console. "All engine power is gone. Tumbling out of control. Trying the attitude thrusters."

This is it, then. Delano swiveled back to his screen. The Ktarran ship had closed the distance between the still-tumbling *Defiant*. In another minute or so the enemy would be within range of the helpless Earth ship.

The Gunny saw the same data. "Damn the luck. Looks like he's coming for us. A pleasure to serve with you, Admiral."

Delano turned toward his friend. "Thanks, Gunny. See you on the other side."

Then the impossible happened. Just before reaching firing distance, the Ktarran ship changed course and began accelerating away at what appeared to be maximum speed.

"What the fuck is that? He's turning away!" The Gunny's voice blared in Delano's earphones.

Delano took a moment to verify the enemy's new course. It was definitely leaving the area, and definitely not headed back toward Earth. At that moment, he didn't care where the hell it was going.

I'm still alive! He might yet die in space, trapped in a ripped-open and airless wreck of a ship, but he was still alive.

*   *   *

For the PDF ships at the Battle of the Line, the carefully crafted, bogus recall order arrived just in time, saving the embattled Destroyers from complete destruction. The Ktarrans had gradually pushed through Peng's screen, and not even the repeated attacks from the Darts could halt their thrust toward the planet. But when the Ktarrans received the supposed order to retreat, more than a few reduced their speed and some even turned to break off the action. Their advance to the planet slowed, then stopped.

It was a godsend at the height of the fighting. Peng knew he might have only a minute or two before the Ktarrans figured out what had happened, but in that time he managed to regroup his ships. In less than ninety seconds, a new line was hastily formed. With the ships working in formation once again, they had temporarily avoided destruction and prevented the attack on Earth.

The Darts, too, used the fake message to recover. Blasting away from the Ktarran ships, they managed to form two separate groups, to prepare for another coordinated assault on the enemy rear. To escape this threat, several Ktarran ships began to retreat. Peng saw that even the vessels attacking the remains of Delano's squadron had received the bogus message and broke off the engagement. They, too, headed for open space, leaving Earth safe for the moment.

Though neither side knew it yet, the Battle of the Line was over, at least for now.

Chapter 52
3 BKA

Aboard the *Zelbinion*, the reaction was far different. When the Grand Commander saw his ships turning back, he roared his anger. On his screens he could see many of his ships breaking contact and accelerating away from Earth orbit. A few moments later, when Veloreck learned of the false recall order, his rage turned to shock. He stared at his ships, most of them moving away from the fight. False or not, the order allowed them to avoid any further battle, and many captains were taking advantage of the respite.

Furious, Veloreck ordered the immediate cancellation of the retreat order, but the powerful transmitters on Earth and the Moon, following Sir Nigel's instructions, were now jamming most of the Ktarran communication channels.

Out of contact with his ships, Veloreck suddenly found himself on the front line, facing the regrouping Earth ships. They had less than half the original eighty Destroyers, but they were more than enough to take care of the lonely *Zelbinion*.

With a snarl of frustration, Veloreck ordered his ship to move away from the planet before the *Zelbinion* found itself cut off and destroyed. For those Ktarrans who continued fighting, many remained unsure of what to do. Still out of contact with their commander because of Earth's radio jamming, they saw the *Zelbinion* leaving the field. They decided the recall order was real and obeyed their commander. That ended the fighting. The last few ships still engaged broke contact and followed.

The Battle for planet Earth had ended, temporarily at least.

*   *   *

Colonel Peng put aside his relief at the enemy withdrawal. Half his Destroyers were gone, and forty percent of his Darts were out of action, unaccounted for, or destroyed. But the respite gave him what he needed most – time.

Even before the orders came from the *Enterprise*, Peng began organizing a counterattack. To be effective, a counter strike needed to hit the retreating enemy before they could reorganize. In moments, he had five battle-ready Destroyers and their Darts ready to go.

"Don't wait to form up," Shuvalov ordered. He understood the tactical importance of a rapid counterattack. "You can do that on the way. Concentrate your force on the stragglers and overwhelm them. Don't give them time to regroup."

"We're still jamming all Ktarran comm channels," Welsh added. "I've ordered Moon base to put every kilowatt of power into those transmitters."

"Keep that up for as long as you can," Peng said. "The more confusion, the better."

*   *   *

Grand Commander Veloreck tried to halt the retreat. But the regular communication channels were sporadic, and not all the ships had switched over to the close-range backup frequency. He ordered the *Zelbinion* to accelerate, to catch up with those ships already ahead of him. That, unfortunately, caused other ships, still in doubt of what to do, to assume the recall order was correct. They began to accelerate, too, following what they thought to be their commander's order and example.

By the time Veloreck reestablished communications, he'd left Earth half a million kilometers behind. The flight finally slowed, and his technicians managed to get the backup frequency working. But before he could reorganize the fleet, the humans in their puny ships arrived.

Targeting the rear of the new Ktarran formation, more than eight of the small ships attacked before two Ktarran stragglers could prepare their defenses. In a straight, high speed run through, the human ships were almost impossible to target. Operating at high velocities, they concentrated their projectiles against two enemy ships.

Within moments, both injured battleships were destroyed by the concentrated fire, and another badly damaged. Right behind the tiny ships came the larger Destroyers, finishing off the wounded battleship and then turning their weapons against the next target of opportunity.

Plagued by communications glitches, the Ktarrans wasted precious time trying to establish a cohesive battle line. The moment they did so, the Earth ships broke off the attack and retreated toward their original positions orbiting the planet.

* * *

Peng received Shuvalov's retreat order, and for a moment was tempted to continue the attack. But the old Russian was right. The odds of success had dropped, and it was time to get back to Earth orbit.

"Send half your Darts to the Moon for refueling and re-arming," Shuvalov said.

More so than Peng or anyone actually fighting in the fleet, Shuvalov had been watching the power drains on his ships. He knew the Darts especially needed to replenish their supplies of helium-3 and rail-gun projectiles.

Aboard the *Enterprise*, Colonel Welsh watched the departing Darts, racing for the Moon. Almost all needed combat resupply. Nevertheless, he kept half with the Destroyer formation. If the Ktarrans thought all the Darts were grounded, they might return to the attack.

Then he and Shuvalov waited. They had no more missiles, even on the Moon, and the helium-3 fuel stocks were low. With half the Darts heading for the lunar surface, the defense line was vulnerable. One more determined Ktarran attack and the PDF forces would be finished.

* * *

On the *Zelbinion*, Grand Commander Veloreck also took stock of his capabilities. He still had almost thirty ships combat ready. Added to that number were another twenty-two reporting various levels of battle damage. Exactly how many of those were capable of fighting remained unknown.

Veloreck smashed his fist against his chest. "Order all ships to hold position here."

He wanted to resume the attack, break the puny human fleet before they could recover and rearm. Even without the pitiful survivors of Teeg's squadron, Veloreck still had ships capable of continuing the fight. However, their captains and crews, badly shaken by the unexpected heavy casualties, needed time to recover their nerve.

Meanwhile, his specialists informed him that many human ships were landing and taking off from Earth's moon, and others lifting up from the planet as well. Even if he disregarded the enemy's re-supply preparations, his own fleet had turned into little more than a mob of disorganized ships.

Teeg was dead and most of his ships destroyed. Jothe's ship had been badly damaged from a near miss by an enemy missile, as well as five strikes from the cursed projectile weapon that the humans utilized so effectively.

The idea that a miniature ship, one small enough to fit inside a battleship's shuttle compartment, could defeat an enemy more than twenty times its size had unnerved his battle captains to the core.

No, Veloreck decided. He had to wait until his crews regained their nerve. More than that, he needed a new plan, something that would counter Earth's unconventional ships and tactics.

What he did not want was another communications disaster. Veloreck still had not figured out how his ships received a false message ordering an immediate retreat. How could the humans decipher the Ktarran codes in the middle of a battle? He had to solidify and safeguard his communications, something no Ktarran warship had ever needed in the past.

If he attacked, and were forced to retreat again, an Earth counterattack might mean the destruction of Veloreck's remaining ships. With another snarl of frustration, he issued a new set of orders.

"Have all the captains report at once to the *Zelbinion* for a conference and to give details of damage. We need to find a new way to attack these humans."

Until then, Veloreck would hold at this position. Now, when he needed most to communicate with home world, the cowards who were supposed to guard the wormhole had fled, taking with them his link to Ktarra. That was the first order of business. There would be no further fighting until communications with Ktarra were reopened.

*   *   *

Delano, still belted in his chair, watched Pilot Captain Seanna try to steady the *Defiant*, which was continuing to pinwheel through space with a sickening motion that made it nearly impossible to move or think. With the main power gone, there was no artificial gravity, and the tumbling motion tortured his head and stomach.

He must have blacked out, for he didn't remember the *Defiant* starting to spin. His head throbbed and he had trouble focusing his left eye. Slowly his brain began working. Something must have slammed into his helmet. Now that he thought of it, Delano saw a pair of zig-zag cracks in the tough plexiglass. Whatever had struck the helmet had come that close to finishing him.

He rolled his eyes to the right, and saw Captain Chan and Flight Engineer Cook slumped in their seats. Delano couldn't tell if they were dead or merely unconscious. As far as he could see, only Seanna seemed capable of movement.

The *Defiant* continued spinning, but Delano thought it might be slowing down. He called Seanna's name, but it came out as a garbled croak. He swallowed, and tried again.

"Seanna, what's our status?"

She didn't bother to glance at him. "Main engines gone, we've a major hull breach, and we're tumbling through space. Trying to correct using the attitude jets."

With the main engines down, she had nothing else to control the ship, which meant figuring out which maneuvers could be effectively undertaken before those small thrusters exhausted themselves of fuel. If that happened, they would be helpless.

Delano still felt dizzy, but now he understood why. He realized he was slumped down in his seat, and pushed himself upright. The effort exhausted him, and he needed a moment to recover. Then he looked around the bridge. *What's left of it.*

The back end of the Defiant was open to space, a jagged gash in the hull about ten feet long, as if the ship had been twisted apart. He scarcely recognized it. Control stations had been ripped from their mounting and sucked out through the opening. Anything touched by the energy beam had been burned black.

Jeez, how many are dead? The thought shocked him alert. He could see at least four stations missing, which meant that Gun stations One and Three were gone, taking their operators with them. So four dead there. Their flight suits would never have withstood being dragged through the opening. The Dart crews were missing, but that might not mean anything. They could still be safe on their ships. But Communications Specialist Jerome Cowan and Power Engineer Wang Chen were dead, their suits ripped open by the blast and resulting decompression.

The seats for Senior Engineer Kosloff and Navigator Peter Tasco were empty, but Delano noticed that their seat belts had been unfastened. He remembered Linda, the med-tech. Her jump seat was empty, retracted against the wall. Somehow she must have dragged the two men back to the still-intact Med Lab. That hatch could be sealed and filled with air.

With a guilty start, he turned toward the Gunny. Whatever had hit Delano had struck the Gunny first. But he looked alive and his suit remained intact. Turning his head, Delano checked out Steve. The Comms specialist was also breathing, his body twitching though his eyes remained closed.

So six dead, four missing, and eleven survivors out of a crew of twenty-one.

Trying to take it all in, Delano noticed the *Defiant* had definitely slowed its erratic tumbling. He heard Seanna muttering to herself as she worked the thrusters, balancing one against the other, shifting power in turn to regain some control. In another minute, the ship stabilized. It was still moving through space, but at least the tumbling and turning had mostly stopped.

Seanna sagged back in her seat, then glanced at Delano. "That's the best I can do, Admiral." She looked around at the destruction, and her eyes widened.

"How bad is it?" Might as well get it out in the open, Delano thought.

"We're on emergency power, but that's going fast. I've got the heat to the suits working, so we haven't frozen to death yet. If that holds up, we may last another twenty, maybe thirty minutes before the oxygen runs out."

Well, that's not good. "Any chance of a rescue?"

"Main antenna gone. Steve got the Mayday beacon on line before he passed out, so there is a chance somebody might have heard it."

That supposed there were any other surviving Earth ships. For all Delano knew, they could be the last survivors of the entire PDF fleet. Not that he expected any rescue. Before communications went down, he'd seen Colonel Peng's outnumbered forces in a desperate struggle to hold back the enemy.

"Any idea of how the main battle went?"

"Nothing, not a guess," Seanna said. "But even if we drove them off . . ."

She didn't need to finish the thought. Even with a partial victory, Earth likely didn't have any ships to waste searching for survivors of destroyed ships, and certainly not in the next thirty minutes.

So we're toast. Delano clenched his jaw. He'd been a great commander. Killed almost half of his first command in the initial encounter, then finished them off with two more actions. Worse, all his planning and work to save Earth had probably failed, so he could list the planet's destruction as another of his achievements.

Well, he wouldn't have much time to brood. Guiltily, he thought of Lian. At least she'd probably survived the initial attack. The bunker in West Virginia was solid, and she might even have a chance to escape off planet.

"Owww!"

Steve's voice cut through Delano's gloomy thoughts. He saw his Comms officer straighten up in his chair. "Steve, you awake? You OK?"

"Yeah, I think. There's something . . . on the emergency channel. I can't . . . holy crap, it's the *Meseka*! Horath's ship! Wants to know if we're still alive!"

"Where is it?" Seanna had heard Steve's excited words.

"He's . . . it's Ahvin. She says the *Meseka* is coming along side now." Steve paused. "Something about extending the screens?"

Before Delano could grasp the reality of being saved, he felt something bump against the *Defiant*. A moment later, "Ahvin says to hurry," Steve said. "Horath is afraid our ship might blow up at any moment."

"Tell Ahvin that we need some help, that we're still in our seats."

"OK, she's got it. Ahvin says we should prepare to be . . . extracted? I think that's what she said."

Suddenly two Halkins wearing full space suits squeezed carefully through the gash in the hull. Help had arrived.

The extraction took fifteen minutes. Delano and Linda were the last to leave, making sure that everyone, living or dead, got off the *Defiant*. Despite the ship's tumbling, Linda had dragged two wounded men into the Med Lab and managed to keep them alive.

Delano had decided to make sure everyone got off the *Defiant* first. But Linda ended up helping Delano when he started feeling faint. He must have blacked out, because he never remembered crossing over to the Halkin ship.

Aboard the *Meseka*, they assisted Delano to a bunk, where he promptly passed out again. When he recovered, he looked up to see Captain Horath towering over him, Ahvin at his side.

"This second time we rescue you," Horath said. He spoke a passable English. "Not wanting to be a habit."

Delano reached out and clutched the big Halkin's arm. "But you are so good at it. Did we drive the Ktarrans off?"

If the physical contact offended Horath, he didn't show it. "Not knowing. So cannot say," Horath said. "Much confusion still. Rest now. Much to do."

Amen, brother. Delano nodded, closed his eyes, and drifted off to sleep.

*   *   *

Colonel Welsh and Marshal Shuvalov stared at their screens, not sure what they were seeing. Almost thirty minutes earlier, the Ktarran fleet had paused in its attack on Earth, and withdrawn. They hadn't gone far, but they put enough distance between themselves and Earth's powerful radio broadcast to regain control of their communications.

The fake message ordering their withdrawal had occurred at the peak of their attack, when the issue was still in doubt. The enemy ships had stopped approximately half a million kilometers away, obviously to regroup. But before long they retreated even further, doubling the distance between themselves and Earth to a million kilometers.

"They want to get out of range of Earth's transmitters," Shuvalov said. "Next time we'll make sure we have stealth radio beacons much farther away from Earth."

"Yeah, if there is a next time. Do you think they have had enough?" Welsh asked the question, though he didn't really believe what he was seeing. "According to Sir Nigel in Crypto, Veloreck has ordered all his captains to report to the *Zelbinion*."

"If they're as good at blaming each other as we are," Shuvalov said, "that will keep them busy for hours, maybe a day."

"Right. First they have to decide who to blame, then argue

over who did what, who fought bravely." Welsh knew the after-action drill well enough. "Then they'll blame everything that went wrong on Commander Teeg, since he's conveniently dead."

"If we are very lucky, Colonel Welsh," Shuvalov said, "they may want to report their status to their home world. They cannot be happy being out of touch with their leader."

"To do that, they'll have to send ships back to the wormhole, enough ships to chase Tanaka's guys away," Welsh said. "That will give us all the time we need."

"Yes. I suggest you order the rest of the Darts to return to the Moon for refueling and rearming as soon as possible. And order the supply Jumpers to deliver whatever they can to the Destroyers."

"I think they've finished working on a handful of missiles," Welsh said. "I'll see if I can get them to the Destroyers as well."

"Remind everyone that each minute is precious." Shuvalov sighed. "I'd hoped the battle would end in a victory for Earth. This seems more like a draw."

"For now, I'll take what I can get," Welsh said. "I'll start the ball rolling."

*   *   *

Grand Commander Veloreck did indeed have his problems. His captains screamed at each other, each accusing another for the failure to achieve a decisive victory. Such a fiasco, such a disaster, had never happened in Ktarra's history. The unconquerable Ktarran military had suffered a major setback and failed to achieve its objective. The unspoken presence of Pannoch Staleeck hung over the conference.

"Silence!" Veloreck screamed the word and every argument ceased. "We are still out of touch with Ktarra. I want five ships to return to the wormhole, and get rid of the Earth ships there. That should be enough to destroy them. It is possible a reserve force can be summoned once we reestablish communications with home world."

The idea of communication with home world did nothing to ease the tension.

"Jothe, is your ship ready for action?" Veloreck snapped.

"No, Grand Commander," Jothe said. "Six of my weapons systems are severely damaged, and many sensors are burned out.

It will take some time to repair them."

"But you still have full power?"

"Yes, the projectile that destroyed the weapons power cables did not affect the drive units."

"Good. Then pick four ships that can still fight and head for the wormhole. Choose the least effective and make repairs along the way. Eliminate the humans guarding the gate and reestablish communications with Ktarra."

Veloreck didn't dare waste any time communicating with the Emperor, not with the threat of death hanging over his head. "We must establish an open channel to Ktarra. I will have a message ready by the time you get there. Go. Leave now."

"Yes, Grand Commander," Jothe said, no doubt glad to be out of the meeting before blame was assigned. He called out the names of four of his captains and they departed.

"With those five ships gone, we still have twenty-five ships." Veloreck glared at his subordinates. "I want to launch another attack on the humans as soon as possible. Whose ship is not ready to return to the fight? We can't give the Earth animals time to rearm and repair any damage."

At first no one spoke, then one captain gestured. "My ship's power drive failed when we reached this place. It cannot be repaired quickly."

That opened the floodgates. One by one, another seven captains reported severe damage.

"Then we still have seventeen ships that can fight," Veloreck said. "That should be enough to finish off the humans' ships."

One captain, braver than the others, spoke up. "If they rearm with missiles, and use their smaller ships as before, seventeen ships may not be enough to defeat them. We all saw how tenaciously they fought. The small ships are almost impossible to target."

Like the captain, Veloreck had never seen ships as maneuverable as those pesky Darts, a word he'd recently become all too familiar with.

Another captain spoke up. "We should first make sure all our communications are secure. The humans have figured out our codes and how to interfere with our transmissions."

Veloreck hesitated. Fighting was one thing, but repairing and safeguarding the communications system required the use of technical slaves, who might not be in any rush to complete such a task.

"Very well," Veloreck said. "Perhaps it will be better to wait until all our ships are ready for combat. Order the slaves to deal with the communications issue immediately. Kill anyone who doesn't work as hard as possible. In the meantime, while you're repairing your ships, try to find a workable defense against their Darts. Go!"

They emptied the chamber, moving far more rapidly than dignity demanded.

Veloreck stared down at his clenched fists. Emperor Staleeck would be furious at the failure of the fleet to destroy Earth. If Veloreck attacked again, he might win the battle and destroy the planet, but Ktarra would have no fleet left. The Empire would be open to attack from several worlds. Ktarrans had no friends and many enemies.

Sensing weakness, conquered systems might rebel. Ktarra's authority depended on the enormous firepower of its great ships, and many of them had just been destroyed.

That reminded him that the Emperor would blame him for the loss of so many ships, no matter what happened. But dying in battle above the planet Earth didn't appeal to Veloreck either. The *Zelbinion* had been attacked, and only luck had saved it from serious damage. Perhaps it would be better to report what had happened, and learn about any available reserves. Staleeck would be furious, but he couldn't very well blame the entire disaster on Veloreck.

He decided to wait. Hopefully the humans had expended their stocks of nuclear missiles. Veloreck didn't understand how a world virtually without space travel could possess so many atomic weapons. Without them to frighten his captains, the planet would fall. Yes, Veloreck would wait until he could speak to the Emperor.

*   *   *

Shuvalov kept watching the Ktarran fleet, still hanging motionless one million kilometers away from Earth. During their initial withdrawal, they'd halted half a million kilometers from the planet. But after he'd sent a few Darts out on reconnaissance and raid, they moved farther away.

He'd been in the battle center of the *Enterprise* for more than forty hours, leaving only to relieve himself. The pains in Shuvalov's chest were more frequent, what the doctors would call a warning about slowing down and getting some rest.

He ignored the discomfort, just as he ignored his doctors. Shuvalov had no intention of leaving the game now. The Ktarrans were repairing their ships, getting ready for the next attack. Or possibly waiting for communications with home world to be re-established. He knew they had dispatched five ships out to the wormhole, more than enough to deal with Tanaka's squadron, now without any missiles. The Ktarrans would drive them away, then communicate through the wormhole.

What would the new orders be? Return to base or continue the attack? Shuvalov didn't know, and he would bet that Grand Commander Veloreck didn't know either. Whatever home world decided, Tanaka would intercept the message and perhaps the Crypto people could decipher it.

All that mattered now was time. Half of his Dart fleet was already refueled and rearmed, though unfortunately there were no missiles for them. In another two hours, the other half of the Darts would rejoin them. Meanwhile, Jumpers from Earth and the Moon were bringing fuel and supplies to the Destroyers. Already Colonel Peng's Destroyer had been fully prepared for battle.

With two or three Destroyers and all the Darts, Shuvalov would order another raid on the Ktarrans. The Darts could remain out of effective beam range and fire their rail guns at the largely stationary Ktarrans. Odds of a hit would be small, but Darts carried more than adequate stocks of projectiles, and the Ktarrans wouldn't enjoy just sitting there being targets.

Three hours later, Shuvalov lifted himself from his chair. The PDF fleet was as ready as possible, but if the Ktarrans hadn't returned by now, they would almost certainly be waiting for communications to be reestablished with home world. If they could summon more reserves to join the battle, Earth was doomed.

"Colonel Welsh, please take command of the fleet," Shuvalov said. "I need to rest. Call me if anything urgent arises."

"Of course, Marshal," Welsh said. "Get some sleep while you can. You deserve it. I'll wake you the minute something happens."

But Shuvalov decided the likelihood of anything happening in the next few hours remained small. Defeated armies need time to recover their nerve, and there would be many arguments put forth as to why breaking off the fight, temporarily of course, would be the wisest course of action.

Some things never change, and it would take a strong leader to order soldiers back into the fight. The Ktarran leader would soon be faced with that decision. Whatever it was, humans would learn that much more about their enemy.

He put all thoughts of the battle aside. Shuvalov returned to his cabin to get some rest. If the Ktarrans started toward Earth, Welsh would wake him. Then he would see what needed to be done.

Chapter 54
4 AKA

Delano found himself floating, drifting on a warm breeze, enjoying the pleasant sensations that touched his body. For a few minutes he luxuriated in the feeling, then his eyes opened and he woke up from the induced sleep of the latest happy drug. The feeling of floating translated into a soft bed on the Moon, and the warm breeze turned out to be a heated blanket that covered his body.

"Glad to see you're finally awake, Admiral." The man wore the white jacket of a doctor, and he studied his tablet. "Time to get up and get moving."

Fully alert now, Delano studied the doctor, but didn't recognize him. The red name tag on his chest said "Dr. Sanjay Desai," but that meant nothing to him either.

Delano tried to sit up, and the motion confirmed his earlier guess than he was at Moon Base.

"What happened?" *Stupid question, you idiot.*

"Let's see," Dr. Desai said. "Two days ago, the Halkin ship dropped you and the other injured personnel from the *Defiant* at the JovCo medical facility. Your med-tech said you had a concussion and some injuries, so we just put you to sleep and let your body recover."

"How long was I asleep?"

"About forty hours. First we had to . . ."

With a rush, Delano remembered the battle. "The Ktarrans! What happened to the attack?"

"Take it easy, Admiral. The Ktarrans are gone, left the solar system about six hours ago. Didn't even leave a goodbye message. Nobody is saying anything for sure, but it looks like they've given up, at least for now."

"I need to get contact Lian," Delano said. "Linda and the others, I have to. . ."

"You need to take it easy for another few days, unless you want to kill yourself," Desai said. "Everything is under control. In fact, someone is waiting to see you. He'll tell you everything you want to know."

Delano slumped back onto the bed, trying to get control of his excitement. The Ktarrans gone . . . what did that mean? When would they be back?

The door opened and a tall, overweight man stood there dressed in a hospital gown. Delano needed a moment to recognize Field Marshal Shuvalov, out of uniform for the first time in Delano's memory.

The Russian moved cautiously to the side of the bed, and carefully eased his bulk into a bedside chair almost too small for him. He took a deep breath. "It is good to see you again, Colonel Delano. I'm very glad you survived the battle."

"What happened, how many did we lose, where . . . "

"Stop talking. I will tell you everything."

And Shuvalov did, describing the Battle of the Line, the tricks from the Crypto Department that saved the day, and the eventual Ktarran return back through the wormhole.

"So we think they are gone, at least for a few months. They need to take stock of their situation and recover their nerve. The communication from Ktarra translated to only three words – return to Ktarra." He laughed. "It's always the shortest message that carries the most pain. They lost many, many ships. Only thirty-five went back though the wormhole."

"So we won?"

"Not really. We just held them off. But the next time we will beat them. More Destroyers and Darts are being assembled every day. Some mad scientist from India claims he can increase the beam weapons energy by twenty percent." He shrugged. "It may even be true. Pilots and crews are in training. In a few months, all our losses will have been replaced. A month or two after that, we will double the fleet."

"Unless they come back first," Delano said. "Or they bring more ships."

Shuvalov shook his head. "No, I don't think so. For us, the battle was a draw. For the Ktarrans, it is a disaster from which they may never recover. Remember Midway."

Delano knew that the Battle of Midway had turned the tide in the Pacific War. The unstoppable Japanese lost the offensive and never regained it. "I hope you're right, Marshal Shuvalov."

"Trust me." The old Russian smiled. "You'll see. Already we are taking offensive action against them." He told Delano of the plan for Tanaka and the Halkins to attack a construction base deep inside Ktarran territory.

Suddenly Delano remembered his manners. "Why are you in the hospital? Is anything wrong?"

"No, just the usual. I drink too much vodka, don't sleep enough, don't eat proper meals." He laughed. "Doctors are fools. But when the *Enterprise* led the reserve force into action, the acceleration, eh, caused problems. So I am stuck here, on the Moon, perhaps forever."

"I'm sorry to hear that," Delano said, and meant it. "Russia needs you."

"No, Russia has Demidov and Borodin. They will guide its future, if they can work together without killing each other. There will not be a need for an old army general. The days of great land battles in Europe and Asia are over."

Delano nodded. The Ktarrans had accomplished one positive thing – united the major powers on Earth. As long as there were the slightest threat to the planet, the PDF and the Alliance would present a solid front. No one would ever argue again that Earth didn't need a single voice to speak in its defense.

"You may come to like the Moon, Marshal Shuvalov," Delano said. "Low gravity has some advantages."

Shuvalov waved his hands. "What about you? Are you still planning to leave Earth and join the Colonizer?"

"Yes, unless Lian changes her mind. We've made too many enemies on Earth, even if we did help drive the Ktarrans back."

"I think that is best," Shuvalov agreed. "No one rewards visionaries or the agents of change." He smiled. "Your Destroyer should be ready in a day or so. It's a new one, fresh off the line, and it will take you to your ship. Some fools wanted to keep it here, but Colonel Welsh and I overruled them. One more Destroyer won't change anything."

"And the *Centauri* needs it," Delano said, referring to the big Colonizer.

"Then I wish you well on your new journey," Shuvalov said, carefully rising to his feet. "It is almost time for my medicines, so I must hurry back to bed before they miss me."

Delano reached out his hand. "I want to thank you for all you've done, for me, for Lian, for the planet. We would not have survived without you."

Shuvalov shook hands. "Who knows what may happen? Perhaps I will join a Colonizer myself, a new adventure for an old man."

"Maybe we can stay in touch through the QuantC. I'd like that."

"Then consider it done. By the way, you'd better call Colonel Welsh. He's back on Earth dealing with the Alliance. He wouldn't want you to leave without speaking with him."

"I will, Field Marshal," Delano said. "Now you just take care of yourself."

*   *   *

Two days later, Delano stood inside the hangar at the JovCo Lunar Base, watching the Jumper disgorge its passengers. Lian was the seventh and last to exit, recognizable despite the bulky space suit. The arrivals didn't have far to walk, and within moments, the interior airlock started cycling.

He helped her remove her helmet, and as soon as it cleared her head she wrapped her arms around him. They kissed, ignoring the others removing suits and greeting friends. The embrace lasted some time, until they needed to breathe.

Delano saw the tears in her eyes, and his own were just as moist. A smiling dock worker joined them, and helped remove her suit. Delano had her hand in his, and neither spoke as he guided her through the descent passageways and down into the hotel portion. He kept a firm grip on her, since she hadn't visited the Moon in some time. When they reached his quarters, the guard opened the door, then closed it behind them.

"Lian, Lian, it's been so long." He held her close, and her arms remained tight on his neck.

Nearly a month of hectic war preparations, followed by the frenzy of battle, had passed since they'd been together. After the battle, they'd spoken several times by phone, but that remained as unsatisfactory as ever.

Finally she pushed away. "I thought you were supposed to stay in bed? What did the doctor say?"

"He checked me out again this morning. No evidence of damage. It was just a mild concussion. He said to take it easy for a few days."

"Then you need to rest," Lian said. She put her arm around him and guided him to the bed.

"Bed, yes, that's a good idea." Delano pulled her down

beside him. "Lots of bed, that's what I need."

"That's not what I meant!" She frowned at him. "But if you're strong enough . . ."

"Don't worry. I'll let you do all the work."

They spent the rest of the day in the hotel, letting the staff deliver dinner and refreshments. When the last of the dessert was finished and the empty dishes collected, Delano held her in his arms.

"Did you tell your uncle?"

"Yes, and my mother," Lian said. "She was horrified, but Uncle Liu explained to her that it was probably the safest plan of action. She finally accepted the arrangement."

"It must be hard for her."

"My mother understands the danger. Uncle Liu has gotten almost as many threats. But he is lucky that China did not receive any more damage from the Ktarrans. Otherwise, I don't think he could survive." She sighed. "In a year or two, the people of China will hail him as a hero."

The Ktarran strike on western Europe and Africa could have been much worse. Another assault on China or the United States might have crippled either country. Fortunately, when the Ktarran missiles were launched, their angle of attack meant they could only target a small portion of the planet, from the eastern Atlantic to Africa.

Delano touched her cheek. "You still want to do this?"

"Yes! More than ever. I cannot stand living like this any more. Better the unknown than trying to defend the PDF." She straightened up. "And the others? Do they still intend to join us?"

"Yes. Gunny was the last one. He's been thinking about it for the last few weeks. But he's on board now. Decided there was nothing back home to hold him. And that he needed to keep me out of trouble. Steve was onboard from the get-go."

"I wish Sergeant Shen could join us. But his wife cares for both their parents." She sighed. "When do we leave?"

He knew Lian would miss her friend and bodyguard. "I just checked this morning. The Destroyer – its name is the *Kestrel* – will be ready in two days. It will be crowded with the six of us plus the crew, but Peter, Linda and Steve can pull regular duty. We should make contact with the *Centauri* in about a week. It's holding position, waiting for us. It won't proceed without the *Kestrel's* protection."

"What does the name *Kestrel* mean?"

"It's a small desert hawk," Delano said. "But a good hunter and fighter for its size."

"I'm surprised they're letting us have a ship."

"Yeah, me too. If it wasn't promised to the *Centauri*, I doubt we'd be getting it. Hopefully one less Destroyer won't make that much of a difference. The Ktarrans seem to be standing down, for now."

"Then we will be a new family, the six of us. You and me, and Peter and Linda, the Gunny, and Steve."

"We'll be closer than most families," Delano said, "after what we've been through together."

He put his arms around her and pulled her close. "That's enough talk for now."

*   *   *

"So you're still determined to go," Colonel Welsh said, his voice sounding odd coming from the video phone. "Can't believe you want to quit in the middle of the war."

Delano laughed. "Nice try, but Lian and I've done more than our part. Even Klegg admits that. By the way, he wished us both luck. Now it's time for you to step up. You've worked with Horath and Talmak, and they'll accept you as one of the leaders of the PDF. And I agree with Shuvalov, naming Minister Borodin as the other PDF leader will keep him busy and out of President Demidov's hair."

"You're sure that China will buy into that?"

"As long as you reappoint General Zeng to be the PDF's military specialist. It will really be the three of you, but we won't tell the Halkins that."

"How's Shuvalov doing?"

"Not well. He's staying here at the JovCo hospital. The doctors say going back to Earth's gravity will kill him. I don't think he cares. He keeps smiling. We would never have made it without his support."

"Roger that. Give him my best," Welsh said. "Anything else you want me to do?"

"Yes, two things. First, take care of Sergeant Shen. He's a valuable asset. He'd make an ideal bodyguard for General Zeng."

"OK, can do that. What else?"

"Lian and I would like to know the result of Tanaka's new mission. The *Kestrel* will have the QuantC comm device. It's part of the test the scientists want to conduct, to see how far we can actually communicate over interstellar distances."

"Yeah, maybe we'll use it to recall the *Centauri*," Welsh joked. "I'm biting my nails about the whole idea of you leaving. I still think it's way too early to start something like that. You should stay at least until we learn what happens to Tanaka."

"Sorry, no can do. The *Centauri* needs to get moving again, and you may not hear from Tanaka for another four or five days. Whatever the outcome, you'll know what to do."

"OK, gotta go now," Welsh said. "There's another crisis in Europe."

Delano laughed. "Always is. Good luck and take care."

"I'll miss you, Delano. Always something exciting happening around you."

"Exactly my point. Don't forget to watch your back."

After he broke the connection, Delano turned to Lian. "I really do feel bad about ducking out before . . . Tanaka gets back."

Lian took his hand. "He may never return."

"I know. But it's still a good mission for him, and now is the best time to do it. We may never get another chance like this."

"Then let's stop worrying about what we can't control," Lian said. "For us, it's a new adventure. It's time to start packing."

"Yes, my love. Time for a new adventure, and maybe this one will be a little less exciting." *Hope for the best, prepare for the worst.* Possibly, just possibly, this time it wouldn't be the worst.

Yeah, right!

Chapter 55 – Epilog 1

Captain Raizo Tanaka took his position, second in line behind Captain Horath's ship, the *Meseka*. Behind Tanaka's *Naganami* were two more Destroyers, the *Agamemnon* and the *Poltava*. Each Destroyer carried its two Darts, and a compliment of special weapons.

The *Naganami* would be the first Earth ship to enter a wormhole, but the mission was military, not scientific. The little squadron intended to strike a blow against the Ktarran Empire. With luck, it would be a serious assault, one intended to give Earth more time to prepare for the next stage of the Earth-Ktarran War.

The idea for the mission had come from Horath several months earlier. Despite all the hectic preparation for the Ktarran invasion of Earth space, enough resources had been made available to prepare for the contingency that Earth would survive and have the capability to mount a counterattack.

For Horath's *Meseka*, much new equipment had been installed, including computers, enhanced communications technology, and some operation-specific weapons.

The mission itself was a raid, an attempt to catch the Ktarrans off-guard, and disrupt their ability to construct new ships and repair existing ones. Within the Empire, the Ktarrans had established a major construction facility on a world named Litigara. Ships regularly arrived and departed transporting all the supplies and slaves necessary for its functioning.

Many cycles earlier, the planet had been home to a primitive and peaceful agrarian society. But the Ktarrans had ruthlessly hunted them down, dropping the helpless indigenous population from a hundred million to less than a million. These survivors eked out a wretched existence in the remaining forests, still hunted for sport by the occasional Ktarran visitor.

The construction facility dwelt at the base of a mountain adjacent to a river and only a few miles from one of the inland seas that dotted the planet. The river and sea provided an ideal place to dump highly-contaminated waste material, and of course the Ktarrans cared nothing about the ecology they were destroying. The nearby mountains were mined by slaves for materials needed to forge the giant battleships so prized by the Ktarrans. Litigara, however important to the Empire, was mostly undefended, except for a ship or two orbiting the planet.

Even so, Horath estimated that almost a third of all Ktarran spaceship construction occurred on Litigara. The facility occupied an area about sixty square miles. That included factories, energy generation, and housing for the Peltors and Dalvak slaves who built the ships. The work was arduous and toxic, killing the laborers within a few years.

Near the sea, a small enclave offered luxurious housing for the few hundred Ktarrans who directed the hundred thousand or so slave workers. Due to health concerns, the Ktarrans rotated in and out of Litigara every cycle, to avoid the poisons circulating in the local environment.

Horath's plan proposed a raid on Litigara with the intention of destroying the facility. Best of all, the planet was only two jumps away from Earth. If a small force could get past the wormhole's guardians, it could reach Litigara. A few nuclear weapons would destroy the complex, and indirectly aid the indigenous survivors by eliminating the source of contaminants and periodic hunts. At least, that's what Horath claimed.

Earth's supply of nuclear materials and missiles remained critical, and none could be spared from their main tasks of defending Earth from another attack. But where mass destruction was concerned, Earth's nations had developed alternatives. With typical human ingenuity, the PDF scientists found a way.

Meanwhile, the PDF High Command grudgingly approved the use of three Destroyers for the raid, and provided the necessary enhancements to the Destroyers and Horath's ship.

Less than eight days had elapsed since the Ktarran fleet departed Earth space. Months earlier, the PDF had developed an operation plan and allocated resources. With the enemy fleet driven off, the actual implementation took little time.

Now the four ships formed a column five hundred kilometers from the wormhole. Horath's ship would lead the way, and the three Earth vessels would be close behind, with only three hundred meters separating each ship. The idea was to surprise and eliminate any Ktarrans at the other end of the wormhole, then traverse the distance through physical space to the nexus of another wormhole that led to Litigara.

In the seventeen months that Captain Horath and his ship lingered in Earth orbit, he shared much of his weapons and engineering skills with the PDF. It proved to be a good exchange. Meanwhile Earth had several key technologies that Horath lacked, and he received many of them. The first of these was communication enhancements, with better and more secure radios and messaging systems.

The second item was an EMP generator. A basic EMP device consists of a capacitor, transformer, trigger, and a coil of copper wire. Creating a major pulse that would disrupt enemy ships from miles away needed a good-sized nuclear device. But strong EMPs could also be produced using electronics, especially when powered by a ship's anti-matter generators.

The device manufactured for installation on PDF ships had transformers the size of an SUV and contained miles of tightly wrapped copper wire. The device was expected to be used at close range, but would be capable of overloading at least temporarily any unshielded electronics within fifty to one hundred kilometers.

The plan called for the four ships to travel through the wormhole. Ktarrans, of course, would be at the other end, guarding the entrance to prevent any unauthorized travel to Earth's system. They would also be watching to see if anyone exited the wormhole, but Horath believed they would not be as vigilant. The Ktarrans likely assumed that Earth had no ships capable of wormhole travel.

No one knew how many Ktarran ships would be on guard duty. If the number turned out to be large, the Earth ships would immediately turn around and try to escape back to Earth's system. But if any Ktarran patrol ships could be overwhelmed and destroyed before they could broadcast news of the Earth ships' arrival, then the next stage of the plan could be set in motion.

Horath gave the signal, and his ship headed for the wormhole, Tanaka and the others following. All the Earth crews had been briefed on what to expect inside the space-time distortion that made up the wormhole. As his ship entered, Tanaka felt the momentary disorientation that accompanied the transition to hyperspace.

The prepared crew suffered few ill effects. Fortunately, the journey through hyperspace didn't last long, less than ten minutes of ship's time. But during that interval, the ships could not communicate with each other. Then they were through, and Tanaka's stomach quickly readjusted itself.

The radio came to life. Horath was at least fifteen seconds ahead of Tanaka's ship. ". . . two ships . . . one battleship . . . destroyer . . . pulse effective."

Tanaka's screens came to life, and he saw Horath's *Meseka* accelerating directly toward the battleship, less than sixty kilometers away. The plan called for the second ship through to attack the second Ktarran vessel. If there were more than three enemy ships, the squadron would abandon the operation, return to the wormhole and travel back to Earth space.

The second Ktarran vessel was somewhat further away, but Tanaka's pilot was already on course to attack it. A focused EMP pulse was aimed at the smaller ship, and a second would follow, as soon as the capacitor could be recharged, a process that took about fifty seconds.

By that time Tanaka intended to be well within firing range. His Darts were already released and would add their firepower. If the EMP were effective, the Ktarran ships would be blind and relatively helpless. More important, the would almost certainly be unable to communicate, either with each other or the home planet.

The two Ktarrans vessels had no chance. Caught by surprise, by the time they reacted to Horath's arrival, the *Naganami* had fired its own EMP. With most of their sensors burned out, the enemy tried to use its beam weapons, but their crews needed time to react, and power had to be rerouted. By then Tanaka's weapons were pouring energy into the ship's defensive screens.

The Darts had it just as easy. Before the Ktarran ship could get under way or its shields strengthened, both Darts were sending projectile after projectile into the helpless vessel. Within seventy seconds after Tanaka's arrival, the second enemy ship exploded.

The other two Earth ships had followed Horath's attack on the battleship. That action took a few seconds longer, but it too ended with the destruction of the enemy vessel.

In just over two minutes, both Ktarran ships were destroyed and the PDF had control of the wormhole.

"Captain Horath, did the ship broadcast a message?"

A moment later the voice of Ahvin responded. "No, Captain Tanaka. The moment we came through the wormhole we activated the EMP device. And again when it recharged."

Tanaka's own comms crewman reported the same finding. No enemy messages were sent. Tanaka breathed a sigh of relief. So far, so good.

"Captain Tanaka," Ahvin's voice came again. "Horath is ready for the second phase. Are you prepared to follow?"

The always impatient Horath was right. There was no time to waste. "Yes, we are ready. *Naganami* and *Agamemnon* will accompany you. The *Poltava* will remain here to guard the entrance."

No sooner was the message received when Horath started accelerating away from the wormhole. The two Earth ships took after him at maximum speed. They had a journey of at least six hours to reach the proximity of another wormhole. This one should be unguarded, and it would take them directly to the Ktarran slave planet.

Tanaka's nerves were on edge during the journey. If a large enough force showed up, the three ships would be alone and helpless, caught between wormholes. Whether or not the Ktarrans had any long-range sensors capable of monitoring local wormholes remained anyone's guess. Horath believed that they didn't, but he'd been out of touch with the Empire's technology for the last year and a half. He'd thrown his lot in with the humans, and risked his ship and his crew to help them.

For this raid, however, the potential reward outweighed the risks. If Tanaka's force could get to Litigara undetected, they should be able to strike a blow powerful enough to slow down the Ktarrans for some time. Certainly long enough for Earth to build more ships and train more crews.

The PDF needed time. Even more important than ship construction was the need to process nuclear materials into fission bombs that could be added to new missiles. Despite advances in nuclear engineering, the process still took months to produce weapons-grade material. The brutal fighting around Earth had nearly wiped out the planet's nuclear arsenal, and it needed to be replenished.

Even with all three ships accelerating at top speed, the chronometer on the *Naganami* seemed to crawl. But the time passed, and Tanaka's crew reported no presence of enemy ships. Finally the ships began to slow, and a little after six and a half hours the squadron, still following Horath's ship, detected the presence of the second wormhole.

Horath approached this new event horizon at maximum safe speed. Once again the Earth ships entered a wormhole. This trip seemed to take longer, and Tanaka registered nearly twenty-two minutes of elapsed time before they emerged, now deep in Ktarran space.

Once again the Halkin ship emerged from the opening first, but when Tanaka followed, there were no enemy ships in sight.

Tanaka ordered the *Agamemnon* to guard the wormhole, and the *Naganami* and the *Meseka* headed toward the planet. Another six or seven hour journey awaited them, as they traveled closer to this system's sun and moved toward the second planet.

Tanaka expected to encounter ships, hostile ships, but he had a plan for that. The *Naganami* and the *Meseka* activated another new piece of technology. This one enabled them to modify their defense screens so as to mimic that of a small Ktarran supply ship. Hopefully any ships or instruments orbiting the planet would not challenge the two inbound vessels.

United States and Russian sea-going military vessels had possessed this capability for years. Under the right conditions, a watchful satellite might easily mistake a destroyer for a merchant ship, or even a large yacht.

Whether the device was functioning effectively, or the Ktarran forces at the planet didn't bother to check, no challenge occurred. If a challenge were issued, Ahvin was ready to reply in the Ktarran language.

Tanaka hoped that Horath's second wife could pull it off. But that, too, was out of his control. He resumed his study of the chronometer, resisting the urge to show any signs of nervousness in front of his crew, no matter how queasy his stomach felt.

When they were closer, sensors detected three ships orbiting Litigara, all arranged around an orbiting ship assembly platform. Two were quickly identified as supply ships, most likely unarmed. The third was another Ktarran battleship, but one of the smallest Tanaka had seen. The platform, empty now, was used for final assembly and testing for the newly constructed ships.

Using a tight and low power radio band, Horath confirmed the data. The Halkin used few words to convey the plan. He would attack the military ship while Tanaka delivered the packages. Tanaka's two Darts would also assist Horath.

Tanaka would be on his own if anyone else showed up. By this time he could see the planet and make out its land masses. The Ktarran base was easily visible, like a giant sore on the edge of a large land mass. As they drew closer, Tanaka could see the skeletons of several ships under construction.

Horath's ship continued traveling at a leisurely speed, heading for a low-planet orbit, just as any other cargo ships would be doing at this point. Tanaka's nerves were wound tight, and he had to force himself to maintain the air of imperturbability that warship captains displayed, or whatever he thought they should exhibit.

The battleship remained stationary, and exchanges of radio messages with Horath's ship began. Tanaka hoped Ahvin was doing a good job fooling the Ktarran. By now they were close enough to the planet and the Ktarran ship. A plume of air pollution, large enough to be easily visible from orbit, trailed off to what Tanaka called the western region. The Ktarrans really were killing the planet. At this rate, another fifty years would see the end of all life on Litigara.

"Just a little more," he muttered, unaware he'd spoken out loud. Horath should have attacked by now. Any moment the Ktarran would become suspicious and raise its shields. But the *Meseka* continued its slow pace, and now the two ships were less than forty kilometers apart, almost close enough for visual identification and well within the range of the EMP weapon.

Suddenly Horath's ship swung toward the Ktarran and accelerated. Tanaka's sensors recorded the EMP. "Launch the Darts," he ordered. Three seconds later both Darts blasted away at top speed, aiming toward the Ktarran and spitting projectiles. "Attack speed. All beam weapons engage."

Horath's beam weapons also activated, and his three beams focused directly on the Ktarran control bridge, or where it should be, Tanaka noted. There were now eight beam weapons blasting at the enemy, and still the Ktarran hadn't replied or even taken any evasive action.

The EMP pulse must have blinded them, Tanaka guessed. Whatever the reason, the Ktarran was doomed. Before the

Naganami and *Meseka* had closed within fifteen kilometers, still firing their weapons, the battleship exploded.

Tanaka watched the incandescent debris slowly fade in the coldness of space. One look told him that the ship was dead. "Darts, attack the supply vessels. Don't let them get away."

Tanaka ignored the final stages of the battle. Instead he focused on maneuvering his ships closer to the planet, maintaining orbital position fifty thousand meters above the industrial complex.

"Targets selected," his weapons chief called out. "Missiles ready for launch."

"Launch in sequence," Tanaka ordered. A moment later he felt the ship lurch as the first missile broke free of the *Naganami*. Actually, it wasn't much of a missile, more like a laser-guided fusion bomb in a heat-resistant case. The bomb drifted leisurely away from the ship, its tiny brain and rocket motor focused on the laser beam now emanating from the specially-constructed laser antennae. It would follow that beam all the way to the target, and explode a thousand meters above the factory complex.

The second and third bombs soon followed, each launched ten seconds apart. The three twenty-five megaton bombs would blast the entire complex to rubble. Nothing usable would survive the multiple blasts. Fascinated, Tanaka watched the bombs detonate, their nuclear flash dazzling at that altitude. Within seconds, huge mushroom clouds formed, and rivers of fire spread from the many combustible storage tanks.

He realized the crew was cheering. The Darts were already returning to the *Naganami*. The radio came on, and Tanaka heard Ahvin's voice.

"Captain Horath sends his congratulations," she said. "We have destroyed the construction platform, and are now leaving to return to our home world. He suggests you do the same."

Horath had a twelve-hour journey to reach the wormhole that would, after a series of jumps, take him back to his home planet, a place he had not seen in almost nineteen months.

"Many thanks to your captain, Ahvin," Tanaka said. "We will also return home."

She didn't bother to acknowledge, and already the *Meseka* was moving away. Horath's ship still faced a dangerous voyage ahead of her, and there was not a moment to waste. The

Ktarrans could arrive from several directions and at anytime.

"Set course for the *Agamemnon*, full speed," Tanaka ordered, sinking gratefully into his chair and relaxing for the first time in what seemed like days. "We're going back to Earth."

Even if none of the ships ever returned, the raid had been a success. At least a third of the Ktarran manufacturing and construction capabilities were gone, and they would not be easily replaced. This site on Litigara could never be used again. Earth had bought itself valuable time.

If and when the Ktarrans returned to Earth space, they would find plenty of PDF ships waiting for them. If the Ktarran Empire waited too long, Earth ships would soon be roaming their territories, as the PDF struck back at its enemy. As Admiral Yamamoto said before the raid against Pearl Harbor, "It is not wise to arouse the sleeping dragon."

The war was far from over. It wasn't the beginning of the end, but it was the end of the beginning. Perhaps in some way, the war would be a blessing, uniting the people of Earth in a common effort, maybe even ending the nationalistic ways that had plagued the planet with violence and endured since the days of the Babylonian Empire. And maybe helping a few cousin species in the stellar quadrant in the process.

Whether such a scenario would happen or not, Tanaka couldn't say. But he intended to work toward that goal for the rest of his life.

Chapter 56 – Epilog 2

The Almighty Ruler of Ktarra, Pannoch Staleeck, glared at the groveling Commander Veloreck kneeling before him. This was Veloreck's second appearance before his Emperor. The defeated commander had expected to be eaten at his first appearance, and no doubt had been surprised to find a somber ruler who had listened in great detail to the report of the invasion of Earth's space and the subsequent battles.

That had been a bad day for Staleeck, the worst day of his rule, the worst day in the proud history of the Ktarran Empire. A mighty fleet had been dispatched to finish off the defiant humans, and scarcely twenty percent of those ships had returned. These war-like animals had proved to be far different from the usual species inhabiting the stellar quadrant.

Today's news had only increased the size of the disaster.

"The base on Litigara has been destroyed." Staleeck's usually harsh voice had a different tone. "The destruction is total, and the area is no longer usable due to high levels of radiation."

A stunned Veloreck lifted his eyes. "How is that possible? What could . . ."

"Three ships in orbit were also destroyed, two freighters and a battle cruiser. A satellite recorded the arrival of two freighters who launched the attack. With Litigara destroyed, Ktarra has lost almost forty percent of its ship fabrication facilities."

"Who could have done it?" Veloreck's voice expressed as much dismay as his leader. "Which of the slave worlds . . ."

"After the destruction of the three ships," Staleeck went on, "one of the freighters launched three missiles. According to those ships who responded to the attack, each missile contained more explosive power than we have ever seen before, greater than our own nuclear weapons. The scientists suspect these were fusion bombs."

"So it must have been the humans," Veloreck said. "But how could they have responded so quickly after our attack on Earth? Their fleet was nearly destroyed, and all of their nuclear missiles expended."

"After the missile launch, the two ships departed in different directions," Staleeck went on, ignoring Veloreck's question. "One headed for a wormhole that could take it back to Halkin space. The other returned to the Earth gate, where we discovered another one of our battle cruisers destroyed."

"These humans . . . they could mount a counterattack so fast?" Veloreck sounded dazed. "And somehow they used massive weapons? How did they even know where Litigara was, or how to get there?"

"I'm sure that the Halkins guided them to Litigara. They probably suggested the attack."

"We must warn our other bases," Veloreck said. "They may also come . . ."

"The warning went out just before you arrived," Staleeck said. "All ships and planets in the Empire are on alert. We will not be caught by surprise again."

Veloreck shook his massive head. "These humans are cunning fighters. They attacked our superior numbers without fear or hesitation. They used tactics we have never seen before, and fought with coordination and speed that we did not expect."

"Enough of that," Staleeck snapped. "That is why you are here. We must begin our preparations for the next attack. Earth must be destroyed. This time it is we who will utilize new tactics and weapons. If we cannot destroy these animals, they will destroy us."

"You want to attack them again?" Veloreck seemed confused. "By now they have already strengthened their defenses. Their small fighters with their projectile weapons are probably easy to construct. They will be ready for another attack."

"Yes, I understand. They are ready and we are not, not yet. But Earth is at the end of that particular wormhole. I want you to station ten of your ships to guard that exit. If they get through that portal, they can attack us anywhere."

"Then I am not relieved of my command?"

"No, nor will you be eaten," Staleeck said. "I have reviewed your battle report and spoke to Jothe and others. You did what you could in the face of these new ships and tactics, and nearly destroyed the planet. I do not believe you will make the same mistakes or assumptions again. You are fully aware that we are matched against a new kind of opponent, one as likely to destroy us as we are to eliminate them."

"We must build many new ships, different types of ships, to

deal with this new enemy."

"Yes, we will do that," the Emperor answered. "There may be another way to destroy their planet. Meanwhile, I have ordered our other bases to speed up battleship construction. But we will need time to recover from the defeat, build new ships, and train our fighters in these new battle techniques. That will take many cycles. For the first time in our history, we face a long war, possibly a never-ending war. The wormhole to Earth will remain open for now, and then it will close again. The next time it reopens we will be ready."

"I will do my utmost," Veloreck said.

"If you do not, if you do not succeed, you and I, and the Empire will probably be destroyed. Earth must be defeated, crushed, or the same fate will fall upon Ktarra. There will be no other outcome."

"We will succeed, my Emperor. The Ktarran Empire cannot be defeated."

"No, it cannot," Staleeck said, hoping his words were true. "It cannot."

The End

Acknowledgement

My thanks, as always, go to my wife, Linda, for all her help in the editing and proofing of this book. Her keen eye caught every mistake, and her determined quest for clarity ensured that the text is as readable as I could make it. It is no exaggeration to say that this book would not have been possible without her help.

More thanks are due to Bill Morgan, my friend since the first grade. He gave the book an early read and spotted the lingering typos, and, as usual, under the rush of getting the book completed and ready for publication. Other early readers who provided great input were my niece, Laura Groch, and Richard Lynch, an Eskkar and sci-fi fan. Final draft was reviewed by Dr. Julie Schifferli, D.C., and Prescott Valley Artesian Thomas Schifferli. Many thanks to all.

Of course our three cats – Varney, Jake, and Alice – all helped out. Varney often climbed onto my lap, forcing a break in the writing process, but restoring a sense of calm to the author.

Sam Barone
Prescott, AZ

About The Author

Born and raised in Queens, New York, Sam Barone graduated from Manhattan College with a BS degree. After a hitch in the Marine Corps, he entered the world of technology.

In 1999, after thirty years developing software, Sam retired from Western Union International, as VP of International Systems. He moved to Arizona, to take up his second career as a writer.

Seven years later, the author's first Eskkar story, *Dawn of Empire*, was published in the USA and UK. Five more novels and two short stories followed, bringing the Eskkar Saga to 1.2 million words.

Next came Sam's first science fiction, a novella entitled *Jettisoned*, the basis for *Sentinel Star* and *Earth Besieged*.

All of Sam's stories are available in print or Kindle at Amazon.com

History and reading have always been two of Sam's favorite interests. He considers himself more of a storyteller than a writer. "I write stories that I would enjoy reading, and it's a true blessing that others have found these tales interesting, informative, and entertaining."

Sam and his wife Linda, and their three cats (Varney, Jake, and Alice) enjoy life in beautiful Prescott, Arizona.

Sam's books have been published in nine languages and he has readers all over the world. Sam enjoys hearing from his readers, and invites them to visit **www.sambarone.com**.

Made in the USA
Las Vegas, NV
17 October 2021